P O W E R S A T

POWERSAT

BEN BOVA

A TOM DOHERTY ASSOCIATES BOOK
NEW YORK

POWERSAT

Book design by Mary A. Wirth

A Tor® Book
Published by Tom Doherty Associates, LLC
175 Fifth Avenue
New York, NY 10010

www.tor.com

Tor® is a registered trademark of Tom Doherty Associates, LLC.

Library of Congress Cataloging-in-Publication Data

Bova, Ben, 1932-
   Powersat / Ben Bova—1st hardcover ed.
     p. cm.
   "A Tom Doherty Associates book."
   ISBN 0-765-30923-8 (acid-free paper)
   EAN 978-0765-30923-5
   1. Satellite solar power stations—Fiction. 2. Terrorism—Prevention—Fiction. 3.
Scientists—Fiction. I. Title.

PS3552.O84P63 2005
813'.54—dc22

                                                              2004056261

First Edition: January 2005

Printed in the United States of America

0 9 8 7 6 5 4 3 2 1

This book is dedicated to
those who gave their lives
on the high frontier.

POWERSAT

FLIGHT TEST

California in sight."

Test pilot Hannah Aarons saw the coastline as a low dark smudge stretching across the curving horizon far, far below. Beyond the cockpit's thick quartz windshield she could see that the sky along that horizon was bright with a new morning coming up, shading into a deep violet and finally, overhead, into the black of infinite space.

The spaceplane arrowed across the sky at Mach 16 and crossed the California coast at an altitude of 197,000 feet, precisely on course. Through the visor of her pressure suit's helmet, Aarons saw that the plane's titanium nose was beginning to glow as it bit into the wispy atmosphere, heading for the landing field at Matagorda Island on the gulf coast of Texas. She began to hear the thin whistle of rarified air rushing across her cockpit.

"On the tick, Hannah," she heard the flight controller's voice in her helmet earphones. "Pitch-up maneuver in thirty seconds."

"Copy pitch-up in thirty," she answered.

The horizon dipped out of sight as the spaceplane's nose came up slightly. All she could see now was the black void of space high above. She concentrated on the display screens of her control panel. The digital readout of the Mach meter began to click down: 16, 15.5, 15…. The shoulder straps of her harness cutting into her by the *g* force, Hannah heard her breath coming out harsh, labored. Out of the corner of her eye she saw the leading edge of the plane's stubby wings turning a sullen deep ruby. In seconds they'd be cherry red, she knew.

Suddenly the plane pitched downward so hard Hannah banged her nose painfully against her helmet visor. Her neck would have snapped if she weren't in the protective harness. She gasped with sudden shock. The air outside her cockpit canopy began to howl, throwing streamers of orange fire at her.

"Pitch-down excursion!" she yelled into her helmet mike as she pulled at the T-shaped control yoke at her left hand. Her arms, even supported in their protective cradles, felt as if they weighed ten tons apiece. The plane was shaking so badly her vision blurred. The controls seemed locked; she couldn't budge them.

"Servos overridden," she said, her voice rising. Through the fiery glow outside her cockpit she could see the ground far, far below. It was rushing up to meet her. Stay calm, she told herself. Stay calm!

"Going to wire," she called, thumbing the button that activated the plane's backup fly-by-wire controls.

"No response!" The plane continued its screaming dive, yawing back and forth like a tumbling leaf, thumping her painfully against the sides of the narrow cockpit.

"Punch out!" came the controller's voice, loud and frantic. "Hannah, get your butt out of there!"

The plane was spinning wildly now, slamming her around in her seat as it corkscrewed back and forth in its frenzied plunge toward the ground. She could taste blood in her mouth. The inflatable bladder of her *g* suit was squeezing her guts like toothpaste in a tube.

"Hannah!" A different voice. "This is Tenny. Punch out of there. Now!"

She nodded inside the helmet. She couldn't think of what else to do. No other options. This bird's a goner. It took a tremendous effort to inch her right hand along its cradle to the fire-engine red panic button. Just as she painfully flicked up its protective cover the plane's left wing ripped away with a horrible wrenching sound, flipping the plane upside down.

Hannah's arm snapped at the wrist. White-hot pain shot all the way up to her shoulder. She was still trying to push the eject button when the spaceplane broke into half a dozen blazing pieces and fell to earth in smoky meteor trails, scattering wreckage over several hundred square miles of flat, scrubby west Texas.

MATAGORDA ISLAND, TEXAS

Dan Randolph stood at the broad window of his office, staring grimly at the hangar floor below. A pair of technicians was bringing in a twisted bit of wreckage from the truck parked outside in the hot summer sunshine, carrying it as tenderly as if it were the body of a fallen comrade. Part of the wing, it looked like, although it was so blackened and deformed that it was tough to be sure.

The sleek outline of the spaceplane's original shape was laid out across the hangar floor in heavy white tape. As the chunks of wreckage came in from the field, the technicians and crash investigators from the FAA and the National Transportation Safety Board laid them out in their proper places.

"Once they get all the pieces in place," Dan muttered, "they'll start the autopsy."

Saito Yamagata stood beside Randolph, his hands clasped behind his back, his head bowed in sympathy.

"Might as well do an autopsy on me, too," said Dan. "I'm as good as dead."

"Daniel, you are much too young to be so bitter," said Yamagata.

Dan Randolph gave his former boss a sour look. "I've earned the right," he said.

Yamagata forced a smile. No matter what, he almost always smiled. Founder and head of a young but vigorously growing Japanese aerospace corporation, Yamagata had much to smile about. He wore a Saville Row three-piece suit of sky blue, with a tiny pin in the jacket's lapel: a flying crane, the family emblem. His dark hair, combed straight back from his broad forehead, was just beginning to show a touch of gray at the temples. He was the tallest member of his family within living memory, at five-eleven, more than an inch taller than Randolph. Once Yamagata had been as slim as a samurai's blade, but the recent years of living well had begun to round out his belly and soften the lines of his face. His eyes, though, were still probing, penetrating, shrewd.

Dan was in his shirtsleeves, and they were rolled up above his elbows. A solidly built middleweight, he had a pugnacious look to him, in part because his nose had been broken a few years earlier in a brawl with a trio of Japanese workmen. When he smiled, though, women found his rough-hewn face handsome, and he could be charming when he had to be. He felt far from charming now. His gray eyes, which had often sparkled as if he were secretly amused at the world's follies, were sad now, bleak, almost defeated.

The spaceplane had been his dream; he had bet everything he had on it, everything he could beg or borrow. His company, Astro Manufacturing Corporation, was going to show the world how private enterprise could make money in space. Now that dream lay twisted and broken on the hangar floor below.

Dan saw a small, slight figure off in the far corner of the hangar: Gerry Adair, the company's backup pilot, slim and spare; from this distance he looked like a sandy-haired, freckle-faced kid. Adair was staring silently at the wreckage being deposited on the floor. He had often clowned around with Hannah Aarons; she had been the serious one, he the exuberant, playful joker. He wasn't clowning now. He simply stood there like a forlorn teenager as the technicians brought in the blackened, twisted pieces of what had been a machine he might have piloted.

Dan turned away from the window. "Today is Astro Corporation's fifth anniversary, Sai. Probably its last, too."

The office was cluttered with papers and reports that were piled high on Randolph's massively grotesque old Victorian black walnut desk. Even through the thick, double-paned window they could feel the deep, heavy vibration of the overhead crane as it lugged the blackened remains of the spaceplane's cockpit section across the hangar to the team of technicians waiting to set it into its proper place in the outline on the floor.

As he stood beside Randolph, Yamagata laid a hand gently on the younger man's shoulder and said, "Dan, if you allow me to buy you out, you can continue to run the company."

Randolph grimaced. "Into the ground."

"You need capital. I'm offering—"

"Sai, we both know that if I let you buy me out, within a year I'll be out on the street, no matter how reluctant you'd be to can me. A company like Astro can't have two masters. You know that, and I know you know it."

Yamagata's smile turned slightly down. "You are probably right," he admitted. "But you must do something, Dan. Wasn't it one of your own presidents who said that when the going gets tough, the tough get going?"

"Yeah, to where the going's easier," Randolph muttered.

Yamagata shook his head. "You have great assets, Daniel. The power satellite is nearly finished, isn't it? That could be worth several billions by itself."

"If it works."

"You know it will work. The Yamagata demonstration model works, doesn't it?"

Randolph nodded reluctantly. He had helped to build the Japanese power satellite, working as an employee of Yamagata. Then he had used the demonstration satellite's success to win backers for his own start-up company, Astro Manufacturing Corporation. Yamagata had been angered, but as soon as he heard about the accident he had flown in from Tokyo. To offer his help, he told Randolph. To scoop up the competition at a distressed price, Dan thought.

"Your company wouldn't be the first to encounter difficulties because its founder was too optimistic, too much in love with his own dreams."

"Dreams? I don't have any dreams. I'm a hard-headed businessman," Randolph growled. "Not a *good* businessman, maybe, but I'm no starry-eyed dreamer."

Yamagata looked at this American whom he had known for almost ten years. "Aren't you?" he asked.

"No," Dan snapped. "The spaceplane is an important part of the picture. If we don't have cheap and reliable access to orbit, the power satellite isn't much more than a big, fat, white elephant in the sky."

"White elephant?" Yamagata looked puzzled for a moment, but before Randolph could explain, he said, "Ah, yes, a useless extravagance."

"You've got it, Sai."

"So you intend to continue with the spaceplane?"

"If I can."

Yamagata hesitated a heartbeat, then said, "I can provide you with enough capital to last for another three years, even at your current level of losses."

"No thanks, Sai. I'll be double-dipped in sheep shit before I let you or anybody else get their hands on my company."

With a theatrical sigh, Yamagata said, "You are a stubborn man, Daniel."

Randolph touched his crooked nose. "You noticed that?"

The office door swung open and Randolph's executive assistant stuck her head in.

She started to say, "Joe Tenny's here. Mrs. Aarons's funeral is set for—"

Tenny barreled past her, a short, stocky, scowling man in an open-neck shirt and a tight-fitting, silver-gray blazer over a pair of new blue jeans. "Time to get to Hannah's funeral, boss," he said, in his abrupt, no-nonsense manner. "I'll drive."

KHARTOUM, SUDAN

Asim al-Bashir sat calmly with his hands folded over his middle as the others around the table gleefully congratulated themselves. Fools! he thought. But he kept a carefully noncommittal expression on his round, dark-bearded face.

They called themselves The Nine. No poetic names for them, no declarations of bravery or daring. Merely The Nine. They worked in secret, planned in secret, even celebrated their victories in secret.

Here in this squalid hotel conference room that smelled of pungent cinnamon and rancid cooking oil from the kitchen down the hall, most of the others wore their tribal robes, including their Sudanese host, who sat at the end of the table muffled in a white djellaba and turban. Here in the crumbling capital city of backwater Sudan they were comfortably safe from the prying eyes and hired assassins of the West. At least, they thought so. Al-Bashir was dressed in a Western business suit, although he disdained to wear a tie.

"We have stopped the American," said the tall, bearded Saudi, his eyes glittering happily. "His dreams are smashed into as many pieces as his so-called spaceplane."

"But they don't realize that we are responsible for the crash," said the deeply black Sudanese. "They believe it was an accident."

"So much the better," the Saudi replied. "Let the unbelievers think so. We have no desire to draw attention to ourselves."

The others murmured agreement.

The Iraqi exile, once a general and still dressing in an olive-green military uniform, was the nominal chairman of this group. They met rarely, furtively. It was not wise for all of them to be together for very long. Despite all their precautions, despite all their successes, the Yankees and their lapdogs still had a powerful arsenal to use against them.

"The purpose of this meeting," the general said, his deep, rich voice loud enough to quiet the others around the table, "is to decide where to strike next."

"Randolph is done," said the Egyptian, who had masterminded the sabotage of the spaceplane. "Astro Manufacturing Corporation will be in receivership within three months. Perhaps sooner."

Al-Bashir raised a hand in protest. "We may be congratulating ourselves too soon."

"What do you mean?" the Saudi demanded, his lean, hawk-nosed face darkening with displeasure.

"Randolph is a resourceful man," said al-Bashir.

"What of it? His project is crippled now," the Egyptian countered, his round bald head slightly sheened with perspiration despite the fans that turned lazily overhead. "Randolph is finished, I tell you."

"Perhaps," al-Bashir conceded mildly.

The general, sitting up at the head of the table, asked with narrowed eyes, "What is troubling you, my brother?"

My brother? al-Bashir thought disdainfully. These zealots and religious fanatics are no brothers of mine. Yet he kept his contempt hidden. I must convince these maniacs of the seriousness of the situation, he told himself.

He pushed his chair back and got to his feet. All eyes were on him, the room was completely silent now.

"As I said, Randolph is a resourceful man. And his Astro Corporation still possesses the power satellite, up in orbit. It is almost completed."

"But without the spaceplane his project can't possibly succeed," the Egyptian countered. "It will be too expensive to service the satellite, to send crews up to repair and maintain it. He nearly went bankrupt merely assembling it in space with ordinary rockets."

"True, the spaceplane is the key to operating the power satellite profitably," al-Bashir admitted. "But the satellite itself is worth several billion dollars, is it not? That is a considerable bargaining chip for a man with Randolph's talents of persuasion."

"Then we'll blow it up," said the Saudi, slapping the tabletop with one long-fingered hand. "That will finish him for good and all."

"That will finish us," al-Bashir snapped.

The others stared at him, almost openly hostile.

"Let me point out that each of our peoples' victories against America has come at a very high price. September eleventh was followed by the destruction of the Taliban in Afghanistan. Saddam Hussein's intransigence led to the invasion and humiliation of Iraq. Even our greatest victory, the Day of the Bridges, has brought nothing but devastation and the Americans' permanent 'protection' of the Persian Gulf oil fields."

"They have not occupied Iran's fields!" the mullah snapped.

"Nor Arabia's," added the Saudi.

"That will come," al-Bashir warned, "if we strike openly again."

"But they don't know that we are responsible for the spaceplane's failure," the general pointed out. "The entire idea of such a plane has been discredited by the crash."

"That is all to the good," said al-Bashir. "But if we blow up the power satellite, what retribution will the furious Americans take upon our people?"

The room went silent once again. At length, the general spoke up. "What do you recommend, then?"

Al-Bashir suppressed an urge to smile. I have them now, he knew. Keeping his face perfectly serious, he replied, "I recommend that we *use* the power satellite. For our own purposes."

SOLAR POWER SATELLITE

It floats in silent emptiness twenty-two thousand three hundred miles above the equator, a mammoth flat square two and a half miles long on each side. At that precise altitude over the equator its orbit is exactly the same as Earth's daily rotation: the power satellite remains over the same spot above the Earth's surface always. From Texas it appears as a bright star in the south, almost halfway between the horizon and zenith. If you know precisely where to look, often you can see it in full daylight.

To the crews working on the powersat it looks like a big square island. The side facing the Sun glitters darkly, its panels of solar cells greedily drinking in the sunlight's energy and silently converting it to electricity. The satellite's underside, the side facing Earth, is studded with microwave antennas and pods that house power converters and magnetron tubes, as well as temporary shelters for the workers. Dwarfed by the sheer size of the powersat, the spacesuited workers buzz around the huge structure on broomsticklike flitters, little more than a small rocket motor and sets of stirrups to anchor their booted feet.

Far below, on empty desert land leased from the state of New Mexico, stands a five-mile-wide field of receiving antennas, looking like thousands of metal clothes poles set into the ground. The rectennas, as the engineers call them, wait for the microwave beam that the powersat will someday transmit.

In 1968 Dr. Peter S. Glaser, an engineer with Arthur D. Little, Inc., of Cambridge, Massachusetts, invented the Solar Power Satellite.

Glaser's concept was simple. Solar cells convert sunlight into electricity; they had been used on spacecraft since the original *Vanguard* satellite of 1958. Why not build a satellite specifically to generate electricity from the uninterrupted sunlight in space and beam it to receiving stations on Earth? The basic technologies were already in existence: solar cells, such as those used to power pocket calculators, to generate the electricity; and microwave transmitters, which are the heart of microwave ovens, to transmit the energy to the ground. Receiving antennas on the ground would convert the microwave energy back into electricity.

The one technical drawback was that Solar Power Satellites would have to be *big*: several miles across. But they could generate thousands of megawatts of electrical power and beam it to Earth. With no pollution, because a power satellite burns no fuel. The system's power plant is the Sun, some ninety-three million miles from Earth.

In the 1970s NASA and the Department of Energy conducted a joint study of the feasibility of Solar Power Satellites, and concluded that such an orbiting power plant would cost many billions of dollars. The SPS idea was quietly put aside by the American government.

Not so in Japan. In February 1993 Japan's Institute of Space and Astronautical Science conducted the first experiment in space in which microwave power was beamed from one spacecraft to another. The power level was only 900 watts and the experiment took less than a minute. But that was the first step in Japan's Sunsat program, aimed at building an experimental Solar Power Satellite capable of beaming ten megawatts of electrical power to the ground.

By the second decade of the twenty-first century, the global electrical power market had grown to more than one trillion dollars per year. Most of that energy was supplied by fossil fuels: coal, natural gas, and oil that came principally from the Middle East. In Japan, where private corporations and the national government are intimately intertwined, the Sunsat program was quietly handed over to the newly formed Yamagata Industries Corporation, which constructed the demonstration solar power satellite in low Earth orbit. It delivered twelve megawatts to a receiving station built in the Gobi Desert. Yamagata's program was international in scope; the corporation employed engineers and technicians from many nations, including Daniel Hamilton Randolph, a newly graduated electrical engineer from Virginia Polytechnical Institute.

Despite the fact that a Solar Power Satellite uses neither fossil fuels nor radioactives such as uranium or plutonium, many environmentalists objected to transmitting a powerful beam of microwaves through the atmosphere. They drew pictures of birds being roasted alive as they flew through the beam and claimed there would be damaging effects on the long-term climate. Thus the original Japanese receiving station was placed in remote, sparsely settled Mongolia. And the microwave beam was kept so diffuse that horses could graze amid the receiving antennas without harmful effect.

Once the demonstration satellite was operating successfully, Dan Randolph flew back to his native United States and founded Astro Manufacturing Corporation. Pointing to the success of the Japanese, he convinced a consortium of American and Western European financiers to back his company's effort to build a full-scale SPS, capable of delivering ten thousand megawatts to the ground. He hammered home to them that while the capital costs of building the orbital power station would be some four or five times the cost of a nuclear power plant, the operating costs would be so low that the power satellite would begin showing a profit within three years of its start-up. And once the first full-scale power satellite was operational, capital costs for the next ones would go down appreciably.

Saito Yamagata's supporters in the Japanese government told him that the American's betrayal was what he should have expected from a foreigner. Yamagata held his tongue and his patience. In silence he watched Randolph driving his fledgling corporation at a breakneck pace to produce a practical solar power satellite, while his own efforts proceeded much more slowly.

Carefully avoiding funding from any governmental entity and the crippling regulations that came with it, Randolph hired hundreds of workers. He rented time and expertise from NASA to train his team, and convinced aerospace giants such as Boeing and Lockheed Martin to mass-produce rocket boosters that lifted construction crews and equipment into orbit. Even with the benefits of mass production, the costs of the operation drove Astro Corporation to the edge of insolvency.

While the massive power satellite took shape several hundred miles above the Earth, and then was boosted to its final orbital position above the equator, Randolph pushed an elite team of engineers to perfect a spaceplane, a vehicle that lifted off on a rocket booster and then could land like an airplane at any major airport, capable of carrying a small payload or half a dozen workers into orbit. That was the key to operating the solar power satellite economically, profitably. Without it, servicing the huge powersat with human repair and maintenance teams would be too expensive to be practical.

Now Randolph had his solar power satellite. Its construction was almost complete. But the spaceplane project was in a shambles, and he had run out of sources for more funding.

Except for Yamagata's offer.

TAOS, NEW MEXICO

Dan sat across the aisle from Joe Tenny, his chief engineer, while Gerry Adair flew the aging twin-jet Cessna Citation to New Mexico and Hannah Aarons's funeral. Tenny busied himself with his laptop computer, content to let his boss work out his feelings in silence.

At last Dan asked, "Who's watching the store?"

"Lynn Van Buren," said Joe. "She'll keep everything under control until we get back."

"She was a friend of Hannah's, too, wasn't she?"

"Hell, Dan, ninety-nine and a half percent of the staff was a friend of Hannah's. We can't have 'em all trooping out to New Mexico for the funeral."

The chief legal counsel of NASA had regretfully turned down Dan's request to have Hannah Aarons honored with other fallen astronauts. "She wasn't a NASA employee," he explained reluctantly. In the telephone screen Dan could see the pained expression on the man's face and decided not to press the issue. Aarons's alma mater, the Naval Academy, suggested she could be buried at Arlington National Cemetery. But her family wanted her with them, so Dan flew to Hannah's hometown of Taos, above Santa Fe, for her funeral.

The ceremony was brief and dignified. The Aarons's rabbi spoke of Hannah's unquenchable spirit. A high school choir sang the sailor's hymn, "Eternal Father, Strong to Save," adding the verse written for fliers:

> *Lord, guard and guide all those who fly*
> *Through the great spaces of the sky.*
> *Be with them always in the air,*
> *In darkening storms or sunlight fair;*
> *Oh, hear us when we lift our prayer,*
> *For those in peril in the air!*

Standing in the crisp morning breeze beneath a warming Sun, Dan noticed that Hannah would be buried not far from the grave of Kit Carson. Not bad, kid, he said to her silently. You'll be with another frontier scout. Good company.

The sky was bright and clear. The sunshine felt good, comforting, on his shoulders. Dan thought of all the energy that the Sun beamed out continually for billions of years. If we could convert even a tenth of 1 percent of that sunlight into electricity, the world would never have a power shortage. Ever. And we could turn off all the fossil-fuel and nuclear power plants on Earth.

Adair spoke haltingly of his admiration for Hannah and promised he would finish the work that she had started. Then it was Dan's turn to say a few words, and he wondered if he could do it without breaking up. He walked up to the grave, murmured his regrets and condolences to Hannah's husband, her ten-year-old daughter, and her wheelchair-bound mother. Crumpling the speech his public relations man had written for him, Dan said simply:

"Home is the sailor, home from the sea. And the hunter, home from the hill."

He couldn't say more. Not without bawling like a baby.

When it was all finished and Hannah lay beneath the freshly turned earth, Dan, Tenny, and Adair started toward the cemetery's gate, following the Aarons family. A cluster of news reporters and camera crews were hovering outside the cemetery like a humming swarm of bees. Only a few close friends and coworkers and Hannah's immediate family had been allowed past the steady-eyed Native American men who guarded the cemetery gates with loaded shotguns.

Dan knew he would have to face the reporters. There was no way around it.

"You want me to run interference for you?" Tenny asked gruffly as they trudged toward the iron gates.

Dan almost grinned. Tenny was built like a football guard, not all that big but just as burly. Dan pictured the engineer knocking down reporters like a bowling ball going through tenpins.

"No," he answered, looking at the little crowd waiting on the other side of the gates. "Time for me to try to put some positive spin on this."

Tenny grunted. "Lotsa luck."

As soon as the guards swung the gates open the reporters swarmed around him. Dan knew what their questions would be, they were always the same after an accident:

Do you know what caused the crash?

Does this mean your project is finished?

What are you going to do next?

He spread his arms to quiet them, then said in his clearest, most authoritative voice, "We have the best investigators in the world working to determine what went wrong with the spaceplane. At this point in time, all I can tell you is that there might have been a fault in the control system."

"Will Astro Corporation be able to continue the solar power satellite project?"

"We intend to."

"But our information is that you're broke."

"Not quite." Dan gave them a rueful grin. "In fact, we've already had an offer of funding to carry us through the next couple of years."

"An offer of funding? From who?"

"I'm not at liberty to say," Dan replied, silently asking Sai Yamagata to forgive him.

The questions went on, many of them repetitious. Dan thought of himself as a swimmer in the middle of the ocean, surrounded by sharks who were circling, circling, smelling his blood in the water.

At last Tenny broke in. "Hey, we've got a plane to catch, boss."

Dan nodded vigorously. "That's right. Sorry, people. If you need anything more you can call my office at Matagorda."

The reporters grudgingly backed away while Dan, with Tenny and Adair at his side, half-sprinted to the rental car they had picked up at the Taos airport.

When they arrived at the airport, though, Dan was surprised to see another reporter waiting for him on the concrete apron where their plane was parked.

"I'm Vicki Lee," she said, sticking out her hand before Dan could say a word. "Global Video News."

She was almost Dan's height, with a generous figure that edged close to being plump. What do the Jews call it? he asked himself. *Zaftig.* Not quite voluptuous, but good-looking enough to be a news anchor some day, Dan thought. If she skinnies down a little. Not as young as she dresses, though, he told himself as he took in her snug jeans and loose-fitting pullover sweater. Heart-shaped face that dimpled nicely when she smiled. Chestnut hair cut short and spiky; eyes the color of sweet sherry wine.

"How'd you get out here before us?" Dan asked as he took her extended hand. Her grip was firm. She's been practicing, he decided.

Vicki Lee smiled brightly. "I ducked out of the crowd at the cemetery early. Their questions and your answers were pretty predictable, actually."

"Uh-huh," said Dan. He saw Adair and Tenny clamber up the ladder and disappear inside the Cessna.

"I figured I could get better information out of you by myself, without the rest of those twinkies and bozos pushing at you."

Despite himself, Dan grinned. "Okay, here I am. You've got about ten minutes, max."

Her eyes flashed, but she quickly reached into her handbag and pulled out a miniaturized video camera. Dan unconsciously squared his shoulders and tugged at his jacket to make certain it didn't gap. I must look pretty ragged, he thought, but what the hell—I've just come back from a good friend's funeral.

"Mr. Randolph," Vicki began, looking at him through the camera's eye-piece, "is there any truth to the rumor that you and Hannah Aarons were having an affair?"

Dan felt as if she'd hit him in the gut with a monkey wrench. "What is this, a tabloid smear job?"

She put the camera down. "Actually, I'm on the utterly boring financial news desk."

"Then what the hell are you trying to do?"

Perfectly calm, she replied, "I'm trying to get a story, Mr. Randolph. My boss thinks Astro's about to collapse. But I've heard that you and your test pilot were sleeping together."

"Well you've heard dead wrong," he snapped angrily. "Hannah was a married woman with a ten-year-old daughter, for double-damn sake. She and her husband had a fine marriage and she didn't sleep with me or anybody else except her husband."

"Really?"

"Really. And what kind of an idiot do you think I am, sleeping with an employee?"

She shrugged. "But the rumor is out there, Mr. Randolph. Maybe you should allow me to put it to rest."

He shook his head. "I'm not going to dignify a piece of crap like that. No comment at all."

Her expression turned impish. "Not even to deny it?"

Dan stared at her. "You're enjoying this, aren't you?"

"Righteous indignation always tickles me."

"Son of a bitch," Randolph muttered.

"You may have noticed," Vicki said, "that I turned off the camera several moments ago."

"So?"

"So I'm not here to smear you or Mrs. Aarons or anyone else. I'm merely trying to get a story."

He planted his fists on his hips and told himself to calm down. Play her right or she'll do a hatchet job on you.

Adair stuck his head out of the Citation's cockpit window. "Should I start crankin' her up?" he called.

Dan gestured for him to wait without taking his eyes off Vicki Lee. "What kind of a story are you looking for?" he asked her.

She didn't hesitate an eyeblink. "One that can get me off the damned financial desk. I'd really love to work for *Aviation Week*."

"That's setting your sights pretty high."

"Why not? I'm worth it."

"Really?"

"Really and truly, Mr. Randolph."

Jabbing a thumb toward the plane, Dan said, "Okay. You want to fly back to Matagorda with us? We can talk without interruption for a couple of hours."

She broke into a wide smile. "My bags are in the car. I've got to drop it off at the rental office."

Dan started walking beside her toward the burgundy Corolla. "I'll get somebody to drop off the car for you."

"Can you?"

"Sure. No problem. Always happy to cooperate with the news media." He laughed, wondering how cooperative she would be with him.

COUNTDOWN TO LAUNCH

Very, it turned out.

Once they landed at the company airstrip on Matagorda Island, instead of taking Vicki to his own one-room apartment halfway down the hangar catwalk from his office, Dan drove her to the Astro Motel, a few miles away from the airstrip.

"A Jaguar convertible," Vicki said, impressed, as he tossed her luggage and his own battered travel bag into the trunk.

"Ten years old," he gruffed as he slid in behind the steering wheel. "I spend more time under the chassis trying to keep it running than I do driving her."

Vicki nodded as if she thought he was merely making an excuse for an extravagance.

The motel was legally owned by Astro Corporation, but operated quite independently by a local Calhoun County family who had gladly added the hospitality industry to their generations-long business of renting fishing boats and guiding tourist hunters through carefully stocked "safaris" across Matagorda Island. Despite being less than five years old the motel already had a slightly seedy, run-down look to it. The family who ran it was hardly ever there; they far preferred to take their profits to Las Vegas and hand them over to card dealers and slot machines.

Vicki didn't seem to notice the motel's slightly tacky décor. She didn't demur when Dan registered her as a corporate guest and toted his own travel bag along with hers into the room. Two queen-sized beds, same as every room in the place. They ate dinner together in the motel's restaurant; she hardly paid attention to the food as she pumped Dan for the story of his life. He thought that her indifference to the cooking was a good thing, considering its quality, while he spun out a carefully edited version of his days working in space for Yamagata and his goal of making the first working solar power satellite here in the United States of America.

She seemed to take it for granted that they would sleep together. Dan had no objections; in fact, he worried that if he didn't have sex with her she'd get sore. Hell hath no fury, he reminded himself. Besides, it had been a long time since he'd had a sexual romp. Months. Seemed like years.

When Dan awoke the next morning, Vicki was still sleeping soundly beside him. He slipped out of bed and padded to the bathroom, wondering if this little tumble in the hay would help silence the rumor about him and Hannah or make things worse. Every time you think with your gonads, he berated himself, you screw nobody but yourself.

As he looked back at Vicki's fleshy naked body entangled in the sweaty sheets, he laughed inwardly. And damned well, too, he added.

Lifting his toiletries kit from the travel bag he'd left on the unoccupied bed, Dan closed the bathroom door softly and went through his morning shower, brushed his teeth, and started to shave. As he stared into the mirror at his lathered face, though, he thought of Jane.

Haven't seen her in—what is it now, five years? No, damned near six. And you're still thinking of her. Last night in bed with Vicki he had fantasized about Jane Thornton, the woman he had fallen in love with all those years ago, the woman who had moved out of his life and gone back to her native Oklahoma to be a United States senator.

He nicked himself. Damn! Love hurts, he thought.

When Dan came out of the bathroom Vicki was sitting up in bed, the sheet modestly tucked across her bosom, chattering into her cell phone. She smiled at him without missing a syllable.

Dan motioned for her to put the phone down. She did, covering the tiny mouthpiece with her free hand.

"I've got to get back to my office in Houston," she said, "or else—"

"Don't you want to see the rocket launch?"

"Rocket launch?"

Nodding, Dan said, "If the weather holds we'll be launching an OTV around ten this morning."

"What's an OTV?"

"Orbital transfer vehicle. A little shuttle bus that can take crews from low Earth orbit up to geosynch, where the power satellite is."

"Geosynchronous orbit," Vicki said, as if answering a test question. "That's the twenty-four-hour orbit. Twenty-two thousand miles above the equator."

It's twenty-two thousand and three hundred, Dan corrected silently. But what the hell, she's got the basic idea.

"They want me back at the office as soon as I can get there," she said.

"You want to get connected with *Aviation Week?* Cover this launch for them as a freelancer. Make an impression."

He could see the wheels churning in her head. It took her all of three seconds to put the phone back to her ear and say, "I'm going to stay for Astro's launch of a rocket.... Yes, a rocket launch. They're putting up an OTV. Orbital transfer vehicle. It'll make great footage."

By eight-forty-five they were back in the forest green Jaguar, speeding along the empty road the few miles to the Astro complex. Dan had the top down. It was cloudy and cool, with the wind whipping past. Hope there's no problem with the weather, he said to himself.

Once in his office, Dan's executive assistant brought them a breakfast of coffee and English muffins, an obvious frown on her face. Jealousy? Dan wondered. No, he decided. April was young and popular and so good-looking that even the rednecks forgot she was an African American. Could she be suspicious of this news reporter? April's damned sharp, Dan said to himself. She's got sensitive antennae.

When he led Vicki up to the roof of the hangar, the clouds were breaking up and the Sun was beginning to heat the morning. To his surprise, Dan saw a thin haze of fog over by the beach.

"Are all these buildings yours?" Vicki asked, turning a full circle.

"All my domain," Dan replied. "As far as the eye can see, almost."

"Wow."

He pointed to the wall of live oaks and pines off to the right. "Those trees mark the end of Astro Corporation's property and the edge of the state park."

Turning, he identified for her the office building that rose four stories on one side of the hangar, the hangar B on the other side, and the machine shops and assembly buildings beyond it.

"And there," Dan stretched his arm, "is the bird we're going to launch this morning."

Two miles distant, the rocket booster stood tall and slim against the brightening morning sky. It was painted stark white with a big ASTRO corporate logo stenciled in Kelly green along its upper length.

"That's not the spaceplane," Vicki said.

"No, this is an unmanned launch. We're putting up an OTV, like I told you."

"There are people up there?"

Shaking his head, "Nope, the satellite's unattended now, waiting for a crew to go up and finish the final assembly tasks before we turn her on and start generating energy."

"When you send a crew up, they'll go in the spaceplane?"

"Right. As soon as we find out what went wrong in the test flight and get the fault fixed."

"But the spaceplane only goes to low orbit," Vicki said, obviously trying to get her facts straight, "while the power satellite's up in geosynch orbit."

"Which is why we need the OTV," said Dan. "To transfer work crews from the low orbit to geosynch."

She nodded her understanding and then turned to look out at the booster. Dan expected the usual comment about a phallic symbol. Instead, Vicki said, "I don't see any vapor coming from it. No frost where the liquid oxygen tanks are."

His estimation of her climbed several notches. "It's not a liquid-fueled rocket. Solid fuel, like the old Minuteman missiles. Just a big, dumb, cheap booster. Fire it off like a skyrocket."

"Oh."

Pointing again, he explained, "The upper stage has all the sophistication: guidance, rendezvous and docking systems, all that. The first stage just belts her the hell off the planet and then plops down into the Atlantic."

"You mean the Gulf?"

"No, the Atlantic, nearly a thousand miles from here. We send a command to break up the booster shell once she's exhausted her fuel and disengaged from the upper stage. Pieces burn up in the atmosphere, mostly. Some small debris falls into international waters."

"Then why do you need the spaceplane?" she asked.

"To carry people safely and economically. The big dumb booster's fine for carrying freight. We need something better to get people up there. And back down again."

"Oh. Back down."

"That's the trick. We've been leasing Russian spacecraft and launching them from an oceangoing platform that a private company operates. Damned expensive. If we're going to generate electricity at a competitive price, we've got to bring down the costs of sending people to the powersat. That's what the spaceplane is for."

"I see," said Vicki. She took her miniature camera from her handbag, then slipped the bag over her shoulder. "How long until the launch?"

Dan fished his cell phone from his shirt pocket and called the launch center. Everything was going on schedule. Solid-fuel boosters were simpler to operate than the more complex liquid-propelled rockets. The launch countdown was going smoothly.

Vicki began panning across the skyline of square, blocky buildings. She took close-ups of Dan and zoom shots of the booster standing on its launch-pad. The clock ticked down.

April came up at T minus ten minutes with two of the FAA investigators with her. Dan saw little knots of people clustering on the roofs of Hangar B and the office building.

"Five…four…"

Dan felt his innards tightening. No matter how many launches he had seen, how many he had participated in, there was always this heart-thumping anticipation.

"…one…zero."

A blossom of flame flared at the bottom of the rocket's tall cylindrical shape. Dan felt the building beneath his feet rumble. The rocket stirred, lifted slowly, majestically. The roar of a million demons carried across the miles be-tween them, growling louder as the rocket rose higher, higher, gaining speed, a brilliant stream of fire rushing from its tail. Wave after wave of throbbing, pulsing sound washed over them, a physical thundering that shook the bones and tingled every nerve in the body. The rocket was hurtling through the sky, up, up, up, growing smaller, the throaty roar of its engines diminishing now, deepening into a rolling distant thunder.

And then it was gone. The tiny blazing star of the rocket exhaust winked out; the sound dissipated. The sky seemed suddenly empty, the launchpad de-serted.

It took Dan a few moments to get his breathing back to normal. When he looked at Vicki Lee, he saw that her eyes were full of tears.

"I've never seen anything…" she said in a near whisper, her voice falter-ing. "It's an experience…"

Dan nodded and suddenly realized that Jane had never seen a rocket launch. Not one.

MATAGORDA ISLAND, TEXAS

Within a few minutes, though, Vicki recovered from the emotional rush. Suddenly she was in a mad hurry to get back to her office in Houston. Chattering frantically into her cell phone as she scampered back down to Dan's office, Vicki grabbed a gulp of warm orange juice that had been left on his desk and then headed for the door. Dan hustled after her, asking April to set up a corporate plane to take Vicki to Houston, then drove her to the airstrip in his convertible.

"Thanks, Dan, that was wonderful," she said as he walked her to the waiting twin-jet Citation. She gave him a peck on the cheek. No sentimental good-byes, no "When will I see you again?" Just as well, Dan said to himself as he followed her down to the parking lot. Just as well.

Dan watched the plane take off, then drove back to his office the long way, around the airstrip and along the shore road, with the Gulf of Mexico lapping placidly against the white sand of the beach. Much of Matagorda Island had once been a ranch, its scrubby vegetation used as grazing for cattle. Decades earlier, a real pioneer in the space industry had launched a rocket from the is-land, one of the very first launches by a private industrial firm rather than a government agency. Dan had bought the old ranch when he first started Astro Manufacturing Corporation. He had bulldozed a three-mile-long landing strip and thrown up the hangars, test stands, and cinderblock office buildings that comprised Astro's headquarters complex. The region's environmentalists howled, but the local building inspector hesitantly okayed the buildings as tenable under the county's hurricane safety code. The inspector departed from the Astro complex with a large bulge of cash in his pocket.

A hurricane—that's all we need, Dan thought as he parked his forest green convertible in his personal space. He tried to keep the ten-year-old XJS in mint condition; before the spaceplane crash he had often tinkered with the auto himself. Not now, though. He walked briskly past the DON'T EVEN *THINK* OF PARKING HERE sign that marked his slot, eager to get out of the hot, humid air. Hurricane season coming up, he reminded himself.

Inside the air-conditioned hangar Dan clanged up the steel stairway to his office on the catwalk that ran across three sides of the big open barnlike structure. The spaceplane's wreckage was spread across the floor, one lonely technician squatting on his heels in the middle of it, looking puzzled. Dan thought about how much it cost to air-condition the whole hangar. The building wasn't insulated, either, he knew: just bare metal walls frying in the sun. Be cheaper to keep just the offices under air. But as he looked down at that one technician Dan realized that cutting the air-conditioning bill wasn't going to save Astro from bankruptcy.

He smiled at April as he passed her desk. She looked happier now that Vicki was gone. Dan closed his office door behind him and slid into the ultra-modern leather swivel chair behind the heavy, ornately Victorian desk. His grandfather had given Dan the desk when he'd first started Astro Corporation. It had been the desk of *his* father, Dan's great-grandfather, when he'd been a genteely impoverished young minister in rural Virginia. Dan had promised to use it as his very own. So now it dominated the cluttered office like a dark brooding castle looming over an untidy little hamlet.

Dan booted up his desktop computer and punched up his schedule for the remainder of the day. And frowned at the screen. One P.M.: Claude Passeau, Federal Aviation Administration. That'll take the flavor out of lunch, he thought.

He's coming here to close me down, Dan thought. What he didn't know was how he might talk the man out of it.

It was precisely twelve minutes after one when Dan's phone buzzed.

"Mr. Passeau to see you," April announced. Dan thought again of how fortunate he was to have April as his executive assistant. The woman was smart, hard-working, and good-looking, to boot: tall and leggy, with skin the color of creamy milk chocolate and glossy shoulder-length dark hair. She ran his office, his social calendar; she could even program his computer with cool efficiency.

The memory of Vicki Lee's accusation about an affair with Hannah flicked into his memory, annoying him all over again. If I was going to take an employee to bed it would be somebody like April, Dan said to himself. Not my top test pilot.

His office door opened and Claude Passeau stepped in. He was a small man, almost dainty, wearing a lightweight beige suit and a neat bow tie of blue and yellow stripes. Clip-on, Dan guessed. Passeau looked to be about forty, forty-five. Too young to be worried about his retirement benefits yet. He had a trim little moustache; his hairline was starting to recede, but his hair was still dark brown, although thinning.

Dan got to his feet and came around the desk, his hand extended. "Mr. Passeau."

"*Doctor* Passeau, actually," he said in a smooth voice that almost purred. He smiled pleasantly as he spoke.

Gesturing the man to the little round conference table in the corner of his office, Dan asked, "Doctor of engineering?"

Passeau brushed his moustache with a fingertip. "Psychology, I'm afraid. It was the only curriculum I could get in the school's distance-learning program."

"Oh. I see." Dan started to ask which school he'd gone to, then thought better of it, realizing that Passeau had bought his doctorate from a diploma mill.

"The doctorate looks good on my resumé," Passeau said as he sat at the chair Dan proffered. "The government doesn't really care where it comes from or what subject it's in. Just being able to claim a doctorate from a reasonably reputable school is enough to boost your salary category."

Dan grinned as he sat next to him. Either this guy is charmingly honest or he's a damned slippery customer, he thought.

April stepped into the office. "Can I get you gentlemen something? Coffee, maybe?"

"Thank you, I've had my lunch," said Passeau.

"I'll have coffee," Dan said.

"In that case, so will I," Passeau reconsidered.

As April shut the door behind her, Dan leaned slightly toward Passeau and said, "My people seem to be working well with your investigators. I think they'll find the reason for the accident in a week or so."

"More like a month or two, I'd say," Passeau replied.

Dan said nothing, but grumbled to himself. More like six months, if I don't light a fire under this bureaucrat.

Passeau asked, "Do you intend to build another spaceplane?"

"We've already got one nearly finished. It's over in the next hangar, if you want to see it."

"You realize, of course, that you will not be permitted to fly it until our investigation into the crash is concluded."

Dan leaned back in his chair. "It could take a year to finish all the paperwork."

"At the very least," said Passeau.

"I was thinking that once you found the fault, we could fly the new bird without waiting for the paperwork to be finished."

Passeau began to reply, but April came in with a lacquered tray bearing an insulated stainless steel jug of coffee and two delicate-looking china cups.

"I'll pour," Dan said, shooing her out of the office with the expression on his face.

Passeau said, "I know you're anxious to get a successful flight, but the Federal Aviation Administration has rules, you realize, and those rules must be obeyed."

And rain makes applesauce, Dan said to himself. Aloud, he asked, "Can't we bend those rules a little?"

"And kill another pilot? What would that gain you?"

WASHINGTON, D.C.

t's a mistake, Senator."

Jane Thornton said nothing; she merely continued walking along the side of the reflecting pool, her back to the giant phallic Washington Monument, her eyes on the classic beauty of the Lincoln Memorial. The smell of freshly cut grass filled the air. It was a warm afternoon; tourists and office workers were strolling along the lawn or sprawled on the grass, soaking up the sun. Jane wondered inwardly, How many of them are federal workers who should be at their desks? She smiled slightly at the thought that "federal worker" could be regarded as the biggest oxymoron of them all.

The man beside her was grossly overweight, sweating heavily in his summerweight suit, tie pulled loose from his wilted collar. He misunderstood her smile.

"You think it's funny?" asked Denny O'Brien. "It isn't, you know. We're talking about your political future."

"I understand that," Senator Thornton said, without taking her eyes off the distant Lincoln Memorial. Squinting, she thought she could make out the form of the heroic statue inside the graceful Greek columns. Hidden by a grassy knoll off to the right was the Vietnam Wall. To the left, the Korean Veterans' Memorial.

"I mean, you back a dark horse and win, you're a genius," O'Brien went on, wheezing slightly. "But you back a dark horse and lose, like Scanwell would lose, and you're an idiot."

Very few people could speak that way to Senator Thornton. O'Brien was one of them. He had engineered her campaign for reelection to the Senate. Now he was worried that she was going to throw it all away.

"Scanwell hasn't got a chance, Senator."

Senator Thornton at last turned her eyes to the globulous O'Brien. In high heels she was inches taller than he, and even though she was wearing comfortable flats at the moment, she still looked down at him. Her long auburn hair was done up off her graceful neck in a stylish swirl. Her skirted suit of pale green was modest, yet heads still turned as she strolled along the pool. She was not merely beautiful: Jane Thornton was regal, tall and stately, possessed of the porcelain-skinned, green-eyed beauty of a Norse goddess. Yet she had a reputation for being cold, aloof, a hard-headed, no-nonsense Ice Queen.

O'Brien was becoming frustrated by her frosty silence. "Come on, Senator, face it: Scanwell's a nobody!"

"He's governor of Texas," she said calmly.

Squinting in the sunshine, O'Brien countered, "Not every governor of Texas becomes president of the United States."

"Morgan Scanwell will."

O'Brien looked as if he wanted to hop up and down in frustrated fury. He'd give himself a heart attack if he did, Senator Thornton thought.

"You *can't* declare for him! It'd be political suicide!"

"Not if he wins, Denny."

"Which he won't," O'Brien retorted sullenly.

"Denny, there's no sense our going around this bush any more. I want to back Morgan Scanwell. I want to throw the entire Oklahoma delegation to him at the convention—"

"He won't make it to the convention. He'll be wiped out by Super Tuesday. Maybe by the New Hampshire primary."

"If you knew him you wouldn't feel that way," said Senator Thornton.

"He's just a hick from the sticks, Senator! A rube from nowheres-ville."

"That's what they thought in Dallas and Houston," she replied. "And in Austin. But he won. He beat them all and won the governorship. And he can win the White House, with the proper backing."

"No way."

She stopped walking and turned to face O'Brien. His face was dripping sweat. He seemed to be visibly melting, like a snowman in the sun.

"Denny, I'm flying to Tulsa tomorrow night. Come and join me there. Meet the man. Is that asking too much?"

O'Brien gave her a mistrustful look. While many in Washington thought that Senator Thornton's physical appearance was her greatest asset, O'Brien and a handful of other insiders knew that the senator's ability to convince people, her skill at changing the minds of erstwhile opponents, was the true key to her success.

"Overnight?" he asked warily.

"I'll be gone for the weekend. One day in Tulsa to keep my home fences mended, and then at home at the ranch."

"I'll come to the ranch," O'Brien said. "Okay?"

"Fine," she said.

"Great. Now let's get out of this sun!" O'Brien stalked off toward the nearest bar.

MATAGORDA ISLAND, TEXAS

As Dan walked along the catwalk from his one-room apartment to his office and the breakfast tray that April would have waiting for him, he saw Passeau coming in from the morning sunlight through the hangar's big open sliding double doors. The FAA inspector already had his jacket off and folded neatly over one arm. With his free hand he slowly unknotted his bow tie and unbuttoned his collar as he stood there staring at the wreckage of the spaceplane on the hangar floor.

From this distance it was hard to see the expression on Passeau's face, but from the slump of his shoulders the man seemed to be downcast, depressed.

Dan forgot about going to his office and clattered down the steel steps to reach Passeau's side.

"It's so heartbreaking," Passeau said, once he recognized Dan. "I hate to see the wreckage of a plane. It saddens me."

"Come with me," Dan said. "I'll show you something that'll cheer you up."

Passeau followed Dan without argument, back into the burning brightness of the summer morning. Dan felt the warmth of the sun soaking through his short-sleeved shirt. We can make electrical energy out of you, he said silently to the Sun. We can use your energy to light up the world.

"Where are we going?" Passeau asked, walking beside Dan.

Pointing to hangar B, a huge metal box looming a few dozen yards from them, Dan replied, "Right there."

This hangar's sliding doors were shut, but there was a man-sized doorway in the nearer of them, with an armed security guard standing just inside it, in the shade.

"Hi, Mr. Randolph," said the guard, smiling. He was portly, jowly, looked out of condition. But he wore a nine-millimeter pistol on his hip.

"Morning, Frank," Dan said. "This is Dr. Passeau. He's with the FAA."

Passeau fingered the ID card he wore on a cord around his neck and the guard peered at it. "Dr. Pass-oh," the guard drawled. "Right."

It took a moment for their eyes to adjust to the much lower light level inside the hangar. And then Passeau sucked in his breath.

"So that's it," he said, almost in a whisper.

"That's it," said Dan.

Sitting in the middle of the hangar floor was a sleek, silvery, stub-winged spaceplane, the twin of the one that had crashed. A single tail fin flared up from its rear end, atop a pair of rocket nozzles. Its nose was pointed like a stiletto, with a raked-back windshield above it showing where the cockpit was. The spaceplane rested on three wheels, two where the stumpy wings joined the fuselage, the third beneath the nose.

Passeau slowly walked around it, admiration clear in his eyes, his expression. He reached out his free hand and touched the smooth metal skin, like a worshipper touching a statue in a cathedral.

"Hey, yo! Hands off!" a deep voice bellowed.

Passeau jerked his hand away as if it had been scalded.

Dan saw a skinny black man in spanking white coveralls advancing from the shadows beneath the catwalk balcony, his dark face scowling. "Don't touch the hardware, man."

"Claude, this is my chief technician, Niles Muhamed. Niles, this is Dr. Passeau of the Federal Aviation Administration."

Muhamed's demeanor changed by a fraction. "Pleased to meet you, Dr. Passeau. But please keep your hands off Oh-Two."

"I'm sorry," Passeau apologized. "I should have known better."

"Niles is the head honcho in this hangar," Dan explained. "Nobody lifts a finger in here without Niles knowing about it."

"It's a beautiful creation," Passeau said, gesturing toward the spaceplane.

"It's almost ready to fly," said Dan.

"'Nuther week," Muhamed said. "Maybe ten days. We're checkin' ever'thing twice. Just like Santa Claus."

"Good," Dan said. Passeau said nothing. He simply stared admiringly at the backup spaceplane.

"Come on, Claude," Dan said at last. "Time to get back to work."

Muhamed nodded approvingly. He didn't like having strangers poking around in his hangar. Or the boss, either, for that matter.

He's not such a bad guy, Randolph thought as he watched Passeau getting involved deeper and deeper with Joe Tenny in a discussion of the crash investigation.

"The telemetry data is pretty clear," Tenny was saying, pointing to a jagged series of spiky lines weaving across his desktop screen.

"The forward attitude jets fired," Passeau murmured, nodding.

"But they weren't programmed to fire at that point," Tenny said, his finger pecking at the keyboard. "See? This is the program, on the left, and on the right's the actual."

Passeau stared at the screen as intently as if it were the Mona Lisa. Or a *Playboy* centerfold, Dan thought.

He had taken the FAA official down to Tenny's office, where Passeau could compare notes with the beefy engineer on the crash investigation. Tenny had complained that so many people from the FAA, the NTSB, and half a dozen other government agencies were crawling over Astro's headquarters that he was spending all his time "babysitting the red-tape gang." Yet it had to be done. You don't have a crash, especially a fatal one, without government hounds sniffing everywhere. Even NASA had sent in a team of advisors, although the spaceplane was strictly a private endeavor.

Dan had ordered Tenny to cooperate fully with the investigators. Reluctantly, the engineer turned over most of his tasks to his top aide, Lynn Van Buren, and devoted himself full-time to working with Passeau and the other government people.

Tenny's office was the opposite of Randolph's: almost exactly the same size, but as neat and ordered as Randolph's was cluttered. The only thing out of place was a painter's easel standing in the far corner of the room, a half-finished acrylic of a tropical beach at sunset done in bold, blaring primary colors.

As soon as the two of them began talking technical details, Passeau's demeanor—his entire personality—had changed. In my office he's a bureaucrat winding red tape around my dead body, Randolph said to himself. But here with Joe he's an engineer trying to figure out what the hell went wrong with the flight.

"May I see the high magnification video again?" Passeau asked.

"It's pretty grainy," Tenny said as he grabbed the computer's mouse in a meaty hand.

"Yes, I know, but I want to see that pitch-down maneuver. Perhaps the video can be enhanced enough to show the puff from the attitude jet."

Tenny nodded, impressed. "Yeah, come to think of it..."

Randolph got up from the chair Tenny had given him, thinking, Better to leave these two alone. The longer Passeau's with Joe, the less he'll bother me.

"Gentlemen," Dan said, "if you'll excuse me, I have a business to run."

They barely acknowledged his exit, their heads together as they watched the video of the spaceplane's breakup. Dan couldn't stand to watch it again.

Glad to be out of there, Dan pulled his cell phone from his pants pocket and checked his schedule. Meeting with his public relations director at ten. It was a few minutes past the hour, he saw. Hurrying down the hallway, mumbling greetings to the employees he passed, he saw the P.R. director ambling up from the opposite direction, toward him.

Len Kinsky was a tall, gangling native of New York, where he had worked as an editor and writer for technical magazines for several years. He had left the city in the middle of a nasty divorce proceeding and accepted a job "in the boondocks," as he put it, because he needed more money than a journalist made to pay for his divorce lawyer and his ex-wife's constant demands.

But although he had taken himself out of New York, he could not take the New York out of himself. He prided himself on being a native of the Big Apple. At least once a day he declared to anyone who would listen that the entire state of Texas wasn't worth a single block of Manhattan's worst slum. He had absolutely no faith in rockets, no interest in space exploration or power satellites or anything more complex than a beanbag chair. Which made him a damned good public relations man for Astro Corporation, as far as Dan was concerned. The worst trap a P.R. guy can fall into is believing his own propaganda. Kinsky wasn't even sure he believed in airplanes.

His face was long and horsy, with startling ice-blue eyes that peered out suspiciously from under heavy reddish brows. His ginger-red hair was a thick tangle, like a jungle underbrush, almost. Kinsky was known to call attention to himself at parties by whipping out an ancient Ronson cigarette lighter and setting his hair on fire. Randolph had seen him do it. As everyone gasped and staggered, Kinsky would put out the little blaze with a couple of pats of his hand, grinning and saying, "Wasn't that sensational?"

He wasn't smiling now as he approached Randolph, and his Ronson was in his pocket.

"How's it going, Len?"

Kinsky reversed his course like a soldier doing an about-face and fell into step with Randolph. The two men strode swiftly down the corridor toward Dan's office.

"Not good, boss. *The New York* fucking *Times* ran their usual editorial about keeping people out of space. Practically blamed you for murder."

Randolph snorted disdainfully. "So what else is new?"

"The *Wall Street Journal* says pretty much the same, but in a more businesslike way."

"How so?"

"They say the powersat could be operated entirely by remotely operated machinery; no need for humans in space."

"Yeah," Dan groused. "And rain makes applesauce."

"They quoted three different university professors."

Dan banged through the door to his outer office, startling April at her desk. "The day any one of those double-dome geniuses starts to operate his own laboratory on campus entirely with remotely operated machinery, without using grad students or any other humans, *then* I'll believe we won't need human crews at the powersat."

He pushed through the door to his private office and threw himself into the sculpted chair behind the big ornate desk.

"You know that, boss," said Kinsky, dropping into the upholstered chair in front of the desk, "and maybe even I know it. But the media doesn't and neither do the public."

"Fatheads and fools," Randolph muttered.

"But if you want the government to be on your side—"

"The double-damned government!" Randolph snapped. "I've got a guy from the FAA sitting in Tenny's office. He's all set to shut us down. For good."

"You need friends in high places, boss."

"Maybe I should build a church?"

Kinsky's long face took on a crafty look. "Or see the governor of the state."

"The governor?"

"Governor Scanwell. There's talk that he's considering running for president next year."

"What good's that going to do me?" Randolph demanded.

"Well," Kinsky said, "Scanwell's a dark horse, an outsider to Washington politics. He's going to need some issues that the Beltway bandits haven't taken for themselves yet."

Randolph made a sour face. "No major politician has made an issue of space since Kennedy."

Shaking his head vigorously, Kinsky said, "No, no, no, boss. It's not space. It's energy."

"Energy."

Hunching forward in his chair eagerly, the P.R. director said, "Look. The U.S. is more dependent on oil from the Middle East every year, right? Europe, too."

"Right," said Randolph.

"Every President since Nixon has made noises about energy independence, right? But every year we buy more oil from the Arabs. That oil money funds dictatorships, slavery, attacks on Israel, you name it."

"And terrorism," Randolph muttered.

"Right!" Kinsky agreed. "And terrorism. Okay, so here's you, with Astro Corporation. What are you trying to do?"

"Stay afloat."

"No! You're trying to open up a new source of energy for the U.S. of A. Solar power! Enough energy from one solar power satellite to replace all the fossil fuel and nuclear power plants in all of Texas!"

"Or California."

"Or New York!"

Dan sank back in his softly yielding chair. "Okay, so we're offering a way off the oil teat. There's nothing new in that."

"But the governor of Texas could use it as a campaign issue. It would bring him instant national attention. International attention!"

"You think he'd buck the oil lobby?" Dan scoffed. "In your dreams."

Kinsky retorted, "He's already bucking them with the environmental legislation he's pushed through. He won the governorship without oil money!"

"By a hair."

"But he won. He beat them."

"Yeah. And with a little luck maybe a terrorist will blow him up."

"So much the better!"

Dan shook his head warily. "The politicians have backed away from us, Len. You know that. God knows I've tried to get political support in Washington. They're just not interested."

"That's because you're too goddamned independent for them. And NASA sees you as competition. Nobody in Washington is going to back a new private venture against an existing government agency."

"But we're not competition . . ."

"As you say it, boss: And rain makes applesauce."

Randolph stared at his P.R. director. "Did you know that that phrase came from NASA's first director of public relations? He used it in a children's book he wrote."

Kinsky shrugged carelessly. "Boss, you should meet the governor."

"I already did, once. Didn't I?"

"At the rollout ceremony for the spaceplane, yeah; he was here for that."

"So what do I do now? Go to the governor with my hat in my hand and ask him for a handout?"

"No! You get him to invite you to Austin. And when you get there, you tell him how you can help him get into the White House."

Despite his doubts, Dan smiled. "Okay. How do I get him to invite me to Austin?"

"Leave that to me, boss. That's what I get paid for."

KHARTOUM, SUDAN

The Sun was setting over the dusty, picked-bare hills. Standing alone at the window of the now-empty conference room, Asim al-Bashir watched the molten red ball sinking slowly, slowly into the parched and dying earth, turning the cloudless hot sky into a bowl of burnished copper, sending long purple shadows across the decaying old stone fortress, the ancient mosque of the city's central square, the modern office and apartment blocks that were already crumbling gradually into disrepair.

After three days of sometimes bitter discussion, the others of The Nine had left the hotel to go their separate ways. They had listened to al-Bashir's plan, incredulous at first, but with slowly increasing understanding. None of them were enthusiastic about it, but at last they had reluctantly given their approval. The power satellite would be used for *their* purposes, and the Americans would not even realize they have been attacked. But this attack would kill thousands, tens of thousands, and it would humble the arrogant Americans mercilessly. They will turn on themselves after this, al-Bashir thought, rending each other in an eruption of accusations and recriminations. They will do our work for us.

And the very idea of a power satellite will be damned forever. Al-Bashir smiled to himself as he saw a future in which the West became even more dependent on oil from the lands of Islam. Oil is power, he told himself. Nothing must be allowed to challenge that power.

The cry of a muezzin came wailing faintly from the loudspeakers in the distant mosque's minaret:

"Come to prayer. Come to salvation. Allah is most great. There is no god but Allah."

Al-Bashir turned, ready to go back to his hotel room upstairs. He had no intention of taking a chance on being seen outside the hotel, especially at the hour of prayer, when a man in an expensive Western business suit was something to stare at.

He was startled to see the Sudanese who had hosted the meeting of The Nine standing in the doorway of the conference room, silently watching him.

"Will you pray with me, my brother?" The Sudanese's voice was surprisingly soft and gentle for such a stoutly built man. In his white djellaba and turban he looked like a mountain of snow, except for his deeply black face. They think of themselves as Arabs, al-Bashir thought, and lord it over their neighbors in the south of the country who have not surrendered to Allah.

"I will be honored to pray with you, my brother," said al-Bashir. Prayer was not foremost in his thinking, but he agreed to the Sudanese's simple request out of respect for the greatness of Islam, where men of all races were equals. Neither wealth nor poverty, neither family nor the color of a man's skin nor the land of one's birth should stand between those who have accepted the faith.

The Sudanese led him down a corridor of the hotel to a small private office, which he unlocked with an old-fashioned metal key. He went to a filing cabinet and withdrew two prayer rugs from its bottom drawer. The rug he handed al-Bashir looked threadbare, almost fragile.

"My grandfather's," the Sudanese murmured. "It was all he had left after the rebels took his village. They raped all the women and slaughtered all the younger men."

Civil war, al-Bashir knew. Sudan had been torn apart by civil war for two generations and more. North against south. Moslems against the nomadic pagan tribes who camped in their tents atop billions of dollars worth of oil deposits. It was the oil that counted, al-Bashir knew. In the end, all wars are fought over wealth, even civil wars.

After their prayers, the Sudanese carefully rolled up the rugs and placed them back in the filing cabinet drawer from which he had taken them.

"Tell me, my brother," he said softly, looking away from al-Bashir, toward the blank and silent computer screen on the desk, "this thing with the power satellite—it will kill many?"

Al-Bashir nodded. "Many thousands. Tens of thousands, perhaps even more."

"But the Americans will not know that we of the faith have done this to them? They will believe it was an accident?"

"Yes. An accident that will cripple their efforts to steal energy from space."

"Which will make them more dependent on oil from the lands of Islam?"

"Indeed so. If all goes as I believe it will, we will be in a position to demand a return of the oil fields the Americans now control. We will drive them out of the Persian Gulf region altogether."

"But it will kill many thousands? Truly?"

"Truly," said al-Bashir.

The Sudanese appeared to think about that for a few silent moments. At last he said, "It is good, then. Hurt them. Hurt them as we have been hurt. Let them suffer as we have suffered. Let them know the pain and blood that have made my life into an endless hell. May God's will be done."

"Indeed, brother," said al-Bashir. And he thought, Keep the Americans dependent on our oil. That is our power over them. As long as they need our oil they must bend to our will. But we must be subtle. We must be as silent as the snake. And as deadly.

THORNTON RANCH, LOVE COUNTY, OKLAHOMA

From her bedroom window in the sprawling old ranch house, Jane Thornton could see the Red River winding through the wheat fields and, off in the distance, the greener pastures where cattle still grazed. Texas lay on the other side of the river, but here along its northern bank stretched the family ranch, as it had for generations.

Easterners thought of Oklahoma as oil country, even now, a quarter century after most of the oil had been pumped out of the ground. All through the oil boom of the twentieth century the Thornton family had tended its acres, growing wheat and beef, the staples that people needed no matter who was getting filthy rich from oil. Now, with the oil just about gone, the wheat and cattle remained to feed the hungry—at a price that kept the Thorntons in luxury and provided the money to send a Thornton to the U.S. Senate.

Jane's father had been a senator and had groomed his eldest son to take his seat when the time came. But Junior had killed himself, his wife, and both children in the crash of his private plane. Dad saw to it that his blood alcohol level was never revealed to the public, but neither money nor influence could heal the pain and shock of the tragedy. Then Dad died in office from a massive stroke, and the governor that he had maneuvered into office in Oklahoma City appointed Jane to fill out his unexpired term.

She had met a headstrong young engineer named Dan Randolph and fallen into a whirlwind of romance with him, but then he'd run off to Japan to follow his own wild dreams and Jane had gone to Washington.

Jane found that she enjoyed being a United States senator. She enjoyed the power of belonging to that exclusive little club of one hundred men and women. Quickly she latched onto Senator Bob Quill, the "silver fox" who chaired the Senate Finance Committee. He became her mentor, and there were even occasional rumors that they were having an affair, rumors that never got far because the standard wisdom on Capitol Hill was that Quill was the straightest arrow in the quiver, and Jane Thornton was the Ice Queen, beautiful but cold and aloof.

Both those characterizations were very far off the mark, although Jane and Quill kept their relationship strictly nonsexual. Jane had a lover, but no one knew it. She went to great lengths to make certain that no one—not even her closest staff aides—knew about her love life.

Dan Randolph had popped into her life again briefly, disastrously. They had parted for good, she thought, on the Day of the Bridges.

She turned from the window and began to dress for dinner: denim skirt and short-sleeved white blouse. Ranch casual. No need to be fancy. She didn't have to impress anyone—that would be Scanwell's objective, not hers.

She was tugging on her slingbacks when she saw Scanwell's car coming down the long driveway from the main road from Marietta. Right on time, she thought, smiling. How like the man.

When she got downstairs, Denny O'Brien was already in the entry hall introducing himself to Scanwell. The governor had come to this meeting alone, flying his own plane from Austin and then driving a Thornton car from the airport outside Marietta. He looked tired, Jane thought; he could use a weekend of rest.

"The senator's told me a lot about you, Governor," O'Brien was saying. He had to look up; Scanwell towered over him.

The governor of Texas looked like the Hollywood image of a cowboy: tall, rangy, with a craggy yet handsome face and sky-blue eyes that twinkled boyishly when he smiled. He was wearing whipcord slacks and a suede sports jacket. And well-worn tan boots.

Jane had to smile at the contrast between pudgy, globular O'Brien and the lean, lanky Morgan Scanwell. He had been a special agent with the Federal Bureau of Investigation when Jane had first met him, but he had quit the FBI in disgust over the political infighting with the Homeland Security Department that had hamstrung the Bureau. Guided by the philosophy, "If you can't beat 'em, join 'em," Morgan Scanwell had entered politics, swiftly rising from a councilman in suburban Houston to governor of Texas—with the advice and substantial financial help from the Thornton family in neighboring Oklahoma.

Jane guided them to the bar off to one side of the spacious living room. The butler served drinks as they made themselves comfortable, Jane in her favorite wing chair, where she could tuck her feet up off the carpeted floor, Scanwell in the big, plush sofa, O'Brien in the armchair facing him. Morgan's drinking bourbon and water, Jane noticed. He must be edgy.

"So, Governor," O'Brien said, sipping at his tonic and lime juice, "Jane tells me you're thinking about running for president."

Scanwell smiled, glanced at Jane, then replied, "I'm thinking about it."

"Think you can win?"

"I wouldn't contemplate running if I didn't think I could win." Jane thought that Scanwell's voice, normally a pleasant light baritone, sounded just a little high, tense.

"Really? Sometimes people toss their hats in the ring just to get the party to pay attention to them."

Scanwell's smile tightened. "Mr. O'Brien, I—"

"Denny. Call me Denny."

"All right, Denny." Scanwell took a breath. "I wouldn't put my people through the stress and labor of a campaign merely to feed my own ego." Before O'Brien could object, he continued, "Or to make some political points within the party. I'm not in this to win concessions from the party. I'm in it to become president of the United States."

O'Brien sank back in his chair, then took a long sip of his drink. Stalling for time while he thinks, Jane realized.

"Okay, then," O'Brien said at last. "What do you have to offer that none of the other potential candidates have?"

Jane relaxed and picked up her vodka martini. It's all right, she thought. Morgan's passed the first test. Denny's impressed.

MATAGORDA ISLAND, TEXAS

So what've you come up with?" Randolph asked.

Tenny scowled at him. "Hey, it's only been a few days, boss. These things take time."

"Time is the one thing I don't have, Joe. I need an answer fast."

Dan was sitting on the edge of his chair, toying nervously with the sleek silver-painted model of the spaceplane that he kept on his desk alongside the square, flat replica of the power satellite. When he realized what he was doing he put the model down as if it was a hot coal.

Seated backward on one of the conference table chairs, his beefy arms across its back with his chin resting on them, Tenny said, "It's gotta be the attitude thruster. Damn thing misfired and pitched the nose down."

"You're sure?"

"Hell no! But it's gotta be that. Nothing else makes sense. Telemetry shows everything going fine, everything nominal until the goddamn nose pitches down. At that point in the reentry it was the worst thing that could happen. Absolutely the worst."

"The telemetry shows that the thruster fired?"

"The friggin' telemetry doesn't show shit!" Tenny snapped, waving his arms angrily. "At that point it goes blooey. Just turns into fuckin' hash. Not worth a thimbleful of piss."

Randolph leaned back in his chair. He had seen Tenny in many different moods, but never had the engineer been so crude.

"We need to find the thruster in the wreckage," Tenny said, more calmly. "So far we haven't recovered the nose section."

"So what makes you think—"

"It hadda be the thruster. Just at the wrong goddamn instant. Talk about Murphy's Law! If the thruster had fired a coupla seconds earlier, or even later, Hannah could've compensated, got the bird back under control. But it hadda go right then, right at that fuckin' microsecond. Put the bird into a dive that nobody could recover from. Heat load, aerodynamic load, goddamn structure broke up."

"And the telemetry went out?" Randolph asked again.

"Yeah. Just went into hash, like it was being jammed or something."

"Jammed? You mean, like somebody was jamming the frequency?"

"Yep. Just like that." Tenny sunk his chin back onto his hairy forearms.

"Deliberately jamming?"

Tenny's brows went up. "Deliberately?"

Randolph nodded.

"Jesus Q. Christ," Tenny muttered. "You think somebody did it on purpose?"

"You tell me."

The engineer sat up straighter. "If it was deliberate..."

"Sabotage," said Randolph. "Murder."

"Whoever did it would have to know our telemetry codes."

"Could that be done?"

"The thruster's controlled by the flight computer. You'd have to know the whole friggin' computer code, then override it and put in a new command to fire the thruster at that point in time."

"Maybe it wasn't jamming," Randolph suggested. "Maybe it was the new command, sent in from an outside source and strong enough to override the existing program."

Tenny looked as if he had just discovered ants crawling over his body. "They'd have to know the whole computer program, all the codes, the time sequence... everything."

"That means it's somebody on the inside. Somebody here."

Shaking his head hard enough to pop vertebrae, Tenny replied, "Naw. It couldn't be. We know everybody here. We've worked with 'em for years, Dan. None of them would do it, kill Hannah. It couldn't be!"

Randolph felt a wave of anger rising in him. *Somebody here, somebody who's worked for me for years, deliberately sabotaged the spaceplane. Deliberately killed Hannah. Some sonofabitch that I've trusted.*

"They wouldn't have to know that the plane was going to crash," he said slowly. "They'd just be selling information to make some extra bucks."

"Corporate espionage," Tenny growled.

Keeping his voice calm, flat, Dan asked the engineer, "Can you come up with a better explanation?"

Tenny swung a leg over the chair he'd been sitting on and got to his feet. "When I do, I'll let you know."

He started for the door. Dan saw that both his hands were balled into fists. "Joe."

Tenny stopped and turned back toward Randolph.

"Keep this between you and me. If we do have a rat in with us, I don't want him to know that we suspect anything."

"Yeah. Right."

"Nobody else, Joe. Not even Lynn. And especially not Passeau. Just you and me."

"That's gonna slow things down, if I have to do all the checking myself."

"Nobody else."

Tenny nodded, accepting it. "Gotcha."

WASHINGTON, D.C.

The Senate dining room was quiet; only a few tables were occupied this late in the afternoon. The strong aroma of freshly brewed coffee wafted in from the kitchen as Senator Quill toyed with a fruit salad, waiting for Jane Thornton to show up.

Robert Quill was a man with an embarrassment of riches. Like most of his fellow senators, he had been born to considerable wealth: His forbears had made the family's original fortune in railroads and steel, and sent their sons to the Wharton School of Business to learn how to preserve the family's money and add to it. They invested in aluminum and aircraft, later in titanium and electronics. Each generation sent one of their sons to the United States Senate; protecting the fortune was as important as increasing it.

Bob Quill was known as a liberal senator. He fought for civil liberties and equal rights, as long as they didn't seriously endanger his family's interests. To his credit, he bent corporate managers and directors (including his own siblings) toward better treatment of minorities, including Native Americans.

His biggest political problem was the thick seams of coal deposits that underlay Montana's Great Plains region. For years Quill had earnestly tried

to convince his fellow senators, and even a president or two, that this coal rep-
resented an untapped reserve of energy as large as all the oil in the Middle
East. But nobody wanted Montana's coal. The environmentalists pointed out
that coal, especially the high-sulfur-content coal in Montana, was an ecological nightmare. Mining it would devastate croplands and pastures; burning it
would pollute the air unconscionably. The oil interests didn't want Montana's
coal competing against them. And the automotive industry pointed out that
although coal could be converted into liquid fuel for transportation purposes,
the cost of doing so was so high that only a national emergency (and plenty of
federal funds) could possibly justify it.

Quill was brooding on these matters when Jane Thornton finally arrived
at his table.

"I'm sorry to be late, Bob," she said softly. People tended to speak in whispers when the dining room was almost empty. "The subcommittee chairman
wouldn't let go of us until five minutes ago."

Quill got to his feet and helped her into a chair. He was a small man,
slight and light-boned, almost like a dancer. Despite his Western origins, he
dressed like a Philadelphia banker in a dark gray three-piece suit. With his
trim moustache and sleekly coifed silver hair, news reporters almost always
described him as dapper.

A waiter immediately brought a menu but Jane waved him off. "I had
lunch in my office," she explained to Quill.

He smiled at her. Senator Thornton had been his protégé since she'd first
arrived on Capitol Hill. They had fought battles against the radicals of both
the right and the left, and won more times than anyone had a right to expect.
The occasional rumors about their being lovers buoyed Quill's ego, even
though there was no truth to them.

"I've only got a few minutes, Jane," he said apologetically. "I've got to talk
on the floor. C-SPAN's covering it."

Jane understood. It was common practice to give a speech late in the day
to a nearly empty Senate chamber. The voters back home would see their senator on C-SPAN, holding forth on some issue that was important to them.

"Energy?" she asked.

He shook his head. "Farm price supports."

"Oh. Good luck."

Quill pushed his half-finished fruit salad away. "So, what do you want to
tell me?"

"I want to ask you something, Bob."

He cocked his head slightly to one side. "Go ahead and ask."

"I want your support for Morgan Scanwell."

He smiled. "I thought so."

"He can win it, Bob," she said earnestly. "With the proper support he can
win the nomination."

Quill glanced at his wristwatch. Knowing he could trust Jane Thornton, he said, "Let's cut to the chase. What can Scanwell do for me?"

"He's thinking about making energy independence a major plank in his platform."

"Western coal?"

"And the high-tech systems that will allow us to use Western coal without ruining the environment."

Quill fell silent for all of five seconds. Then, "I'll have to meet him. Talk to him. Size him up."

"You can trust him, Bob."

"I'll still need to press the flesh."

"Yes, of course. I'll tell his people to contact your people."

"Quietly," Quill added. "I don't want anything leaked before I'm ready to make a public statement."

"Quiet as a mouse," Jane said, smiling.

"Quieter," said Senator Quill, completely serious.

Hours after sunset, Senator Thornton was still in her office, talking intently with one of Governor Scanwell's aides in Austin. On her desktop screen, the aide looked no more than a teenager, young and earnest and full of energy. She had a big Texas cheerleader's toothy smile and golden blonde hair. It might even be naturally blonde, Jane thought.

The door from the outer office opened and Denny O'Brien shambled in, looking as if he had rolled all the way from Bethesda, as usual. Jane suppressed a frown and reminded herself that Denny's brain was sharp even if his outward appearance wasn't, and it was his brain that she depended on.

"Very well, then," she said to the smiling aide on the desktop screen. "I'll leave it to you to contact Senator Quill's office."

"Oh, yes, ma'am, Senator Thornton. I'll get on the horn right away!" gushed the aide.

"Good. Thank you." Jane cut the connection and turned to O'Brien, who was rummaging through the refrigerator set into the wall below the bookshelves.

"Don't you have a home to go to?" she asked good-naturedly.

"Nope. I sleep in the streets. Keeps me closer to the real people." O'Brien pulled a bottle of carbonated water from the refrigerator and came over toward the desk, struggling with the cap.

"You look as if you sleep in the streets," Jane said as he slumped into one of the leather chairs facing her desk.

"Speaking of sleeping," O'Brien said, finally getting the cap open, "are you sleeping with the governor of Texas?"

Jane had expected him to ask sooner or later. But the question still caught her unprepared. For several moments the only sound in the office was the fizz of O'Brien's drink.

O'Brien broke the silence. "I mean, he flies *alone* to your ranch? Not even a state trooper or a bodyguard? And stays overnight?"

"You stayed overnight, too, Denny."

"Yeah, but I didn't tiptoe into your bedroom. I think maybe he did."

"It's none of your business, Denny."

"The hell it isn't! If the news media find out that you're sleeping with Scanwell, you can kiss his candidacy good-bye."

Jane bristled. "I don't see why. Neither of us is attached to anyone else. We're both adults."

O'Brien wagged his head back and forth, making his fleshy cheeks waddle. "Senator, the public goes apeshit over politicians with hidden love affairs."

"It didn't hurt Clinton."

"Except to get him impeached. Except to get all his programs and ideas torn to shreds. He didn't accomplish diddly-squat after the Monica thing went public."

She fell silent again, thinking, My god, he's making me feel like a guilty little kid.

Hunching forward in the chair so far that Jane feared he would spill the bottle onto the carpeting, O'Brien said, "Look, Senator, it would damage your credibility and his if you two are screwing around."

"We're not *screwing around!*" Jane snapped.

"Excuse me. Having an affair."

"Not that, either."

"Well, for god's sake, don't give the appearance of having an affair," O'Brien insisted. "Once the media latches onto the slightest hint, the tiniest little whiff, they'll be all over the both of you. Any hopes you have for him and the White House will go right down the toilet."

"We're not having an affair," Jane said, knowing that while it was true, it was not the whole truth.

FLASHBACK: THE DAY OF THE BRIDGES

It was the Fourth of July, and the day was clean and warm and dry as Dan drove Jane Thornton in the rented convertible down Route 101 after a morning of wine tasting in the Napa Valley vineyards. She was Senator Thornton now; during the fourteen months he'd been away in Japan, Jane had been appointed to the U.S. Senate. Yet she was just as beautiful and desirable as the day he'd left, and she appeared to love him as much as he loved her.

Dan's gray eyes sparkled happily; his nose hadn't yet been broken. As they sped along the highway, the warm wind ruffled her auburn hair while the brilliant sunshine made the waters of the bay shimmer. Over the rush of the wind Dan rattled away about the work he'd been doing in Japan.

"It's only a demonstration satellite," he said, his voice raised to be heard above the wind, "but we've got it working, actually sending energy to the ground."

Jane nodded and smiled and said nothing.

When they passed Sausalito, Dan pulled off onto Bunker Road.

"We're not going back to the city?" Jane asked, shouting.

"I want to show you the prettiest site in the country," he yelled back. "Point Bonita."

When he finally pulled into a parking area, Jane saw that he'd been right. They were high above the ocean; the Pacific glittered before them, and, on their left, the bridge arched gracefully across the Golden Gate, glowing like molten gold in the late afternoon sun.

"Point Bonita," Jane said, as they walked slowly along the grassy height. "The name fits."

"Sure does."

She looked at him. "So you're going back to Japan."

Nodding: "And when I finish my contract with Yamagata I'm coming back here and start to build a *real* power satellite. Full scale. Deliver twenty giga-watts to the ground. Maybe fifty."

"For Yamagata?"

"For me. For the U.S. of A. For anybody who's smart enough to invest in the project."

"That'll take some doing," she said.

"I can do it, Jane. I know I can. I can do this. It's important, and I can make it work."

Jane smiled at him.

"Don't give me that condescending smile," he said, grinning back at her. "We can generate energy from space. Lots of energy."

"If anyone can, it would be you," she conceded.

Feeling uncertainty rising inside him, Dan tried to explain. "Jane, this is important to me. To the whole world. I wasn't born rich, like you. I had to scratch my way through college. Yamagata hired me because I *believed* in what he's doing. Now I want to get out on my own, I want to *be* somebody. This is my chance, Jane, my chance to accomplish something nobody else has been able to do."

"Except Yamagata," she pointed out.

"Pah! His little demo satellite isn't enough. Nowhere near it. I'm going to build the big one, the prototype for all the powersats to come."

"If you can get the financial backing."

"I'll get it," he said fervently. "You just watch me."

Jane smiled again, but this time it was more admiring. "I believe you, Dan. I believe you will. You won't let anything stand in your way, will you?"

"Not a damned thing," he said. Then he pulled her into his arms and kissed her. "But I need you with me, Jane. This past year has been miserable without you."

"I've missed you, too, Dan."

"Will you marry me?"

Her eyes went wide. "Marry you?"

"I love you, Jane Thornton. I love you madly," he said. "And sanely."

She leaned her head against his shoulder. "You're sure?"

He grinned down at her. "From the first time you flashed those gorgeous green eyes at me I was a goner."

"That's very flattering."

"I mean it. Of course, I didn't know you were going to become a senator. And you *were* the first person I'd seen in that convention hall who wasn't smoking a cigar."

Jane laughed. "I love you, too."

"Really?"

"Of course. What woman wouldn't? You can charm a snake out of its skin—when you want to."

"Now *that's* flattery!"

"You can be awfully stubborn, too."

"I'm not stubborn. I'm a man of principle. Other people are stubborn, not me."

Jane laughed. But then, "Seriously, Dan. Marriage is a serious step. Are you prepared to be Mr. Senator Thornton?"

Now he blinked with surprise. "But I thought you'd come back to Japan with me."

"And resign my seat in the Senate?"

"Well . . . maybe when your term is finished, then."

She fell silent. They walked along the crest of the height, their arms entwined about each other's waists.

Dan took a breath. "Jane, you're the most fantastic person I've ever met. You're smart, strong, beautiful, wealthy—but most of all, you're honest. Straight up-and-down honest. You never play games with anyone. You say what you mean and you mean what you say. So what's your answer? And don't tell me you weren't expecting this."

"Frankly, I wasn't."

"I told you not to tell me that," he joked.

"I didn't realize you were the marrying kind, Dan. I thought you were in love with your power satellite."

"I am," he admitted. "But I love you more. I need you. I don't want to go back to Japan without you."

Her face grew serious, almost sad. "I've got to make a decision about running for reelection."

"Reelection? But I thought—"

"I was wondering, Dan," she asked, almost wistfully, "how would you feel about being a senator's husband?"

"Move to Washington? Quit Yamagata?"

"It wouldn't be easy for you, I know. But you could start your own company in Washington, couldn't you? I could help you; I know a lot of very influential people."

"I've got to finish my contract with Yamagata," he said. "I can't run out on him. Bad enough I'm going to go into competition with him afterward."

"You don't really have to go back to Japan, do you?"

"You've definitely decided to run for reelection?"

She hesitated a heartbeat. Then, "Not set-in-concrete definitely, no."

Dan squinted at the lowering Sun, then abruptly turned back toward the parking area. "We'd better talk about this over dinner."

She glanced out toward the ocean. The sun was close to setting. Already the sky was turning flame red. He needs time to think about this, she realized. He's made a major step in asking me to marry him. Now I'm asking him to completely scramble his plans.

"Over dinner," she agreed. Reluctantly.

In the bathroom of the suite they'd taken at the St. Mark's, Dan was slathering foamy white lather across his face, wearing the fluffy terrycloth robe that the hotel provided. Quit Yamagata's project and move to Washington, he was thinking. Become Senator Thornton's husband. He picked up his razor. She'd never come to Japan; it'd be stupid for me to ask her to give up everything she's achieved just to marry me.

The explosion came like a clap of thunder, sharp and so hard that Dan dropped the razor. Dan not only heard it, he *felt* it. The floor jumped. Earthquake? he wondered. But now he heard a long rumbling growl.

"What the hell was that?" Dan called, his face covered with lather.

"A sonic boom?" Jane answered from the bedroom, where she was dressing for dinner.

"Didn't sound like a sonic boom," Dan said, reaching for his razor. This was earthquake country, he knew, although nothing seemed to be shaking. Just that one shock. The roll of toilet paper wasn't even swaying.

From far away he heard the wail of a siren. A fire truck, maybe, or an ambulance. Then another.

"Oh my god."

He wasn't certain that he'd heard Jane correctly.

"What did—"

"Dan. Come here."

"What is it?"

"Come in here! Now!" He'd never heard Jane's voice sound so urgent. "Now, Dan!"

He grabbed a towel and started wiping the lather off his face as he stepped into the bedroom. More sirens were screaming down on the street outside. Jane had turned on the television. The screen showed the Golden Gate Bridge. The middle of its main span was covered in billowing black smoke. Where the suspension cables come down from the towers, Dan realized.

The sound was muted. Dan looked for the remote control. Then he saw the central span of the bridge split in two and both sides sagged into the water, slowly peeling away from each other like two limp strips of cardboard and plunging down, cars and trucks and buses sliding along their collapsing lengths, falling, splashing into the cold deep water far below.

"Jesus H. Christ," Dan gasped.

Jane stood horrified, her fists pressed to her face, her eyes filling with tears.

The remote was on the floor, Dan saw. Jane must have dropped it there. She stood frozen in front of the TV screen, half dressed, unmoving, unspeaking.

Dan sat on the edge of the bed, suddenly feeling very weary, drained, as if all the energy had been sapped out of him. He bent down and retrieved the remote, thumbed on the sound.

"...no telling how many have been killed," a voice-over was saying, shocked, hollow. The screen showed the bridge span dangling into the strait, objects still splashing into the water. "Our traffic helicopter was apparently caught in the explosion. We've lost contact with it. I guess it's down there with all the other wreckage."

Jane sank down onto the edge of the bed beside him, still stunned into silence. The screen was showing people in the streets now, dazed, staring, as billows of dirty gray smoke wafted into the bright blue sky. Police cars were arriving. Fire trucks pulled up, the firefighters looking bewildered, perplexed, with really nothing to do except stare at the shattered bridge in helpless anger.

A frightened-looking young man in his shirtsleeves appeared on the screen, obviously in the television station's studio. His hands were trembling as he held a flimsy sheet of paper.

"We've just received word," he said, his voice shaking, too, "that the Brooklyn Bridge in New York City has also been blown up. And the Sunshine Skyway Bridge over Tampa Bay in Florida has been attacked, as well."

"Those sons of bitches," Dan muttered. "Those murdering sons of bitches."

For hours Jane and Dan sat there watching the horror. Three bridges destroyed. Thousands killed. Bits and scraps of information were added as the Sun sank into the Pacific, slowly turning their hotel room dark except for the flickering TV screen. A huge supertanker filled with liquefied natural gas had blown up precisely as it passed beneath the Golden Gate Bridge. The same tactic blew up the Sunshine Skyway Bridge across Tampa Bay. In New York, three trucks loaded with chemical fertilizers had stopped precisely in the center of the Brooklyn Bridge and then exploded. The terrorists presumably went up in the blast. Three bridges. Thousands killed.

At nine P.M. the president of the United States appeared on television from his home in Florida, where he'd been spending the holiday weekend.

"This is a tragic Fourth of July," he said, his face ashen, bleak. "The American people will not forget this day. Nor will we stop until the terrorists and their sponsors are rooted out and destroyed. I have ordered the secretary of defense and the Joint Chiefs of Staff to meet with me tonight...."

Once the president finished his grisly little speech, Dan clicked off the television. The only light in the room came from the window. Down in the streets sirens still wailed like lost demons keening for the dead.

Beside him, Jane stirred. "No. Turn it back on. I want to see—"

"We've seen it a couple dozen times, Jane. There's nothing new to show."

"We drove over that bridge," she said, as if just realizing how close they had come to death. "An hour or so later and ..."

"We'd be dead, along with the rest of them."

She nodded.

"But we're not dead, Jane. We're alive. And I love you. I'll protect you. We'll be all right, I promise."

She rested her head on his shoulder and he held her tightly. "It's all right, Jane. We're safe. Don't be afraid."

"I know," she murmured. "I love you, Dan. I don't ever want to be separated from you."

He lifted her chin gently. In the shadows he could see a wisp of terrycloth fiber that clung to her cheek. He brushed it off, then kissed her.

"Let's get married," he said. "Right away. Tonight."

Dabbing at her eyes, Jane made a weak smile. "You want to make an honest woman of me?"

"I want to marry you, Jane Thornton. I want you to come to Japan with me."

"You're going back to Japan? Now?"

"I've got to," he said. "Yamagata's demo satellite is almost finished, but there's still a lot of work to do. And I'm under contract. I've got to go back."

She said nothing for a moment. Then, "And I've got a reelection campaign to start planning for."

"But that's years away, isn't it?"

"There are only one hundred senators in the world, Dan. I'm not going to give that up. I can't."

"But—"

"Dan, it's my career. My world. Now, with this terror attack, I've *got* to be there."

He nodded glumly.

"You can get out of your contract with the Japanese."

"But I don't want to."

"You don't? Why?"

"That power satellite is vital. More important now than ever."

"With this terrorist attack, and more to come, you think playing in outer space is important?"

"It's not playing! Jane, if we can get electrical power from space, we can thumb our noses at the Arabs and their oil."

She stared at him as if she couldn't believe what he was saying. "Dan, that will take years! If ever. We have to fight the terrorists *now*."

"As long as we're dependent on oil from the Middle East they'll have us by the short hairs."

"And you think going into space is going to help us?"

"Yes! Generate power from space—"

"In a hundred years, maybe."

"Ten! Five, maybe, if we push it."

"Ten years," Jane said. "My god, Dan, ten years is as good as a century in politics."

"If we don't start now, we'll never have it!"

"The costs," Jane muttered. "Everything NASA does costs so much."

"It can be done cheaper."

"It will still costs billions, won't it?"

Feeling exasperated, trying not to lose his temper, Dan replied, "Give me ten percent of what the oil industry spends on digging dry holes each year, and I'll put up a full-scale powersat."

"It can't be done," she said, shaking her head.

"It can't be done unless somebody goes out and does it!"

"And that's what you want to do? With everything else that's happening, you want to go play in outer space."

He bit back the reply he wanted to make. Instead, he said simply, "I'm going back to Japan. I've got to."

"For how long?"

"A year, maybe a little less."

"A year."

He clutched her by her bare shoulders. "Jane, come with me. Forget this political crap. Come with me and help build the future!"

Even in the darkened room he could see her eyes blaze. But only for a moment; then she softened. She put her head back on his shoulder, murmuring, "I wish I could, Dan. I really wish I could."

"But you won't."

"I can't."

"Will you marry me?"

"With you in Japan or up in a spaceship someplace?"

He smiled. Sadly. "It's only a few hundred miles up, Yamagata's demo satellite."

"My place is in Washington, Dan."

"But what about us? You love me, don't you?"

Dan could feel his heart thumping beneath his ribs. For many beats Jane was silent. At last she said, "We'll talk about that when you come back from Japan."

The room fell silent except for the continuing wailing of sirens.

AUSTIN, TEXAS

Dan was on his cell phone with his corporate counsel as the limousine inched past the state capitol in the crowded rush-hour streets. The six flags of Texas hung limply on their poles in the soggy August heat. Len Kinsky, his public relations director, sat beside him in the air-conditioned limo, trying to look as if he weren't listening.

"The liability suits are coming in," the lawyer was saying, his voice like the whine of an annoying mosquito. "It's going to add up to billions, Dan."

"But nobody got hurt," Dan said, feeling exasperation rising in him as he always did when talking to lawyers. "The wreckage hit one shed, from what I've been told. Otherwise it all fell on open land."

"Owners are still suing," the lawyer replied. "Property damage, emotional pain and suffering. One woman's claiming you caused her to miscarry."

"Double-damn it to hell and back," Dan groused.

"Insurance won't cover, either," the lawyer went on. "The carrier's canceled all your policies."

Dan leaned back against the limo's plush seat and tried to control his temper. He remembered Mark Twain's advice: When angry, count to four. When very angry, swear.

Instead, he said into the phone, "We don't settle with anybody. Understand? Not a cent. Not until we find out what caused the accident."

"Dan, it's Astro's responsibility no matter what the cause of the accident was."

Dan almost said, Not if the spaceplane was sabotaged. But he held back. "No settlements. None. Not until I tell you. Understand?"

"It's foolish, Dan. It's just going to run up your legal fees."

"Better spend it while you can, then," Randolph said. "Before we declare bankruptcy."

He said good-bye to the lawyer and snapped the phone shut.

"Lawyers," he grumbled to Kinsky.

The P.R. director scowled back at him. "Tell me about it. My divorce lawyer just bought himself a Lamborghini."

Before Dan could slip the phone back into his jacket pocket, it began playing "Take Me Out to the Ball Game" again. Dan huffed and peered at the tiny screen. Joe Tenny.

"Good news for a change, boss," Tenny said without preamble. "Divers recovered the nose cap. Fell into Lake Travis, near Johnson City."

Randolph saw that the limo was at last pulling into the driveway of the Hyatt Regency. He pressed the phone to his ear harder and tried to keep from saying anything he didn't want Kinsky to know. "That is good news, Joe. How banged up is it?"

Tenny caught on immediately. "You're not alone?"

"That's right."

"I haven't seen the piece yet. The Texas authorities are 'coptering it down here. But I saw the dive team's video. Handheld, kinda shaky, but the thruster assembly's recognizable, at least."

What the hell does that mean? Dan asked himself. Aloud, he said, "I'm going to this party of Governor Scanwell's now. I'll call you from my hotel room afterward."

"Gotcha," said Tenny. The phone went dead.

Dan never felt comfortable in a tuxedo or a dinner jacket, which he was now wearing. At least I blend in with the crowd, he thought as he followed Kinsky across the hotel's spacious lobby, up one flight of moving stairs to the huge atrium, with tier upon tier of balconies circling around it. Dan craned his neck, gawking, for a few seconds. Then Kinsky tugged at his sleeve.

"Come on, boss. You're here to meet the governor."

Dan followed his public relations director. Len looks relaxed enough in his straitjacket, he thought. Then he grinned. He looks like the best-dressed scarecrow in town.

There was a reception line. The atrium was crowded with women in expensive gowns and sparkling jewelry, men in dinner jackets and bow ties. Randolph spotted a few daring guys who wore no ties, only a diamond stud or a piece of Navajo turquoise at their throats. Conversations buzzed and laughter echoed across the broad atrium. Waiters carried trays of drinks. Dan asked one of the prettier waitresses for a glass of amontillado. From the perplexed look on her face he figured he'd never see her again or his drink at all. But as they edged along the creeping reception line she came back, all smiles, and handed him a tumbler filled with Dry Sack. On the rocks.

Be grateful for small miracles, Dan told himself as he sipped the drink. Kinsky, he saw, had a martini. You can take the man out of New York, Dan thought, but you can't take the New York out of the man.

It wasn't until he was giving his name to the flunky who was setting up the introductions for the governor that he saw Jane. As the flunky whispered into his pin mike, Dan saw her standing beside Scanwell, tall and straight and beautiful as a princess out of a fairy tale, her copper hair falling to her bare shoulders, her strapless gown of emerald green showing her enticing figure to great advantage.

Dan's insides went hollow. It was like being in space, in zero gravity, that feeling of falling, endlessly falling. She's more beautiful than ever, he thought. The years have been good to her. His eyes followed the graceful curve of her bare shoulder. How many time had he kissed that skin, caressed her flesh, made love to her as if no one else existed in the entire universe?

"Boss?" Kinsky nudged him gently. Dan saw that the couple ahead of them had shaken hands with the governor and it was his turn to step up and meet his host for the evening. And the woman standing beside him.

Another flunky with a tiny plug in his ear said over the hubbub of the crowd, "Governor, Senator, may I present Mr. Daniel Hamilton Randolph and Mr. Leonard Kinsky. Sirs, allow me to introduce Senator Jane—"

"Hello Jane," said Randolph.

She kept her self-control, except for a moment's flash in her sea-green eyes. "Hello Dan," she said, allowing herself a cool smile.

"You two know each other," Governor Scanwell said, looking slightly perplexed.

Dan said, "We're old friends. At least, we used to be."

"Dan and I met years ago," Jane said to the governor, "when I had just started in politics. Then he took off for outer space."

"Outer space?" The governor offered his hand to Randolph. His grip was firm without being overly powerful. He's had lots of practice, Dan thought. Scanwell looked like a rangy, weather-beaten ranch hand in a monkey suit and cowboy boots. All he lacked was a Texas ten-gallon hat. Then Dan realized the governor was no older than he himself, and his cowboy look must be carefully cultivated.

"Dan lived in orbit for more than a year," Jane was saying.

"Really?"

"I helped to build the Japanese power satellite," Dan explained.

"And now you've built one for the United States," Scanwell said, showing that at least he had been briefed about Dan. "We'll have to talk about that later on."

That was the cue to move away and let the people behind him shake the governor's hand.

"Yes," Dan said. "I'd like to talk to you about that."

Another of the governor's aides ushered Dan and Kinsky away from Scanwell. And Jane.

"Let's hit the buffet line and get some appetizers," Kinsky said, tugging at his collar. "I'm starving. And dinner's going to be stupid, I bet. No pastrami. No blintzes. Nothing but dumb Texas steaks."

"You go. I'm not hungry." Dan stood in the milling, swirling crowd and let the chatter and laughter and clink of glasses surround him as he kept his eyes riveted on Jane, standing beside Morgan Scanwell. She never looked his way. Not once.

NEW YORK CITY

Asim al-Bashir traveled on a Tunisian passport. Tunisia was a moderate Arab nation, not known by Western intelligence to have links with international terrorism. Al-Bashir had actually been born in the city of Tunis, and kept a sumptuous home there, which eased any suspicions that an investigator might have.

Moreover, al-Bashir was a member of the board of directors of one of the largest oil companies in the world. As a director of Tricontinental Oil Corporation, he had legitimate business in America. The quarterly board meeting was scheduled to take place in Houston within two days.

His traveling secretary directed an assistant to handle al-Bashir's considerable luggage while he escorted his employer to the white stretch limousine waiting for them at curbside. Without waiting for the luggage, the limo pulled into JFK's thrumming, snarling traffic and headed for the Queensboro Bridge and Manhattan.

With the male secretary sitting up front with the chauffeur, al-Bashir leaned back patiently and watched the dreary traffic speed its growling, fume-spewing way past the gray and dismal houses huddled along the highway. The

Americans prized their individual houses and their automobiles, their televisions and other luxuries. All dependent on energy, he thought. Energy from electricity. Energy from oil. America grows fat and prosperous on Arab oil. Most of the other people of the world could only dream about the luxuries Americans take for granted. Dream and be envious. Envy is a powerful emotion, al-Bashir thought. Envy can breed hatred, and hate is the greatest motivator of them all.

He dozed slightly, but awoke when the limo's tires suddenly changed the tone of their sound against the paving. They were on the Queensboro Bridge, he saw. He shifted in the seat and looked out to find the United Nations building. There it stood, by the East River. From where he was, al-Bashir could not see the ruins of the Brooklyn Bridge. The Americans were rebuilding it to look exactly as it had before the attack knocked it down.

My colleagues thought it a glorious day when the bridges were destroyed, al-Bashir remembered. A magnificent day. The faithful around the world celebrated their great victory. The Nine were overjoyed at their success. Al-Bashir had smiled and congratulated them, especially the Egyptian, who had brilliantly directed the complex operation.

Three bridges destroyed. Nearly five thousand Americans killed, many of them Jews. A day of wild celebration.

But to what end? he asked himself. The Americans swept into the Middle East in overwhelming force and no one would gainsay them, not even other Moslem nations.

Terrorism is the tactic of the desperate, the weak against the strong. Like a child throwing a stone through the window of a mansion. Yet it has its uses, al-Bashir conceded. In this long war we can use terrorists, both suicidal fanatics and brilliant planners like the Egyptian. But the war will be won as all wars are eventually won, by economic power. Mao Zedong wrote that power comes out of the barrel of a gun, but one must have the money to buy the guns. We will win this war because we will control the economic power of the oil industry. We must ruthlessly suppress any challenge to that power. Ruthlessly.

Two days later al-Bashir was in Houston, sitting at another conference table, much longer and more gleamingly polished than the one in the dilapidated Khartoum hotel. The boardroom of Tricontinental Oil reeked of wealth. Its walls were paneled with redwood. Its long sweeping windows looked out on the city of Houston, far below the lofty level of this skyscraper. The room was air-conditioned to the point where al-Bashir felt chilly. Texans and their air conditioning, he thought. Conspicuous waste of energy. Flaunting their affluence.

A table laden with drinks and finger foods ran across the back wall. The opposite wall was completely taken up by a new kind of computer screen that the technical people called a "smart wall." Unfortunately, it wasn't working properly this day. The board members had to rely on the small screens set into the table at each seat.

Like the other men around the table al-Bashir wore a conservative Western business suit and tie. Even the women were dressed in tailored blouses and skirted suits.

But crusty old Wendell T. Garrison, sitting in his powered wheelchair at the head of the table, was in shirtsleeves and a black onyx bolo tie, its silver-tipped strings hanging halfway down his wrinkled shirt front. He looks like an evil djinn, al-Bashir thought: shriveled and wizened, his bald pate speckled with liver spots, the wisps of his remaining hair dead white. But he has great power, enormous power. Just the touch of his fingertips can move nations.

This is the man I must defeat, al-Bashir told himself. To gain control of Tricontinental Oil, I must overcome Garrison.

The board meeting had been quite routine. The only real item of contention was over the corporation's involvement in Iraq, where Tricontinental was rebuilding the Iraqi oil fields under contract to the U.S. government. The profit margin was slim, but Garrison insisted that they renew the contract at the same rate.

"When the reconstruction is finished and we start pumpin' oil again," he said in his grating, rasping voice, "*that's* when we up the ante with the feds."

One of the women halfway down the table pointed out that Washington had promised to turn the oil fields back to the Iraqi government once the reconstruction was finished.

Garrison gave her one of his patented sour looks. "Yep, they'll hand it back to the Iraqis, all right. And specify that we run the operation."

"Under contract to the Iraqi government," the woman added.

"Under terms that we set," Garrison said flatly.

Al-Bashir said nothing. No one asked his opinion. He was content to leave it at that.

Finally Garrison rasped, "That's it, then, 'less there's some new business."

Al-Bashir raised his hand.

Garrison had already started to back his chair away from the table. Frowning, he said, "Mr. al-Bashir." He pronounced it "awl-Basher."

"There is the matter of the solar power satellite to be considered."

Brows rose around the table.

"Astro Corporation?"

"They had that spaceship crash, didn't they?"

"They're finished. Going bankrupt."

Garrison's flinty eyes went crafty, though. "What about the solar power satellite?"

"I believe we should invest in it."

That brought actual gasps of surprise.

"Invest in the competition?"

"Help that madman Randolph?"

"He wants to drive us out of business!"

Al-Bashir folded his hands on the table's edge and patiently waited for them to quiet down.

Garrison made a hushing gesture with both his blue-veined hands, then asked, "Why should we invest in that pipe dream?"

Smiling at the board chairman, al-Bashir calmly replied, "There are several reasons. First, it would make very favorable publicity for us. The public sees us as the big, bad corporate giant. For years they have been fed stories about how the oil companies suppress any invention that threatens their grip on the world's energy supply."

One of the older directors humphed. "The pill that turns water into gasoline. I've heard that one all my life, just about."

"Exactly," said al-Bashir. "By lending Astro Corporation a helping hand, we show that we are not such monsters. We show that we are interested in the future."

"Mighty expensive public relations," Garrison grumbled. "Randolph's going to need a billion or more to pull out of the hole he's dug for himself."

"There is another reason, also," al-Bashir said.

All eyes were on him.

"What if it works? What if this solar power satellite actually proves to be successful? Shouldn't we own part of it?"

"I get it! A strategic partnership," said the youngest member of the board, down at the end of the table.

Garrison frowned at the junior director and pointed out in his rasping voice, "If we don't bail Astro out, the power satellite won't work because Randolph will be busted. So there's no danger of it being successful."

"I beg to differ," al-Bashir said. "Even if Randolph goes bankrupt, the power satellite will still be up there. Someone else might buy it on the cheap and make it work. Then *they* will get the glory—and the profits. Not we."

"Who would be that crazy?"

"The Japanese, perhaps," al-Bashir replied mildly.

Silence fell in the boardroom. One by one the directors shifted their gaze from al-Bashir to the head of the table, to Garrison.

The chairman was staring straight at al-Bashir and tapping his fingernails on the tabletop, obviously thinking it over. No one said a word. For long moments the only sound in the boardroom was Garrison's absent tap-tap-tapping.

"We maybe could pull a billion out of the exploration budget," the old man said at last. "Send a few geologists back to their universities for a year."

The directors stirred to life. A few argued, mildly, against the idea. But al-Bashir knew that it was merely a formality. Garrison had accepted the idea of buying into a possible competitor. Al-Bashir was pleased. It will be much easier to destroy the very idea of power satellites from inside Randolph's Astro Corporation.

MATAGORDA ISLAND, TEXAS

For a suit, you're not a bad engineer," Tenny said, his dark jowly face dead serious.

Dan took it as a compliment. He was kneeling alongside the twisted wreckage of what had once been the spaceplane's nose cap. Tenny was squatting on the hangar floor, facing him. Claude Passeau stood on the other side of the nose cap, looking almost elegant in his neatly creased slacks and jacket, although he had pulled his bow tie loose from its collar.

Even this late at night the hangar had been buzzing with government investigators and Astro technicians. With Passeau's help Dan had shooed them all home. Now only the three men remained in the brightly lit hangar.

The twisted bits of remains from the spaceplane were laid out precisely in their proper places inside the taped outline of the vehicle's swept-wing shape, exuding a faint odor of charred metal. Every time Dan looked at the wreckage he felt his guts wrench. But he forced a rueful grin.

"Coming from you, Joe," Dan replied, "that's pretty high praise."

Passeau said, "Your degree was in engineering, wasn't it?"

"And economics," Dan replied. "Double major."

"And then you went to Japan to work for Yamagata Corporation."

Dan got to his feet. "You know a lot about me."

With a shrug, Passeau said, "You interest me, Mr. Randolph."

"Dan."

"Thank you." Passeau touched his moustache with a fingertip, then said, "Why did you go to Japan? Weren't there jobs in the States?"

"Not the kind of jobs I wanted. The U.S. space program was just spinning its wheels: scientific research but not much else. Yamagata was building a power satellite. Just a demo, of course, but it meant I could get into space and work in orbit. Real work, building something practical up there three hundred miles high."

Tenny clambered to his feet, too. "I never been up there. You get space-sick?"

"A little woozy the first hour or so," Dan admitted. "After four or five flights, though, you learn to adjust. Then it's terrific."

"Zero gravity, you mean," Passeau said.

"I hear the sex is terrific," quipped Tenny.

Dan laughed. "I wouldn't know. We were in spacesuits most of the time."

"You spent weeks up there on each mission, didn't you?" Passeau asked.

Nodding, Dan said, "Yep. But there were only a handful of women up there and they were all Japanese. They wouldn't have anything to do with a *ketoujin*."

Tenny smirked. "That's how he got his nose busted."

"Really?"

"No, but Joe likes to think so."

The three men laughed mildly. Then Tenny brought them back to the here-and-now.

"The nose thruster's fuel control valve is wide open," he said, jabbing a thumb at the twisted wreckage. "It should be shut."

"It might have been jarred loose when it hit the ground," said Passeau.

"Maybe," said Tenny. "But take a look at it. It's locked in the open position."

Dan took the battered assembly from Tenny's hands and tried to close the valve. It refused to budge. "Joe's right," he said to Passeau. "It's locked in the open position. If it had banged open from the crash it'd be flapping loose."

Passeau fingered his moustache again, thinking. "Then the thruster must have fired during reentry."

"And kept on firing until all its fuel was exhausted," Dan added.

"What could have caused that?" asked Passeau.

Dan shot a warning glance at Tenny.

"That's what we've gotta find out," the engineer said.

"And quickly," Dan added.

Tenny puffed out a breath. "Well, we ain't gonna find it standing around here until the sun comes up. I don't know about you guys, but I've got a home and a family that expects to see me now and then."

Sighing, Passeau said, "I'm living in your wonderful Astro Motel, the only facility between here and civilization, until this investigation is finished." He glanced at his wristwatch. "And their bar closed two hours ago."

Dan thought of all the nights he had spent at hotel bars, and the women he had picked up at them. "You're not missing much, Claude," he said.

Passeau hiked his brows suggestively. "One never knows. To give up all hope would be a tragedy."

Laughing together, the three men began walking slowly out of the hangar, leaving the wreckage behind them. Dan nodded to the uniformed security guard standing at the tightly closed hangar door. Two more guards were supposed to be on duty, he knew. Probably making the rounds.

He walked Passeau and Tenny to the parking lot, where the FAA inspector got into his rental Buick Regal and Tenny hauled himself up into his remodeled Silverado. The only pickup in Texas that ran on hydrogen fuel. But then, only someone who had access to Astro's hydrogen facility could find enough fuel to run the truck. Not even the NASA center near Houston had a hydrogen generation system.

Dan waved the two men good night and headed for his own compact apartment up on the catwalk back inside the hangar.

The thruster's fuel valve was commanded to open and lock during reentry, he mused as he started up the steel stairs. Somebody sent a bogus signal to the bird.

He stopped halfway up the stairs, his footfalls echoing off the hangar's metal walls. Which means, Dan said to himself, that somebody really did deliberately sabotage the spaceplane. Hannah's death wasn't an accident. It was murder.

Slowly, he started up the stairs again, running it through his mind. Which means that somebody was able to override our command codes and radio the bogus signal to the plane's computer. Which means that the saboteur had access to our command codes.

As he opened the door to his one-room apartment, Dan came to the inescapable conclusion: Which means that there's a spy in my company somewhere. A saboteur who wrecked the spaceplane and killed Hannah.

DAN RANDOLPH'S APARTMENT

The apartment was always neat and clean when Dan came back to it from his day's work. His office was barely fifty yards down the catwalk that circled three walls of the hangar, but Tomasina, his dour-faced, stocky cleaning woman, always managed to get in and straighten the place, even if Dan was gone for only a few minutes. She cleaned his clothes, washed his dishes, and kept the apartment shipshape, all without getting in Dan's way. Most of the time he didn't even know she'd been there, except that the place was spotless and tidy. Once in a while she'd leave him a note in neat, large block letters, ordering cleaning supplies that were running low.

As he undressed, Dan wondered what he should do about the problem he faced. I've got a spy working somewhere in the company, he kept repeating to himself. How do I find him? Hire a private investigator? Tell Passeau about it? He could get the FBI in here, I suppose.

Yet he hesitated, uncertain. Who can I trust? he asked his image in the mirror as he brushed his teeth. Joe Tenny, I know. Joe's put as much of himself into this project as I have. Hannah was like a sister to him. No, more like a grown-up daughter.

As he climbed into his king-sized bed, Dan realized that his list of people he could trust ended with Tenny. He didn't know anybody else in the eight-hundred-odd men and women he employed well enough to trust them implicitly. Any one of them could be the spy, the saboteur.

Wait, he said as he clicked off the bedside lamp. Whoever it is has to be technically trained. It couldn't be April, for example. She can run the office all right, but she's no engineer.

But then he thought, That could all be an act. A saboteur wouldn't have to show his technical skills. Or hers. What do they call them in the spy business? Moles, he remembered. I've got a mole in my organization.

He lay on his back in the darkness, his mind spinning. Stop thinking, he commanded himself. Get to sleep. Let your subconscious work the problem. By the time you get up tomorrow morning you'll probably have the answer you need.

He decided he had given himself good advice, turned over onto his side and closed his eyes. But sleep did not come to him. Instead, he remembered seeing Jane again, with Governor Scanwell.

The fund-raiser in Austin had been such a big bash that Dan thought he'd never be able to speak privately with the governor, but Len Kinsky kept telling him to be patient.

"Half the people in Texas are trying to see Scanwell," Kinsky said over the buzz and clatter of the crowd as they stood by one of the bars that had been set up across the spacious sweep of the hotel's atrium.

"That's what I'm afraid of," Dan grumbled, sipping at his disappointing Dry Sack. "We'll hang around all night and never get to talk to him."

"Wait it out," said Kinsky. "Hang in there. The drinks are free, aren't they?"

"And so's dinner," Dan admitted.

Kinsky made a sour face to show what he thought of Texas cuisine.

Dan wanted to leave. He didn't like seeing Jane standing there beside Scanwell. It bothered him, annoyed him. This is the life she chose, he told himself. She's a politician and she loves all this. Dan wanted to run away.

Instead he weaved through the crush of strangers, nursing his drink and smiling mechanically at the men in their dinner jackets and the begowned and bejeweled women. He didn't know any of them and none of them knew him. He deliberately moved away from Kinsky, who was talking to a young blonde, a wolfish grin on his face. Wandering through the crowd, Dan wondered why he was wasting his time; he wanted to get away but knew he would stay until the bitter end.

He saw a young redhead who seemed to be equally out of place, alone, clutching a long-stemmed glass of champagne in one hand and an expensive-looking beaded bag in her other. She wore a glittering short-skirted outfit of red and black sequins.

"You're wearing my high school colors," Dan said to her, by way of introducing himself.

She was deeply unimpressed, and after a few words Dan drifted away from her. No sense of humor, he decided.

Kinsky found him again when they went into the ballroom, where a sea of round tables had been set up for dinner. Dan and his public relations director sat with eight older men and women. When one of them asked Dan what he did for a living and Dan began to explain it, he quickly changed the subject to golf.

Teams of harried-looking waiters and waitresses slapped dishes onto the table. Broiled steak and baked potatoes, with a medley of overcooked vegetables. Dan glanced at Kinsky: the P.R. director looked like a martyr heading toward the scaffold.

Scanwell made a few remarks from the head table about the wonderful charity this dinner was supporting. Dan hardly heard him. He watched Jane, sitting there beside the governor's place. She was splendid, completely in her element, smiling and chatting with the others at the head table.

The speeches seemed endless to Dan, a succession of men and women congratulating one another on the wonderful work they were doing. Yeah, Dan said to himself, and not one of them gives a good god damn about the wonderful work *I'm* trying to do.

He was startled when Kinsky tapped him on the shoulder.

"I told you he'd come through," Kinsky whispered, leaning so close to Dan that he thought the man was going to stick his tongue in his ear. Kinsky was holding a small white card on which was scrawled the numbers 2335.

"He wants to meet you in his suite," Kinsky whispered.

Dan took the card in his hand and turned it over. It was the governor's calling card, complete with the seal of office, his "hotline" phone number, and official e-mail address.

Scanwell didn't stay for all the speeches. He got up, shook every hand along the head table, and made his apologies for leaving early. Jane went with him.

"Come on," Kinsky said, nudging Dan again.

Feeling as if he really wanted to get out of this hotel, out of Austin altogether, Dan pushed his chair back and got to his feet. He followed Kinsky up the glass elevator to the twenty-third floor.

When they got out of the elevator a pair of unsmiling uniformed state policemen big enough to play in the National Football League checked their IDs and directed them down the hall. Dan pushed the doorbell button; an aide in a dinner jacket and black tie immediately opened the door and ushered them into the suite. It was richly carpeted, furnished in big plush pieces and polished oak. The drapes were drawn over windows that spanned two walls of the sitting room.

Scanwell was sitting back on the long sofa, his jacket off, his tie loosened, and a cut crystal tumbler of bourbon in his hand.

"Hello, Governor," Dan said. "It's good of you to give us some of your time."

"Come on in," Scanwell called to Dan and Kinsky. Gesturing to the bar, "Have a drink." The governor perched his booted feet on the coffee table.

Jane was nowhere in sight. Two more aides were standing by the bar, the man wearing slacks and a light brown sports jacket, the woman in a tailored pantsuit. Obviously neither one of them had been at the dinner downstairs. Then Dan noticed the butt of a pistol inside the guy's jacket. Bodyguards.

Dan reached for the San Pellegrino water from the row of bottles lined up atop the bar.

"There's beer in the fridge if you prefer," the male aide said. "Lone Star longnecks."

Dan made a smile and poured the water. "Thanks anyway," he said, thinking that he'd better stay sober through this meeting.

"I think y'all can wait outside in the hall," Scanwell said to his aide and the bodyguards. "I'll yell if I need anything."

As they were leaving Jane came in from the bedroom, smoothing her hair. Dan's breath caught in his throat. She smiled uncertainly at him, then went to the sofa and sat beside Scanwell.

"C'mon over," Scanwell said, waving to Dan. "Make yourself comfortable."

Dan took the upholstered chair on the opposite side of the glass coffee table. Kinsky sat off to one side.

Scanwell gave Dan a friendly grin. "What I'd like to know," he said, "is how you talked my parks department into letting you lease part of a state park and turn it into your rocket base." Dan realized that the governor's voice was slightly hoarse. Too much talking over the noise of the crowd, he thought.

Grinning back at the governor, Dan replied, "They needed the cash. Budget deficits and all that. But it still wasn't easy. I had to sweet-talk sixteen different staffs of bureaucrats to let me use the old Wynne ranch property."

Scanwell shook his head. "I caught a lot of flak over that when I ran for re-election."

"But Calhoun County voted for you very solidly," Dan countered. "They appreciate the new jobs."

"How many engineers do you have down there?"

"It's not just the engineers. It's the people who run the new ferry. And the motel. And the truck drivers and road crews and building trades people. They all vote, and they all like the paychecks they're getting."

"But how did you ever get it past my environmental protection people?"

Dan's smile widened. "Governor, NASA's big Kennedy Space Center sits right alongside the Cape Canaveral National Wildlife Reserve. Launching rockets doesn't bother the pelicans."

Scanwell cocked his head slightly to one side. "Well maybe so. Still, you must be a very convincing guy...."

"Dan can be extremely convincing," Jane said without a smile, "when he wants to be."

"Jane's been telling me about your project," Scanwell said.

"I'll be frank with you, Governor," Dan said. "My company's in deep financial trouble."

Scanwell nodded sympathetically. "So I hear."

"But if I can make it work," Dan went on, "if I can start to deliver electrical power from the satellite, it will change the energy picture for America. For the whole world."

"That's a big if, though, isn't it?"

"Not as far as the technology is concerned. We know how to make the satellite work. It's the economics that's a bitch."

Scanwell laughed. "Isn't it always?"

Jane said, "Energy independence could be a major part of Morgan's campaign."

Morgan, Dan thought. She calls him by his first name.

"It's not going to be easy," Scanwell said, his brows knitting. "Making energy independence a major campaign issue will mean the oil interests line up solidly against me. A lot of money there."

"And power," Dan agreed.

"You've fought against them before," Jane pointed out. "And won."

Scanwell grinned forlornly. "Yeah, I squeaked past 'em for governor. But Garrison and his people will work their butts off against me now."

"Garrison?" Dan asked. Then he realized that of course Garrison of Tricontinental Oil would be against any candidate who threatened his power.

"It'll be tough, but I'm willing to slug it out with them," said the governor, "if I can show that we have a practical alternative to importing foreign oil."

Kinsky offered, "Well, I think we can help you there. Solar power satellites could play a major role in making America independent of overseas oil."

"That so?" Scanwell asked, looking squarely at Dan.

"Yes, it is, Governor. With power satellites and nuclear plants we—"

"People are scared of nuclear," the governor objected.

Dan groused, "Yeah, they'd rather have blackouts."

"Power satellites don't present any environmental problems," Kinsky said, trying to bring the conversation back on point. "It's solar energy. Nobody's scared of solar energy."

"But you're in trouble now," Scanwell said to Dan.

"Deep trouble," Dan admitted. "To be perfectly honest, I need all the help I can get, Governor."

Before Scanwell could reply, Jane said, "The support of a major presidential candidate would help you to raise money, wouldn't it?"

Dan nodded warily. "Sure, once your campaign gets underway. Problem is, I need help now."

"And a promise of government funding after Morgan's elected," Jane added. "That would be even better in the long run, wouldn't it?"

"Wellll," Dan said, drawing out the word, "government funding could be a two-edged sword."

Scanwell's brows knit in puzzlement.

Kinsky jumped in, "What Dan means—"

"What I mean is that federal funding will bring all sorts of government oversight and red tape. NASA will want to run the show. Every congressional committee this side of the Moon will want to stick their fingers in."

Jane looked nettled, but Scanwell broke into a big grin. "You're completely right. But what else could the government do to help you, once I'm elected?"

Hunching forward in his chair, Dan said, "Offer backing for loans. The same way the government did for Lockheed and Chrysler when they were in trouble."

"That was a long time ago," Jane said.

"Loan guarantees," Scanwell mused, glancing at her.

"It won't cost the taxpayers a cent," Dan said. "The federal government just guarantees that any loans to Astro Corporation will be backed by the U.S. Treasury. Wall Street will do the rest."

"Do you think you could raise the capital you need to finish the project?" Jane asked.

"From the private money markets, yes, sure. If the government guarantees the loans."

"But what if you fail?" Scanwell asked.

"That's not the problem," Dan countered. "The problem is that we need money now. With all due respect, Governor, I can't wait until your campaign starts. Or until you're in the White House. I have a payroll to meet and a powersat to put into operation. Right now."

Scanwell stared into Dan's eyes for a long silent moment, as if trying to see what was going on in his mind.

"You need funding to tide you over," he murmured at last.

"That's the size of it," said Dan.

Jane said, "It could bring national media attention to you, Morgan. A bold new idea. A new way to unleash the power of American industry in space. The road to energy independence. It could get you the kind of attention that you need."

"The oil interests won't like it," Scanwell murmured.

"They'll accept it if we play our cards right," Jane said. "We can show that it's the patriotic thing to do."

The governor made a pained smile. "They're not patriots, Jane. The oil industry isn't American; it has no loyalty to any nation."

"Oil money funds terrorism," said Kinsky.

"That's why we need power satellites," Dan said. "To cut down their power over us."

Scanwell nodded slowly, yet Dan could see the question that still lingered in his eyes: *But what if you fail?*

"We can do it," Dan repeated. "If I can just get the money to move ahead before I have to shut down the whole operation."

The governor got to his feet and stuck his hand out. "You've given me a lot to think about, Dan. Let me see what my people can come up with. I'll get back to you in a few days."

Standing, Dan took his extended hand. "I appreciate anything you can do, Governor."

Dan knew he was being dismissed. He glanced toward Jane but she refused to meet his eyes.

Scanwell looked almost embarrassed. Without releasing Dan's hand, the governor said, "Uh, come on over here with me for a minute, will you, Dan?"

Dan allowed the governor to lead him into the suite's spacious bedroom. The bed was neatly made; there was no sign of clothing or luggage in sight.

Nudging the door shut, Scanwell said, "Dan, Jane's told me what you two meant to each other years ago."

Surprised, Dan didn't know what to reply.

"Do you still love her?"

Dan nodded dumbly, not trusting himself to say what he truly felt.

Scanwell's craggy face edged into a rueful smile. "Well, I do, too, you know. She means the world to me."

"More than the White House?" Dan blurted.

The smile faded. "I sure hope I never have to choose between them."

Damn! thought Dan. Why's he have to be so goddamned honest? This'd be a lot easier if he was a sonofabitch.

MATAGORDA ISLAND, TEXAS

It took an effort for Dan to keep his mind on business. *Scanwell loves Jane,* he kept thinking. *And she's right there, by his side almost every day, while I'm down here trying to sort out the wreckage.*

"So was it sabotage or not?" Dan snapped.

Tenny, seated backward on a chair with his chin resting on his hairy forearms, hiked his dark brows at his boss's impatience. "I'm damned sure it was. But I can't prove a friggin' thing."

Dan got up from his desk chair and walked to the window. Down on the hangar floor a dozen men and women were still moving among the twisted bits of wreckage, more than half of them in blue work shirts with FAA or NTSB stenciled on their backs.

"They're never going to leave, are they?" he muttered.

"Federal employees, boss," said Tenny. "They can spend another year on this."

"While we go broke."

"That's not their concern."

Turning back to the engineer, Dan blurted, "Joe, what the hell do we do? Tell Passeau about it? Call the FBI? What?"

"Passeau's coming around to the sabotage idea on his own. Give him another couple days."

"And then what?"

"Then he'll call the FBI, I guess."

"And *then* what?"

Tenny shrugged. "They find the skunk in the woodworks."

Heading back to his desk, Dan said, "Joe, I want a list from you of everybody on our payroll who might have done it. Everybody with the technical smarts to sabotage Hannah's flight."

"That's not gonna do much good, boss. Anybody smart enough to knock off the spaceplane is smart enough not to let us see how smart he is."

"I still want the list," Dan said, knowing it was most likely nothing more than busywork.

With a stubborn shake of his head, Tenny replied, "You're on the wrong track. It isn't one of our tech people."

"Says you."

"Says logic," Tenny snapped. "Remember logic? Thinking with your brain instead of your glands?"

Dan plopped down in his desk chair and waited for the engineer to continue.

"If it was a spurious command to the thruster that caused the crash, it had to come from a ground station or a plane in flight along the reentry ground track. That means outside people. People who are organized. People who have high-tech toys to work with."

"Not one of our employees?"

"Our people were all here, Dan, on the job. Everybody in their places with bright shining faces."

"So how'd the bastards get our command codes?"

Tenny grimaced. "Bribery. Blackmail. Threats. How the hell do I know."

"You're saying that somebody in the company sold the command codes to an outsider."

"Or gave them. Maybe under duress."

"Who in the Seven Cities of Cíbola could it be?"

"Anybody who had access to the codes. Not just techies, either. Secretaries. Cleaning crew. Anybody."

Dan huffed out a breath. "That's a big help."

"That's the facts, boss."

"They'd have to know the ground track of the reentry path, too. And the timeline. They'd have to know where the plane was when it started its reentry maneuver."

Tenny's brows rose. "Right! Now you're starting to think."

"So whoever sold us out had to be somebody with access to the command codes *and* access to the flight's timeline and ground track."

"That narrows it down," Tenny said. He jumped up from the chair and headed for the door. "Okay. Now I've got a small-enough list to work with."

"Keep me informed," Dan called after him. Silently he added, And don't tell anybody else about this. He thought Tenny already knew enough to keep quiet.

As soon as Tenny breezed out of the office April appeared at the door, looking cool and in charge of herself. Dan thought of the old aphorism, If you can keep your head when all about you are losing theirs—it shows you don't understand the seriousness of the situation.

"You got two calls," April said, "while you were in conference with Dr. Tenny."

Dan tapped the keyboard on the credenza that extended from the left side of his desk. The computer screen showed a call from Wendell T. Garrison of Tricontinental Oil. And a call from Senator Jane Thornton in Washington, D.C. His breath caught in his throat.

Suddenly embarrassed, he waved April out of the office with a gruff, "Okay, thanks, kid," and clicked his mouse on Jane Thornton's name and number.

She wasn't available, of course, but a serious-faced young aide told Dan that the senator would call him back. Telephone tag, Dan fumed as he clicked on Garrison's name.

To Dan's surprise, the old man himself appeared on the screen.

"Mr. Randolph," Garrison said in his creaky, raspy voice, smiling genially. "Nice of you to return my call so quick."

"It's good of you to call," Dan responded, wondering how much bullshit they would have to throw at one another before they got down to serious talk.

"My board of directors is interested in your powersat project," Garrison said.

Surprised at the man's directness and even more surprised at his interest, Dan said merely, "Really?"

"Yep. Think you can find the time to come up to Houston and talk to me about it?"

Dan thought, Another shark in the water. Better count your fingers when you shake hands with him. And your toes.

But he said, "I'd be happy to. I'll tell my secretary to set it up with your people."

"Good," said Garrison. "Put your secretary on the line and I'll do the same from this end."

"Right."

Before Dan could switch the call, Garrison added, "I assume you'll want to set this meeting for sometime this week, right?"

"If that's convenient for you," Dan replied.

"I know you're in a bind. No sense wasting time about this."

Nodding, Dan said again, "Right." Yep, he told himself as he blanked the screen, the old shark smells blood in the water and he's moving in.

He went through the motions of doing a day's work while his mind spun the possibilities and unknowns like a wild symphony that would never end. Who's the spy in our midst? Why did they sabotage Hannah's test flight? Can Joe find the bastard or will we have to bring the FBI into this? Yamagata's offered financial help and now Garrison is nosing around. How the hell can I hold onto my own company when the big guys are moving in on me? What's Scanwell going to decide to do?

Why doesn't Jane call back? What's she up to in all this? Does she want to help me, or Scanwell? Or both of us? Why hasn't she called me back?

All day long he kept coming back to that question: Why hasn't Jane called back?

It was nearly midnight when she did. Dan had spent a long evening going over his financial situation with his chief accountant, an exercise that always left him depressed. He trudged along the catwalk back to his apartment, trying to keep his eyes off the wreckage sitting silently in the shadows of the dimly lit hangar floor. Nobody else in the building, he realized, except the security guards making their rounds. Even Tenny's office light was off.

Feeling tired and grimy, he went to the kitchenette without turning on any lights and opened the refrigerator. Pretty bare. Pulling open the freezer door he saw that Tomasina had stacked three frozen dinners in among the pizza slices, ice cream, and instant juice containers.

The phone buzzed. Dan slammed the fridge shut and peered through the shadows at the screen on his night table: the caller ID spelled out SENATOR THORNTON, WASHINGTON D.C.

"Phone answer," he called as he hurried to the bed.

Jane's face appeared. She seemed to be in her office; Dan saw some photographs hanging on the paneled wall behind her. She was wearing a tailored blouse, but her auburn hair hung loosely to her shoulders. After hours, Dan guessed. Alone in the office after a long, busy day.

"Hello Jane," he said, sitting on the edge of the bed.

"I got your call," she said. "I wanted to wait until everybody was out of the office before I called you back."

"Yeah, I figured that's what you'd do." It was a lie, he knew, but now that he thought about it he realized he should have known it all along.

"Morgan was very impressed with you."

"It was good to see you again," he said.

"He wants to work your satellite program into his energy policy, Dan."

"Haven't seen you since the day after the bridges went down."

"Dan, let's stick to the business at hand."

"You're the business at hand, as far as I'm concerned."

She tried to frown at him, but a tiny smile curved the corners of her mouth slightly. "Dan, that was a long time ago."

"Six years, one month and…" it took him a moment to count it out in his head, "…eleven days."

She looked away for a moment, and when her eyes returned to him she had regained control of herself. Completely serious now, she said, "If you want Morgan's support, Dan, you've got to promise that you'll support his candidacy."

"Sure, I know. One hand washes the other; that's politics. But you're the only one I'm interested in."

"And not your power satellite?"

He took a breath. "You come first, Jane."

"I didn't in San Francisco."

"You do now. I'll drop this whole project. I'll sell it off to Yamagata or Garrison or the local junkyard."

This time she really smiled. But her eyes remained sad. "I know you think you would, Dan. But we both know it's not true. You couldn't give up your work, your life."

"Try me."

"And you mustn't sell out your project to the Japanese or the oil interests."

"I'll be a senator's husband. I'll sit home and stay quiet and show up at parties with you and take you home and make love to you all night long and well into the morning."

Her smile faded. "Dan, it's too late for that."

"Why? You tied up with Scanwell?"

"It's just too late for us, Dan. We both have more important things to do."

"I don't give a damn about any of that. I love you, Jane. There's nothing more important to me than you."

"Yes, there is!" she insisted. "Getting Morgan elected president is more important. Getting the United States off its dependence on Middle Eastern oil is more important."

He shook his head. "Maybe it is, but that's not my department. The world will have to take care of its own problems. You're the only one that I'm interested in."

"Dan, the country needs Morgan Scanwell in the White House. None of the other candidates have the guts or the vision—"

"You're sleeping with him, aren't you?"

The question didn't seem to surprise her. She replied stiffly, "That's none of your business, Dan."

"Yeah. Right. And neither is Scanwell. You can both go jump in the Gulf of Mexico."

"Dan, you can't—"

"Good luck on your way to the White House, Jane." He banged the phone's OFF button so hard he nearly knocked the console off the night table.

HOUSTON, TEXAS

As he flew the butter-yellow Beech Staggerwing into the old Hobby Airport, Dan thought that Houston's sprawl of high-rise towers looked like some Hollywood designer's concept of what "the city of the future" should look like. All glass and steel, one building gaudier than the next.

Adair had offered to pilot the plane but Dan told him to stay with the FAA team investigating the accident. He flew to Houston on his own in the company's little "puddle jumper," a venerable Staggerwing biplane. It was slow and noisy, and it vibrated like a kitchen Cuisinart, but Dan loved the old beauty, loved her graceful lines and her faithful reliability. He and Tenny had personally rebuilt it, and he cherished every bump and rattle as he lined up the biplane for final approach, bouncing around in the jet wash of the Boeing 737 touching down ahead of him.

Garrison had a limousine waiting for him on the ramp as Dan taxied to a parking slot. He grabbed his summerweight jacket and stepped down from the plane. The African-American chauffeur, standing next to the limo in the soggy heat, was in black livery; Dan felt sorry for him. As he walked to the limousine the chauffeur opened the back door for him. Dan noticed that the motor was running and the air-conditioning was on full blast. He didn't have the heart to tell the guy to turn it down a notch or two.

Garrison's office tower was also cooled enough to raise goosebumps. Dan was met at the lobby reception desk by a sleek, long-legged brunette with a warm smile and sexy eyes. She led him to an elevator marked PRIVATE, which whisked the two of them nonstop to the top floor of the skyscraper.

When the elevator doors opened, Dan saw that the whole penthouse floor was one single expanse of lush greenery. "Looks like Jurassic Park," he blurted. The brunette's smile turned a little brittle. "Mr. Garrison loves nature," she murmured.

Nature, Dan thought as he followed his escort past trays of colorful flowers and huge tubs that contained real trees. The place smelled like a garden, even down to the scent of fresh-cut grass, but he wondered if it was real or piped in with the cooled air that sighed through vents in the green-painted pipes twined overhead. The ceiling was mostly glass, deeply tinted to keep the place from turning into a solar oven. Garrison's turned the top floor of this high-rise into a by-damn greenhouse, Dan saw. He probably thinks of himself as an ecologist while his riggers are out digging up half the world to find more oil.

Through an archway of carefully pruned greenery they walked, past a pair of desks flanking their green-carpeted path, each occupied by another sleek-looking young woman. Garrison likes his scenery, Dan thought. Or maybe he has 'em here to impress visitors.

They went around a seven-foot-high hedge and there was Wendell T. Garrison himself, sitting in his powered wheelchair behind a desk big enough to land a helicopter on.

Garrison was peering intently into a slim display screen as Dan and his escort came into his view. He looked up and the screen slowly folded itself into the top of his massive desk.

"Dan Randolph," Garrison croaked, his weathered face breaking into a big welcoming smile. He backed the chair away from the desk and drove around it toward Dan.

"Sorry I can't stand up," he said, extending his hand. Dan took it in his own. Garrison's hand felt cool and dry, reminding Dan of a snake's skin.

"C'mon over here," the old man said, driving off toward a corner where a small, round table stood next to windows that ran from floor to ceiling. Dan could see cars crawling along the city streets far, far below. It's almost like being in orbit, he thought.

"You can go now, sugar," Garrison said to Dan's escort. "If I want anything I'll call."

Despite the lush garden and the hothouse atmosphere, the huge room was still cool enough for Dan to keep his jacket on. Garrison wore a gray business suit, his shirt collar unbuttoned and a bolo tie hanging loosely down his shirt front, which was as wrinkled as his wizened face. Dan couldn't make out the greenish gray stone in the bolo, although its setting was clearly silver.

"You want anything? Drink? Lunch?"

"No thanks," said Dan as he sat next to the old man.

"Okay, then let's get right to business."

"Suits me fine."

"You need a cash influx. I'm willin' to put a bill or so into your company. How much of a percentage can I buy?"

Dan was a little taken aback by his bluntness, but decided that he liked the direct approach.

"Mr. Garrison, I don't want to sell any part of Astro Corporation to any-body. I want to keep control of my company."

"Of course, of course. But what you want doesn't jibe with your financial situation, now does it?"

"I'd be glad to borrow a billion from you," Dan said.

"At today's interest rates?"

"LIBOR plus one percent."

"The Brit bankers' rate? How about prime from the good old U.S.A.? Plus two."

"The London interbank rate suits me better."

Garrison laughed, a wheezing cackle. "Well, you got balls, I'll say that much for you."

Smiling back at the old man, Dan replied, "And I don't intend to give 'em away."

Garrison nodded. "Can't say I blame you. How'd you like that cutie that brought you up here, eh? I can fix you up with her for dinner tonight."

"I'll be going back to Matagorda tonight."

"H'mp."

"About that loan . . ."

"Not interested in a loan, son. If I put out money for you I expect a share of your company. That's reasonable and fair."

Dan nodded; he had to admit Garrison was right.

"Who owns Astro now?"

From the look in the old man's flinty eyes, Dan figured he already knew such details. "I do," he answered. "Most of the shares. Sunk every penny I ever saw into it."

"Uh-huh. And who else?"

"A couple of banks. A lot of smaller investors. My employees own a chunk."

Garrison scratched at his chin. "They own how much, fifteen percent?"

Right on the nose, Dan thought. "Just about fifteen, yes."

"Okay, I'll buy fifteen percent. You can take it out of your own shares. I'll pay one point five billion. That ought to raise the value of your stock quite a bit."

"I'd rather have a loan."

Garrison shook his head.

"Yamagata's already offered me a loan."

The old man's eyes snapped. "You don't want to be taking money from the Japs, son. They're out to cut your throat."

Dan admitted, "Yamagata wasn't happy when I started the project. He sees it as competition for his own interests."

Waggling a bony finger under Dan's nose, Garrison said, "If you're worried about somebody musclin' you out of your company, worry about the Japs. Not me."

The two men talked for more than an hour without coming to an agreement. Dan promised to think about Garrison's offer of buying into Astro Corporation. "I'll talk to some of my key board members about it," he said.

"You do that," said Garrison. "And remember, the clock's ticking. You're lookin' at the edge of a cliff, son."

"Don't I know it," Dan said.

Once Dan left, escorted again by the brunette, Garrison muttered to himself, "Got to turn up the screws on that boy. He's too damn stubborn for his own good."

MATAGORDA ISLAND, TEXAS

Later that afternoon, Joe Tenny hustled along the catwalk from his office to Dan's. He burst through the door to the outer office, startling Dan's executive assistant.

"Gotta see the boss," Tenny said.

April quickly regained her poise. "He's in Houston, seeing Mr. Garrison."

"When's he due back?"

She shrugged her slim shoulders. "Later tonight."

"Get him on his cell phone, willya?" Tenny said as he strode into Dan's private office. For a moment April looked as if she wanted to stop him, but instead she turned to her desktop computer and pecked out a command.

Tenny slid into Dan's desk chair. The display screen lit up to show Dan's face. Before Tenny could speak a word, Dan's image said, "I'm not available at the moment. Leave a message and a number where I can get back to you."

Fuming impatiently, Tenny said into the screen, "Boss, I think I got an angle on who's the skunk in the woodworks. I tracked down the people who had access to the command codes *and* the ground track. Call me on my cell right away."

His message finished, Tenny jumped up from the chair and headed out of the office. As he breezed past April once again, he said, "If Dan calls in, transfer it to my cell phone. Top priority."

"Yes, Dr. Tenny," April said, in a hushed voice. Tenny always rattled her, and this day was worse than any previous.

Nine o'clock and still no word from Dan, Tenny groused to himself as he paced the catwalk around the hangar. He glanced over the railing at the wreckage sprawled across the hangar's concrete floor. He had called Dan four times since he'd barged into the boss's office earlier in the afternoon; all he'd gotten was that shit-brained automatic message. What good is having a friggin' cell phone if you keep it turned off all the time?

All right, Tenny admitted to himself, Dan wouldn't want the phone bothering him while he's meeting with Garrison. But he oughtta be flying back by now. He's probably still got the friggin' phone off while he's flying the Staggerwing. Tough enough flying that clunker at night without phone calls interrupting your concentration, he reluctantly acknowledged.

I can't just stand around here waiting! Tenny complained silently. He yanked his own cell phone out of his shirt pocket to make sure it was on and functioning. Okay, he thought as he stuffed it back into his pocket, no sense sitting here with my thumbs up my butt. He started down the steel steps, his boots clattering, echoing in the darkened hangar.

At the bottom he stopped and stared out at the wreckage of the spaceplane. Dirty, shit-eating sonsofbitches, he growled inwardly. They did this deliberately. They destroyed the plane and killed Hannah. Deliberately. In cold blood. Must have taken 'em months to plan it out and get everything set. Friggin' murderers.

Striding toward his shiny black, chrome-trimmed Silverado parked outside the hangar, Tenny pulled the phone out of his pocket again and pecked out the number for the motel where Passeau was staying. An automated answering voice asked him for the name of the guest he was trying to reach.

"Passeau," Tenny snapped. Then he spelled it.

The phone beeped four times. Five.

"The person you are trying to reach is not answering the phone. If you would like to leave a voice mail message, press one."

Tenny thumbed the keypad. When the automated voice gave him the cue, he said, "Claude, it's Joe Tenny. I've got proof that the bird was sabotaged and I know who did it. Call me as soon as you get this message."

Fuming about people who didn't answer their goddamned phones, Tenny opened the door to his Silverado and climbed up into the driver's seat. He turned on the ignition and the engine growled to life. Then he saw the orange warning on the dashboard fuel gauge.

Near empty? he asked himself. Couldn't be; I filled the tank yesterday and I haven't gone anywhere except from here to home and back.

Nettled, worried that the hydrogen tank might be leaking, he put the truck in gear and headed through the night for the hydrogen storage facility on the other end of the airstrip. The Astro base was dark, except for pale lamps spaced along the roadways that connected the various buildings. Glancing out his side window, Tenny saw that the clouds that had been piling up since late afternoon had blotted out the stars. Dan's gonna have to land at the commercial airport, he thought. It's gonna be pouring rain here pretty soon.

The damn fuel tank shouldn't be leaking, he fumed as he drove across the base. The hydrogen bonds to the metal chips in the tank, nice and solid. Maybe some of it baked out of the chips, though; the pickup's been sitting out in the sun all day. Hydrogen gas leaks out the tank's cap, he knew. Sneaky stuff in its gaseous phase; seeps through almost any kind of seal.

He shrugged. No real danger. Hydrogen gas just floats up into the air; doesn't drip and spread and make puddles like gasoline would. Still, Dan insisted that the hydrogen facility had to be stuck out in the middle of noplace. Worried it might blow up like the old *Hindenburg*. No matter how I tell him the stuff is safe, he still worries about hydrogen. Him and everybody else. NASA's been using liquid hydrogen for rocket engines for more'n fifty friggin' years and people are still scared of the stuff.

Shaking his head at human obstinacy, Tenny pulled to a stop at the wire fence that surrounded the hydrogen facility. In the darkness he groped in the glove compartment for the automatic door opener, clicked it once, and the gate rattled open on its metal wheels. He drove in, passed the low building that housed the electrolysis equipment that separated water into hydrogen and oxygen, and pulled up next to the huge spherical hydrogen tank. Bigger than a two-story house, the tank dwarfed Tenny's Silverado. Both it and the smaller oxygen tank next to it had enormous NO SMOKING signs painted across their curving flanks in Day-Glo red.

Tenny climbed down from the truck, grumbling to himself that he would have to check the fuel tank in the morning. Not at the house, though, he decided. I'll drive back out here and park it in the far corner of the parking lot. Maybe I'll have to build a carport to protect the truck from the sun.

"Who's there?"

Tenny jerked with surprise at the sound of a man's voice. Then he saw one of the uniformed security guards walking up to him. Big guy. His shirt stretched, too small for his muscular frame.

"It's okay," he told the rent-a-cop, fishing his ID badge from his shirt pocket. "I work here."

The guard flashed his light on the card, then into Tenny's face. Tenny squinted, frowned.

"Okay, Mr. Tenny. Just doing my job."

"Yeah, fine, but get the light outta my eyes."

"Yessir." The light winked out.

Blinking, waiting for his night vision to return, Tenny stepped around his pickup to find the fuel hose. The big hydrogen tank held liquefied hydrogen, cooled to more than four hundred degrees below zero. To power his truck, Tenny had built a small assembly that tapped liquid hydrogen from the tank, allowed it to warm to a gas, and then pumped the gas into his pickup's tank.

"I didn't know you guys were patrolling out here," Tenny said, as he peered at the dimly lit gauges in the darkness.

"The boss thought we out to check the facility every shift, since the accident," said the guard.

Overreacting, Tenny thought. Scared of hydrogen. Shit, this facility's as safe as the file cabinets in Dan's office.

He found the fuel hose as his eyes readjusted to the darkness of the cloudy night. As he turned back to his truck, the guard smashed the butt of his pistol into Tenny's head, knocking him unconscious. He sprawled on the ground, the hose still gripped in his right hand.

Swiftly, the guard unlatched the safety valve on the hose. Invisible, odorless hydrogen gas began pouring out of it. The guard could hear the pump chugging behind him. He ran out to the wire fence at the hydrogen facility's perimeter, dashed through the gate and raced to his own car, parked up the road. Ducking in behind the steering wheel, he popped the glove compartment and pulled out a small flat metal box. Inside it was a length of ordinary white string that smelled sharply of the oil it had been soaked in.

For a moment he hesitated. He clicked the box closed again and started his car's engine. He wanted to be moving away when the shit hit the fan. He jumped out of the car, uncoiling the oil-soaked string as he ran back to Tenny's Silverado. The engineer was still facedown, moaning, his legs scrabbling feebly. The man pushed one end of the string into the still-hissing hydrogen hose, then uncoiled the string to its full length and lit its other end. He sprinted back to his car, slammed it into gear, and peeled away with a screech of rubber on the tarred roadway.

The hydrogen facility blew up in a massive red fireball, hotter than the pits of hell. The roar of the blast shook the guard's car so badly he nearly drove off the road. As the fireball soared into the night sky, turning the clouds coppery red, the guard drove off and headed for Houston, where his money was waiting for him.

OVER GOOSE ISLAND STATE PARK, TEXAS

Dan saw the fireball as he flew over the state park.

He had just ducked the Staggerwing below the thickening cloud deck, knowing that he wouldn't be able to land at the airstrip at the Astro headquarters. He was receiving landing instructions from the airport at Lamar, on the other side of the bay that separated Matagorda Island from the mainland when the hydrogen facility blew up.

"What the hell was that?" yelled the air traffic controller in Dan's earphones.

The Staggerwing lurched, whether from the explosion's shock wave or Dan's startled response he didn't know. Or care.

"Explosion at my headquarters on Matagorda," he said into the pin microphone that almost touched his lips. "I'm diverting over there to take a look."

Dan felt bile inching up his throat. He knew that the only thing on Matagorda that could create a fireball that immense was Astro's hydrogen facility.

"Christ, not another one," he groaned. First the spaceplane and now this. I'm ruined. They've ruined me.

Circling over the blazing remains, Dan saw that his worst fears had come true. Flickering flames broke the darkness where the hydrogen facility had been. The grass was burning now; a spreading brushfire had already reached beyond the sagging wire fence that surrounded the facility. There's nothing down there but burning wreckage, he saw. Must've broken windows for miles.

Along the road on the other side of the bay from the island Dan saw headlights racing toward the fire. Local firefighters, he thought. Volunteers. They'll have to get the ferry guy out of bed.

Don't let anybody be hurt, he prayed to a god he didn't believe in. Just don't let anybody be hurt. But as he circled around the burning destruction he thought he saw the twisted remains of a truck or some sort of vehicle.

Tenny? Dan's heart clutched in his chest at the thought. Joe powered his pickup on that hydrogen. My god, was he caught in the blast?

"Staggerwing oh-nine," came the voice of the air traffic controller in Dan's earphones. "Report your position, please."

That snapped Dan back to reality. I'm circling over hell, he wanted to say. I've been damned and put in hell.

Dan tried to phone his office from the airport in Lamar but there was no answer at any of the phone lines. He considered driving to his headquarters, but realized that once the ferry had carried the local firefighters to the island it wouldn't be running again until morning. So he bunked down at the airport motel and tried to sleep. Tried to.

First thing the next morning Dan flew from Lamar back to the airstrip on Matagorda, his eyes bloodshot and pouchy. The local morning news had a brief item on the explosion at the Astro base. Radio stations in Houston didn't mention it at all.

Wait till they find out it was a hydrogen blast, Dan thought as he touched the Staggerwing's wheels to the runway. They'll come boiling out here from New York and Transylvania to do stories on how dangerous hydrogen is.

He was in a sour mood as he clattered up the stairs to his office. April was already at her desk, her eyes red and puffy.

"Was anybody—" Dan stopped. One look at his assistant's face told him. "Who was it?"

"Dr. Tenny," April said, bursting into fresh tears.

"Dead?"

She nodded, sobbing.

"Double-damn it all to hell and back," Dan muttered as he went past April's desk and into his own office.

Passeau was already there, in shirtsleeves, standing by the window with a steaming cup of coffee in his hand.

He turned as Dan stepped behind his desk. "Tenny was killed," Passeau said, his voice flat, resigned. Dan saw that the man looked weary, saggy-eyed, as if he hadn't slept all night either.

"He was murdered," Dan said.

Passeau stepped to the fabric-covered chair in front of Dan's desk and sat in it. He took a cautious sip of the hot coffee. "Last night about ten he called me at the motel."

Dan leaned forward, rested his forearms on the desktop.

"I was in the bar, such as it is."

"Joe left a message?"

"He said he knew who had sabotaged the spaceplane. By the time I picked up the message—"

"He was murdered," Dan repeated.

Passeau nodded.

"He must have tried to get me on the phone, too." Dan pulled his cell phone from its clip on his belt. Five messages, he saw, all from Tenny. If I'd left the double-damned phone on, he accused himself, Joe would still be alive.

"The county fire marshal is investigating the accident scene," Passeau said. "You have more investigators sniffing around here than your own working staff."

Dan took a deep breath, trying to calm his racing pulse. "Claude, I need your help."

Passeau notched an eyebrow slightly.

"If Joe said he'd figured out who had sabotaged Hannah's flight, if he was murdered to keep him silent—"

"You need someone to follow his trail."

"Yes."

For a long moment Passeau said nothing. Then he shook his head. "I've already called the FBI office in Houston."

Dan closed his eyes briefly. Okay, he told himself, that was inevitable. Maybe we should have called them last week.

To Passeau he said, "We've got to do more than sit back and let the feds start poking around, Claude."

"You can't expect me to—"

"I'm not asking you to do anything you don't want to do," Dan said impatiently. "I'm going to follow Joe's footsteps. I'd like you to help me figure out the evidence."

"A consultant?" Passeau almost smiled.

"Unpaid."

The FAA investigator did smile at that. "And unannounced, please. I don't want my superiors knowing that I'm doing some freelance work for you."

"You'll do it?"

"You realize that following Tenny's trail could be dangerous for you. They killed him because he was getting too close."

"Who else do I have?"

"The Federal Bureau of Investigation has been known to track down criminals now and then."

Frowning, Dan replied, "By the time I convince the double-damned feds that a crime has been committed, the murderer could be in Timbuktu."

"True enough, I suppose. Officially the spaceplane's crash is still regarded as an accident."

"You know it wasn't."

"I believe that it wasn't an accident, yes. But there isn't a shred of evidence to back up that belief."

"Joe said he had evidence."

"And now he's dead."

Dan said slowly, "You know, Claude, you might go over and give the county fire investigator a hand. My guess is that he's in over his head."

"I suppose I could talk with him. Unofficially, of course."

"Of course."

Passeau pushed himself up from the chair. "Very well. I'm off for an unofficial chat with the fire investigator."

Dan wished him luck. Once Passeau left the office, Dan booted up his computer and began wondering how he could hold his company together. Hell, he thought, I'm going to have a tough time meeting next week's payroll.

By the end of the long, wearying day, Dan sat at his desk, shirtsleeves rolled up, desktop buried in paper, computer screen showing numbers that got steadily worse each time he looked at them.

With enormous reluctance he called April. She appeared at his door, dry-eyed now but still looking as sad as a woman who'd lost her firstborn.

"Get Garrison on the phone for me, will you, please?" Dan said.

"In Houston?"

"Right. In Houston." As she went back to her desk Dan said to himself, You've got no choice. You sell a chunk of the company to Garrison or the whole thing goes down the drain.

KYOTO, JAPAN

Saito Yamagata sat on his haunches upon the tatami mat before the low table, which was lacquered to such a luster he could see his reflection in it. The five other men around the table were all older than Yamagata, white or gray-haired, some of them balding, one of them with his scalp deliberately shaved in the manner of an old samurai. Each of them wore Western business suits, either dark gray or dark blue.

Delicate cups for tea were set at each place, although there was no servant in the room to pour. This meeting was held under the tightest security.

The industrial might of Japan, Yamagata thought. Representatives of the nation's five major corporations. Their joint worth was in the trillions of yen. They ran the government, they ran Japan's major industries, and they ran Yamagata as well.

Saito had no problem with the arrangement. It was all as it should be, he thought. I take the risks of this new enterprise in space. If it fails, it is my fault, not theirs. If it succeeds, they become wealthier and more powerful. If it succeeds, Japan becomes the energy source for the world and the Middle East becomes a backwater once again.

The would-be samurai, kneeling at the head of the table, was saying, "The American effort has met two severe setbacks this month. Their experimental rocket plane crashed during a test flight, and their hydrogen facility exploded, killing their chief engineer."

"That would be three setbacks, then," murmured the oldest man at the table.

"Your arithmetic is impeccable," said the samurai, dipping his head in agreement. The others laughed.

The elder looked toward Yamagata, at the foot of the table. "These regrettable accidents will drive your competitor from the field, I suppose."

Yamagata took in a hissing breath before replying, "Perhaps not. The American is tenacious almost to the point of foolhardiness. I know him well."

"He worked for you several years ago," said one of the others.

"Yes. I came to like him. I still do."

"But he is a competitor."

"True," said Yamagata, thinking: A valuable competitor. Without Dan Randolph's mad drive to build an American powersat, these five old men would still be dithering over financing my corporation.

"Can he be eliminated now?"

Yamagata said, "He is in financial need. My information is that he has agreed to sell a small percentage of his company to Tricontinental Oil in order to raise the capital he needs to continue."

"Garrison?" asked one of the men, clearly shocked at the news.

"Garrison," replied Yamagata, in a near whisper.

The samurai said, "If Tricontinental gains control of the American power satellite they have the resources to push the project through to completion."

"And do it at least three years before our own satellite can begin operating."

"This is unwelcome. Not acceptable," said the elder.

"The deal with Garrison has not been finalized," Yamagata told them, "although it is moving swiftly toward completion."

"Can it be stopped?"

"Is there something we can do to stop it?"

Yamagata waited, head bowed, until they ceased their chatter and all turned to him.

"I believe I have a solution," he said meekly.

No one spoke, waiting to hear what he had to say.

Yamagata began to explain, "The American powersat is almost completed. What Randolph needs more than anything else is transportation to and from the satellite. That is why he was developing the rocket plane."

"But it crashed."

"Just so," Yamagata said. "That leaves Dan Randolph with the problem of getting people and material to his satellite in the most economical manner possible."

"He can use NASA shuttles, can't he?"

Suppressing a smile, Yamagata replied, "The American government does not interact well with private companies. They suspect that any organization which strives to make a profit is somehow crooked and must be dealt with at arm's length."

A few chuckles and grins went around the table.

"It would take Randolph many months, perhaps a year or more, before he could work out an agreement with NASA to rent space on their shuttles. That is, assuming that NASA would deal with him at all. In my estimation, NASA simply does not have the capacity to accomplish its own missions and add Randolph's workload as well."

"Then NASA is out."

"It would seem so," said Yamagata. "That means Randolph must go to one or more of the private launch companies in the United States or Russia."

"What about the European Space Agency?"

"Their launch capabilities are limited and fully booked," said Yamagata. "No, Randolph must go to a private company in the States or Russia." He hesitated a heartbeat, then added, "Or Japan."

"Ahhh," said the samurai. "I begin to understand." Even the elder, normally sour and gruff, allowed himself a slight smile.

"I could propose a strategic partnership with Randolph. Yamagata rockets will provide transportation to and from his satellite. The money he takes from Garrison can go into the development of his spaceplane."

"And what do we gain from this?"

Yamagata closed his eyes for a moment. At last he said, "We gain a share of the spaceplane. Perhaps a license to build it here in Japan. With such an advanced transportation system we could shave perhaps a full year off the development of our own power satellite. And reduce our costs significantly."

"But the American spaceplane is a failure. It crashed."

"It crashed," Yamagata agreed. "Most new aircraft crash. Most new rockets blow up. But the spaceplane is basically sound. And valuable."

The five older men rocked back on their haunches. No one broke into applause or even hissed appreciatively, but Yamagata knew he had won the day.

MATAGORDA ISLAND,
TEXAS

Following Tenny's trail wasn't as simple as Dan had hoped it would be. The engineer kept no notes, no record of his hunt for the traitor among Astro's staff. Dan ransacked Tenny's office, spent hours each night poring over his computer files, searched for keywords, clues, hints. He could find nothing. Dan even went to Tenny's home to ask his widow and teenaged sons, as gently as possible, if he'd discussed the matter with them. Nothing.

At last he tried a different tack. Late at night, alone in his own office, Dan called up the computer's personnel program and began to search for signs showing that Tenny had hit a particular individual's file. Now he began to discover too much material. Tenny had delved into dozens of files. Dan sorted the hits by date. Joe had evidently started with the technicians on the launch team, then the flight controllers, and branched out to all sorts of people. Even Niles Muhamed and Dan's executive assistant, April, were on Tenny's hit list.

He scrolled through the personnel department's directory of all the company's employees. Eight hundred and sixty-four men and women, he saw. Then he corrected himself: No, make that eight hundred and sixty-three; they haven't taken Joe's name off yet. Eight hundred and sixty-three people. One of them's a traitor. Maybe more than one. But who is it? Which of them has sold me out? Which of them is a murderer?

He knew a lot of the employees by first name, knew them well enough to listen to their family troubles, well enough to joke with them. April was always bringing in tidbits about romantic entanglements, who was chasing whom, who was breaking up, who was expecting a baby. Maybe she could help me track down the killer, Dan thought. Then he laughed at the idea. Shows how desperate I am, he told himself. April is terrific with the in-house gossip; a detective she ain't.

He fell asleep at his desk, waking only when the morning sun lanced through the window that looked out onto the parking lot.

Bleary-eyed, he stumbled along the catwalk from his office to his apartment. Half an hour later, showered, shaved, dressed in a freshly pressed shirt and slacks, he went back to his office. Can't beat the commute, he said to himself. I never have to worry about the morning rush traffic. A few people were already down on the hangar floor. He didn't see Passeau among them.

April was at her desk, brushing her silky dark hair. Dan gave her a smile that was almost a grimace. Why can't she do her hair before she comes in to work? he grumbled to himself. Then he remembered that she drove a baby blue Dodge Sebring convertible that half the guys in the company drooled over. Cool car, but it made a mess of her hairdo.

"Breakfast?" she asked as Dan went into his office.

"Just grapefruit juice," he said, then added, "And coffee." Start the day with the two major food groups: vitamin C and caffeine.

Dan sat at his desk and took a deep breath. "Let's see if you can get through the day without going broke," he muttered.

He saw that April had already booted up his computer and displayed his morning's appointments and incoming calls. The insurance carrier, of course. Passeau. Somebody named Neil Heinrich, of Tricontinental Oil; one of Garrison's flunkies, most likely. Saito Yamagata, calling from Tokyo.

Dan jiggled his computer's mouse until the screen showed the global map that displayed time zones. Cripes, it's midnight in Japan, he saw. But he moved the pointer to Yamagata's name and clicked on it. The phone program automatically dialed the number in Japan. Dan expected to get an answering machine, still he knew it would be good form to return Sai's call as soon as he received it. Politeness is important to the Japanese.

To his surprise, Yamagata's round, flat face grinned at him from his screen. "Daniel, you're at your office early."

Grinning back, "And you're at your office late, Sai."

Yamagata threw his head back and laughed heartily. "Two workaholics, that's what we are."

"Maybe," Dan agreed, thinking that you had to be a workaholic when your company was sinking beneath the waves.

Yamagata's face grew more serious. "I heard about the accident and your chief engineer's death. My condolences."

Dan hesitated, then thought, what the hell; why try to keep it a secret? "It wasn't an accident, Sai. I don't think the spaceplane crash was an accident, either. Somebody's trying to knock me out of business."

There was always a half second of delay in response when a call was relayed by satellite. Even moving at the speed of light, the message had to travel to the commsat up in synchronous orbit and then back again. This time, though, Yamagata hesitated much longer than the normal time lag before replying.

"I wondered about that, Dan. There are powerful forces opposing us. The international oil interests don't want anyone to succeed with a power satellite."

"You mean the Arabs," Dan said.

Yamagata shook his head, dead serious. "I mean the international oil interests. Arabs are part of the bloc, of course, but there are others, including Americans right there in your state of Texas."

"Tricontinental? You mean Garrison?"

"Among others."

"He wants to buy into Astro Corporation," Dan said.

Yamagata hesitated again, obviously thinking fast. "Remember the story of the Trojan horse, my friend."

Now Dan hesitated. He remembered his father's advice: Whenever somebody calls you friend, check your pockets. At length he asked, "Have you had any problems like this? Sabotage, I mean."

"No," Yamagata said, a trace of a smile curving his lips slightly. "We are not as far advanced on our program as you are. And our workforce is entirely Japanese now. No more *gaijin* workers, such as you."

Dan thought, That's one way to keep internal security tight: hire only people you know.

"I called to give you good news," Yamagata said, his smile widening. "My board of directors has approved my suggestion that we offer you our help. We can provide you with transportation to and from your powersat on Yamagata rockets."

"From Japan?"

"Yes, our launch center at Kagoshima."

"At what price?"

Yamagata said, "As I understand it, the heavy lifting is finished. What you need now is primarily transport for engineers and technicians."

Nodding, Dan added, "Plus their life-support supplies and some materials, electronics assemblies for the most part."

"Yes, that's what I thought."

"At what price?" Dan repeated.

"Zero."

Dan leaned back in his desk chair. "Sai, should I start counting my fingers or my toes?"

Yamagata laughed again. "You don't trust your old friend? The man who hired you when you were just a puppy?"

"And threw me in with a bunch of roughnecks whose idea of fun was busting a *gaijin*'s nose?"

"You look better for it," Yamagata said jovially. "You were too pretty before."

"Sai, what do you want in exchange for free rocket rides?"

Yamagata's smile faded a little. "A strategic partnership between Yamagata Industries and Astro Manufacturing."

Dan hesitated just long enough to show Yamagata his respect. Then, "On what basis?"

"You grant us license to manufacture your spaceplane in Japan."

Alarm bells began tingling in the back of Dan's mind. "That would bring your costs down when you start assembling your powersat in orbit."

"Yes, of course. That is why you developed the spaceplane, isn't it? That is why we need it."

"So you can compete against Astro more efficiently."

Yamagata shook his head slowly, like a teacher disappointed with a student. "Dan, Dan, the global energy market is worth trillions of U.S. dollars. Together, you and I, we can carve out a big slice of that pie. We can corner the solar power satellite segment of the market."

Dan gave him a grin. "Sai, I can grab a big part of the solar power satellite market all by myself."

"If you don't go broke first," Yamagata retorted, with an upraised finger.

"There is that," Dan admitted.

"Work with me on this, my friend. Why should we compete when together we can make many, many billions?"

Yeah, Dan asked himself, Why should we compete? But he heard himself say, "Sai, I appreciate your offer. I truly do. But I'll have to think about it. Give me a few days?"

"Of course," Yamagata said generously. Then his expression hardened. "But remember the Trojan horse."

"I will, Sai. I will," Dan said, thinking that the Trojan horse might well be Japanese.

HOUSTON, TEXAS

In his lush penthouse orangery of an office, Garrison sat back in his powered wheelchair and studied the man sitting in the leather-covered armchair before his desk.

Asim al-Bashir had been on Tricontinental's board of directors for almost five years. He'd never made much of a fuss about anything at the board meetings; Garrison thought that the man had worked steadily to win friends for himself among the other board members. No, not just friends, Garrison thought: allies. For five years he's been gathering supporters, forming his own little clique on the board. And now, at the quarterly meeting of the board he pipes up and takes the initiative on this power satellite business.

At least he's not the oily rug-merchant type, Garrison thought, looking al-Bashir over. I can't picture him in one of those bathrobes and hoods those sneaking A-rabs wear. Al-Bashir looked quite normal in a regular business suit and tie. His face was round, with his dark brown hair slicked straight back from the forehead. His skin was the color of light cigarette tobacco. His beard was neatly trimmed, not one of those long bushy things, and his eyes were light and clear, not shifty at all.

Yet there's something about him, Garrison said to himself. He's too damned relaxed, too cool, like he knows a lot more than he's telling.

Garrison had checked out al-Bashir six ways from Sunday when the Tunisian first joined Tricontinental's board. The man owned enough stock to deserve a seat on the board, but Garrison didn't trust any Moslem. Or Christian, for that matter. He even pulled strings in Washington and had the feds investigate the man's background. No trace of a problem, no connections to terrorism or radical Islamic movements. As far as Garrison could find, Asim al-Bashir was a very successful Tunisian businessman, nothing more.

Over the years al-Bashir had sat quietly at board meetings, seldom raising his voice, usually voting the way Garrison wanted. He wasn't a troublemaker. His major interest seemed to be making money. And slowly, quietly, building a power base for himself, Garrison thought.

Leaning back in his wheelchair, Garrison said, "Well, Randolph's taken a bite of the apple."

For a moment al-Bashir looked puzzled, which pleased Garrison. Then he said, "Ah, Adam and Eve in the Garden of Eden."

Garrison chuckled. "Not much gets past you, does it?"

Al-Bashir dipped his chin slightly, accepting the compliment.

"How long're you gonna be in Houston?" Garrison asked.

"I have a meeting in Singapore in two days. It's not terribly important, though. I can postpone it if necessary. But next week I must be in Beijing."

"The coal deal?"

"Yes. I believe the Chinese government is ready to accept our terms. By this time next year we could be selling Chinese coal across half of Asia."

"I don't like it," Garrison said flatly. "We'll be competing with ourselves. We're in the oil business; why should we be selling coal to people who oughtta be buying our oil?" He pronounced the word "oll."

"We are in the energy business," al-Bashir countered. "Our aim is to make profits. If we can do that by selling coal, we will sell coal. Or camel chips, if we can make a profit at it."

"I still don't like it," Garrison insisted. "Why, if we just—"

"It makes no difference what you like, old man," said al-Bashir, suddenly as hard and sharp as a steel blade.

Garrison actually flinched back in his chair as if he'd been slapped. But he recovered quickly. "Nobody talks to me like that, sonny."

"I do. You may be the patriarch of this corporation, but it's time for a new generation to take the leadership of Tricontinental."

"New leadership? Meaning you?"

"Of course." Al-Bashir made a frosty smile. "Oh, you can remain as chairman of the board. I wouldn't humiliate you by voting you out. But you must understand that I have the votes and, if necessary, I will call on them."

"Why, you—" Garrison stopped himself before he began uttering the string of epithets that heaped into his mind. Instead he said, "I've made this company what it is. I've brought it up from nothing, from a dinky li'l wildcat outfit drilling holes out in West Texas—"

Smiling like a rattler, al-Bashir said, "You inherited a profitable company at a time when the oil industry was booming. You rode the wave, quite successfully, I admit. But it took no great genius to achieve what you have."

"If I could stand on my feet—"

"You can't, and we both know it. Times are changing, old man, and Tricontinental must change with them. I will see to that."

Garrison stared at the man, his chest heaving, his heart thundering.

"Come, come," al-Bashir said, his smile warming slightly. "We shouldn't be enemies. We both want the same thing: power and profits for Tricontinental Oil."

"And you make all the decisions," Garrison muttered.

"Most of them will be exactly as you would make them, I assure you."

"Except for this goddamn Chinese coal business."

"In the long run, Chinese coal will make our oil more valuable, not less. Every ton of coal we sell in Asia this year means thousands of barrels of oil we can sell at higher prices in years to come."

"The goddamn environmentalists don't like coal."

"That's of no consequence," al-Bashir said. "Besides, oil is crucial to the petrochemical industry. It's much too valuable to burn."

"By Christ, you sound like that pantywaist Shah of Iran."

"Pahlavi? He was right about that."

"Lot of good it did him."

Al-Bashir dismissed the subject with an impatient wave of his hand. "No matter. We must think of the future."

"Like this power satellite contraption?"

"Yes," al-Bashir replied, his tone changing noticeably. "The power satellite is important to my plans."

The two men stared at each other for a long, silent moment: Garrison wrinkled, old, slumped in his wheelchair but determined to hold onto his power; al-Bashir smooth, elegant, obviously enjoying this moment of revealing his true strength.

At length Garrison said, "Reason I asked about your travel plans was I wanted t'know if you could be in Austin this Saturday."

"Why should I go to Austin?" al-Bashir asked with just a touch of haughtiness.

"The governor of Texas is gonna announce that he's running for president."

"Scanwell?"

"Morgan Scanwell," said Garrison. "And he's gonna make energy independence a big part of his platform."

Al-Bashir stroked his beard absently. Garrison could see the wheels turning behind his eyes. "Energy independence," he murmured.

Pointing a bony finger, Garrison asked, "I want to know what your real reason is for wanting us to buy into Randolph's power satellite."

For just a flash of an instant al-Bashir's eyes flared. And Garrison said to himself, Ah-hah. There *is* something going on!

Quickly regaining his composure, al-Bashir said smoothly, "I believe it is important for Tricontinental to diversify. Coal, nuclear power, natural gas, even this far-out idea of a power satellite—we should be involved in every form of energy production."

"Save your pretty speeches for the public relations flacks," Garrison snapped. "What's the real reason?"

Al-Bashir smiled, revealing teeth so perfect that they had to be the result of expensive orthodonture.

"Well?" Garrison demanded.

"Very well then." Al-Bashir hunched forward slightly. Garrison leaned toward him and placed both his liver-spotted hands on his desktop.

"As I told you, Tricontinental is in the energy business, not merely oil," al-Bashir said in a near whisper. "It is vital to our long-term interests to control as much of the energy market as possible. Not merely oil. We must control all the possible competitors against oil, and that includes Randolph and his powersat."

"Control 'em," Garrison muttered.

Al-Bashir nodded gravely. "Yes. Not merely invest in them. Not merely dabble in them. We must *control* the world's energy supplies." And he closed his right hand into a tight, hard fist.

He's right, Garrison said to himself. The sumbitch is right. And now he's out in the open. He thinks he can shove me aside, make me into a figurehead. He wants power, pure and simple, and he's smart about getting it. But he's dead wrong if he thinks I'm gonna lay down and let him walk over *me*.

As al-Bashir rode in his limousine back to his hotel suite, he called his travel secretary to cancel his meeting in Singapore and make accommodations for him in Austin for the weekend.

Folding his cell phone and slipping it into his jacket pocket, he picked up the intercom microphone. Up front, on the other side of the soundproof glass partition, his chauffeur glanced into the rearview mirror at him.

"Roberto, the business of the Astro technician must be finished."

The chauffeur nodded.

"You say that Randolph is tracking down the same leads that Tenny followed. Sooner or later he will find our man."

"Yeah. The pigeon's gettin' pretty damn spooked. He wants more money so he can leave the country."

"Give him what he wants. Then terminate him when he least expects it."

"Right."

"And make it look like an accident this time. No more explosions."

Al-Bashir could see little more of Roberto in the rearview mirror than his dark eyes. It seemed to him that Roberto smiled.

"You wanted t'make people think that hydrogen stuff is dangerous, di'n't you? That blast knocked off two targets all at one time."

This Latino is becoming impertinent, al-Bashir thought. But he smiled back and said mildly, "No more explosions. I want the man's death to look like a suicide. From remorse."

"Yeah, sure," said Roberto grudgingly as he swung the limousine into the hotel's busy driveway.

MATAGORDA ISLAND,
TEXAS

The setting sun was low enough to send a shaft of light lancing through Dan's office window. He saw that it was in Lynn Van Buren's eyes, making the woman squint painfully, so he got up and lowered the blinds.

"Whew, thanks," said the engineer.

"Why didn't you say something?"

She grinned at him. "Didn't have to, chief. You caught my body language."

Lynn Van Buren was an unlikely engineer. Her education at Caltech had been in biophysics, with a minor in mathematics. She'd been an experimentalist, a lab rat who enjoyed getting her hands dirty and tinkering with balky equipment that frustrated less-patient researchers. She got into the engineering end of the business when she started working on biophysics experiments that were going to be performed in space, completely automated after riding into orbit aboard a rocket booster.

In time, she found herself more fascinated by the rockets than by what they carried. She was one of the earliest hires when Dan started Astro Manufacturing Corporation. Within the first year of the company's operation she became Joe Tenny's top assistant.

Lynn Van Buren sat before Dan's desk now, a feisty grin on her face. She was in her early forties, short and chunky, dimpled chin, her mouse-brown hair cut short, her hazel eyes bright with good-humored intelligence. She was wearing a dark blue pantsuit with an incongruous string of pearls around her neck.

"So what's the latest from Hangar B?" Dan asked.

"That's why I wanted to see you, chief. Number two's ready to fly."

Despite everything, Dan broke into a smile. "She's ready?"

"We did the final checkout this afternoon. I just had to rush over and tell you in person."

Dan's elation quickly faded. "The FAA won't be finished with their investigation until hell freezes over."

"They won't let you fly her until they're done?"

"Yep. Can't say I blame them...."

Van Buren's expression turned crafty. "Even if the flight's crewless?"

"Unmanned?" Dan asked.

"Crewless," Van Buren replied firmly. "We can fly the bird remotely. We did it for the first one, remember?"

"Before Hannah took it up, right."

"So the FAA won't stop you from flying it crewless, will they?"

Dan mulled it over for a moment. "I don't know. I'll have to talk to Passeau about it."

Near midnight, the hangar was quiet and deserted except for Dan Randolph, sitting in his darkened office, the only light coming from his desktop computer's screen. He stared at the invitation that had just arrived via e-mail:

> The Honorable Morgan Scanwell, Governor of Texas, requests the pleasure of your company at a cocktail reception and dinner Saturday, August 28...

The invitation was accompanied by a video mail message from Jane: "Dan, please come and join us. Morgan's going to announce his candidacy the following Monday morning, and we want to bring together a group of supporters for a personal evening with him."

And rain makes applesauce, Dan said to himself. Why should I go to Austin? To help Scanwell? He hasn't done a thing to help me.

In all honesty, he thought, what can the governor of Texas do for me? Maybe if he ever gets to be president of the United States he can help, but until then it's all talk, all smoke and mirrors. And Astro will be in receivership by the time the next president takes the oath of office.

But he stared at Jane's face, frozen on his screen. And he knew he would go to Austin, or the South Pole, or Mars, to see her again. No matter what the pain.

Clicking on the REPLY icon, Dan put on a smile and said jovially, "Thanks for the invitation, Jane. I'll be there, in dinner jacket and black tie and dancing shoes."

Then he blanked the invitation. The screen showed what he had been poring over before Jane's message arrived: a list of the names compiled from the personnel files that Tenny had checked into the day before he was killed.

The anger burned up inside him again. Killed. Joe didn't die in an accident. He designed that double-damned hydrogen facility. He knew every weld and flange. It wasn't an accident. Somebody blew it up. Somebody murdered Joe. And Hannah. Maybe I'm next.

Strangely, that thought calmed him. You want to come after me? he silently asked the unknown murderer. Okay, you try it. In the meantime, I'm coming after you. I'll find you, you gutless sonofabitch. Me. Myself. I'm going to nail your balls to the wall.

He thought of Passeau and the swarm of government investigators working on the spaceplane crash. They're still working under the assumption that there was something wrong with the plane. Passeau knows better, but he hasn't convinced the rest of his crew that it was sabotage. Maybe he's not trying to. Maybe he's in on it.

No, Dan told himself, shaking his head. He couldn't have had anything to do with the crash. He was in his office in New Orleans. At least, that's what he said. Maybe I should check that out.

The list on his screen showed the names of the staff people whom Tenny had called over the weeks since the spaceplane's crash. I have to retrace his steps, Dan thought wearily. I'll have to go through every double-damned one of those names. Without consciously thinking about it he commanded the computer to rearrange the list in chronological order. Last one first, he thought. I'll talk to the people Joe called the day he was killed and work backwards from—

He stopped, staring at the screen. The last people Joe had checked on! he realized. Three names were listed for that date. Joe talked to these three people, and that night he was killed. One of them is it! Has to be!

Elyana Mechnikov.

Peter Larsen.

Oren Fitch.

One of them is it, Dan repeated to himself. Maybe more than one of them. Maybe all three!

Despite his queasiness at being on the water, Roberto took the last ferry to Matagorda Island and drove the battered pickup truck he had borrowed to the motel a few miles up the road from the Astro Corporation's fenced-in compound. No one paid much notice to a Hispanic man in work-stained coveralls checking in there, despite his size. The greatest difficulty Roberto had encountered the last time he'd come on the island was getting through the Astro main gate, but even with the spaceplane crash less than a month behind them, the guards at the gate hardly glanced at his phony ID. They saw the security guard uniform he wore and assumed that he was what he claimed to be, a new hire reporting for the night shift.

For this job he didn't even have to get inside the Astro facility. The prey would come to the hunter.

Roberto parked the pickup in front of the dimly lit front door of his motel room, went inside, and dropped his overnight bag on the sagging bed. Then he walked back to the bar that adjoined the motel's reception desk. He was a big man, with a weightlifter's shoulders and thickly muscled arms. He kept his face clean-shaven and the sleeves of his gray coveralls buttoned at the cuffs so that the tattoos he had acquired during his street-gang youth in Los Angeles would not show.

Downhearted country music twanged out of the speakers set into the ceiling above the bar. The barmaid was a tired-looking bleached blonde, trying to look sexy in a push-up bra. "Yew want dinner, the kitchen closes in ten minutes," she said over the nasal whine of a cowboy singer.

"No thanks," said Roberto. "Jus' a beer. Dos Equis dark."

"We got Bud, Bud Lite, Michelob, Mick Lite, and Corona."

Roberto sighed. "Mick."

"Lite?"

"No, heavy."

She poured the beer and placed the mug on the bar in front of him on a round paper coaster. "Kitchen closes in ten minutes," she reminded him.

"You tole me that."

"Oh, yeah."

"What time do you get off?"

She gave him a wordless sneer and walked down the bar to start talking with a trio of Anglos. Roberto stared down into his beer, hiding his rage. Sure, spit on the greaser, he seethed inwardly. What would she think if I went over there and kicked the cojones off those three assholes?

He took a long pull of the beer. Stay cool, man. You don't want nobody to notice you. You get paid to be invisible. Wait. You got a job to do.

The job walked into the bar, looking uncertain, worried.

Peter Larsen was a short, slight, middle-aged man with thinning hair, bulging thyroid eyes, and the beginnings of a potbelly. Despite the jeans and biker-style denim jacket he wore, he looked every inch the techie geek, down to the square MIT ring on his left hand like a wedding band. Roberto saw him in the mirror behind the bar and thought that Larsen looked more like a frightened little bird than anything else. I could snap him like a wishbone, he told himself.

Larsen didn't come up to the bar. He just looked around until he recognized Roberto sitting alone, separated by several stools from the guys the barmaid was talking to. Then he walked out, quickly.

Roberto finished his beer, left a five on the bar, and walked out into the night. It was still hot and muggy, the sky overcast. Crickets were chirping and Roberto saw swarms of insects flitting around the lamps that stood on high poles at the corners of the parking lot.

One of the cars flicked its lights. A boxy gray Volvo. Roberto went to it and slid into the passenger's seat. He felt cramped, confined.

"We've gotta talk," Larsen said, his voice whining, high-pitched.

"Tha's why I came, man. I know you're worried."

"I didn't expect you to kill Tenny!"

Feigning surprise in the darkness of the car, Roberto said, "Me? Wrong, man. It was an accident, pure and simple."

"Pretty lucky accident, for you."

Roberto shrugged.

"I mean, Joe starts asking me questions, so I call you. That night Joe gets killed in an accident."

"Shit happens, man."

"I want out of this," Larsen said, urgency in his voice. "I want to get as far away from all this as I can."

"Can't say I blame you."

"I'll need money. Cash."

Roberto pulled in a deep breath, then let it out in a long sigh.

"Well, what about it? If you don't—"

"Hey, man, simmer down. You'll get cash. You wan' it, I got it for you. Le's drive over to your place. More private than a fuckin' parkin' lot."

Larsen had an apartment in the company-built low-rent housing six miles down the road from the motel, on the other side of the Astro complex. The next morning his landlady found him dead, hanging from the broken ceiling fan in his living room. The police suspected suicide, especially after playing his phone messages and hearing a threatening voice demanding that Larsen pay his gambling debts or else. The voice, of course, belonged to Roberto, who slept late in his room that morning, quite tired after walking the six miles from Larsen's apartment complex back to the Astro Motel.

SEATTLE, WASHINGTON

It was drizzling again, after a cheerfully bright sunny morning. Rick Chatham looked out the rain-spattered windows and wished he were back in Arizona, where rain was as rare as sunshine here in Seattle. The house he was staying in looked out over the working harbor, where freighters from China and Japan unloaded their cargoes of toys, appliances, automobiles and god knew what else. Globalization. Chatham hated the idea. Americans are supporting sweatshops and slave labor camps just so they can pay a few dollars less for their luxuries.

He had been christened Ulrich, which in German means "wolf rule." The name pleased him, although he never told anyone about it. There was a lot about himself that he never told anyone. Rick Chatham was a man of secrets.

He hardly looked the part. He was a bland-seeming man in his late thirties, so average in stature that he could fade into a crowd without anyone noticing him. He wore his long, sandy hair in a ponytail and kept a neat little beard ringing his unexceptional face. He had a tiny diamond stud in his left earlobe but no other jewelry. Chatham's great talent was his mind, his intelligence; he prided himself on seeing farther than others, and on understanding how to rally people to his point of view.

When the Astro Corporation spaceplane had crashed, Chatham had barely paid attention to the news coverage. Until he discovered the enormous ecological havoc that a solar power satellite could wreak. He discovered it quite by accident: one of the TV news broadcasts covering the spaceplane accident and its aftermath gave a brief, animated explanation of how a powersat would work. That was enough to set Chatham firmly against the very idea of allowing a solar power satellite to go into operation.

"It beams out microwaves," he was telling the small group of people who had assembled to listen to him. "Microwaves, for chrissakes! Like you use to cook! They could cook *you!*"

There were eight other people in the living room, sitting on the overstuffed sofa, the New England rocker, or on pillows strewn across the polished oak floor. This was the next-to-last stop on Chatham's itinerary. One more little gathering like this in L.A., and then back home to Tucson.

"Microwaves?" asked one of the women.

"Microwaves, just like you use in your kitchen," Chatham replied.

"The government wouldn't let them do that," she said. The others around her snickered.

Chatham explained patiently. "They tell you that a power satellite is clean and environmentally friendly. Doesn't burn any fuel. Uses solar power. Yeah, right. But how do they get the energy from the satellite up there in space down to us on the ground? They beam it down with *microwaves*. Five or ten billion watts' worth of microwaves!"

"They can't do that!"

"They will unless we stop them."

"Now wait a minute," said the lean graying man who was Chatham's host. He and his wife wore matching bulky gray cable-knit turtleneck sweaters. "They're going to send the beam down to an isolated area, aren't they? White Sands, from what I remember."

"Yeah, that's what they claim they're going to do," Chatham admitted.

"And the beam will be spread out over a dozen square miles or something like it, so it won't be strong enough to hurt anything."

"If you believe what they say," Chatham replied. "They claim that birds will be able to fly through the beam without being hurt."

"So what's the problem?" His host smiled to let Chatham know that he was merely playing devil's advocate.

Chatham smiled back tightly. "The problem, sir, is that we have no idea of what the long-term effects will be. Remember, ecology is the science of understanding consequences—"

"Frank Herbert wrote that," one of the others murmured, loud enough for everyone to hear. Admiration shone on her face.

"And he was right," Chatham snapped. "Suppose a bird circles around in the beam. How many circles can it make before it's cooked? Or blinded?"

"Blinded?"

Warming to his subject, Chatham said, "Back in the nineteen fifties the U.S. Defense Department put up a string of big-ass radars, up above the Arctic Circle, in Canada and Alaska. They were supposed to provide early warning of an attack from the Soviet Union."

"What's that got to do with power satellites?"

"Let me tell you," said Chatham. "Eskimos found that the area around those huge radar antennas was warmer than the rest of the region, so they started setting up their camps near the radars. And pretty soon they started going blind."

"Blind?" asked a woman.

"Blind. Those radars were pumping out microwaves. That's why it was warm near them. The microwaves cooked the Eskimos' eyeballs. Hard-boiled them."

"Oh my god!"

Almost triumphantly, Chatham added, "And the microwaves those radars put out are *puny* compared to what the powersat will be beaming to the ground."

One of the younger men, wearing a scruffy-looking UCLA sweatshirt, objected: "But I've seen pictures of cows grazing in a field where the power satellite's receiving antennas are set up."

"Drawings, yeah," Chatham said. "If they try that in reality they'll be cooking their steaks on the hoof."

That brought a few distressed laughs.

Chatham went on, "What's more, nobody's done any studies of what the long-term effects on the atmosphere will be if we start beaming gigawatts of microwaves all over the place. Nobody."

"You mean it might affect the weather?"

"Does a bear sleep in the woods?" Chatham replied, grinning.

"The point is, I think," said the group's host, "that we've got to do whatever we can to stop this threat to our environment."

"No," Chatham snapped. "We've got to do *whatever it takes* to stop the power satellite."

MATAGORDA ISLAND, TEXAS

Dan found out about the apparent suicide when he tried to phone Larsen at his cubicle in the engineer's building that stood next to Hangar A. The man wasn't at his desk, so Dan asked April to track him down.

She came into Dan's office nearly half an hour later, her face drawn.

"What now?" Dan asked.

"Pete Larsen hanged himself."

"What?"

Without Dan telling her to, she sank into the chair before his desk. "I talked with a sergeant I know from the county sheriff's office. He said that Pete committed suicide. The Mafia or somebody was after him."

"The Mafia?"

April nodded. "He owed a lot of money from gambling."

"Pete Larsen?" Dan asked again, incredulous. "He wouldn't even bet on the Super Bowl pool."

"That's what the sergeant said. He hanged himself because he owed money to gamblers."

Dan frowned at his assistant. "April, you knew Pete. Was he a gambler?"

"I didn't think so. But the police said he was."

"And rain makes applesauce."

"But—"

"No buts, kid. Look. Hannah gets killed in the crash. Joe Tenny thinks it's sabotage and Joe was trying to figure out who did it. He talked with Pete the afternoon he was killed. That night, boom! Joe is murdered."

April flinched visibly at hearing the word *murder*.

"Now Pete's dead," Dan continued. "If you ask me, I'd say Pete was involved in the crash, and when Joe started sniffing too close they killed him. Then they killed Pete to keep him quiet and shut off any chance of our finding out who's behind all this."

Staring back at him, April asked, "Is that what happened?"

"That's what I think." Then Dan realized how tenuous it all was. "Of course, I could be having paranoid delusions. I could be chasing my own tail."

"Oh no," she said, her gold-flecked eyes wide and earnest. "You must be right, Mr. Randolph. I mean, I knew Pete Larsen pretty well. I even dated him a couple of times. He didn't strike me as a gambler. Not at all. And it doesn't seem right that Dr. Tenny would have an accident with the hydrogen equipment. He designed it himself, didn't he?"

Dan nodded.

"What are you going to do now?" April asked. "Do you want to talk to the county sheriff about Pete?"

He shook his head. "I don't think that'd do any good. They're calling it suicide. Let it rest there. If I try to make a fuss the cops'll think I'm a crank or, worse, a nut case."

"And it would alert whoever killed Pete that you're still after them."

"Right," Dan said, his estimation of April rising another notch. Are you part of this? he asked her silently, locking his gaze onto her's.

"But you can't track down the killers by yourself, Mr. Randolph. You should get the FBI into this. Or maybe the Texas Rangers."

"The FBI's supposed to be investigating the crash. I haven't seen any action from them, though. Have you?"

Her brows knit slightly. "All right, then. What about a private investigator?"

"I've thought about that. I just don't think that a private gumshoe would be much help. They're mostly involved in divorce cases, tapping phones and photographing husbands with telephoto lenses."

"Mitch O'Connell? The head of your security department?"

"Useless for anything more than hiring rent-a-cops and filling out forms. Hell, if our security was any good we wouldn't be in this fix."

"I suppose," she said, sounding disappointed.

"Maybe I ought to talk to the local FBI office and try to goose them up," Dan said halfheartedly. "I don't know what else to do."

April's slender jaw set in a look of determination. "Let me talk to my father, back in Virginia. He's a county district attorney and he might know an investigator here in Texas who can do something more than peep through keyholes."

She didn't wait for Dan to agree. Instead, April got up from the chair and went straight to the office door, so firmly intent that Dan just sat in his desk chair, speechless.

But he was thinking: Is she one of them? Being my assistant is a good spot for a mole. Is she calling her father, or one of the guys who killed Hannah and Joe and Pete?

April Simmonds was cursed with good looks. From the first beauty contest her mother had put her into, when she was five years old, she had found that she could smile and dimple and everyone would admire her. But as she grew into a shapely teenager and began to understand the power of sex, she started to realize that being beautiful was not enough. Not for her. Yes, the good-looking girls got picked first for the cheerleaders' squad and teachers excused them for being late with assignments or forgetting their homework. That was fine. But April learned soon enough that others—especially men—didn't expect anything from a beautiful woman except for her to be pretty. And compliant. They were frightened by a beautiful woman with brains.

April had a first-class brain. At first she didn't realize this because when she got As in class she (and everyone else) assumed it was because she smiled brightly and caused her teachers no trouble. No one was more surprised than April when she sailed through the toughest courses in high school, including algebra and trig, without the slightest difficulty.

It was much the same in college. Yes, there was some racial trouble now and then, especially when she dated white men. But she handled it without letting it blow up into a major confrontation. She found that she was actually interested in learning about history and English literature and even the dreary courses in economics. Her only difficulty came when she was pledged for a sorority chapter and some of the sisters were unhappy with a tall, good-looking, almond-eyed charmer who made them look shabby by comparison. But she won them over and by the time she was a senior she was elected president of the chapter.

Men were a problem, though. She could manipulate them easily enough: her high school boyfriends were so driven by testosterone that she could have made them bay at the Moon for her, or rob a bank. In college she began to date older men, including professors from the faculty. She wanted to learn from them, learn about the big world beyond the campus, learn about what life had in store for her. Instead, they patted her on the head (or elsewhere) and made it clear that all they expected from her was to be pretty. And compliant. When she tried to talk politics, or art, or anything deeper than the latest Hollywood flick, their eyes went wide with apprehension. And they seldom asked her out again. She got a reputation for being a snob.

She graduated with a degree in English literature and an ambition to do something interesting. The first job she took was as an editor on the magazine published by the state's tourism bureau. That lasted less than six months. She was asked to leave after showing the editor-in-chief how he was missing some major stories and allowing the magazine to fall into a boring rut. Unemployed, she spotted a news story about a private company in Texas that was building a solar power satellite. Interesting, thought April Simmonds. She e-mailed her resumé (with photo) to Astro Manufacturing Corporation and applied for a secretarial job, the only position she felt qualified for. Within twenty-four hours she received a return e-mail inviting her to fly down to Matagorda Island for an interview.

The personnel chief was a tough-looking older woman with hard, probing eyes and a no-nonsense attitude. But after talking with April for ten minutes, she smiled and said that the CEO and founder of the company needed an executive assistant. April accepted the offer, determined to do her job well but never to let her boss see how smart she truly was.

Then she made her first mistake. She fell in love with her new boss, Dan Randolph. He was one of those rare men who was not intimidated by an attractive woman with brains. In fact, she thought he seemed uninterested in her looks. April got the feeling that he was in love with someone else, someone unobtainable. That made her love him even more.

Now she was determined to help Dan find the people who had killed Hannah Aarons, Joe Tenny, and most likely Pete Larsen, as well. She knew this would be difficult. What she never stopped to consider was that it would also be very dangerous.

AUSTIN, TEXAS

The cocktail reception was held not at the governor's mansion, nor in the capitol, nor even in one of Austin's major hotels. For this quiet little get-together with his major backers, Morgan Scanwell used the home of the University of Texas's chancellor.

As he drove his rented Lexus sedan up the driveway Dan saw that it was a lovely house, nestled in the deep shade of a garden steeped in vivid beds of azaleas, begonias, and jacaranda. The air was heavy with the sweet scent of jasmine. A pair of kids in T-shirts and jeans were serving as parking valets. Students, Dan guessed. Smart of Scanwell to have the party here; no snoops from the news media, and he gives the university brass the impression that he owes them one.

Plenty of security, Dan saw. Blank-faced men in sports jackets and business suits were scattered around the garden and standing at the front door. Dan thought that they probably had enough firepower under those jackets to take out half the student body.

There were only a dozen people in the spacious living room, the men in ordinary suits, as Dan was, the women in dresses or slacks. Scanwell was nowhere in sight. Neither was Jane.

A young woman in a maid's dark outfit proffered a tray of champagne flutes. Caterer, Dan thought, although she might be a student working for the caterer. He thought briefly about asking for a glass of amontillado but immediately figured it would be an exercise in frustration and accepted the champagne. Then he saw that several of the men had shot glasses in their hands. Stronger stuff was available.

"Daniel Randolph?"

Dan turned at the sound of the man's voice and saw a shortish, solidly built man with a round face fringed by a neatly trimmed dark beard. His skin was about the same shade Dan's would be after a summer in the sun. The man wore a light gray suit with a pastel green tie carefully knotted at the collar of a figured white-on-white shirt. Expensive. Dan thought of Polonius's advice about apparel: rich, not gaudy.

"I'm Dan Randolph," he said, smiling politely.

"I am Asim al-Bashir," the man said, extending his hand. He had to shift his cut crystal old-fashioned glass to his left hand; his fingers felt cold to the touch.

"Pleased to meet you," said Dan, thinking, He looks Arab, his name sounds Arab, but he's drinking alcohol. Not much of a Moslem, then.

"I'm on the board of Tricontinental Oil," al-Bashir said. "Mr. Garrison wants me to go over the details of our agreement with you."

Dan replied, "I spent the morning talking to Yamagata's people. They want to buy into Astro, too."

Unruffled, al-Bashir replied, "I'm sure they do."

With a rueful chuckle, Dan said, "As long as I've got that powersat up there, I'll never be lonely."

"Until you go bankrupt," al-Bashir countered pleasantly.

"There is that," Dan admitted.

Scanwell entered the room with Jane at his side. Dan felt his face settle into a frown. With an effort, he forced a smile. She's always with him, he thought. Like they're living together. No, he tried to tell himself. It's just that you only see her when she's meeting with him. Yeah, he retorted silently. And she's meeting with him all the time.

Everyone turned to greet the governor. He wore a lightweight tan suede jacket over darker brown slacks, a bolo string tie hanging from his open shirt collar. Jane was in a midthigh cocktail dress, tropical flowers on a pale blue background. She looks gorgeous, Dan thought. Smiling and happy and gorgeous. She caught his eye momentarily but quickly looked away and began chatting with the couple nearest to her and Scanwell.

The governor started working the room, smiling and shaking hands, going from one guest to the next, Jane constantly at his side.

When he came up to Dan and took his hand in his strong grip, he said softly, "I'm glad you came, Dan. I hope you can stay after this shindig winds up. Jane and I need to talk with you."

Dan nodded. "Fine. Can do." But he was thinking, Jane and him. Jane and him.

"Good." Scanwell turned his smile to al-Bashir.

After expertly working his way through the guests, Scanwell placed himself in front of the empty, dark fireplace and held up both his hands to silence the buzz of conversations. Once everyone had turned their full attention to him, he smiled broadly.

"You probably already know," he began, "that I've got a news conference set for Monday afternoon. It's no secret that I'm going to announce my candidacy for president of the United States."

Everyone broke into applause. Scanwell looked properly humble, stared at his boots for a moment, then looked up again.

"This won't be an easy fight. I'll be facing powerful opposition within the state, within the party, and once I've won the nomination—well, you know what a national campaign is like."

"You can do it, Morg!"

"Hear, hear!"

He laughed modestly and made a silencing motion with his hands. Big hands, Dan saw. An athlete's hands. Cowboy hands.

Then he looked at Jane and wondered if she'd let him put those hands on her. He didn't want to know the answer.

"Well now, you know that a candidate needs a first-rate campaign manager. I wanted to let you know before the rest of the world is told that I'm going to have the best campaign manager in the country." And he turned to Jane. "Senator Jane Thornton, of Oklahoma!"

Everyone clapped as hard as they could. Everyone except Dan. He heard one of the women shouting over the noise of the applause into the ear of the woman beside her, "Don't they make a lovely couple?"

Dan grit his teeth.

"As some of you already know," Scanwell was going on, "I intend to make energy independence a major issue in the coming campaign. The United States has been held hostage by Middle Eastern oil for too long. It's time for us to cut that umbilical cord and become energy independent."

All the lights went out.

"Damn!" somebody grumbled.

"Not another blackout!"

"Looks like it."

"They must have heard me." Scanwell's voice, with a slight chuckle.

"I don't see any lights on outside."

One of the caterer's men came with a candle that guttered uncertainly in his cupped hands. "I'm sorry, ladies and gentlemen. It seems to be a major blackout."

"Again?"

"That's the third one this year, and we're not even halfway through the summer."

Scanwell took the candle and placed it on the mantle. While the servants brought in more, he said forcefully, "See what I mean? This country needs an energy policy that *works*—twenty-four hours a day, seven days a week, and fifty-two weeks a year!"

Everyone cheered in the flickering shadows.

"We need to end our dependence on imported oil and start developing energy sources that are reliable, renewable, and under our own control!"

They cheered harder.

"Now, to accomplish that, I'm going to need all the help I can get," Scanwell resumed. "Most of you have supported me very generously in the past. I'm going to need you to open your checkbooks again."

"Oh, damn, Morgan, I forgot to bring my checkbook!" joked one of the elderly men.

"It's too dark in here to write a check anyway," someone else called out.

Scanwell grinned at them. "That's okay. We know where you live. And where you bank."

The crowd broke into laughter. Dan thought, I didn't bring my checkbook, either. Even if I did, I'd have to write with red ink.

The reception went on by candlelight, but within an hour people began leaving. The streets outside were still dark and Dan heard the hollow wail of sirens now and then. It's going to be an interesting drive back to my hotel, he thought. Keeping one eye on Jane, who never left Scanwell's side, Dan spent most of the time talking with al-Bashir: strictly getting-to-know-you banter, no business.

"What is it like, working in outer space?" al-Bashir asked, his face half-hidden in the flickering shadows. "There's no gravity, I'm told."

"Zero gee," Dan said, nodding. "The scientists call it microgravity, but to us working stiffs it's zero-*g*."

"You float like a balloon?"

"You're weightless, yep. It's not that there isn't any gravity, but the motion of your orbit cancels the effect of Earth's gravity. You're falling, really, but your forward speed keeps you from hitting the Earth."

Al-Bashir shook his head, puzzled. "I'm afraid I don't understand."

How could you? Dan thought. You have to be there. You have to experience it for yourself. And once you do you'll never be completely happy pinned down to this Earth again.

The first time Dan went into orbit, as a Yamagata employee, he got sick. He was keyed up for the rocket launch, excited and a little scared about riding a rocket into space. Yamagata had bought out a bankrupt American firm that launched rockets from a huge seagoing barge, so Dan had to fly out to the mid-Pacific along with five Japanese coworkers who eyed him with suspicious silence.

Big as it was, the launching barge heaved and swayed in the long rolling swells of the Pacific. Next to it was the command ship, a converted super-tanker that had towed the barge to this precise position on the equator. Dan couldn't help grinning when he saw that his fellow workers were getting queasy from the barge's motion. He had never been seasick, not even on his first boyhood ventures in a borrowed Sunfish out on Chesapeake Bay.

It all went exactly the way it had in training. Wriggle into the cumbersome spacesuit, pull on the helmet and lock the visor down, plod in the heavy boots to the elevator that lifted the six workers to the top of the rocket, crawl into the capsule and shoehorn yourself into the padded couch.

The capsule was like a metal tomb. No windows, no panels of instruments or controls. Six couches jammed into the cramped confines like a half-dozen biers for mummified bodies.

Lying there with nothing to see but the underside of the couch six inches above his visor, Dan waited, his pulse beating faster with each tick of the countdown clock, while he listened to the bang of valves and the gurgle of propellants surging through pumps. The rocket was coming alive, stirring like a slowly awakening beast. At T minus three seconds Dan felt the low, growling vibration of the engines' startup.

Then an explosion and a giant fist smashing into his spine and they were hurtling up, pressed into the couches by the enormous force of acceleration. Dan's vision blurred, and he grit his teeth to keep from biting his tongue in half. The world outside his helmet was a rattling, shaking, roaring haze of pain.

And then it stopped. Just as suddenly as a light switch flicking off, it all stopped. Silence. No sense of motion at all. Dan sucked in a deep double lung-ful of canned air, realizing that he had been holding his breath for god knew how many seconds. He saw his arms floating up off the couch's armrests, lifting slowly like ghosts rising from their graves. He turned his head inside the helmet to look at the Japanese worker beside him, and his insides suddenly lurched. Dan felt bile burning up his throat. He broke into a sweat and fought to keep from upchucking.

No use. He vomited inside the helmet, as wretchedly sick as any landlubber in his first storm at sea. His coworkers immediately reacted. They all laughed uproariously.

Smiling at the memory, Dan said to al-Bashir, "You have to be there to really appreciate it. Once you get accustomed to zero-g it can be really exhilarating."

Al-Bashir smiled back, slightly. "I understand that sex under weightless conditions is fantastic."

Dan thought, No sense disillusioning him. "You've got to be pretty damned ingenious; you're both floating around like a couple of feathers. But, yeah, once you get the hang of it, it's incredible."

"I suppose I'll have to try it some time."

"Sure. Everybody should."

Looking around in the guttering light of the candles that had been placed through the room, Dan saw that most of the other guests had already left. Scanwell was in the entryway, bidding good evening to a white-haired couple. With Jane still at his side.

Al-Bashir peered at his wristwatch, which glinted in the shadows. Solid gold, Dan thought. He must get his daily exercise for that arm just by lifting it to see what time it is.

"I have a dinner engagement," he said to Dan.

Walking with him toward the entry hall, Dan said, "I can have one of my people fly you down to Matagorda on Monday, if you'd like to see our operation."

"I fly my own plane," said al-Bashir. "But Monday will be fine. Say, eleven o'clock?"

"Eleven it is," Dan replied, thinking, This guy's not an early riser. Almost as an afterthought, he asked, "What are you flying?"

"Oh, I've rented a T-38 for my stay here in Texas. It's old but serviceable."

The kind of jet that NASA astronauts used, Dan realized.

"How's it fly?" he asked.

"Like a willing virgin," said al-Bashir.

Turning, he stepped up to Scanwell to say his good-bye. Dan watched the short, brown-skinned, al-Bashir shake hands with the lanky, craggy-faced governor while Jane looked on, smiling her politician's fixed smile, full of phony sincerity and artificial warmth. He knew what her *real* smile was like.

As the front door closed behind al-Bashir, Scanwell turned to Jane. "That's the last of them, isn't it?"

"Yes," she said, relieved.

"Good. Let's get somebody to make us some sandwiches. I'm starving." He laid a meaty hand on Dan's shoulder and started back into the candlelit living room. "Dan, we're going to make your power satellite a part of our energy independence program. What do you think of that?"

Dan looked from Scanwell to Jane and back again. "I think it's great. I just hope I'm still in business by the time you get into the White House."

"We can help you, Dan," Jane said.

"How?"

One of the caterer's waitresses came into the living room. "Is there anything else I can get for you, Governor?"

Scanwell grinned wolfishly, then said, "If the food in the fridge hasn't spoiled yet, maybe you could rustle up some sandwiches for us, honey. And beer, if it's still cold." He turned to Dan. "Beer okay for you?"

Tempted to say he preferred wine, Dan instead nodded. "Beer's fine."

"I wonder how long this blackout will last?" Jane murmured as she went toward the sofa.

"Last one was two whole days," said Scanwell.

Dan felt glad that his complex on Matagorda had its own backup generators. And several days' worth of fuel for them.

The waitress went back into the kitchen. Scanwell pulled off his jacket and tossed it onto a chair, then loosened his bolo as he plopped himself onto the sofa beneath a Remington painting of cowboys herding cattle out on the range beneath scudding clouds lit by a glowing full Moon.

Jane took the armchair angled at the end of the sofa. Dan pulled up a straight-backed chair and sat facing her.

"So how're you going to help me, Jane?"

Scanwell's eyes narrowed slightly at Dan's tone. Dan wondered how much the governor knew about the two of them.

Unruffled, Jane replied coolly, "The last time we talked you mentioned the concept of having the government back long-term, low-interest loans for private corporations."

"That's right," Dan said.

She turned toward Scanwell, "Morgan, did you know that the big power dams of the West were financed that way? Hoover Dam, the Grand Coulee: they were built on money raised privately for fifty-year loans at two percent interest."

"Two percent?" Scanwell asked, his brows rising.

"I think it was two."

"And the federal government guaranteed the loans?"

"Yep," Dan broke in. "The dams got built. They provided irrigation water for desert areas and generated enough electricity to light up Las Vegas and a lot of other cities that wouldn't exist otherwise. And everybody made money out of it."

"After fifty years," Scanwell muttered.

Jane said, "Dan, I intend to introduce a bill in the Senate that will offer federal backing for similar loans for you."

For a moment, Dan didn't know what to say.

He didn't need to say anything, because Jane went on, "I'm going to have to be a little creative with the language so that it won't appear that the bill is aimed specifically at helping Astro Corporation. It'll say the government will back loans to any private entity engaged in building major structures in orbit. Something like that."

"Make it any private group engaged in developing new forms of renewable energy resources," Scanwell suggested.

"A pretty thin disguise," Dan muttered.

"My staff people are pretty good at making up disguises, don't worry."

"Fifty years at two percent?" Scanwell asked.

With a slight shrug, Jane replied, "Again, my staff people will come up with numbers appropriate for today's money market."

Scanwell rubbed his chin. "If you make the wording too loose, some other corporations could line up at the trough."

"I can't specify Astro Corporation," Jane said. "The bill would be shot down in committee as a special-interest job."

"Wait a minute," said Dan. "Jane, I appreciate what you're trying to do, but by the time you get a bill through both houses of Congress and onto the president's desk, I could be in a soup line somewhere in downtown Houston."

"And that's assuming that our current president would sign it," Scanwell added. "Which I doubt."

Jane gave them both a pitying look. "Neither of you understand the bigger picture."

"Enlighten me," Scanwell said.

"Simply offering the bill will make it easier for Dan to raise money now. The prospect of government backing—"

"Will mean that anybody who's thinking of loaning me money will wait until the feds come in with their guarantee," Dan interrupted.

Jane countered, "No, we'll word the bill so that people who have already loaned money to Astro can apply for federal guarantees for their existing loans once the bill becomes law."

"You can do that?" Dan asked. "It's legal?"

Smiling knowingly, Jane said, "You'd be surprised at what's in the fine print of most bills."

"But the White House won't agree to it. He'll veto the bill," Scanwell said.

"Good. Let him."

Before Dan could object, Scanwell asked, "Let him veto it? Then why . . . oh, I get it."

"This bill gives you a powerful tool for your energy independence program, Morgan," Jane said, leaning toward him. "You can tell the voters that your plan won't be funded out of their tax dollars; it will be paid for by private investors."

"And if the President vetoes it . . ."

"You've got an issue to club him with," Jane said, almost triumphantly.

Dan sank back in his chair and stared at the two of them grinning at each other. She's not doing this for me, he realized. She doesn't give a hoot in hell about Astro or the powersat or energy independence. She's doing it for *him*, to help him get elected. Not for me. For him.

MATAGORDA ISLAND, TEXAS

Mr. Randolph?"

Dan looked up from his desk.

April said, "The control tower just called. Mr. Al-Bashir is landing."

Dan got to his feet and looked through his outside window. Sure enough, a sleek little T-38 was making its turn for the final approach to the runway, glinting silvery in the late morning sunlight. Dan saw thunderheads building up out over the Gulf. We'll have boomers this afternoon for sure, he thought.

"Do we have somebody at the airstrip to ferry him over here?" Dan asked.

"That's all taken care of," April assured him.

"Good. Thanks." Now all I have to do is wait and look like the busy executive when he gets here.

Once he had returned from Austin, Dan had looked up al-Bashir on the Internet. Not much there, he found. Born in Tunis of a filthy rich family, on the boards of a dozen big multinational corporations. Nothing in the tabloids about him. Either he's not a playboy or he's got enough money to keep his exploits out of the scandal sheets.

Dan asked April to straighten up his office in preparation for al-Bashir's visit while he took a walk around the hangar floor. Still more than a dozen FAA and NTSB people down there, measuring and weighing fragments of the shattered spaceplane. And more in the office building next to the hangar, running analyses on their laptops and driving up Astro's phone bill with calls to Washington.

By the time he'd returned to his office he hardly recognized it. Everything neat and clean, sparkling, almost. His desk was bare, Dan saw with some astonishment. I'll never be able to find anything, he thought.

April announced, "Mr. al-Bashir to see you," precisely on the tick of eleven A.M. I always heard that Arabs had no sense of timing, Dan thought as he got up from his chair and came around his desk, hand extended.

Al-Bashir smiled as he stepped into Dan's office, but he took a good long look at April before turning to accept Dan's proffered hand. He was dressed like a fashion model in a light gray suit and pale blue tie. Dan felt almost shabby in his shirtsleeves and creaseless slacks. They sat at the circular little table in the corner of the office, next to the window that looked out on the parking lot and the trees beyond it. April brought in a tray of coffee and juices, smiling prettily as she put the tray down on the table and left. Al-Bashir followed her with his eyes, a curious little smile on his lips.

"Your secretary is quite lovely," al-Bashir murmured as April closed the door behind her.

Dan nodded offhandedly. "Yep, I guess she is."

"Is she married?"

His attitude riled Dan. Keeping his tone pleasant, he lied, "No, but she's got a steady boyfriend. Local police officer and martial arts champ. Big guy, mean as a hungry bear."

Al-Bashir's smile faded.

"Coffee?" Dan asked.

Half an hour later, Dan was impressed with how much al-Bashir knew about the technology of solar power satellites. He's no engineer, Dan thought, but he's pretty damned smart.

"Power satellites will never replace petroleum entirely," the Tunisian was saying, "but they should be able to take over a large percentage of base-load electrical power generation."

"Yep," said Dan. "If we get a dozen or so powersats up there we'll be able to shut down most of the fossil-fuel electrical power plants on the ground. Maybe all of 'em."

"Only the fossil-fuel plants? What about the nuclear?"

Dan hesitated a moment, wondering how much he should tell his visitor. Then he said carefully, "Fossil-fuel plants put out greenhouse gases. Nukes don't. Burning coal and oil and natural gas is causing global warming—"

"Many eminent scientists don't agree that global warming is real."

"Yeah, I know. But global temperatures are creeping up every year. If we could shut down the fossil-fuel power plants around the world—"

"An enormous if," al-Bashir interrupted, with an upraised finger.

Dan chuckled. "Okay. Okay. Let's concentrate on getting *one* powersat up and running."

"What do you think of Scanwell's dream of making the United States independent of imported petroleum?"

"It's no dream," Dan replied. "It's a necessity."

"Really?" Al-Bashir's brows rose. "How so?"

"As long as we're tied to Middle Eastern oil we're tied to Middle Eastern politics. We're hostages to the terrorists and nutcases who want to wipe out Israel and the United States because we support Israel."

Al-Bashir smiled blandly. "And if the United States no longer needs to import petroleum from the Middle East? What then?"

"That's their problem, not mine."

"And Israel's?"

Dan said, "Israel will have to solve its own problems."

"I see," murmured al-Bashir. Then he fell silent.

You stuck your foot in it, Dan angrily told himself. You're talking to an Arab, for double-damn's sake, a Moslem. Why can't you put your brain in gear before you rev up your mouth?

Well, he asked for it, Dan thought. He pushed the door open. So now what?

Al-Bashir sat before Dan's desk, his face expressionless, his deep, dark eyes on Dan.

"Look," Dan said, feeling uncomfortable, "I'm not a politician. I'm a businessman. I'm not trying to save the world. I just want to get this power satellite going and make an indecent profit out of it."

Al-Bashir broke into laughter. "Indeed, that's what we are all seeking, Mr. Randolph."

"Call me Dan."

Nodding, al-Bashir said, "It's very rare to find one so honest as you are, Dan."

Dan shrugged.

Growing serious again, al-Bashir said, "Very well. Mr. Garrison is prepared to buy fifteen percent of Astro Manufacturing for a price of one point five billion dollars."

"And what else?"

"Tricontinental Oil will want to have one of its board members sit on your board of directors."

"Would that be you, Mr. al-Bashir?"

"It will be me, yes."

"I would much prefer a loan," said Dan, "without diluting my holdings of Astro stock."

Al-Bashir leaned back in his chair and said nothing.

"Senator Thornton plans to introduce a bill that will provide government guarantees for loans to Astro."

"And other firms, as well," said al-Bashir.

He knows about Jane's plan! Dan felt surprised. But he kept his voice level as he added, "The bill is intended to help Astro."

"The loans will be at very low interest," al-Bashir pointed out.

"Two percent of a billion and a half is still—"

"Much less than the money would earn elsewhere."

"But it would be guaranteed," Dan pointed out. "Zero risk."

Al-Bashir had the look of a cat playing with a mouse it had captured. "Dan, be serious. You can't expect us to hand you a billion and a half dollars and get nothing for it but two percent interest over a ten- or twenty-year time span. It's ridiculous."

"Then I'll have to go elsewhere, I guess," said Dan. "Maybe Saito Yamagata will be more willing."

Al-Bashir's expression turned pitying. "Dan, my friend, if you're worried about having your corporation snatched out of your hands, worry about Yamagata and the Japanese, not Tricontinental."

Inwardly, Dan agreed. Sai is willing to help, he knew. But the price of that help would be to allow Yamagata to get its hands on the spaceplane design.

"You can't get the kind of money you need without giving up something, Dan," al-Bashir said, quite reasonably. "What is it the scientists talk about, some law of thermodynamics?"

"The second law," Dan muttered. "You can't win, and you can't even break even."

"There's no free lunch, Dan. All Garrison wants is a seat on your board so he can stay informed of what you're doing. One seat isn't going to change your board. I won't be able to take over your company with only one vote."

"I suppose not," Dan admitted. But a voice in his head asked, Then why do you want that seat so badly?

WASHINGTON, D.C.

Senator Thornton!"

Jane turned at the sound of the voice. She didn't recognize the young man elbowing his way toward her against the crowd streaming down the crowded marble corridor of the Hart Senate Office Building. Denny O'Brien, walking beside her, looked over his shoulder and whispered, "Gerry Zisk, *Wall Street Journal*."

It was almost four o'clock, the nominal end of the working day for staffers, and already the corridors were jammed with office workers on their way to the homeward-bound traffic rush. The young man striding briskly against the human torrent looked too scruffy to be a reporter for the redoubtable *Journal*. He was balding but had a silly-looking goatee springing from his chin. He wore slacks and a baggy pullover shirt and, Jane noticed, expensive Bierkenstock sandals that looked as if they had seen plenty of miles. But no socks.

"He covers high tech, science, that sort of stuff," O'Brien explained before she could ask.

Zisk reached them and stuck out his hand. "Thanks for waiting up for me," he said, grinning happily. "I just want to ask you a few questions about the bill you introduced on the Senate floor this afternoon."

"Why don't we go over to my office, where we can be comfortable?" Jane suggested.

Zisk nodded enthusiastically.

As they started walking upstream, with Zisk between Jane and O'Brien, he asked, "Is this bill part of Governor Scanwell's plan for energy independence? I mean, it's aimed at helping to raise capital for high-tech companies, isn't it?"

"Yes, to both halves of your question," said Jane.

They rounded a corner and went to the SENATORS ONLY elevator. O'Brien pushed the button, muttering about how the elevator stops on every floor when the staff were emptying out of the offices on their way home.

"Do you really think it's possible for the U.S. to become totally independent of Arab oil?" Zisk asked.

The elevator arrived and a fresh flood of employees streamed out, forcing Jane and the two men to retreat back away from the doors. Jane thought of the old saw about Civil Service employees: How many people work in this office? About a third of the staff.

They got into the elevator and Zisk repeated his question as the doors slid shut.

"Totally independent of oil imports?" Jane mused. "That's our goal. How close we can get to it, and how quickly we approach that goal, depends on who's leading the nation."

Zisk grinned at her. "I'm covering technology, Senator, not politics. Is it possible, technologywise?"

"Of course it is. A lot of the necessary technology already exists, and we can develop what isn't ready today."

They reached the top floor and headed down the corridor for Jane's suite of offices. Instead of going in through the outer rooms, Jane pecked at the electronic lock on the door to her private office.

Zisk seemed unimpressed by the handsome, dark mahogany furniture. He barely glanced at the window and its view of the Supreme Court building.

"You're really confident we can develop stuff like this solar power satellite?"

"We got to the Moon, didn't we?" O'Brien snapped, heading for the refrigerator hidden beneath the ceiling-high bookshelves.

"And it cost twenty billion bucks."

Jane took one of the green-and-white-striped upholstered chairs near the window. Zisk sat in the facing chair.

"You want something to drink?" O'Brien called, hoisting a chilled bottle of spring water.

"Beer?" Zisk asked.

"What kind?"

"Lite anything."

"I'll have a tonic with lime," Jane called to her aide.

"Coming up," O'Brien replied.

Hunching forward in his chair, Zisk asked again, "Do you really think this power satellite can work?"

Jane hesitated. The reporter didn't have a notepad in his hand. There was no evidence of a recording device, unless he had one burrowed inside his pullover or jammed into a pants pocket.

"Are you recording this?" she asked.

He tapped his temple with a forefinger. "I've got a good memory."

Jane gave him a wintry smile. "Then perhaps I'd better make a record of what we say." As O'Brien handed her a tall glass of tonic, she asked, "Denny, would you turn on the machine?" Looking back at Zisk, "We can provide you with a copy, if you like."

"Whatever," he answered, shrugging carelessly. "Now, about your bill: this is a bailout for Astro Corporation, isn't it?"

O'Brien shot her a warning frown as he headed for her desk. Jane waited until he had clicked on the digital recorder before replying.

"My bill is intended to provide help for struggling companies in areas of new energy technology without costing the taxpayers a penny."

"Unless a company like Astro defaults on the loans."

"The government has done this before," Jane pointed out. "For Chrysler Corporation, for Lockheed. It's nothing new."

"But it *is* intended to bail out Astro, isn't it?"

"It should help Astro, certainly. And other companies struggling to establish private ventures in renewable energy technology."

"Name two," Zisk said, grinning.

"Rockledge Industries has plans to build a hydrogen fuel facility, I hear," Jane replied immediately. "And several companies are looking into the possibilities of establishing windmill facilities—wind farms, they call them."

Zisk's grin widened. "What about Sam Gunn and his zero-*g* honeymoon hotel?"

"That's not a form of energy technology," said Jane coolly.

Zisk changed his tack. "Word we get is that Astro's going to sell out to Tricontinental Oil. Or maybe Yamagata. Looks to me like they won't need your help, after all."

Jane had a technique for hiding her surprise. She took a sip of the drink she'd been holding, then smiled as pleasantly as she could manage for the reporter, all the while thinking furiously of what her reply should be.

At last she said, "If that's the case, then Astro won't need the assistance my bill offers. But there are other new, struggling high-tech companies that will."

Zisk nodded, his grin wider than ever.

That evening, Dan was sitting in a booth at the Astro Motel bar with Claude Passeau. They had shared a mediocre dinner and decided that some strong drink would be better than the desserts the restaurant offered.

"You must come to New Orleans," Passeau said. "The food is infinitely better than here."

"At least I got them to put in a halfway decent brandy," Dan said, swirling his tumbler of El Presidente.

Passeau shook his head. "You should try Armagnac, Dan. Much better."

"Armagnac?"

"It comes from the region of France next to Cognac, but it's smoother and better tasting." Passeau placed a hand on his chest. "That's my opinion, of course."

"Armagnac," Dan muttered. "I'll have to remember that."

Passeau looked around the place. A couple of Hispanics were at the bar, quietly drinking beer. The barmaid was on the phone, talking intently, her free hand gesturing as if she were being hysterical in sign language. Country music seeped from the speakers set into the ceiling, some guitar-strumming lament about lost love.

"Whatever made you decide to build your headquarters here?" Passeau asked. "It's like the end of the Earth."

Dan sipped at his brandy. "We can launch over the Gulf of Mexico from here. And I had an uncle who was able to sweet-talk the parks department into letting us lease this half of the island from the sovereign state of Texas."

"Ahh," said Passeau. "Money talks."

"Especially when it's in unmarked bills being passed under the table."

Passeau laughed. "You're really something of a scoundrel, aren't you?"

Feigning surprise, Dan replied, "I didn't bribe the parks people. My uncle did that."

"And look where it got you."

"It's not exactly a tropical paradise, is it?" Dan admitted.

"I've been to Cape Canaveral," Passeau said. "I thought that was run-down. But this . . ." He waved his hand vaguely toward the bar.

"This will be a metropolis someday," Dan said, grinning.

"Not in our lifetimes."

With a shrug, Dan conceded, "Maybe not."

"You worked for the Japanese, didn't you?"

"Yep."

"Up in space?"

"I wasn't an astronaut, technically. I was what they call a mission special ist. In my case it meant being a construction worker in zero gravity."

"Hmm. Did you like it?"

"Loved every minute of it." Touching his nose lightly, "Even the fights."

The look on Passeau's face was somewhere between disbelief and fascination.

Dan let him take a swallow of the scotch he was drinking, then hunched forward slightly on the booth's table and said in a lowered voice, "Claude, we're ready to fly the backup spaceplane."

Passeau backed away slightly. "I can't authorize another test flight until we definitively prove what made the first plane crash."

"We know what made it crash. Sabotage."

"You may believe that, Dan. As a matter of fact, I believe it myself. But we haven't any proof."

"That's because the proof isn't in the wreckage."

"Then where is it?"

"In Pete Larsen's skull."

Passeau pulled in a breath. "Then it's permanently beyond your reach."

"Look," Dan said, hunching even further over the table. "Pete had access to the command codes for the plane's control systems. And he knew the ground track. He sold that information to somebody. That somebody operated a radio transmitter that sent the command to fire the nose thruster. They knew how to activate the plane's control system and they knew where and when to do it."

"But the pilot could have overridden the command."

"Not during reentry!" Dan whispered urgently. "Every microsecond is crucial at that point in the flight. Hannah had just started the pitch-up maneuver that angles the plane so the heat shield on its underside takes most of the reentry heat. Firing the thruster that pushed the nose down knocked the plane out of control. No pilot could've recovered. The plane was doomed."

"Why didn't she eject?"

"She probably tried," Dan said.

"This is all conjecture," Passeau said.

"If we flew the backup and nothing went wrong, that would prove that the crash was caused by sabotage, wouldn't it?"

"No, it wouldn't. There could be—"

"I want to fly the backup." Dan insisted. Then he added, "Unmanned."

"Without a pilot?"

Dan said, "Completely automatic. But this time we keep the command codes to ourselves and we don't tell anybody what the ground track's going to be."

"You can't fly like that, even unmanned," Passeau objected. "There are other planes in the sky, you know. You've got to clear a flight path, get the FAA to allow—"

"That's your end of the game, Claude. I need a big swath of airspace, wide enough so the murdering sons of bitches won't know exactly where the plane's going to be on reentry."

"That's impossible. You're asking the FAA to clear half the continent of North America for you."

"Just for half an hour, during the reentry phase of the flight. While the bird's in orbit she'll be all right."

"It can't be done, Dan. I'm sorry, but it can't be done."

"You mean you won't—"

Dan's cell phone began playing "Take Me Out to the Ball Game." He grimaced, plucked the phone from his shirt pocket, and flicked it open.

Jane's face was on the tiny screen. She looked decidedly unhappy.

Before Dan could begin to say hello, she said, "Dan, we need to talk."

With a glance at Passeau, he asked, "Face-to-face?"

"Yes."

"I could fly up to Washington for the weekend, I guess."

"No, not here. At the ranch."

Dan hesitated and looked at Passeau again. He was making a great show of trying to catch the eye of the barmaid, who was still gesticulating with the bar phone pressed to one ear.

Lowering his voice, Dan asked, "Will Scanwell be there?"

Jane said, "No. He's got to run up to New Hampshire."

Breaking into a smile, Dan said, "I'll be there Saturday in time for lunch."

Jane said, "Come alone." And abruptly cut the connection.

THORNTON RANCH,
OKLAHOMA

The Staggerwing was too slow to suit Dan for this trip, and from the way Jane had looked on the phone, he figured that she wanted this meeting between them to be kept as secret as possible. So Dan unlocked his bottom desk drawer and fished out the driver's license, Social Security card, and credit card for Orville Wilbur, a phony identity he had established years earlier, when credit card companies were hounding him to become their customers. He found it ridiculously easy to establish a false identity. No wonder terrorists can sneak around the country at will, Dan thought. It had started as a lark, but Dan found times when it was convenient to have an alternate persona. Such as now.

That Friday night Dan drove to Corpus Christi. Orville Wilbur registered at a motel near the airport and from the phone in his room purchased an electronic ticket from Southwest Airlines, round trip from Corpus Christi to Oklahoma City on the earliest flight out, with a commuter link to Marietta. When he got there, Orville Wilbur rented an SUV and drove out to the Thornton ranch.

As he drove through the fancy carved wooden gate of the Thornton ranch, well before noon, he saw another van some distance behind him spurting a rooster tail of dust as it followed him along the road that led to the ranch house. Security? Dan wondered. Hope it's not news media.

Pulling up in front of the low, sprawling house, Dan stepped out into the late morning sunlight. It was hot and dusty, the Sun high in a bright blue sky that had hardly a wisp of a cloud in it. Squinting, Dan saw contrails etching across the blue, people on their way somewhere, six miles above the ground. Then his eye caught the faint, ghostly image of a crescent Moon, just a trace of its lopsided smile visible.

I know, Dan said silently to the Moon. I'm an idiot for coming out here. But what the hell.

His SUV was the only car parked in front of the house. No one seemed to be stirring; the house seemed silent, empty. Dan rapped on the door and waited for someone to answer. Turning, he saw the van that had followed him growling up the gravel driveway. It crunched to a stop in a swirl of gritty dust.

And Jane got out.

She was dressed in jeans with a white blouse tucked into the waist, decorated with a trio of cardinals across its front. Her hair was pinned back, off her neck. Wide leather belt with a silver and turquoise buckle. Well-scuffed cowboy boots.

"You got here before me?" Jane said, surprised.

"I camped overnight," Dan joked.

She stepped toward him. He wanted to take her in his arms but she walked swiftly past and pulled an electronic key card from her jeans.

"Nobody's here," she said as the door clicked open. "I gave the staff the weekend off." No smile, no warmth, no hint of a suggestion of any kind. Just a statement of fact. Jane seemed as cool and businesslike as a stranger. Hell, Dan grumbled to himself, our two vans are parked closer together than her and me.

"Come on in," she said.

"What's all the secrecy about?" Dan asked as he stepped into the cool shadows of the entryway.

Heading down the corridor toward the kitchen, Jane said over her shoulder, "I've introduced a bill that is clearly intended to help you, Dan. The news people are sniffing around, trying to find a personal link between us."

"They don't have to look all that far," Dan said, following her.

"I've made no secret of our past relationship," she said, flicking on the fluorescent lights set into the kitchen ceiling. "But I can't afford to be seen with you now."

"Unless Scanwell's around," Dan muttered.

She turned to face him. "That's right: unless Morgan's around."

"Is he your chaperon or your bedmate?"

Jane's eyes flared angrily, but she quickly regained control of herself.

"He's a candidate for president of the United States, and I'm not going to do anything that might damage his chances."

Dan grunted. "Spoken like a lawyer."

"That's what I am, Dan. A lawyer. You knew that...in the old days."

There were a million things he wanted to say. Instead, he went to the breakfast bar and perched on one of the stools.

"Are you going to cook lunch for us?"

"I can cook," she said.

"I can help."

She seemed to relax a fraction. "All right. Let's see what's in the fridge."

As they pulled eggs and sausages out of the refrigerator, Dan said, "So why'd you ask me up here, Jane?"

"How's the accident investigation going?" she asked.

"Slow. Too double-damned slow. I'm pushing the FAA honcho to allow us to fly the backup spaceplane—"

"I understand the FBI is involved also."

"If they are, they're invisible."

"They're good at that," she said.

Dan waited until the eggs were sizzling in the skillet and two places had been set on the small table in the breakfast nook. Jane was setting down two glasses of orange juice. The aroma of brewing coffee wafted through the kitchen as the coffeemaker gurgled busily.

"So why'd you ask me here?" he asked again.

She took up the spatula and shoveled eggs and sausage onto a serving platter. Dan waited until she set the platter on the table, then he took her by the shoulders and turned her to face him. *Those cool and limpid green eyes.* He always recalled the line from the old song when he looked into her eyes: *A pool in which my heart lies.*

"Jane," he said, holding her, "for god's sake—"

She brushed his hands away. "I asked you here to talk politics, Dan. Nothing else."

"Nothing else?"

"Politics. That's all."

"All right," he said, with a theatrical sigh. It was pretty much what he had expected of her. He pulled out a chair for her. "So talk."

"You're making a deal with Tricontinental Oil."

"Against my gut instincts," he said, sitting down opposite her.

"Don't do it, Dan."

"And what should I do? Make a deal with Yamagata?"

"Give me a chance to get this bill through the Senate. We want you to raise the money you need from American sources."

"Tricontinental *is* American."

"Garrison is an American—"

"A Texan," Dan pointed out, managing to grin.

"—But Tricontinental is a multinational corporation. You know that. It's as much Arabian and Venezuelan and even Dutch as it is American."

"What of it?"

"Garrison isn't interested in energy independence. He's going to fight Morgan every inch of the way."

Dan nodded.

Ignoring the food cooling on the platter, Jane said earnestly, "Dan, the reason for my bill is to get American funding for you. It's part of Morgan's energy independence program."

"I don't give a hoot in Herzegovena about Scanwell's energy independence program! I'm trying to save my company!"

"And we're trying to help you!"

"But I need help *now*," Dan insisted. "Not after the Senate finishes tinkering with your bill. Not after Morgan Scanwell becomes president, if he ever does. Now!"

"You could put your operation in low key for a year, couldn't you? Lay off some of your staff? Mothball your equipment."

"Jane, I've got a two-mile-wide satellite hanging up there in orbit, doing nothing but soaking up money and getting dinged by orbital debris. I can't just let it hang there for a year."

"Why not? It'll still be there a year from now, won't it?"

"Yeah, and Yamagata will own it. Or Tricontinental."

"Not if you don't make a deal with them."

"And what am I supposed to do for a year? Sit around with my thumbs up my butt? Besides, the election's more than a year off."

"Fourteen months."

"I can't lay off my staff and expect them to come back fourteen months later. They'll find other jobs."

"Please, Dan. Be reasonable."

"Reasonable? You want me to put my whole operation in suspended animation for more than a year in the hope that your dark-horse candidate will get himself elected?"

"Yes. That's what's best for all of us."

Dan took a deep breath. Then he counted to ten. At last he said quietly, "It might be best for Scanwell. And you. But not for me or the people who're working for me."

"Dan, the country needs Morgan Scanwell in the White House. You don't know him, he's a great man, a wonderful man."

"Yeah, yeah. Okay, I like him, too. He's a very likeable guy. What of it?"

"If you only knew the pressures he's under, the battles he's fighting. The oil interests are dead-set against him. Even in his own state he's fighting an uphill battle."

"And you're sleeping with him, aren't you?"

Her chin went up. "That's got nothing to do with it."

"The hell it doesn't."

"Please, Dan. Wait. Let us get Morgan into the White House and then you'll be able to do everything you want to do. He's a great man, he really is."

"I don't care about him! You're the only one I'm interested in."

She didn't seem surprised. Or angered. Or even distressed. "No, Dan," she said, very softly. "That was finished a long time ago."

"I'll drop the whole double-damned project. I'll sell it off to the highest bidder. I don't care about it anymore."

"You don't mean that."

"The hell I don't."

"Dan, that project is your life, your work."

"And what's it got me?" he answered bleakly. "Three people killed and the project's going down the toilet. What good is any of it? I don't want to bury any more of my friends. I want out. I want you. Nothing else matters. You forget Scanwell and—"

"Don't!" Jane snapped. "We're talking about the future of America, Dan. The future of the world! Can't you understand that? Can't you see? The future of the whole world is at stake!"

"Your world, Jane. Not mine. I don't give a damn about any of it if you're not part of the deal."

She looked at him, her cool green eyes steady, clear, dry. "I'm working to save America from being bound hand and foot to the oil interests. I thought you were, too. It seems I was mistaken."

"No," he said, low, defeated. "I'm working for that, too. It's just...I love you, Jane. Nothing else makes any sense to me if we can't be together."

For long moments Jane said nothing. Then, with a slow shake of her head, she replied, "We can't be together, Dan. That's over and done with."

Dan realized that she was very, very sad. And so was he.

HOUSTON, TEXAS

Dealing with any government agency usually drove Dan slightly crazy. The Houston field office of the Federal Bureau of Investigation was no different.

He had spent the Sunday after his brief, bitter meeting with Jane back at his office at Matagorda Island, going through the motions of catching up on his work, but actually mulling over his options. Accept Tricontinental's offer? Al-Bashir seemed decent enough, genuinely interested in the powersat. *Okay, so I sell Garrison fifteen percent of the company's stock. At a billion five, that drives up the stock's price very nicely. What have I got to lose?*

Your company, answered the sardonic voice in his head that always tempered his fantasies. *Garrison will start with al-Bashir on your board and then before you know it you'll be out on your ear, wondering how the hell they did it to you.*

Well, there's Yamagata, Dan countered. *Sai's been interested in power satellites right from the git-go. Hell, I got turned on to the idea by him. A strategic alliance between his corporation and mine makes a lot of sense.*

Right, sneered the voice. *Until Yamagata sucks the guts out of your* operation. He wants that spaceplane design. He might be a buddy, but he's a businessman first. He'll feel bad about it, maybe, but he'll step over your dead body if he has to.

Dead body, Dan thought. He made a mental note to phone the Houston office of the FBI to see how their investigation was going. The following morning, after several levels of bureaucratic double-talk, he finally reached Special Agent Ignacio Chavez, the man in charge of the Astro investigation.

Chavez seemed polite and businesslike on the phone. On Dan's desktop screen he looked serious, but not officious. Solid, chunky face; heavy black moustache; thick black hair. He offered to fly down to Matagorda to meet with Dan.

"That won't be necessary," Dan said, studying the agent's square, strong features. Plenty of Native American in him, Dan thought as he went on, "I have a business appointment in Houston on Thursday. Can we meet then?"

Chavez agreed to a meeting first thing in the morning: seven-thirty A.M. Dan flew to Houston Wednesday evening and stayed overnight in a hotel, only to find the next morning that the federal building was closed to everyone except government workers. Two overweight security guards sat behind the reception desk in the lobby.

"Offices don't open until eight-thirty," said the fatter of the two. "You must of heard the time wrong."

Frowning with impatience, Dan insisted, "No, he said seven-thirty. Can't you call his office?"

Obviously unhappy about it, the less corpulent of the guards leisurely looked up Chavez's number and phoned. "No answer. He's not in yet."

Dan huffed. "Okay. I'll wait."

"Not inside the lobby, sir," said the bigger guard. "Security regulations."

"I can't sit here and wait for him?"

"No, sir. Security regulations."

Dan opened his sports coat. "I don't have any explosives wired to me, for double-damn's sake. You can search me if you want to."

"Regulations, sir. You'll have to wait outside." The second guard put his hand on the butt of his pistol.

Grumbling and fuming, Dan stomped across the lobby and pushed through the glass doors. It was already feeling steamy out on the street. Cars and trucks were growling sluggishly along. Why do they call it the rush hour? Dan asked himself. Nobody can move faster than ten miles an hour.

Nettled, Dan groused outside, glancing up at the clouds that threatened rain. He had a lunch meeting with al-Bashir and Garrison. The car he had rented at Hobby Airport was parked in the garage across the street. The parking attendants were up and working at seven-thirty. Why isn't the double-damned FBI?

"You must be Mr. Randolph."

Turning, Dan recognized Chavez from their phone conversation. The man was carrying a white paper bag with the McDonald's golden arches logo on it.

"Right on time," Chavez said, with a smile that showed gleaming white teeth.

Dan glanced at his wristwatch. Its digital display showed precisely 7:30. He'd arrived a few minutes early, as usual.

Feeling better, he followed Chavez back into the lobby, suppressing a triumphant sneer as he signed the visitors' register at the reception desk, and then went with the agent into the elevator.

"The guards told me the offices don't open until eight-thirty," Dan said as the elevator doors closed.

"That's right," said Chavez. "I like to come in early. I can get a lot done before everybody else arrives and the phone starts ringing."

Chavez's office was a cubbyhole, but it had a window. Nothing to look at but the blank wall of the parking garage across the street, Dan saw, but in the bureaucratic world of government agencies a window was an indication of some status in the pecking order.

Chavez slid behind his desk, pulled a cardboard box from the bag, and opened it. Dan saw two small round rolls stuffed with what might have been eggs and bacon.

"I brought an extra one for you," Chavez said. Then he swiveled around in his chair, bent down and opened a cooler. "Coke? Apple juice? Hey, I've even got a bottle of Perrier in here! Wonder who left that here?"

Dan accepted the egg sandwich and the Perrier. Before he could ask Chavez anything, the agent started to boot up his desktop computer.

"I've got to tell you, Mr. Randolph, that our investigation of your accident hasn't gone very far. We're patched into the loop with the FAA reports, but so far there's nothing to indicate foul play."

"That's probably because we haven't been completely honest with you," Dan admitted.

Chavez put down his McMuffin, untouched, his dark brown eyes glittering with sudden interest. "Oh? What do you mean?"

"My chief engineer developed a theory about how the plane was sabotaged. I told him not to discuss with anybody."

"Why in the hell did you do that?"

"We didn't know who in the company might have sold us out. Could've been anybody. So we started snooping for ourselves."

The special agent's face showed what he thought of amateur sleuthing.

"Besides," Dan went on, "as far as we could tell, the FBI's investigation of the accident was strictly pro forma."

Chavez was deadly serious now. "I'll need to talk to this engineer of yours."

"He's dead. Killed in a so-called accident." Before Chavez could react to that, Dan added, "And another of our employees, a guy that my engineer suspected, committed suicide a few nights ago."

"And you're just coming to me now?"

Defensively, Dan answered, "I don't have any proof of any of this. No evidence at all. But it all fits together."

"Maybe," Chavez said. He reached for his McMuffin, took half of it in one bite. "Maybe," he repeated.

"Well, what can you do about it?"

Chavez chewed thoughtfully for a few silent moments. Then, "I've been liaising with the chief of the FAA accident team."

"Passeau."

"Yeah. How much does he know about all this?"

"I've spoken to him about it. He was working with Joe Tenny, my chief engineer, until Joe was killed."

"That hydrogen tank explosion?"

"Right."

"And who's the man who committed suicide?"

Dan went through the entire story with Chavez twice again, even going into technical details about how the spaceplane's onboard computer might have been overridden by a powerful transmitter sited somewhere along the plane's ground track. Chavez had finished his breakfast and a can of Coca-Cola by the time Dan had gone through the story again. Dan's McMuffin lay untouched on its paper wrapper at the edge of the agent's desk.

Shaking his head, Chavez said, "This is a helluva time to come clean with us, Mr. Randolph."

"I guess so. I just didn't know what else to do."

There was a rap on Chavez's door and a pert redhead popped in. "Oh! Sorry. I didn't know—"

"Come on in, Kelly. Mr. Randolph, this is my partner, Special Agent Kelly Eamons."

She looked more like a high school cheerleader than a special agent of the FBI, in Dan's eyes. Knee-length skirt, pretty legs, toothy smile. She sat down and Dan went through the whole tale once again. Eamons listened with complete seriousness.

Then she looked at Chavez. "Nacho, we've got a lot of work ahead of us."

Chavez nodded gravely. He stood up and put out his hand. "Thanks for coming in, Mr. Randolph."

"Dan."

"Okay, Dan. I'm Nacho, short for Ignacio."

Dan took his proffered hand. "Where do we go from here?"

"You go back to your office, or your meeting, whatever. We go to work on your case."

Dan thanked them both and left. As he stepped through the office door he noticed Kelly Eamons picking up his untouched McMuffin with a frown of distaste and dropping it into the wastebasket.

MATAGORDA ISLAND,
TEXAS

Dan and Lynn Van Buren walked slowly around the sleek, needle-nosed spaceplane. Even sitting here in the hangar she looks eager to fly, Dan thought. Dan wanted to reach up and touch her smooth, cool metal skin, but he could feel Niles Muhamed's fiercely proprietary stare boring into his back.

"How'd your meeting with Garrison go?" Van Buren asked as they walked slowly around the craft.

"The old man's sitting tight and waiting for me to cave in," said Dan. "Funny, but I got the feeling al-Bashir is willing to bend a little."

"Are you going to cave in? A billion and a half—"

Dan frowned at her. "Ever hear of Frank Piasecki?"

She thought a moment. "Wasn't he one of the early helicopter pioneers? Invented the heavy-lift chopper, the one they called 'the flying banana.'"

"Right. He got himself into the same fix we're in, needed capital to keep his company going. So he let the Rockefeller brothers stick their nose under his tent."

"Oh-oh. I can see where this is going."

"Yep. Next thing you know, Piasecki's kicked out and the money boys sell his company to Boeing. It's Boeing's Vertol division now and dear old Frank is moldering in his grave."

Van Buren said nothing, but from the expression on her face Dan thought she understood.

"So how's oh-two coming along?" he asked, pointing to the spaceplane sitting on the hangar floor.

"She's ready to go," Van Buren said, grinning. "She's a real flying machine."

He grimaced. "Tell it to the FAA."

"They won't allow it? Not even unmanned?"

Dan looked down at her. Van Buren was a good two inches shorter than he. "Don't you mean 'crewless'? You're getting politically incorrect, kid."

She didn't laugh, didn't even smile. "I'm beginning to understand why you don't want the government involved in anything you do."

"Damn! We've got the best spacecraft that's ever been built, and we can't even get it off the double-damned ground."

Nodding sympathetically, Van Buren said, "Passeau won't allow it?"

With a bitter laugh, Dan replied, "He said he can't stop us from launching it, that's not under his jurisdiction. But he won't give us permission to fly in U.S. airspace. That *is* under his jurisdiction and he won't allow it."

"Damn."

"I can't blame him," Dan admitted. "His higher-ups would fry his balls if he let us fly the bird before the accident investigation has found the cause for the crash."

"Double damn," Van Buren said fervently.

Dan grinned at her. "You're starting to sound like me."

"Great minds run in similar ruts, chief."

Dan ambled slowly around the silvery, stubby-winged spaceplane one more time, thinking of all the red tape he'd been forced to go through to be able to operate his company. He almost laughed when he remembered his chief counsel's face as the lawyer told him they needed a fireworks permit from Calhoun County before they could launch a rocket from Matagorda Island. Fireworks! Dan thought. That's where a sixteen-story-high, twelve-hundred-ton rocket booster fit into the local bureaucracy. Fireworks.

"What's funny, chief?" Van Buren asked as they walked out of the hangar, into the bright hot morning sunlight.

Squinting in the glare, Dan said, "We've got all the permits we need to launch a booster, don't we?"

She shrugged. "Guess so. That's a problem for the legal department, not engineering."

"As long as it's not a crewed launch, nobody aboard."

"The spent booster breaks up over the Atlantic," Van Buren said. "But the spaceplane has got to come back here and land."

"And the FAA won't approve a flight plan, even crewless," Dan repeated.

"What're you driving at, chief?"

Dan quickened his pace, heading back to Hangar A and his office. The plump Van Buren chugged along beside him, puffing.

"Okay. We launch out over the Gulf, same as usual. Can you work out an orbit so that the spaceplane's reentry track isn't over the States?"

"Not over the U.S.?"

"Right," Dan said, pushing through the personnel hatch in the hangar's closed sliding doors. "The bird's orbit can cross the States; it's high enough above controlled airspace so the FAA doesn't have anything to say about it. But when it comes in for reentry it's got to stay out of U.S. airspace."

Following Dan up the stairs toward the catwalk offices, Van Buren puffed, "She's got...some translational...latitude..."

At the top of the stairs Dan whirled on her and pointed his index finger like a pistol. "Work it out, Lynn. Fast. And don't let anybody else know about it."

"But—"

"No buts! Get it done."

She saw how utterly serious he was. "Okay. You're the chief."

"Nobody else on this," Dan warned. "Use your laptop and keep it with you wherever you go."

She grinned at him, her cheeks dimpling. "Even when I go to the toilet?"

"Even when you're making love," Dan answered.

He watched the engineer as she hurried back down the stairs and toward her office, a nondescript woman in a plain dark blue blouse and matching slacks. And a brain that might be the difference between keeping my company or selling out to the sharks, Dan thought.

He breezed into his office, waving hello to April at her desk as he passed. She always looked startled when he bounced in like that. But she didn't try to stop him or tell him that he had calls to answer or meetings to see to. Good, Dan thought as he slid into his desk chair. He booted up his desktop computer and saw that he had a clear agenda right through to two P.M., when the chief accountant was due for his weekly funeral dirge. And then a telephone conference with two of his biggest shareholders, in preparation for the coming quarterly meeting of the board of directors.

So what am I going to tell the board? he asked himself. Do I say we're hanging on by a fingernail or do I tell them the truth and say we're hanging, all right, and not by the neck, either.

The office is so damned quiet! he realized. We're slowing down to a walk. Worse, a limp. In another few weeks we won't even be able to crawl. Unless...

It can work, Dan thought as he swiveled the chair to look out at the midmorning scenery. Quiet outside, too. None of the bustle of trucks coming in and out, people hustling from building to building, boosters being towed out to the launchpad. This company is dying, sinking beneath the waves and gasping for air.

He jumped to his feet and stepped to the window that overlooked the hangar floor. Only a half-dozen FAA people meandering among the bits of wreckage. Dying, he repeated to himself.

Well, by god we'll go out with a bang, not a whimper. Launch the space-plane on its booster. Unmanned. The whole flight under control from the ground. But not from here. From a remote site, someplace where the murdering sons of bitches can't find us. Once the bird's in orbit, shift the orbit so that when it reenters it's not over any part of the U.S. If the saboteurs don't know where the ground track is, they won't be able to screw up the flight.

And then land the bird. Back here in Matagorda? She'd have to fly into U.S. airspace for that. Maybe we ought to avoid that altogether. I'll have to work with Lynn on that.

He laughed aloud. Passeau will shit a brick!

Dan didn't realize how hard he was laughing until April poked her head through his door and asked if he was all right.

QUARTERLY BOARD MEETING

They're all in their places with long morose faces, Dan thought as he gaveled the board meeting to order.

Astro Manufacturing Corporation's board of directors consisted of eight people, five men and three women, plus Dan, who served as chairman as well as the company's CEO. Board politics were delicate: Dan owned the majority of the company's stock, by far, but if all eight of the other board members voted together, they could outvote him. When the company had started, slightly more than five years earlier, Dan had easily gained his way. But as the costs of building the power satellite escalated and profits seemed more elusive with each meeting, running the board became more and more difficult.

This was the first meeting since the spaceplane crash. Dan knew it wasn't going to be easy.

They met in the larger of the Astro Motel's two conference rooms. Despite their grumbling about having to travel all the way out to Matagorda Island, every member of the board was in their seat along the conference table. A bad sign, Dan thought.

Sitting off by the wall, Asim al-Bashir was watching them with a bemused little smile on his bearded face. On the other side of the room, April sat slightly behind Dan with a palm-sized gray digital recorder on her lap.

Standing at the head of the table, all eyes on him, Dan said, "Before we begin the meeting, I'd like to introduce my guest, Mr. Asim al-Bashir. I asked him here to meet you this morning because he represents Tricontinental Oil Corporation, and he has a proposal to make to us."

A few of the board members nodded knowingly. The others glanced puzzledly at al-Bashir. Several members whispered to one another.

Dan tapped the tabletop with his pen and the buzzing stopped. "It's show time," he joked mildly.

They dispensed, as always, with the reading of the last meeting's minutes. Then they moved to delay the usual reports until after a discussion of the company's current situation. Dan was grateful that they weren't in a rush to hear the comptroller's report.

Looking down the table at their faces, Dan thought they were steeling themselves for the bad news. Gray-haired, every one of them, except for the bald men. Two representatives of venture capital companies, four directors of university trust funds, a retired executive from the electronics industry and a friend of Dan's late father, who still treated Dan like a teenager on a toot. Not the sharpest bunch of pencils in the box, Dan thought. But their money does their thinking for them.

"All right," he said. "Here's the company's situation in a nutshell:

"The power satellite is ninety-nine percent completed. We could be generating electrical power from it in a month or less, if we could just finish the last final touches. But the crash of the spaceplane has stopped our operations cold. The government will not allow us to fly the backup until the cause of the crash is determined."

"Meanwhile," said one of the venture capital men, "you're bleeding to death."

"Very vividly put," said Dan, trying to keep the sarcasm out of his voice.

One of the women, a university trust fund executive, asked, "How long will operations be suspended?"

Dan spread his hands. "There's no way of telling. Several months, at least."

"It's already been a couple of months since the crash," said one of the older men.

"These investigations take time," the woman beside him said.

"And while they're taking their time, we're bleeding to death, as Robert said."

"There are some bright spots in the picture," Dan pointed out. "We do have a nearly complete power satellite in orbit, and it's been successfully boosted to its permanent position in geosynchronous orbit."

"But you're not able to send any workmen to it to complete the job."

"For the moment, that's true. But that powersat gives us a very attractive incentive for new potential investors."

"Such as your old friend Yamagata?"

Ignoring the dig, Dan said, "Senator Thornton of Oklahoma has introduced a bill that could help us to raise funding from the private money market."

"But first you have to get the damned bill through the damned Congress," fumed one of the members.

"That's true," Dan admitted. "There are other possibilities, though. That's why I invited Mr. al-Bashir to our meeting."

They all turned to al-Bashir. Dan said, "He has a proposal for us to consider."

Al-Bashir got up from his seat and stepped to the head of the table. Standing beside Dan, he said, "The proposal is very simple. Tricontinental Oil is prepared to buy fifteen percent of the Astro shares now held by Mr. Randolph for a price of one point five billion American dollars."

That stunned them. Dan saw the surprise on their faces and realized that no one was saying a word.

At last one of the university people spoke up: "Will Tricontinental be willing to buy anyone else's shares at the same rate?"

Glancing down at Dan, al-Bashir said, "Not at the present time. But there is always a possibility in the future."

That's it, Dan thought. That's how Garrison will take control of my company. The others will rush to dump their shares. If I sell to him I'll be slitting my own double-damned throat.

MATAGORDA ISLAND, TEXAS

Passeau was smiling, but Dan could see something else in his eyes. Resentment? Anger? Or was it something more subtle: curiosity, maybe. The man sat there in front of Dan's desk, with his floppy bow tie and his little moustache, and he smiled like a cat with a cornered canary.

"You intend to fly the spaceplane?" the FAA investigator asked, his voice a mild purr. "And how will you obtain permission for that?"

"I've already got an FAA license to launch," Dan said, leaning back in his desk chair. "It's still valid." He imagined himself playing poker in the Old West with a slick cardshark who held all the aces in his hands. *I've got to bluff my way through this,* Dan told himself.

"May I point out that a single phone call from me to Washington could revoke any launch permit that you have," said Passeau.

"We'll be launching out over the water, Claude. The booster won't be in American airspace."

With a little nod, Passeau said, "Not for more than a few minutes, I grant you. But still—"

"The spaceplane separates from the booster at an altitude that's miles above controlled airspace. You know that."

Passeau said nothing.

"And the booster breaks up and falls into the Atlantic. Again, way outside of U.S. airspace."

"But the spaceplane must return to Earth. It can't stay in orbit forever. It must land, and for that it must fly through American airspace."

Dan hesitated only for the span of a heartbeat. "If it lands in the U.S."

Passeau's brows hiked up. That got him! Dan said to himself.

"You'd land it outside American territory?"

"Out of the FAA's jurisdiction," Dan said.

Sinking back in his chair, Passeau clasped his hands together as if in prayer and raised them to his lips, thinking hard.

"I suppose you realize that if I allow you to get away with this, my career in the Federal Aviation Administration is absolutely ruined."

Dan had expected that. Very evenly, he replied, "That's why I think you should take some vacation time, Claude. You've been working awfully hard on this investigation. A week or so at a top-flight hotel on the Riviera would do you a lot of good."

Sighing, Passeau said, "Yes, a vacation would be wonderful. If I could afford it. On my salary, the best I could hope for is a Holiday Inn off the beach in Florida."

"I have an uncle," Dan said, straight-faced, "who's taken a suite at the Hotel Beaulieu, halfway between Nice and Monte Carlo."

"Indeed."

"Trouble is, he won't be able to get there. Arthritis or some kind of ailment. He's pretty old, you know."

"That's a shame."

"Well, the suite's paid for and you know the French—they won't refund his money."

Passeau tried to look severe. "Dan, are you attempting to bribe me?"

Dropping the pretense, Dan answered, "I'm trying to save your career, Claude."

"And your company."

"That, too."

"You and your uncles." But Passeau was smiling now.

"I've got a lot of uncles. None of them are named Randolph and all of them have their own credit cards that can't be traced back to me."

Shaking his head, Passeau said, "You're a scoundrel, Dan!"

"Just a businessman trying to survive."

Passeau was smiling now. "It would be wonderful, a week on the Riviera. But it would end with the two of us going to jail."

"Not if we time it right." Dan leaned forward across his desk. "You take a week off. By the time you get back we've run the test flight. You express great outrage that I sneaked it in behind your back. Nobody else knows about it except you and me."

Passeau stared at Dan. He's tempted, Dan thought. It all depends on how much he really wants to help me. He'll be taking a risk, but it's a pretty small one. I'll be betting the farm, the family jewels, and my cojones on the test flight.

"No one else will know about it?" Passeau asked, in a silky whisper.

"No one," said Dan. He realized that April had already made the hotel reservation, but he was confident he could trust his executive assistant.

"And how will you be able to tow your rocket out onto the launchpad and place the spaceplane atop it without anyone noticing?"

"Mating test," Dan replied innocently. "As far as the government is concerned, and the news media, we'll just be testing the connectors between the booster and the spaceplane. Alignment, electrical connections, systems compatibility, that sort of thing."

Passeau said nothing.

"The booster's solid-fueled. We won't need to fill her tanks and go through all that long a countdown. The plane will be crewless, nobody aboard."

A cloud of suspicion crossed Passeau's face. "You promise that? Nobody aboard?"

"I swear it," Dan said.

For long moments Passeau remained silent, obviously thinking, weighing his options, all the possibilities.

"This could destroy me," he said at last.

"I'll hire you if the FAA throws you out."

"We could both go to jail."

"You'll do it?"

Passeau hesitated another few moments, then murmured, "I've never been to the Riviera."

"You'll love it!"

"If this doesn't go well, I may have to stay there and ask the French for political asylum."

If this doesn't go well, Dan thought, there's no place on Earth that I can run to.

ASTRO MOTEL

The Sun was dipping below the scrub pines as April Simmonds parked her baby blue Sebring next to the empty handicapped space and headed for the motel's bar entrance. No sense locking a convertible, she had learned. If anybody wants it badly enough they'll slash the top open. Besides, nobody around here would bother her car. All the Astro people knew it was hers, and none of them were car thieves.

Pushing through the door brought her into the frigid air-conditioning of the bar. It's cold enough in here to raise goosebumps, she complained silently. Then she remembered reading somewhere that they kept topless bars real cold so that the dancers' nipples would be stiff.

It had been a long day at the office, with Dan in a sweat to get a booster set up on the launchpad so that they could mate the backup spaceplane to it. Most of the FAA people had left, though, and a crew of technicians had started gathering up the pieces of the first spaceplane's wreckage to store in precisely marked cartons that eventually would be stacked in a warehouse.

The lounge was jammed with after-work people, most of them crowded around the bar three deep, men outnumbering women at least two to one.

Country music was thumping from the speakers in the ceiling but the conversations and laughter and calls to the barmaids for drinks were so loud she could barely make out the song: "Lay Your Head on My Shoulder," a classic. Dr. Tenny had always called it the transplant song.

Thinking of Joe reminded her why she was here. April wanted to talk to the barmaids, find out what they remembered about Pete Larsen, if anything. She herself had come to this bar with Pete once, on one of her dates with the man. Pete had shown more interest in the computer game console off in the corner than he had in her.

April hesitated just inside the doorway. The thought of worming through the crowd to the bar discouraged her, and she'd never get to talk to the barmaids anyway; they were too busy.

"Hey, April, what're you drinking?"

It was one of the technicians. April recognized his face but couldn't quite place his name.

"White wine?" she said, falling back into the slightly defensive mode of speech that she had inherited from her native Virginia.

The guy dove into the crowd and reappeared a minute later with a glass of wine in one hand and a tumbler of something stronger in the other.

"Haven't seen you around here for a while," he said, guiding her toward an unoccupied booth with a big grin on his face.

She accepted the wine and his hand on the small of her back. "It's been terribly busy."

"Yeah, the crash and then Tenny getting killed. Most of the people in my group are wondering how long we've got before Randolph lays us off."

"He's fighting awfully hard to avoid that," April said, sliding into the booth, resigning herself to the fact that her attempt at detective work was going to result in nothing more than listening to this man's troubles and finding an excuse to get away without hurting his feelings.

Across the crowded, noisy room, though, another Astro employee watched April chatting with the technician. He was a data manager in Astro's personnel department, and he knew that Dan Randolph's executive assistant had been reviewing personnel records for the past several days. She had scanned Pete Larsen's file several times. He had a buddy in Houston who paid good money to be informed about what Randolph was up to. He decided to call his buddy, who worked at Tricontinental Oil, and let him know what April Simmonds was doing. The rumor was that Tricontinental was going to buy Astro out. A lot of money is going to change hands, he thought. I might as well get some of it for myself.

By the time Claude Passeau entered the bar, the after-work crowd had dissipated. April was long gone, driving alone to catch the last ferry of the evening.

The technician who'd bought her a drink drove his own car into the ferry and even followed April partway to her apartment in Lamar, but lost his nerve halfway there and turned back to his own place, a house he shared with three other Astro employees.

A soft instrumental was purring from the music system, a blessed relief from the usual doleful nasalities that the bar's clientele seemed to enjoy. Passeau grimaced at the thought of trying to pick a decent wine from the selection stocked at the bar. Instead he ordered a brandy, longing for a sip of Armagnac but settling for the Presidente that Dan had recommended.

Sitting alone in the same booth that April had occupied, he wrestled with his conscience.

Dan wants to launch his spaceplane, to prove that the crash was sabotage. I can't be a party to that; it would ruin my career. So Dan cleverly offers me a free vacation on the Riviera.

The nerve of the man! Despite himself, Passeau smiled at the thought of it. Out-and-out bribery. We'd both go to jail.

And yet—Passeau admired Dan's drive, his daring, his willingness to risk everything. And, at heart, Passeau agreed that the first spaceplane's crash was no accident. Someone very cleverly sabotaged the plane. Someone with deep technical capabilities and enormous resources. Someone extremely dangerous. If only there were a shred of evidence to show!

A young woman entered the bar. The few men still perched on stools swiveled their heads to check her out. Pert, thought Passeau. That's the kind of woman that defined the word. She was slim, cute, a sprinkling of freckles across her snub nose, strawberry blonde hair cut short. She wore a T-shirt with some sort of slogan across the chest and a pair of ragged cutoffs. Good legs, not much bosom.

She spotted Passeau and walked straight to his booth. Surprised and more than a little flattered, Passeau got to his feet as she approached.

"Mr. Passeau? I'm Kelly Eamons."

Passeau's welcoming smile faltered. "From the FBI office?" he asked, knowing it was a foolish question.

She sat across the table from him and lowered her voice slightly. "Special Agent Kelly Eamons," she elaborated, with a nod. "I work with Special Agent Chavez."

Trying to recover his aplomb, Passeau said, "You seem much too young to be an FBI agent."

She smiled, showing perfectly straight white teeth. "Looks can be deceiving, Mr. Passeau."

He recommended a Presidente for her. Instead she ordered a cherry Coke. Texas girl, Passeau realized.

Once the cola arrived, Eamons ignored it. "I need to get your straight-up opinion on what Dan Randolph's told us."

"About the crash."

"And about the death of his chief engineer, Joseph Tenny."

Passeau nodded.

"Well? What's your take on it?"

He shook his head. How much of my career has depended on going along with the system, keeping quiet, staying out of the limelight? Twenty years of patient servitude, and what has it got me? A wife who has left me; two children who won't even speak to me. A mortgage on a house I'm not allowed to enter. In five years I could take early retirement. Five years more.

Eamons leaned toward him, totally unaware of Passeau's inner turmoil.

"I really need to know," she said earnestly. "Even if you only—"

"I believe the spaceplane was sabotaged," Passeau heard himself say, slightly surprised at his own words. "I have no evidence that clearly shows it, but that is my belief."

Eamons sank back on the booth's bench. She was no longer smiling. "I see," she said. "Then that means there's a chance that Tenny was murdered."

"And *that* means that Astro Corporation had a spy, a saboteur, in its midst."

"Had?"

"The man Larsen. The one who committed suicide."

Eamons nodded, understanding. "Maybe that's where I should start. With him."

They talked until the barmaid came over and unceremoniously announced, "Last call. We close in fifteen minutes."

Eamons got up and left, her original cherry Coke still untouched on the booth's varnished table. Passeau gulped down the brandy that had been sitting before him since the FBI agent had arrived, then he rose, too, and headed for the door.

As he stepped out into the dank, humid, hot night, alive with the buzz of insects and distant groaning calls of lovesick frogs, Passeau finally made up his mind.

I will not go to the Riviera. That would be too obvious. I'll take a vacation week and return to New Orleans. Perhaps my children will consent to let me see them. By the time I return to Matagorda, Dan's test flight will be a fait accompli.

Back in the Astro Motel bar, the barmaid took the untouched coke and delicate brandy glass back to the sink, thinking, A couple of big boozers they were. And he's a lousy tipper, too.

PLANNING

"Venezuela?" Dan asked.

Sitting next to him at the round conference table in the corner of Dan's cluttered office, Lynn Van Buren nodded, her smile bigger than usual because she had found what she'd been searching for.

"Venezuela," she repeated. "We can land the bird at Caracas and we won't even have to alter its orbital track very much."

"It flies over Caracas?"

"Pretty close. On its second orbit."

Dan started thinking out loud. "We could load the ground control staff and equipment onto a ship, I suppose..."

Nodding enthusiastically, Van Buren said, "Use the backup equipment and a skeleton crew. You don't need more than three, four good people."

"Put them on the ship and don't tell them where we're going," Dan mused, warming to the idea.

"Or why."

"That way nobody can tip off anybody outside the company about where we're going to land the bird."

With a laugh, Van Buren said, "We'll sail under sealed orders."

Dan grinned back at her. "That'll give us tight security, all right."

"Then it's Venezuela, for sure."

"Except for one point," Dan said. "How in the name of Snow White and the Seven Dwarfs do we get permission to fly through Venezuelan airspace and land there?"

Van Buren fiddled with the strand of pearls at her throat. "That's not an engineering problem, chief."

"You're right. It's a political problem."

"Know any good politicians, chief?" Van Buren asked. "Or is that an oxymoron?"

Asim al-Bashir returned to Houston after his meetings in Beijing and, with a nonchalant air of superiority, presented to Wendell Garrison a draft agreement with the Chinese government.

"Tricontinental will market Chinese coal in Asia," al-Bashir summarized for the corporate head, "as far west as Pakistan and Afghanistan."

Garrison scowled up at him. The old man wheeled his powered chair out from behind his desk and, without saying a word, led al-Bashir to the curving teak cabinet that stood at the foot of one of the ceiling-high windows. With the press of a stud on the chair's armrest, the cabinet opened smoothly and silently, revealing three rows of bottles.

"Pick your poison," he said grudgingly to al-Bashir. "I suppose you've earned yourself a drink."

Al-Bashir took a modest thimbleful of sherry while Garrison clattered ice into a tumbler and splashed bourbon into it.

"This is gonna put us in competition with ourselves, you know," Garrison grumbled, after they had touched glasses. "We sell a lot of oil to Pakistan."

"It won't affect our oil sales," al-Bashir said. "The Pakistanis want to build new industrial capacity, and they'll power it with Chinese coal."

"Bought from us."

"Indeed so."

Garrison nodded, reluctantly. Al-Bashir did not think it necessary to tell the old man that by delivering Chinese coal to central Asian nations, more oil from Iran and other Persian Gulf fields could be sold to Europe and America. Keep the West dependent on us, al-Bashir told himself. Bind them to us so tightly that they will never be able to escape.

After his drink with Garrison, al-Bashir returned to his hotel suite, looking forward to a restful weekend. Then back to Tunisia and another meeting of The Nine. Several members of the group were showing signs of unease about his plan to use the power satellite. Time to reassure them, al-Bashir told himself.

Roberto was waiting for him at the suite. The man has a look of violence about him, al-Bashir thought. Roberto was big enough to be intimi-
dating, but it was not his size alone that gave the impression of danger. He
radiated anger. His face was always set in a tense rictus; his eyes always
smoldered. He moved with the compact, controlled energy of a stalking cat.
When he spoke, his voice was soft, low, almost gentle. And all the more
menacing for it.

Roberto stood in the middle of the suite's sitting room, a large, heavy-
shouldered man, his arms hanging at his sides, his hands balled into fists. Al-
Bashir felt small and a little frightened next to him, but he knew that Roberto
would never harm him. He had recruited Roberto from San Quentin and personally vouched for him at his parole board hearing, on the recommendation
of the mullah who trolled the California prison system for converts to Islam.
Roberto was no Moslem. But he didn't have to be, as far as al-Bashir was concerned. He had other qualifications.

Indicating the plush armchair at one side of the sofa, al-Bashir said, "Sit,
my friend, and tell me what is happening at Astro's headquarters."

Roberto went to the chair and lowered himself into it like a cat settling
warily onto its haunches, ready to spring up again in an instant. Al-Bashir took
the chair facing him.

"They're talkin' about bringin' out the second spaceplane and stickin' it
on top of one of their rocket boosters," Roberto said, nearly whispering.

Al-Bashir frowned. "They're going to fly the backup spaceplane?"

"They say it's jus' a test to check out ever'thing. No launch."

His suspicions aroused, al-Bashir said, more to himself than Roberto,
"They'd need government approval to try another flight. That's not likely."

Roberto said, "Somethin' else."

"What?"

"Randolph's secretary is askin' questions. The same kinda questions that
Tenny asked."

"The black woman? The pretty one?"

"Yeah."

Al-Bashir ran a hand across his bearded chin. "I don't like that."

Roberto said nothing.

"Keep an eye on her. I want to know what she's up to."

"I'll go down to Matagorda—"

"No," al-Bashir snapped. "You have an informant inside the company,
don't you?"

Roberto nodded. "More'n one. Tha's how I know about her."

"Use your informants, then. You shouldn't be seen down there unless it's
absolutely necessary."

Roberto said, "We might hafta do somethin' about her."

"Perhaps so," said al-Bashir. "Perhaps so."

Roberto smiled, while al-Bashir thought that he might have to pull some government strings to help make certain that Randolph would be allowed to fly his spaceplane.

WASHINGTON, D.C.

Despite the heat, Georgetown's M Street was jammed with tourists and locals sweating and red-faced under the late afternoon sun. Wearing an open-neck shirt and light slacks, Dan weaved through the crowd, heading for the French restaurant where Jane had agreed to meet him.

Not for dinner. She'd been too wary for that. It had taken Dan two days just to get her to talk to him on the phone, and once he had explained that he needed her help but he couldn't say why over the telephone, she had reluctantly agreed to have a drink with him. So Dan had dusted off his Orville Wilbur credit cards, flown to Ronald Reagan National Airport, and taken a modest room at the Four Seasons Hotel.

He found the Bistro Français and stepped gratefully from the hot, crowded street into the cool, shadowy restaurant. Jane wasn't there yet, of course. Dan grumbled to himself that while Admiral Nelson might have claimed that he owed his success in life to being always fifteen minutes early, you spend a hell of a lot of time waiting for other people that way.

The bar was mostly empty and Dan had no problem getting a booth back away from the door, once he explained to the pinch-faced hostess that he was expecting someone to join him, and handed her a five-dollar bill. He ordered a Pernod with water and settled down to wait for Jane.

Half an hour later, when his drink was down to greenish melted ice cubes and he had gloomily watched the dreary news report of the stock market's continuing slump on the television screen above the bar, Jane finally showed up. She was accompanied by a very fat guy in a rumpled gray suit. Rivulets of sweat were trickling down his bulbous cheeks and several chins. Jane looked fresh and cool in a pale lavender skirt and off-white blouse, as if the weather outside hadn't touched her at all.

Dan slipped out of the booth to greet her. Jane smiled pleasantly and accepted a handshake, nothing more, then introduced Denny O' Brien. She's brought a chaperon, Dan thought. Well, at least she's not with Scanwell. Dan felt sorry for O'Brien as he grunted and squeezed into the booth beside Jane. Once they were all seated, the booth felt to Dan as crowded and uncomfortable as the street outside.

The waitress drifted over and Jane ordered a vodka martini; O'Brien asked for a bottle of sparkling water. The waitress asked, "Another Pernod for you, sir?" Dan nodded.

"Denny's my top political advisor," Jane explained as they waited for their drinks. "He's our real campaign manager."

Dan nodded and made small talk about the weather, the stock market, anything except how much he wished Jane had come alone.

Finally, once their drinks were on the table, Jane said, "You sounded kind of mysterious on the phone."

Glancing at O'Brien, Dan said, "I don't want anybody to know what I'm about to tell you."

"You can trust Denny."

O'Brien smiled amiably. "I'm the soul of discretion."

"In Washington?" Dan asked, his amazement only partially feigned.

Jane cut through the badinage. "What's going on, Dan? Why did you want to see me?"

Because I love you, Dan wanted to say. Because I'd march into a horde of fanatical terrorists to get to you.

Instead, he replied, "I need your help. I need to talk to somebody high up in the government of Venezuela."

O'Brien's brows shot up, but Jane's only reaction was a slight smile. "Are you thinking of leaving the country, Dan?"

"You know I'm not."

"Then what's this all about?"

He wasn't prepared to tell the truth. "Sooner or later," he began, "we're going to need secondary landing fields where the spaceplane can land in an emergency."

"'We' meaning Astro Corporation?" O'Brien asked.

"That's right."

"And you want an emergency field in Venezuela?"

"We're working on agreements with Spain, South Africa, and Australia," Dan said. "But Venezuela's closer."

O'Brien glanced at Jane, then said, "You expect to get your spaceplane flying again?"

"Sooner or later," Dan repeated, straight-faced.

"They why the hurry?"

Dan made a lopsided smile. "I've got nothing better to do until the double-damned FAA okays the plane for flight."

Jane obviously saw through his fabrication. "I can ask State for the names of the right people in Venezuela."

"That would help," Dan said. "Could you do it this week?"

"Why this week?" O'Brien asked, clearly suspicious.

Dan hesitated, thinking fast. Then, "Okay, let me put my cards on the table."

Jane smiled as if she knew there was a whopper coming up.

"Please do," she murmured.

"I'm trying to raise money, you know that. Tricontinental and Yamagata both want to buy into Astro. You know that, too. I'm trying to stall them, or at least get them to give me a loan instead of buying in."

O'Brien said, "But what's that got to do—"

"The more I've got this operation nailed down," Dan said, hoping it sounded believable, "the stronger my position against Garrison and Yamagata. If I can show that I've even got emergency landing fields set up for the space-plane, hell, I might even be able to float a big-enough loan from some Ameri-can banks to keep Astro in my own hands."

"When will the spaceplane be ready to fly again?" Jane asked.

Dan almost said it was ready now, but he caught himself in time. "As soon as the double-damned FAA winds up its investigation and gives the backup plane a clean bill of health."

"Months from now," O'Brien said. "Maybe a year or more."

"Maybe," Dan replied tightly.

Jane said, "Denny, could you go to the bar and get a couple more olives for my drink, please?"

O'Brien looked back and forth from Jane to Dan and back again, then said, "Sure." He struggled out of the booth and headed for the bar, which was filling up now with drinkers.

Jane leaned across the table toward Dan. "What are you up to?" she de-manded.

He shook his head. "You don't want to know."

Her lips tightened. "Do you really need to talk to someone in Venezuela this week?"

"Yep."

"Dan, I don't want you doing anything that will hurt Morgan's chances."

"I don't intend to," he answered. Silently he added, I'm fighting for my life here. Scanwell can take care of himself.

O'Brien came back with two green olives on a toothpick, carried daintily in a cocktail napkin. As he grunted back into the booth, Jane said:

"Very well, Dan. I'll get one of my people to contact State first thing tomorrow."

"Thanks," said Dan.

Suddenly there was nothing else for them to talk about. They finished their drinks as quickly as they decently could. Dan spent the time explaining to O'Brien the economics of mass-producing the solid-fuel rocket boosters he used, instead of hand-crafting rockets one at a time. He neglected to tell the man that Astro Corporation had a warehouse full of boosters that the double-damned Internal Revenue Service would not allow them to discount as inventory.

MATAGORDA ISLAND, TEXAS

It was almost noon when April caught a faint trace of jasmine perfume and looked up from her computer screen. A pert, freckle-faced redhead was standing in front of her desk, smiling at her, wearing a white T-shirt and hip-hugging shorts.

"Mr. Randolph's not in," April said. "Can I help you?"

"Randolph went to Washington, didn't he?" asked Kelly Eamons.

"He should be back tomorrow," April replied guardedly.

"Actually, I came over to talk with you, not Randolph." Before April could reply, she fished a slim wallet from the back pocket of her shorts and flipped it open. "I'm Special Agent Kelly Eamons, Federal Bureau of Investigation."

April got to her feet. She was several inches taller than Eamons, leggy and sleek. With the desk between them they looked like a high fashion model and a bouncy Texas cheerleader. If she's carrying a gun, April thought as she looked over Eamons, I can't see where it might be.

"Why do you want to talk with me?" April asked. "I'm only Mr. Randolph's executive assistant."

Eamons surveyed April with clear blue-green eyes. "I bet you know more about what's going on in this outfit than your boss does."

Warily, April said, "That's an old cliché, Agent Eamons: the all-knowing secretary."

"Call me Kelly. And don't pretend to be modest."

Without smiling back at her visitor, April said, "All right. What do you want to know?"

"Why don't we talk over lunch?" Eamons suggested.

"I was planning to eat here at my desk."

"Let's go to the motel. The food's not much, but I've got an expense account. Let Uncle Sam treat."

Wondering if it was a suggestion or a demand when an FBI agent invited you to lunch, April shrugged and answered, "Okay. Why not."

Eamons let April drive to the motel in her Sebring, the top down and the warm, humid air blowing in from the Gulf tousling their hair. The dining room was almost completely empty despite the fact that the nearest competing restaurant was a ferry ride away in Lamar. They took the booth at the end of the row; only one other booth was occupied.

"Catfish?" Eamons asked, looking up from the one-page menu. "Is it fresh, do you think?"

April said, "Look, Kelly, you don't have to put on an act with me. I'll tell you everything I know. I don't need the down-home routine."

Eamons looked genuinely surprised. "But I love catfish! I was practically raised on catfish."

"Where?"

"Little town called Kildare Junction, up in Cass County. Not far from Texarkana."

"You're from Texas, then?"

"Born and bred. Went to Longhorn U., down in Austin."

April relaxed a little. But only a little. When the barmaid sauntered over to their booth, Eamons ordered the catfish. April asked for a salad.

"Somethin' t'drink?"

"Cherry Coke, please," said Eamons.

"I'll have iced tea," April said. "Unsweetened."

"You're a southern gal, too," Eamons said as the waitress left. "Virginia?"

"You've read my personnel file."

"Not yet. It's your accent. I like to peg people by their accents. Southwestern Virginia, maybe? Hill country?"

April had to admit she was right.

"Can I buy you ladies a drink?"

April looked up and saw a technician she knew, smiling shyly at them, a bottle of beer in his left hand. Wally Berardino, she recalled. From the electronics group. Computer specialist.

"We've already ordered, Wally," she said gently.

"Oh." To Eamons, he said, "Do I know you? I don't think I've seen you around here before."

Before April could think of what to say, Eamons flashed a bright smile and said, "I'm new here. Lookin' for a job."

Berardino shook his head sadly. "Man, you've come to the wrong place. We're all wondering when the ol' ax is gonna fall."

Eamons's smile did not diminish by a single milliwatt. "Well, you can't blame a girl for trying."

"Guess not." Berardino seemed to run out of things to say. He smiled back at Eamons and walked slowly back to the bar.

"I don't think it's a good idea to let everybody know I'm from the Bureau," Eamons said in a near whisper. "It intimidates people. Especially guys."

April said nothing. Their meals came and they talked while they ate. Actually April did most of the talking, prodded by an occasional question from Eamons. By the time they had finished their lunches, April was feeling depressed.

"So Dr. Tenny was killed and then Pete Larsen was found dead—"

"Hanged."

"The local police called it suicide."

"But you don't think it was."

"I don't know what to do," April blurted, surprised by how awful she felt. "I want to help Mr. Randolph but I just don't know what to do."

Eamons nodded sympathetically. "That's perfectly all right. It's not your problem, it's mine."

"But I want to help!"

For a long moment Eamons said nothing, studying April with those light blue-green eyes of hers. At last she asked, "Do you really want to help?"

"Yes!"

"Why?"

Now April hesitated a moment. Then, "I liked Dr. Tenny. He was like a big gruff uncle to me. And I dated Pete Larsen. He wasn't a ball of fire but if somebody killed him, murdered him, I want the bastard caught and punished."

"And Dan Randolph?"

A ripple of electricity ran through April. She can see right through me, she realized.

"Randolph's the one who needs your help, isn't he?" Eamons asked gently.

April nodded, not trusting herself to speak without blubbering that she loved Dan.

"All right," said Eamons softly. "I think you can help. It might be dangerous, though."

"Tell me what I've got to do," said April.

CARACAS, VENEZUELA

By god, thought Dan, he looks like some Spanish conquistador, straight out of the History Channel. Put some armor on him and one of those steel helmets and he could play Cortés or Pizarro.

Rafael Miguel de la Torre Hernandez did indeed look like a high-born Castilian. Tall, stately, every inch the patrician, there was no doubt about who he was as he approached the little table on the balcony of the hotel's bar. His cheekbones were high and his nose finely arched. His hair was beginning to gray at the temples, very distinguished, although his full moustache was still luxuriantly dark. But as Dan rose to his feet and extended his hand to greet him, he saw that Hernandez's eyes did not match the rest of his appearance. They were a dull, muddy brown. The eyes of a peasant. The eyes of a man who could be corrupted. Good, thought Dan.

He had waited at the balcony bar for more than half an hour before Hernandez had deigned to make his appearance. Across the street was Bolívar Square with its tall, thickly leafed trees spreading their branches out over the busy avenue. Sloths hung upside down from their hooked claws in the trees, barely moving, hardly showing any signs of life, while chattering monkeys raced through the branches like supersonic Tarzans, zipping around and around the entire square endlessly, as if they were hopped up on amphetamines. Dan had watched them, fascinated, until Hernandez showed up.

"Señor Randolph?" Hernandez asked politely, needlessly, as he took Dan's hand in a lukewarm grasp. He wore an expensive-looking light gray suit. Silk, Dan thought. Beautifully knotted pale yellow tie. Also silk.

"I'm very pleased to meet you, sir," said Dan. As they sat in the wobbly little cast-iron chairs, he added, "It was good of you to take the time to see me."

Hernandez nodded graciously, as if he were accustomed to flattery.

It had taken a tortuous three weeks to get to this meeting. Jane had asked the State Department for someone whom Dan could talk to, as she'd promised. State provided the name of an attaché in Venezuela's embassy who specialized in economic development. Dan had worked his way through the Venezuelan bureaucracy and finally discovered Hernandez, an assistant minister in the government's department of transportation. He had flown to Caracas, only to spend two days cooling his heels until Hernandez finally agreed to see him.

"I apologize for the informality of this meeting, señor," Hernandez said, in slow, accented English. "Considering your desire for confidentiality, I thought it best that we meet outside the departmental offices."

"I agree entirely," Dan said.

A waiter bowed to Hernandez, who ordered a whisky and soda. Dan asked for a refill of his piña colada.

Once the drinks arrived, Hernandez steepled his hands above his glass and asked, "You wish to use our airport?"

Glad that he had at last gotten down to business, Dan hunched forward and said, "I wish to establish a partnership with a man of vision, a man who can understand that there is vast wealth to be found in space."

"Space? You mean out among the stars and such?"

Dan kept a straight face, wondering if Hernandez were truly that naïve or if the man was simply leading him on.

"In orbit around the Earth," he replied. "You've heard of the power satellite that my corporation has built?"

"Naturally."

"Then you know that such satellites can generate enormous amounts of energy. Just one of them could supply all of Venezuela with more electrical power than your entire nation now consumes."

Hernandez's brows arched upward. "Truly? Only one satellite?"

"Only one," said Dan, nodding.

"How can that be?"

So he doesn't know how it works, Dan realized. Okay, he's admitted his ignorance without damaging his dignity. Time for the dog and pony show.

Dan went through his litany of how the satellite uses solar cells to convert sunlight into electricity, then beams the energy to a receiving station on the ground. Hernandez drank it all in as he sipped at his whisky, never objecting or asking a question. He even took the idea of beaming microwaves to the ground without blinking.

"The key to operating such a power satellite economically is the ability to send maintenance and repair crews to it at a reasonable cost," Dan explained.

Hernandez murmured, "Rockets are very expensive."

"The spaceplane we're developing will bring down the costs by a factor of a hundred," Dan said flatly. It was almost true.

"This is the plane that crashed recently."

"We have another. We will flight-test it soon. I would like to have permission to land the plane at a suitable airport in Venezuela."

"Why here?"

"As an emergency precaution," Dan equivocated. "We're negotiating other emergency sites in Spain, Australia, and South Africa."

"I see."

"You have a fine airport here at Caracas."

"It is also quite a busy airport. Many airline companies use it."

Dan nodded. He understands the problem. "If we needed to land the spaceplane at your airport, you would have to stop all other traffic."

"For how long?"

"Half an hour, maybe. Maybe a little more."

Hernandez sipped the last of his whisky, then said, "That is not impossible."

Despite himself, Dan couldn't keep himself from blurting eagerly, "You could do it?"

"It would be an expensive operation," Hernandez said. "There would be many people involved: ground controllers, airline managers, many others."

Bribes, Dan realized. He's talking about bribes. Aloud, he asked, "Could I leave all that in your hands? I'd prefer to deal only with you, and leave the rest of the operation to your discretion."

Hernandez allowed a tiny smile to twitch his lips briefly. "Yes, I suppose that would be the best way to handle it."

"I could give you a retainer to start with, and then you can tell me how much the operation would cost."

"I have a bank account in your national capital. You could transfer the funds there."

No international transfers, Dan said to himself. He's no dummy. "That will be very convenient," he said.

Hernandez broke into an unrestrained smile and signaled the waiter for a refill of their drinks.

"If and when we need to use your airport," Dan said, "I'll have to send a small team of technicians here."

"That is no problem. I can clear that with the foreign office easily."

The waiter brought their drinks, then departed. Dan clinked his glass against Hernandez's and said, "To a successful partnership."

Hernandez sipped, then said, "By the way, your technicians will need hotel accommodations here in the city. My brother-in-law manages the finest hotel in Caracas."

Dan grinned at him. We're going to get along just fine, he thought. Just as long as he doesn't get too greedy.

ASTRO MOTEL

The glass double doors that separated the Astro Motel's pocket-sized lobby from the bar were almost always kept open, so from her vantage point behind the registration desk, Kelly Eamons could see who was coming and going easily enough. Especially who's going, she giggled to herself: the restrooms were on the far side of the lobby.

April Simmonds had pulled a few strings and gotten the motel's manager to hire Eamons as their registration clerk for the night shift: four to midnight. The manager, an overweight son of the family that nominally ran the motel, took one look at Eamons and saw a cute redhead with a glad smile that filled his mind with visions of sugarplums. He himself had been manning the registration desk for the midnight-to-eight A.M. stint, so he moved his night clerk to the graveyard shift and retired to the manager's office to spend his evenings watching television and trying to get Eamons to have dinner with him. The former night clerk quit, though, and the poor man had to go back to his former duties until he could hire a replacement.

He didn't mind it too much. Most of the time there was nothing to do but watch the TV in the lobby, and he got to see Eamons every night when her shift was finished and his just beginning. Many nights, alone behind the desk except for the late-night movies and news broadcasts, he thought about making it with Kelly right there on the big leather couch in front of the TV. Neither he nor anyone on Matagorda Island except April and Dan knew that this attractive, sunshiny redhead was an agent of the FBI.

Eamons smiled and jollied him along while she kept tabs on the patrons at the bar. Almost all of them were Astro employees; April knew most of them and gave Eamons access to the company's personnel files.

April was doing more than that, though. With Eamons watching from the registration desk, April became a regular at the bar. She would come in at the end of the working day for the happy hour two-for-one drinks and stay until the crowd thinned out for dinner. Often she returned later at night, chatting with the Astro technicians and engineers she knew, allowing some of the men she didn't know to buy her a drink or simply sit beside her at the bar and talk.

April always went home alone, as far as Eamons could see. She's smart enough to handle these geek boys, Kelly told herself. Besides, she's in love with Randolph. She's not interested in any of these guys. Eamons had assured April that she could protect her. "I'm just a phone call away," she said, brandishing her cell phone like a miniature club.

Eamons was living with April in the tidy one-bedroom apartment April rented in Lamar. She slept on the pull-out sofa in the living room and shared the tiny bathroom. They always drove to Matagorda separately, of course: April first thing in the morning, Eamons late in the afternoon. They didn't want anyone to know they were working together.

Mornings, over breakfast, they would compare notes, exchange information. The trouble was, Eamons soon realized, that there was precious little information to exchange. April was getting earfuls about who was unhappy with his wife, who was looking for a new job, who was chasing whom. Nothing substantial, though. Nothing that would help with the investigation. Eamons carefully refrained from telling April that Nacho Chavez, back in Houston, was warning her that the Bureau's higher-ups were talking about terminating the investigation for lack of results.

She found that she enjoyed being out of the office, in the field, even if the work was boring and unproductive. She enjoyed living with April and found herself wondering what it would be like to sleep in the same bed with her.

Dan Randolph had returned from Venezuela, full of mysterious smiles, and the engineers were checking out the rocket plane in preparation for its mating to a booster rocket.

Most mornings Eamons made breakfast for the two of them while April dressed for the office.

"Are we getting anywhere?" April asked from the bedroom while Eamons gingerly pulled slices of toast from the pop-up toaster. They never pop the slices high enough, she thought, snatching at the crumbly bread and trying to drop it in the plate before she burned her fingertips.

April stepped through the bedroom doorway, wearing a scooped-neck lilac blouse and a straight-line knee-length skirt of slightly darker hue, tall and sleek and every inch the modern, capable woman. Kelly felt distinctly short and shabby in her shapeless bathrobe.

Eamons thought, That man Randolph is a damned fool. She's really beautiful and he doesn't pay any attention to her. Is it because she's black? Aw hell, men are all crazy, anyway.

"Are we getting anywhere?" April repeated as she pulled up one of the stools before the kitchenette's breakfast bar.

Eamons shrugged and put the toast down on the counter. "You've checked out all of Larsen's friends. He definitely wasn't a gambler."

April nodded glumly. "We knew that the morning after he was murdered."

"My office has sent the recording on Larsen's answering machine to Washington for voice analysis. If the man speaking has ever been arrested on a federal charge, we might have a voice match somewhere in the files."

"That would be something." April picked at her scrambled eggs. Eamons was not much of a cook; try as she might, her attempts at sunny-side up always came out scrambled.

Trying to cheer April, Eamons said, "My grandfather was a stonemason back in Cass County. He used to say to me, sometimes you chip and chip and chip away at the stone but it doesn't crack. Just sits there, stubborn, no matter how hard you've sweated over it. And then, all of a sudden, you hit it one more time and it splits open for you."

"I wish," April said glumly. "I mean, I've talked with just about everybody Pete knew. I've sat at that bar and listened and asked questions until I'm ready to puke. And we don't know anything now that we didn't know the morning after he was killed."

Eamons was tempted to contradict her, but she kept silent. What April said was true enough. But what April didn't know was that her asking questions, her insistent poking around among all those who knew Pete Larsen, might be bothering whoever it was who murdered the man. The people who destroyed the spaceplane and killed Tenny also murdered Larsen. They must have other informants inside Astro Corporation, Eamons thought. They must have eyes watching and ears listening. If April asks enough questions, maybe they'll get worried enough to do something about it.

Or maybe they won't, Eamons had to admit to herself. Their smartest move would be to do nothing. They've done their damage, why stick around? Just get out and stay out and nobody will ever figure out who they are.

On the other hand, Randolph is pushing ahead, struggling to keep his company going. Maybe they'll figure they have to strike again to stop him once and for all.

"I'm off to work." April pushed her unfinished eggs away and got up from the stool.

Eamons walked with her to the apartment's front door. "See you tonight at the motel," she said.

"Right," said April.

Eamons closed the door and leaned against it. It's a helluva plan you're working, she groused to herself. The best thing that can happen is they try to kill her. Some helluva plan, all right.

MATAGORDA ISLAND, TEXAS

Even this early in the morning the thunderheads were piling up over the Gulf, Dan saw. A stiff wind was blowing in from the water as he stood at the edge of the launch platform, Lynn Van Buren beside him, and craned his neck up at the rocket booster standing sixteen stories high, wrapped inside the heavy steel lattice of the service gantry tower.

"The latest weather forecast ain't good, chief," Van Buren said, raising her voice over the gusting wind. "They'll probably be posting a hurricane watch by ten A.M."

"Then what?" Dan snapped. "An earthquake?"

"We can't take a chance on having the booster ride out a hurricane in the open," Van Buren said.

Dan knew she was right. Don't mess with Mother Nature, he told himself. Some mother. Why can't she wait until after we get the bird off?

"Niles has his people tying down the spaceplane in Hangar B," Van Buren said.

Dan chuckled, despite everything. Niles Muhamed isn't going to let anybody put "his" spaceplane in jeopardy. He pictured Niles standing at the door to Hangar B and forcing the hurricane to keep away, like old King Canute trying to stop the tide from coming in.

"She could ride out a storm," Dan shouted over the rising wind. "She's clamped down good and the gantry's holding her. We calculated a booster could stand up to winds of a hundred and fifty miles an hour, didn't we?"

"And what if the calculations were too optimistic?" Van Buren yelled back. "What if we get a hundred-and-sixty-mile-an-hour storm? Or a hundred-and-eighty?"

Dan frowned at her. He dearly wanted to avoid the cost of taking the booster down, towing it back, and setting it up again after the storm.

"And there's the rain, too," Van Buren went on, relentlessly. "Pounding rain for god knows how many hours. She oughtta be inside shelter, safe and dry."

Dan nodded reluctantly, his eyes on the line of trees that marked the edge of the state park. They were tossing fitfully now against the gray clouds scudding across the sky. Soon their leaves will be blowing off, then whole branches. Lots of debris is going to be flying around, he thought.

"Okay," he said grudgingly. "Take her down."

He turned and clambered down the launch platform's steel steps, then walked swiftly to his waiting Jaguar. It took less than five minutes to drive to Hangar A, but Dan thought the sky darkened noticeably in that short time. Once he parked in his slot he pulled up the top on the convertible and locked it down tight. The car had never leaked before, but it had never gone through a hurricane, either.

The sound of the wind was an eerie wail inside the hangar. Now we'll see if these buildings really will stand up to hurricane winds, Dan thought as he hustled up the stairs to his office. We're high enough above sea level so we don't have to worry about storm surges. Then he thought, Unless we get a tidal wave. That would be the finishing touch.

April was at her desk, looking worried. Her computer screen showed an animated weather map. Dan saw the big swirling cyclonic clouds of Hurricane Fernando out in the Gulf moving remorselessly toward the Texas coast.

"Heading our way, huh?" he asked, half-sitting on the corner of her desk.

"Straight toward us," April replied, her voice a little quavery.

"You'd better get out of here while the ferry's still running."

"I've still got to get this order for liquid hydrogen processed."

"It can wait."

With the hydrogen facility destroyed by the explosion, Dan had to purchase liquid hydrogen and liquid oxygen for the spaceplane from a commercial supplier. He had asked April to handle the task, bypassing his purchasing department because he didn't know whom he could trust within his own company.

April said, "I can stay—"

"No. We won't get much work done today. The launch is scrubbed and the crew's going to tow the bird back into its hangar. Get on home, kid."

"What about the others?"

"Get on the P.A. and tell 'em that everybody except the launch crew can go home for the day. If the ferry stops they can stay at the motel, on the company."

The motel was the island's official storm refuge. It was stocked with emergency food and water and had its own auxiliary power generator for electricity.

As April patched her desk phone into the public address system Dan went into his office. Too nervous to sit at his desk, he stood by the window and watched the booster being lowered to its side by the gantry crane.

Feeling helpless, restless, and more than a little scared, Dan paced his office for a few minutes, then headed back out.

April stopped him. "Call for you from Venezuela," she said. "Señor Hernandez."

"He's got a great sense of timing," Dan grumbled, turning back to his office. Over his shoulder he said, "I told you to go home, April. Git!"

Sliding into his desk chair, Dan tapped the phone's ON key. Rafael Hernandez's handsome face filled his display screen.

"Señor Hernandez," Dan said, putting on an amiable smile. "Good morning."

Hernandez smiled back. "*Buenas dias,* Mr. Randolph. How are you this lovely day?"

Dan couldn't see much past Hernandez's head and shoulders. He appeared to be in an office of some kind.

"It may be a fine day in Caracas," he said. "We have a hurricane bearing down on us."

"Indeed?"

"Indeed."

Totally unperturbed by Dan's troubles, Hernandez said calmly, "I have called to inform you that all the necessary arrangements have been made. You may send your technicians to Caracas as soon as you wish. I will see that they meet the airport's director of flight operations and anyone else they will need to interact with."

Dan broke into a genuine smile. "That's very good news, Señor Hernandez."

"I am pleased also, Mr. Randolph."

That means he checked his bank account in Washington and found the money I deposited there, Dan knew.

Aloud, he said, "Please, call me Dan. We're going to be partners, after all."

Hernandez dipped his chin in acknowledgment. "And you must call me Rafael."

They chatted for a few minutes more, then Hernandez pleaded the press of other business and cut the connection. A gust of wind rattled the steel wall of Dan's office. He looked out the window and saw that it was almost as dark as night. No rain, though. Not yet.

Maybe I should get over to the motel, he said to himself. Then he answered himself: No. I'll ride it out here. If these hangars don't hold up to the storm then I might as well be drowned along with everything else.

HURRICANE PARTY

By the time April got to the ferry pier, the last boat had gone. Heavy gusts were lashing frothy whitecaps across the normally tranquil bay. The wind-swept concrete pier was empty, abandoned, a sign bearing a hand-scrawled CLOSED FOR FERNANDO flapping in the gusts.

So she turned her baby blue Sebring around and drove to the motel. Plenty of cars parked there, she saw. April ran through the strengthening wind into the motel's lobby. Thunder rumbled in the distance. Kelly Eamons wasn't on duty at this time of the morning, but the bar was jammed with refugees from the storm, raucous music blaring from the loudspeakers, news coverage of the approaching hurricane on each of the TV screens.

"Hey, April!" one of the men crowding the bar called to her. "Come on over and have a drink."

It was Len Kinsky. All the booths were jammed, and men were packed three deep at the bar, with a scattering of women among them. April recognized most of them as Astro employees. With a resigned shrug, she went to the bar. When they hand you a lemon, her father had always told her, make lemonade. Good idea, she thought. She ordered lemonade, which the men

who quickly surrounded her found uproariously funny. Even the normally
sourpussed Kinsky laughed.

They're already half drunk, April recognized. And it hasn't even started
raining yet.

Kelly Eamons was arguing with the ferryboat skipper at the pier on the
mainland side of San Antonio Bay.

"But I've got to get over to the island!" she shouted over the howling wind.
"I'll lose my job if I don't show up for work!"

The skipper looked up from the line he was tying off. He was wearing a
polyester windbreaker, its hood bunched up around the collar, and a baseball
cap perched on his bald head. His ferry, which had once been a tank-carrying
landing boat for the U.S. Marines, was heaving up and down in the swells,
grinding its truck-tire bumpers against the length of the concrete pier with a
shrieking sound that was almost like fingernails on a blackboard.

"Whattaya think I am, Prince Henry the Navigator? I'm not takin' her out
until this storm passes."

"It's only a few miles," Eamons said.

He turned away from her, muttering, and bent over the line he was knot-
ting. Eamons thought of flashing her FBI badge, but that would blow her cover
completely. A few fat drops of rain spattered down. She retreated to her car,
parked alone in the lot except for a new-looking SUV, which she assumed belonged to the skipper.

She phoned April's office. No answer except for her recorded voice saying the office would be closed until after the hurricane had passed. Eamons
tried April's cell phone.

"Hello?" April's voice, with a lot of noise in the background: voices, music.

"April, it's Kelly. I'm stuck on the mainland. The ferry's not running."

"That's okay. I'm at the Astro Motel. Looks like we'll have to stay here until the storm blows over."

Eamons didn't like the idea of being out of the action. "Is there some way
you can think of that I might get a ride across to the island?"

For a few heartbeats all she could hear was the background of laughter
and voices, mostly male. Then April replied, "Maybe Mr. Randolph could do
something."

"Do you have his cell number?"

"I'll call him," April said.

"No, let me do it. Give me his number and I'll call him."

Again a hesitation, then April gave her the number.

"Okay," Eamons said, "I'll call him. With any luck, I'll get to the motel before the storm hits."

"I think you ought to stay on the mainland," April said.

"I probably will," Eamons admitted. "But I'll give it a shot anyway."

Dan was heading along the catwalk, a rain slicker draped over his arm, listening to the wind roaring and the rain pounding on the steel walls of the hangar like machine-gun bullets. The walls were creaking and groaning. Looking up at the roof, Dan wondered if he'd done the right thing when he paid off that building inspector.

Down below the personnel door flapped open and a solitary figure stepped into the hangar, wrapped in a dripping raincoat and a sodden hat that sagged down over his ears.

Who the hell would be out in this? Dan wondered, starting down the steps as the newcomer walked slowly across the hangar floor, dripping a trail of puddles. He pulled off the sopping wet hat and Dan saw that it was Passeau.

"What in hell are you doing here?" Dan called as he hurried down the stairs. "Why aren't you at the motel? Or off the island altogether?"

Passeau made a weak smile as he unbuttoned his raincoat. "I waited too long. The ferry is shut down."

"Why'd you come back here?"

Looking sheepish, Passeau said, "Actually, I don't know. I was heading for the motel but I drove right past it and came here."

"Helluva spot in a hurricane," Dan grumbled.

"Yes, isn't it?"

"I was going over to Hangar B to check on the plane."

"It's rather wet out there," Passeau said, shaking out his raincoat.

"Yeah, but it's better than sitting around here biting my fingernails. Niles is there and we can commiserate with him."

With a heavy sigh, Passeau struggled back into his raincoat while Dan put on his plastic slicker and pulled up its hood.

"Ready?" Dan asked, striding toward the door.

Passeau slapped his shapeless, dripping hat on his head and nodded unhappily.

Dan had to push hard to get the door open. The wind was like a solid wall, the rain blinding. Lightning flashed and thunder boomed immediately. "Must be right over our heads!" Dan yelled over the raging wind. Passeau said nothing. As soon as Dan let go of the door the wind slammed it shut. The two men trudged to Hangar B, leaning heavily into the wind. Dan felt soaked to the skin despite the slicker. Perspiration, he thought. Double-damned slicker doesn't breathe, makes you sweat. He knew that fear makes you sweat, too.

Once they got to the hangar, its bulk shielded them from the worst of the wind. Dan pulled the door open and the two of them stumbled into the hangar like a pair of shipwreck victims staggering onto a beach.

Gasping for breath, utterly soaked, Dan pushed back the slicker's hood and started to undo its Velcro seals.

"Lordy, lordy," came Niles Muhamed's deep voice, "look what the cat done dragged in."

Wiping water from his face, Dan saw that the four walls of the hangar were piled man-high with sandbags. Another double row of sandbags stood around the spaceplane, like a military revetment.

"When the hell did you do this?" Dan asked, waving at the fortifications.

Muhamed smiled grimly. "If you wasn't traipsin' off to Washington or Austin or goddam Venezuela and stayed around here, you'd know more about what's goin' down."

Dan laughed. "If I stayed around here, you'd have pressed me into your sandhog gang."

Muhamed allowed a glimmer of a smile to break his dour expression. "That'll be the day, you workin' a shovel."

Passeau walked slowly toward the spaceplane, his dripping hat in one hand. "It looks safe enough in here," he said.

"She'd be a lot safer in orbit," Dan said. "Nothing to worry about up there except micrometeorites."

"And radiation," Passeau added.

Dan nodded.

"You white boys need some coffee?" Muhamed asked, jerking a thumb toward a table set up in the far corner of the hangar, next to his desk and workbench.

Heading for the big stainless steel urn sitting on the table, Dan asked, "You alone in here, Niles?"

"Yup. Sent my people home soon's I looked at the weather satellite pictures."

"Let's turn on the Weather Channel and see what's happening," Dan said.

Passeau suggested, "Don't you think we should drive over to the motel, instead?"

"You can go," Muhamed said, with more than a hint of truculence. "I'm stayin' here."

"Not if I—" Dan was interrupted by his cell phone's "Take Me Out to the Ball Game."

As he flicked the phone on and put it to his ear, Muhamed poured steaming coffee into a Styrofoam cup and offered it to Dan.

Dan waved him off as he heard, "Mr. Randolph, it's Kelly Eamons."

While Muhamed gave the coffee cup to Passeau, Dan listened to Eamons explaining that she was stuck on the mainland.

"It's a hurricane, for the love of Neptune," Dan said. "Nobody's going to ferry you across the bay. It's too dangerous. Stay where you are."

"It's not that bad yet," Eamons insisted.

Dan thought a moment, then asked, "Is there some special reason why you have to get over here?"

"No," Eamons replied slowly, hesitantly. "I just want to be where I'm supposed to be."

"Forget it," Dan said. "Take the day off. Everybody else is." Then he saw Niles Muhamed bending over his computer, his long thin finger flicking across the keyboard like a concert pianist's. "Almost everybody's taking the day off," he amended.

ASTRO MOTEL

April had never seen Kinsky look so cheerful. He must be more than half drunk, she thought as the public relations director steered her to an empty corner of the bar and actually began to dance with her to the strains of "The Tennessee Waltz." In a minute or two several other couples joined them on the impromptu dance floor.

"I didn't know you're such a good dancer," she said to Kinsky, surprised at how graceful the gangling scarecrow could be.

Kinsky smiled lazily at her. "There's a lot of things you don't know about me."

April expected a routine come-on line. She'd heard quite a few. Kinsky was divorced, so he couldn't pull the "my wife doesn't understand me" story. No, she decided, he's going to go for the "man of mystery" approach.

The song ended and he walked her, with his arm still around her waist, over to one of the rain-spattered windows. Someone had plastered packing tape across all the windows in big X shapes.

"What are you drinking?" Kinsky asked.

April suppressed an urge to giggle. "Lemonade."

His ginger-red brows shot up. "Lemonade? With vodka?"

"No. Just lemonade."

He shrugged. "Okay. Wait right here. I'll be right back."

As he walked to the crowded bar, April turned and looked out the window. Rain was pelting down so thickly now she could hardly make out her car parked only a few yards away. The wind was blowing the rain almost horizontally. April had never been through a hurricane before; it frightened her a little bit.

Her cell phone buzzed. She fished it out of her purse.

"Hi, it's me, Kelly."

"Did you reach Dan?" April asked.

"Yeah, but it didn't do any good. He told me to stay on the mainland."

Nodding, April said, "Might's well. I'm in the motel. Everything's tolerable here."

"Guess I'll drive back home, then."

"Okay. I'll get there when the ferry starts running again."

"Stay warm and dry," said Eamons.

"Sure."

Kinsky came back, an evil-looking concoction full of fruit in one hand and a tall frosted glass in the other. He placed both drinks on the windowsill, ceremoniously removed the paper parasol from his glass and perched it on the lip of April's.

"Thank you," she said. She picked up the lemonade carefully, but the parasol tumbled to the floor anyway. "Oh, too bad."

Shrugging, Kinsky said, "The story of my life. I try to do beautiful things but it never turns out the way I hoped."

"We all go through that."

"Not like me," Kinsky said fervently. "I go and get Dan a meeting with the governor of Texas and an important U.S. senator and he screws it up. Gets on his high horse and tells 'em they can't help him."

April felt shocked. "Mr. Randolph did that?"

"Not in so many words, but that's what he did, baby. That's what he did."

"I can't believe it."

"Believe it." Kinsky took a long swig of his drink, then stared out at the storm. Trees were bending and lightning flashing in the dark, roiling sky. "We never get crap like this in New York," he muttered.

April tried to lighten his mood. "Are you going to set your hair on fire?"

He almost smiled. "Naw. Not today. Nobody would notice."

"Or you might set off the sprinklers."

He grunted. "Burn the place down. That'd be doing Dan a favor. At least he could collect the insurance."

"I don't think that would help much," April admitted.

"Yeah. The company's going to go belly-up and we're all going to be thrown out on our asses."

"Dan's trying to avoid that."

"Maybe. But it's not going to do him any good. We're going to be out on our rear ends, honey. You and me and all of us. Might as well go outside and let the damned storm drown us."

"It's not *that* bad."

"Isn't it?"

"Dan's working to keep the company going."

"He's rearranging the deck chairs on the *Titanic*, babe. In a few weeks we'll all be on the unemployment line."

"No."

Kinsky took another sip of his drink. "Yes. The ship's sinking. It's every man for himself."

"What do you mean by that?"

"Feather your own canoe, babe. Take care of numero uno because nobody else is going to. Not Dan, not anybody. Nobody gives a damn about the little guys."

April thought that whatever he was drinking, it was making him more morose by the sip.

Abruptly, Kinsky blurted, "April, how'd you like to come to New York with me?"

"New York?"

"Yeah! We could fly up on a Friday and come back Monday. Take a long weekend. We deserve a break from all this."

She blinked at him. Suddenly he was enthusiastic. She said, "I don't think I could afford it on my budget. New York's awfully expensive, isn't it?"

"I'll spring for it. You won't have to put out a penny." Seeing the doubtful expression on her face, Kinsky added, "Or anything else. Separate rooms. Different floors. Different hotels, if you don't trust me."

She had to smile at that. "I've never been to New York."

"Never been...? You've gotta go. You've got to! It's the most fabulous place in the world. The town so big they named it twice!"

"Named it twice?"

"New York, New York!"

"Oh!" She laughed.

"My intentions are completely honorable," Kinsky said, then immediately amended, "Well, maybe not completely, but I won't make a pain of myself, I promise you. It's just... well..." His voice trailed off.

"What?" April asked gently, looking straight into his pale blue eyes.

"I've just got to get out of this dump for a few days. Get back to civilization. Find a good deli, have some real fun. And it'd be great to have you with me, April. I'd get a real kick out of showing you the town. We could go to Broadway shows, see the Statue of Liberty, the Empire State building, all kinds of things."

"It sounds awfully expensive," she repeated.

"So what?"

"Do you have that kind of money to throw around?"

"Hey, I don't have to pay for it. I'll just put it on my credit cards."

April frowned disapprovingly.

"No, seriously," Kinsky said, "I can afford it. I've got more going for me than the salary Dan pays me. A lot more."

"I don't think I can, Len."

"Sure you can. First class all the way. I mean it. I—"

A tree limb torn off by the wind banged against the window. April jumped back, spilling her lemonade over Kinsky's slacks.

"Oh! I'm so sorry, Len."

He grinned sardonically at her. "Hey, if you don't want to go with me just say so. You don't have to douse me."

HANGAR B

Muhamed made a rumbling sound deep in his throat as he pointed to the display screen. It showed an animated weather map. Peering over Muhamed's shoulder, Dan saw the huge circular storm with its well-defined eye slightly off from its center. The sound was down to a whisper; Dan could hardly hear the meteorologist's commentary over the howling of the wind outside and the drumming of the rain.

"Least we ain't gonna get the worst of it," Muhamed murmured.

"This is bad enough for me," Dan said.

Passeau, standing behind Muhamed's other shoulder, smiled wanly. "If you think this is bad you should have been in New Orleans for Hurricane Barbara. The streets were flooded up and over first-story windows. We had no electrical power for six days. Roofs blown off, power poles snapped like soda straws. My own car was totaled: flooded up to its roof and then a tree fell on it."

"You're not making me feel any better," Dan said.

"We'll be okay here," Muhamed said flatly. "Walls are holdin' up and the doors are faced away from the wind."

Dan silently thanked the architects for that. Then he thought that perhaps Niles had decided which direction the doors should face, not the architects.

"There's some water seeping in." Passeau pointed toward the doors.

Muhamed headed there. Over his shoulder he said, "If you two want to make yourselves helpful, you can start totin' sandbags."

Dan had to laugh at the shocked look on Passeau's face. "Come on, Claude," he said. "Lift dat bale, tote dat sandbag."

The storm was dying down, Kelly Eamons saw.

She had spent the long day in April's apartment, worried about her but glad to be on the mainland and high enough to avoid any flooding from a storm surge. Except for the shrieking wind outside and her gnawing fear of the storm, it had been a boring time, with nothing much to do except watch television. Shortly before noon the electrical power went out, and Eamons lost even the doubtful solace of TV.

She tried reading. April had some surprisingly erudite books in the apartment's one bookcase: histories of the Civil War and Reconstruction; biographies of Martin Luther King and Malcolm X; a few historical novels and several romances. Eamons sat in the doubtful light of the window and tried to lose herself in one of the novels. All she got out of it was a headache from eyestrain.

But it was getting brighter outside and the rain was definitely slackening. Then the lights came on and the TV blared to life. The digital clock on the DVD player blinked annoyingly. Eamons got out of her chair to fix it when her cell phone rang.

"Kelly, it's April."

"How's it going out there?"

April said, "A couple of cracked windows but otherwise we're okay. The Weather Channel says the storm's moving inland and breaking up."

Eamons nodded, then realized that April couldn't see it. "We lost power here for a few hours but it just came back on."

"Listen, Kelly," April said, lowering her voice slightly. "I think I've found something."

"What?"

"It might not be important, but you told me we should look for anybody who's getting an unusual amount of money, right?"

"Right."

"Well, as soon as you can get here, I want to tell you about him."

"Who?"

Lowering her voice still further, April said, "Len Kinsky, the public relations director."

Roberto had nothing to do. Al-Bashir had gone back to Africa or some-place, leaving Roberto with instructions to sit tight in Houston and pump his contacts inside Astro Corporation for information about Randolph's plans to fly his backup spaceplane.

But the contacts had run dry. They all claimed that Randolph wasn't telling anyone about his plans. Other than a quick trip to Venezuela several weeks ago, nobody seemed to know anything about what Randolph would do next. Not even his public relations guy had a clue. Or so he claimed.

Then came Hurricane Fernando, and everything was put on hold for a few days while they rode out the storm and cleaned up after it.

Now Roberto sat in his modest apartment and waited for one of his con-tacts to phone him. He hated to wait. *I could be out cruisin' downtown*, he told himself. *What good's the money I'm makin' if I gotta sit here like a punk in a holdin' tank and wait for some damned* pendejo *to phone me? I shoulda given him my cell number.* So he remained in the apartment, sitting in the reclining chair in front of the TV for hours on end, getting up only to trudge to the re-frigerator for another can of beer, or to the bathroom to relieve himself. His anger smoldered, simmering hotter with each passing hour.

If I go out somebody'll call and I'll miss it. He won't talk on the answering machine. So I gotta wait here like a fuckin' moron.

Roberto was asleep in the recliner when the phone rang. Instantly awake, he grabbed it and growled, "Yeah?"

"You told me to call," said the contact's voice.

"So whatchoo got to tell me?"

"Nothing new."

"Nuthin'? Whattaya mean nuthin'?"

"They got a booster back up on the launchpad and they're going to put the spaceplane on it."

"That's somethin', ain't it?"

"It's what they were going to do before the hurricane."

"When they gonna launch it?"

The man's voice hesitated. "This isn't for a launch. They don't have the government's approval for a flight. They're just checking out the connections, making sure the spaceplane and the booster fit together okay."

"And then what?"

"They'll take 'em down, I guess."

"You get paid to do more'n guess, man."

"Randolph's keeping his cards close to his vest. Nobody knows what he's planning to do next."

"Somebody's gotta know."

"Well, yeah. The chief engineer must know. Van Buren. But she's not talk-ing to anybody."

"She ain't talkin' to you, is what you mean."

"She's not talking to anybody! I'm telling you, nobody knows what's coming up next. The whole fucking company could collapse. Randolph could declare bankruptcy and we'll all be out on our asses."

Roberto was not an engineer, nor a technician, not even a high school graduate. But he had the dogged capacity to pursue a course stubbornly and not be deterred by any excuses.

"Lissen to me," he said slowly. "If that engineer knows what's goin' down, then he's the one you gotta pump."

"She."

"He, she, whatever. You find out from her what Randolph's gonna do."

"She won't talk to me about it. I've tried and she shuts up like a clam."

Roberto thought that he could open up a clam, no problem. But he kept his patience and asked, "You mean there's nobody else in the whole fuckin' company knows what Randolph's gonna do?"

A long hesitation. Then the man said, "Maybe his secretary. She makes all his appointments and stuff."

"Lean on her."

"I don't know about that. She—"

"You lean on her, man. Or I'll come down there and do it for you."

"Hey, you don't have to do that."

"Then you do your job."

"I'm not getting paid enough for this."

"You're gettin' paid plenty. Now earn it!" Roberto slammed the phone down. Fuckin' jerkoff.

On Matagorda Island Len Kinsky heard the phone connection click dead. He felt cold and clammy and realized he was sweating. If only I can get April to come to New York with me, he thought, maybe I could get her to tell me what I need to know about Dan's plans.

Of one thing Kinsky was certain. Mating the spaceplane to a booster was no test. Dan was planning to fly the bird. When, where, and how: those were the questions Kinsky needed to find answers for. He knew Roberto would not wait long, and the last thing he wanted was a visit from that Neanderthal.

MATAGORDA ISLAND, TEXAS

Dan craned his neck looking up at the clean, lean line of the gleaming white booster and the graceful silvery swept-wing spaceplane perched atop it, its needle nose pointed into the bright morning sky. The weather had turned friendly, blue sky dotted with fat puffs of white cumulus clouds sailing sedately on the breeze coming in from the Gulf. He could smell the tang of the sea and the sweet odor of the distant pines.

You'd never know a hurricane had blown past here a couple of days ago, Dan thought. The launchpad had been cleaned of the scrub and debris that had littered the area in the aftermath of the storm. The puddles and outright ponds of rainwater had either been pumped dry or evaporated in the sunshine. To Dan's happy relief all of Astro's buildings had survived Fernando with only minor damage. His Jaguar had suffered the most: its ten-year-old fabric top had ripped off in the storm and the car's interior looked like a swimming pool when he went out to check on it.

Could have been a lot worse, he said to himself as he slowly walked around the perimeter of the launch platform, admiring the booster-and-spaceplane combination. The gantry structure had been rolled away from the platform; only the umbilical tower stood beside the booster, with a pair of heavy electrical cables running from it to hatches in the top of the booster and just below the wing root of the spaceplane.

"You look happy, chief," said Lynn Van Buren, pacing along beside him. Like Dan, she wore a hard hat with her name stenciled onto it just below the stylish Astro Corporation logo.

"Rocket's on the pad and all systems check, from what you told me," Dan replied. "Why shouldn't I be happy?"

"What do we do now?" she asked.

Dan leaned his back against the sturdy steel railing of the platform and gazed up again at the spaceplane, thinking, She's built to fly. She shouldn't be sitting here on the ground. She ought to be up in the sky, where she belongs.

"All the checkouts complete?" he asked Van Buren.

"Aye-yup. All the connectors are mated and all systems are functioning. Batteries and fuel cells fully charged."

Dan looked into the engineer's hazel eyes. She seemed amused, expectant, as if the two of them were playing a game and she knew what his next move would be.

"Is the plane fueled up?" he asked.

A hint of a smile curved her lips slightly. "Nossir. The mating test is done with the upper stage empty." He saw in her face that she was thinking, You know that, chief.

Dan played the game, too. He looked around the platform, down to the ground where a trio of technicians were fussing with an auxiliary generator, out to the blockhouse where the launch crew directed tests and launches, then back to Van Buren's anticipant expression.

"I want a full-up test," he said. "A full propellant load in the spaceplane, just as if we were going to launch."

"But we don't have any LOX or liquid hydrogen. The facility blew up, remember?"

Lowering his voice, Dan told her, "There's a truck convoy on its way here with enough LOX and aitch-two to fill the bird's tanks. They'll arrive tonight, after most of the workforce has gone home."

Van Buren looked only slightly surprised. She asked, "So we fuel her up tonight?"

"Yep. With a minimum work crew."

The engineer nodded. "And then what?"

He grinned at her. "And then you and your top five people take a little trip to Venezuela."

Her eyes went wide. "Venezuela?"

"Gotcha," said Dan.

Claude Passeau was in the office that Dan had loaned him, in the engineering building that flanked Hangar A.

Dan popped his head past the office's open doorway and asked cheerily, "Want to go to lunch?"

Passeau was busily tapping at his computer keyboard. Without looking up from the screen, he said, "It's not quite eleven A.M."

"I know," Dan said, stepping fully into the tidy little office.

Dan had given the FAA administrator a corner office with two windows, and Passeau kept it as neat as if it were his permanent residence. The other FAA and NTSB people got claustrophobic cubicles with shoulder-high partitions and barely enough room for a desk and a wastebasket.

Sitting in the hard plastic chair in front of Passeau's desk, Dan said, "I thought I'd tootle over to Lamar for some local frog's legs."

Passeau looked up from the keyboard. "Frog's legs? Really?"

"The size of drumsticks," said Dan.

Passeau stifled a laugh when they walked out onto the parking lot and he saw the rusted, dented old Chevrolet two-door hatchback sitting in Dan's space.

"It belongs to the guy who's fixing my ragtop," Dan explained crossly. "The only loaner he had, he claimed."

Passeau shook his head. "How the mighty have fallen."

Dan shrugged apologetically. "Needs a muffler, too."

As Dan drove the rattling, growling Chevy to the ferry, he said to Passeau, "You know, Claude, you look kind of peaky."

"Peaky?"

"Tired. Overworked. What with the hurricane and all, you must be pretty stressed out."

"Are you saying that this would be a good time for me to take a vacation?"

Driving up the bumpy ramp onto the ferry, Dan said, "I think so. The Riviera's very nice at this time of year."

Passeau smiled knowingly. "Dan, my friend, don't you think it would be just a little conspicuous for an underpaid and overworked government official to take a vacation on the Riviera?"

"Maybe," Dan conceded.

Passeau said nothing as the ferry chugged to life and pushed away from the pier. Dan felt the waves of the bay surging beneath them. Passeau seemed unfazed by the chop.

"Actually," Passeau said mildly, "I believe it's time for me to return to my office in New Orleans. This investigation can be finished up from there."

"No vacation?" Dan asked.

"Not at this time," Passeau replied smoothly. "Perhaps later, after my final report is finished."

"I see."

"If you're still in business by then."

Dan glowered at him.

That evening April and Kelly Eamons planned their strategy.

"This could be nothing at all," April repeated for the twentieth time as she dressed for her dinner date.

"You said he was flashing a wad of money," Eamons said, sitting on April's bed.

"He *talked* about a lot of money," April replied, pulling the sleeveless, sequined gunmetal top over her dark gray slacks. "He was sort of drunk."

"In vino veritas," said Eamons.

"But he wasn't just bragging about money," April said, thinking back to her hurricane-party conversation with Kinsky. "He kept saying he had to take care of numero uno: feather his own nest, that sort of talk."

Resting her chin on her fists, Eamons said gloomily, "It's the only lead we've got."

April fastened a string of faux pearls around her throat, studied them for a moment in the full-length mirror on her clothes closet door. The glittery sleeveless top was high-necked, but she thought it looked kind of sexy, nonetheless. The slim-cut slacks accentuated her legs without looking slutty. Trying to remember how tall Kinsky was, she decided to wear low heels.

Turning to Eamons, she asked, "Do you really think Len might have had something to do with Joe Tenny's death? And Pete Larsen's?"

Eamons's face was puckered into a frown of concentration. "From what you've told me about Kinsky, no, frankly I don't. Probably at worst he's taking money to keep somebody informed about what's happening inside Astro."

"Like a spy?"

"Industrial espionage. Happens all the time. If Tricontinental and this Japanese firm are maneuvering to take over Astro, it makes sense that one of them would want an informant inside the company. Possibly both of them."

April shook her head and went into the bathroom to put the final touches on her makeup.

"That makes me a counterspy, then?" she called through the open bathroom door.

"You just be damned careful with him," Eamons said, getting up and walking to the door. "He might be just an informant, but the people he's talking to could be damned dangerous."

"I know," April said without turning her head from the mirror above the sink.

"Just be your charming self. Listen a lot, talk a little. I'll follow you at a discreet distance."

Pressing her lips together to blot her lipstick, April asked, "Do I look okay?"

"You look terrific," said Eamons, with a sly grin. "I wouldn't mind taking you to New York myself."

April felt her cheeks burn.

HOUSTON, TEXAS

Even though the long-distance connection was scratchy with crackling interference, Roberto could hear sudden anxiety in al-Bashir's voice.

"They've put fuel into the spaceplane?"

"Thass what my contact told me," Roberto said in his stolid, no-nonsense way. "He claims they did it lass night."

He had no way of knowing where al-Bashir was. The Tunisian had phoned him at their regular prearranged time. It was a satellite connection, though, Roberto figured, because there was this little hesitation between his talking and al-Bashir's answering.

"It could be part of a test, I suppose."

"There's somethin' else," said Roberto. Before al-Bashir could respond he went on, "Their top engineer and some of her crew left on the company jet."

Again the brief lag, then, "Left? Where are they going?"

"My contact don' know. He says he's gonna find out tonight. Got a date with Randolph's secretary."

This time the hesitation from al-Bashir was longer than usual. "Perhaps you should get down there."

"Matagorda?"

"Yes. I'll fly to Houston in a day or so. You stay close to your contact—and that secretary."

"You want me to handle her?"

"No! Not yet. But I want you close enough to deal with her and your contact quickly. If the need arises."

"Uh-huh."

"If the need arises," al-Bashir repeated. "You are not to act unless I tell you to."

"So why I gotta go to Matagorda, then?"

He could hear the irritation in al-Bashir's voice. "So that you can be close enough to strike quickly, if and when I tell you to!"

Roberto nodded. "Okay, I'll go down there tomorrow."

"Just lay low. Stay at the motel. Don't draw attention to yourself."

"Yeah, okay." But Roberto heard the words *strike quickly* repeating over and over again in his mind. He had seen Randolph's secretary. Kinsky was a wimp; taking care of him would be a snap. But the secretary was something else. Taking care of her would be fun.

In his palatial home on the outskirts of Tunis, al-Bashir put down the phone, his thoughts swirling. Randolph has the spaceplane ready to launch. But his top engineer and some of her crew have left Matagorda. Why? What is Randolph up to?

He picked up the phone again and jabbed at one of the buttons. The phone buzzed four times before a sleepy voice answered, "Yes, sir?"

One-twenty-three in the morning, al-Bashir saw from the ornate clock on the wall opposite his desk.

"Wake up, Ali," he snapped.

"I'm awake, sir. Fully awake, sir."

"Listen carefully," said al-Bashir. "I want you to contact each member of my special operation team. Tell them they must be ready to move to Marseille within a moment's notice. Do you understand?"

"A moment's notice, yes, sir."

"At eight o'clock this morning you will phone the operations center outside Marseille."

"Eight o'clock, yes, sir."

"Tell them to prepare for receiving my team. Find out how long they will require to be fully operational."

"Yes, sir."

"I'm going to bed now. When I awake I will expect you to have done these tasks."

"They will be done, sir."

"I will expect a full report from you."

"Yes, sir. I will be prepared whenever you call."

"Good."

"Have a pleasant night's sleep, sir."

Al-Bashir detected just the slightest hint of irony in the voice of his faithful servant. Well, he thought, Ali isn't going to get much sleep tonight. He's entitled to a little resentment, I suppose. But heaven help him if he hasn't completed his tasks to my satisfaction.

With that, al-Bashir got up from his desk and headed for his bedroom, trying to decide which of his women he wanted tonight.

Flying thirty-seven thousand feet above the Gulf of Mexico, Lynn Van Buren cranked her seat as far back as it would go and tried to get some sleep. But she was far too excited even to close her eyes. She had never been to Venezuela. Only two of her five-person crew spoke any Spanish at all.

Dan's going to outfox all of them, she thought. He's going to launch the spaceplane, fly several orbits, and land it in Caracas. Hot spit! He's got more balls than the Mongol hordes and the U.S. Marines put together.

The twin-jet Citation couldn't make it all the way from Matagorda to Caracas without a refueling stop in Florida. Van Buren gave up any pretense of sleeping and peered out of the plane's tiny round window at a tropical Moon riding along silvered clouds. Down in the plane's cargo hold was the guidance and control equipment that they would use to monitor the spaceplane's landing. If the bird deviated from its preset flight plan Van Buren and her people could take active control from the ground.

Dan had at first told Van Buren that they would have to work from a boat out in the harbor of La Guaira, the port city for Caracas. But apparently Dan's Venezuelan contact, somebody high up in the local government, had promised them tight security at the airport itself. They could handle the flight much better from the airport, Van Buren knew. Besides, she didn't relish the idea of trying to handle the mission while bobbing up and down in some boat.

The Citation landed at Florida's Southwest International Airport just outside Fort Myers, refueled, and then took off for its run to Caracas. Van Buren finally fell asleep and only woke up when the sudden thump and rushing wind noise of the landing gear being lowered startled her out of a pleasant dream about a picnic with her kids. As she rubbed the sleep from her eyes the plane landed with a screech of tires on the long concrete runway.

Craning her neck to look out at the Caracas airport in the early morning sunlight, Van Buren saw that the plane was taxiing to a remote corner of the facility, far from any buildings or other planes. The only thing out there was a tall wire mesh fence topped by razor wire. And a big, square army truck in chocolate-chip camouflage. As the plane squealed to a stop, a full squad of young soldiers piled out of the truck, automatic rifles in their hands, and formed up in a straight line.

"What's going on?" one of her technicians asked.

"Don't worry," Van Buren assured him. "It's okay. Nothing to worry about." She hoped she was right.

The captain came out of the cockpit, stooped over because of the cabin's low ceiling, and swung the hatch open; a metal stairway automatically unfolded from the plane's fuselage. A trim-looking young soldier immediately clambered up the steps, looking very serious. He had some sort of insignia on the collar of his shirt, a thick dark moustache, and a pistol holstered on his hip.

"Señora Van Buren?" he called out.

"That's me," she replied, heading up the cabin's central aisle toward him.

The soldier was short enough to stand erect at the hatch. "I am Capitan Esteban Guitterez, commandante of your security detail," he said in heavily accented English. Then he smiled brilliantly. "Welcome to Venezuela!"

Len Kinsky wasn't exactly panicked, but he certainly felt nervous. His date with April had been a total waste of time. They spent the whole evening fencing verbally: he tried to find out from her what Dan was up to and gradually realized that she was trying to find out what he was doing. She knows! Kinsky realized, halfway through his bland chunk of dead fish at Lamar's fanciest restaurant. *She's trying to pump* me!

By the time he got home that evening there was a message on his answering machine from Roberto. The big mook was coming down to Matagorda. Great! thought Kinsky. He'd only met Roberto in the flesh once, but that was enough. Plenty, in fact. The guy looked like he should be playing linebacker for some prison football team. Scary.

Roberto wasn't satisfied with the flow of information Kinsky was providing him. Kinsky had to admit that he hadn't much information to pass on. And now April was probably on to him. What to do?

As he drove to the ferry that morning, Kinsky wished he'd never met Roberto, never gone for the money the big lug offered. All they'd wanted was a pipeline into Dan's office. Industrial espionage. Happens all the time. With Astro going down the toilet and his job going with it, Kinsky figured a little extra money on the side was a good bet. Insurance for that inevitable day when Dan called him in and sadly told him he was laid off.

Yeah. Good bet. Kinsky sat and fidgeted while the ferry chugged across the bay. Maybe I ought to just pull up stakes and go back to New York. I can sell some freelance magazine articles if nothing else pans out.

The ferry docked. As he drove the last few miles to the office Kinsky formed a plan of action. Roberto wants the inside poop on what Dan's up to. Otherwise he's going to get nasty. Maybe he was involved in Tenny's death.

Kinsky didn't like to think of that. Focus on the here and now, he commanded himself. Figure out what you've got to do and then do it.

By the time he parked his car he had made up his mind. He strode straight to Hangar A. In the distance he could see that they'd rolled the grill-work gantry structure up to the booster and spaceplane perched on the launchpad. A thin wisp of vapor was wafting from one of the umbilicals connected to the spaceplane. Kinsky stopped in midstride. Christ! They're fueling up the plane! He's really going to launch it!

Kinsky ran the rest of the way into the hangar and pounded up the steps, heading for Dan's office.

BLOCKHOUSE

"T minus ten minutes," the launch director's automated clock announced.

"Propellant top-off complete," said one of the technicians.

"Copy propellant top-off complete," said the launch director as he tapped a keypad on the board before him. He was balding, slightly overweight, so much in control of himself that Dan wondered if he ever perspired. In the corporate organization charts he was Van Buren's assistant, although he had accumulated a career's worth of experience launching ballistic missiles for the Air Force before retiring from the military and coming to work for Astro.

Of the six others sitting at the row of consoles inside the thick-walled concrete blockhouse, three were NASA veterans, the other three recent graduates of technical schools. All of them had headsets clamped over their hair; their eyes were focused on the screens and gauges of their consoles.

There were no windows in the blockhouse, but an oversized display screen that covered one entire wall showed the booster and spaceplane erect on the pad outside with the rust-red tower of the gantry enveloping them protectively.

Dan stood by the blockhouse's steel door, feeling the tightening of his nerves that he always experienced during a launch countdown. Firing off the solid-fuel booster was a simple operation compared to the big liquid-propellant rockets that NASA and other space agencies used. Still, the blockhouse felt hot and stuffy to Dan, damp with perspiration and the smell of tension.

"T minus seven minutes. Gantry rollback in two minutes."

The intercom buzzed, a sudden annoying insect in the midst of the tight, businesslike procedure. The kid handling outside communications pressed one hand against his earphone and whispered into his pin mike. The young man, a graduate student from Duke University, then turned in his swivel chair and motioned for Dan to pick up the phone on the concrete wall.

Frowning with annoyance, Dan yanked the receiver off its cradle.

"Dan? What the fuck is going on?" Kinsky's voice, high, screeching.

"Not now, Len," Dan said tightly into the phone.

"You're going to launch it?" Even higher.

"I'll talk to you when I get back to my office. Wait for me there."

"For Jesus Christ's sake, Dan, you can't—"

Dan hooked the receiver back onto its cradle, then stepped over to the communication guy and tapped him on the shoulder. The kid looked up and Dan drew a finger across his own throat. "No more incoming calls," he said. "No matter who it is."

The young man nodded. Dan walked back to his spot by the door, where he could watch over the shoulders of the whole launch team. *The last thing I need is a phone call from Passeau or some other government pain in the butt telling me I don't have permission to launch.*

"T minus five minutes. Begin gantry rollback."

"Confirm. Start rollback."

Dan saw the big gantry structure begin to move slowly away from the rocket assembly, like the steel framework of a twenty-five-story building rolling on a set of rails. The umbilical tower stood to one side of the launch pad, its electrical power cables and propellant hoses connected to the booster and spaceplane.

What's got Len so geared up? Dan asked himself. And answered, *He's probably warped because I didn't let him know about the launch ahead of time. That must be it.*

Dan suppressed an urge to go outside. The tension was coiling tighter inside him. The launch crew was going smoothly through the countdown, no hitches, no glitches, but still Dan's insides were clenching up just as hard as they used to when he'd been sitting inside a capsule at the top of a big rocket, waiting to be fired off into space, knowing that he was perched atop enough explosive power to blast the rocket and its cargo of human flesh into a roaring hell-hot blossom of flames.

"T minus four minutes. Weather check."

The woman seated to the launch director's right punched several keys on her console, then said, "Weather conditions all well above minimums. No problems."

"Weather confirmed," the launch director said.

Dan knew there would be no need to check weather conditions down-range, nor air traffic, either. The rocket would lift off vertically, then pitch over slightly to head out over the Gulf as it swiftly rose above the altitude that air traffic used. She'll be above controlled airspace in less than a minute, Dan told himself. No sweat for the FAA or anybody else.

"Emergency landing sites?" the launch director asked, peering at the checklist on his console screen.

The three sites in Spain, South Africa, and Australia had been alerted when the countdown had begun, less than an hour ago. Each of the airports confirmed that they were ready to clear all traffic if the spaceplane needed to abort its flight and make an emergency landing.

Van Buren and her team had reported that they were ready at Caracas. Dan had talked to her before coming over to the blockhouse. Lynn seemed to be enjoying her sojourn in Venezuela, even though neither she nor the others with her had left the airport.

The countdown proceeded. A tiny plume of white vapor wafted from the spaceplane's lower body. Liquid hydrogen and liquid oxygen powered its rocket engines, so cold that they condensed the water vapor in the humid summer breeze drifting across the plane's propellant tanks into a miniature cloud of glittering droplets.

His eyes riveted on the big wall screen, Dan saw that the sky outside was as clear as it ever gets, bright blue with only a few fat puffs of cumulus clouds floating slowly past. He licked his lips, clenched his fists, and resisted the urge to pace up and down. Might make the crew nervous, he thought. Still, a quick trip to the toilet won't bother anybody.

The blockhouse lavatory was no bigger than a closet, its walls thin plywood. Dan could hear the countdown clicking inexorably along.

He came out as one of the launch team sang out, "Internal power on."

"Confirm internal power."

"T minus two minutes. Umbilical disconnect."

The cables dropped away from the booster and rocketplane.

Okay, Dan said to himself. It's all on automatic from here on. He clasped his hands behind his back and crossed the fingers of both hands.

The automatic sequencer was counting off seconds now. Dan held his breath. Five . . . four . . .

"All systems go."

Two . . . one . . .

"Ignition."

A bloom of fire flared at the base of the booster and for an agonizingly long moment the big rocket stood unmoving, belching flame from its tail. Then it started to rise, slowly, slowly, like a sedate monarch rising from his throne.

"Go, baby!" somebody shouted.

"Up, up, and awaaay!"

The sound started to roll over them now, thundering waves of raw power reverberating through the blockhouse, rattling the bones and guts deep inside. Dan felt as if he were inside some enormous musical instrument with the whole bass register bellowing away madly.

The wall screen showed a billowing cloud of gritty gray smoke. Dan heard, "Pitch maneuver confirmed."

"She's on her way."

The launch director pushed his wheeled chair back, yanked off his headset, and got to his feet.

"Come on, boss, let's go out and take a look."

Dan followed the heavyset launch director out into the bright morning sunshine and squinted up at the smoky trail of the booster's exhaust, starting to kink slightly where the higher-altitude winds pushed it.

A bright flash of light startled Dan for an instant, until he realized it was the spaceplane's rocket engine lighting off.

From inside the blockhouse they heard, "Separation confirmed. Spaceplane engine ignition confirmed."

The launch director gave Dan a lopsided grin. "Okay. My workday's finished. Think I'll take my crew down to the motel and have a few beers."

MATAGORDA ISLAND, TEXAS

Dan had never seen Kinsky so worked up.

He had driven from the blockhouse back to Hangar A in the beat-up Chevy and rushed upstairs to his office, intent on calling Lynn Van Buren at the Caracas airport. But he saw from the expression on April's face that trouble was brewing.

Before he could ask, she said in an urgent whisper, "Len's in your office."

"Right," Dan said, remembering that he had told the public relations director to wait for him. "I'll handle it."

April gave him an *I hope so* expression as he opened the door and stepped into his office.

Kinsky was at the window, his shirt rumpled, his hair disheveled, his face blotchy red with anger. He whirled to face Dan.

"You launched it! Without telling me!"

Dan went to his desk but remained standing. "I didn't tell anybody except the launch crew."

"That's the dumbest goddamned thing I ever heard of!"

"Len, don't take it personally. I wanted to keep this as tight as possible so nobody from the government could step in and stop me."

"They're going to step in now, you crazy bastard."

"I might be crazy," Dan said calmly, trying to lighten up the mood, "but my parents had been married for years before I arrived."

Kinsky was not placated. "This is a fucking disaster! You can't go firing rockets off whenever you want to!"

Dan sat in his desk chair and tilted back slightly. "Len, you're my P.R. director, not my boss."

"What happens when the plane cracks up? You'll be finished! Wiped out!"

"It's not going to crack up. And there's nobody in the plane. She's flying on automatic."

"How are you going to land it, then?"

"On automatic. If we need to, we can control her remotely for the landing."

Kinsky paced across the office, shaking his head.

"She's not landing here," Dan said. "We won't have any trouble with the FAA about clearing airspace, if that's what's worrying you."

"You should have told me, Dan. I'm supposed to know these things."

"I didn't tell anybody except the launch team," Dan repeated. "Hell, even the service crew didn't know we were going to launch her. I told them this would be a static test."

"I should've been told," Kinsky muttered, still pacing. "How's it look, your P.R. director being kept in the dark. Nobody will believe that. They won't believe I didn't know."

"Len, it's on my head, not yours."

"The hell it is! They're going to lean on me. People expect me to know, Dan! I get paid to know!"

"You get paid to handle public relations for Astro Manufacturing Corporation." Dan tried to smile. "I think I've just handed you the juiciest news story of your career, Len. You'll have the media crawling all over you in a couple of hours."

"The hell I will," Kinsky growled. He stopped his pacing and glared at Dan. "I quit! I'm getting out of here."

Stunned, Dan heard himself say, "You can't quit. I need you more than—"

"I quit!" Kinsky shouted. "I'm out of here!"

"You're going back to New York?"

"No! It's none of your business where I'm going."

He banged the door open and practically ran out of Dan's office and past April's desk. Sitting with his mouth hanging open, Dan could hear the clanging of his footsteps echoing off the hangar walls out there.

April appeared in the doorway, looking apprehensive.

"What in the nine billion names of god got into him?" Dan asked, puzzled.
April shrugged. "Are you all right?"

"Yeah, sure," Dan said, still bewildered at Kinsky's rage. With a shake of
his head, he thought that Len would probably come back once he'd cooled off.

"I've got to talk to Van Buren in Caracas," he said to April, returning to
business. "No interruptions while I'm on the horn with her."

April nodded and returned to her desk. She saw Dan's private phone line
light up on the desktop phone console. Picking up her own phone, she quick-
dialed her home number, hoping that Kelly hadn't gone out.

Kelly Eamons was sitting on the unmade sofabed in the living room of
April's apartment, arguing with her partner Chavez on her cell phone.

"You've got to get back here, Kelly. The brass upstairs wants you back in
the office, pronto."

"We're getting close to a break, Nacho. I can feel it."

Chavez's image in the tiny cell phone screen looked like a darkening thun-
dercloud, though his voice was quietly intense. "You know what I'm feeling? I'm
feeling the hot breath from all the way upstairs right on the back of my neck."

"Hold them off for a few more days."

"We don't have a few more days. Upstairs wants you back here in the office. They say there's no budget for field work on this case."

"Nacho, there's something going on here. Really there is."

"You've got to get back here, Kelly. No fooling, kid."

"Give me two more days."

"I can't give you anything."

"Tomorrow, then."

"Today. I need to see your smiling face here in the office before close of
business today. *Comprende?*"

The apartment phone rang. Saved by the bell, Eamons thought. "I've got
to run, Nacho."

"You damned well better be running back here, partner. You're making
me look bad, you know."

"Right. See ya." Eamons clicked the cell phone off with her thumb and
picked up the phone from the table beside the sofabed.

"Kelly?" April's voice. She swiftly told the FBI agent of Kinsky's nearly
hysterical shouting at Dan.

"He said he's leaving. Quitting the company."

Eamons thought a moment, then asked, "How deep do you want to get
into this?"

"What do you mean?" April asked.

Shifting the phone to her other ear, Eamons replied, "Are you willing to
call Kinsky? Are you willing to go over to his apartment?"

Roberto saw that some kid had scrawled WASH ME across the dust-covered back doors of the panel truck he was using. With a sullen growl, he pulled the checkered bandana from the back pocket of his coveralls and erased the graffito. Better to have a clean spot. Somebody might remember a WASH ME message, identify the truck maybe.

Inconspicuous. Roberto tried to stay as inconspicuous as possible. His size worked against him, but he wore a workman's frayed coveralls and drove an ordinary pickup truck. Just another Hispanic working man, as far as anyone could tell. The region was full of Latinos, greasers, spics, dark-skinned men with moustaches and sad brown eyes, old before their time because they had to do the shit jobs that the Anglos wouldn't touch. Roberto seethed with anger as he drove southwest out of Houston. The multilane expressway petered into U.S. 59, a dual-lane highway as far as Victoria, where he would turn off onto route 77.

He kept to the speed limit. No sense getting picked up by some Texas Highway Patrolman who'd like nothing better than to run in a Latino ex-con. Cars, busses, even semi rigs roared past him. Roberto snarled inwardly at the rich guys in their fancy convertibles and sports coups. A blonde woman in a silver BMW zipped past him, chattering away on the cell phone she had plastered to her ear. Bitch! Roberto thought. I've stolen better cars than yours.

The cell phone was a good idea, though, he had to admit. He pulled his own out of the breast pocket of his coveralls and called Kinsky's office. He got Kinsky's voice mail: "I'm either out of the office or on another line at the moment. Please leave your name and number and I'll get back to you as soon as I can."

Roberto didn't leave his name or number. Not then, and not the next two times he called, either. He simply said, "It's me. I'm comin' down to see you. Be at your place eight o'clock."

By late afternoon, with the lowering sun lancing through the trees blurring by, Roberto began to think Kinsky wouldn't be in his office all day. I better go straight to his apartment, Roberto thought, before I check in at a fuckin' motel.

CARACAS, VENEZUELA

Except for the toilet facilities, it wasn't so bad living at the airport overnight, Van Buren thought. The Venezuelan soldiers patrolling around the area were stiffly polite; their captain—the only one who spoke English—was friendly and as helpful as possible. Two portable toilets had been wheeled up on the back of an army truck; one whiff of them and Van Buren avoided them as much as she physically could. She and her crew slept in the Citation's cabin: not all that comfortable but not bad once the army rolled up a portable generator to keep the plane's air conditioner going.

Van Buren talked with Dan Randolph every hour or so and was in constant touch with her launch crew back in Texas. She and her team worked from laptop computers networked to the command and control equipment stowed in the plane's cargo hold. Using the laptops, they could follow the spaceplane's flight as it orbited serenely three hundred miles up, circling the Earth every ninety-six minutes. That's the theory, Van Buren said to herself. We'll see if it works in the real world. Everything was happening in such a rush, they had to check out the laptops' links with the command system while in flight from Texas.

It'll work, Van Buren silently reassured herself. Then she added, God looks out for fools and drunks.

The plan was to bring the plane down on its sixth orbit, nine hours after its launch, which meant Van Buren's people would have to send a signal to the spaceplane's control system, ordering it to make a maneuver that would alter its orbit so that it would be aligned properly for a landing at Caracas.

Van Buren sat in a seat in the rear of the Citation's cabin studying the display screen of the laptop wedged behind the chair in front of her. Its keyboard rested on her lap and she had a headset clamped over her short mouse-brown hair.

Everything's going fine, she saw, peering at the readouts from the space-plane's internal sensors. They could get data from the bird only when it was within range of Matagorda or Caracas; Dan had refused to ask NASA to allow them to use the agency's TDRS satellites to relay the plane's telemetry signals.

As the signal from the spaceplane faded out over the horizon, Van Buren looked up at her cohorts, each of them bent uncomfortably over a laptop just as she was.

"One more go-round," she called out, "and we bring her home."

They responded with a faint smattering of approval. "Yahoo," was the strongest term she heard, and that sounded sarcastic, tired.

The incoming message light in the corner of her screen began to flash yellow. Van Buren touched a key and saw HQ: DAN RANDOLPH scroll across the bottom of the screen.

She clicked on his name and Dan's image appeared on the screen. He looked tired, too. He hasn't slept any more than I have, Van Buren realized.

"How's it going?" Dan asked.

"Fine," she replied. "Except for the Porta Potties. I don't think they'll last another whole day."

He grinned at her. "Bring the bird in and you can spend the night in the finest hotel in Caracas."

"On the company?"

"Sure. What's a little more red ink?"

In Washington, Senator Thornton awoke from a troubled sleep. She vaguely remembered a dream, something about Dan being in space, soaring weight-lessly away from her while she watched from the ground, helpless, her feet mired in mud or cement or something; it took all her energy to take a single step while Dan floated like a child's balloon farther and farther away from her.

She sat up in bed, reached for the TV remote control unit on the night table, and turned on one of the twenty-four-hour news channels.

More bombing in Israel. She saw a shattered building, bloody bodies sprawled in the street. Smoke and the chilling wail of ambulance sirens. Not waiting to find out who did what to whom, she clicked through a dozen channels.

Local news, children's cartoons, a cooking show, a pair of political analysts discussing the approaching season of primary elections. As if they know anything about it, Jane groused silently.

Nothing about the spaceplane. Nothing about Dan.

She went back to Fox News, turned up the volume, and went into the bathroom. Half an hour later she was showered, combed, dressed in a light blue skirted suit with a pale lavender silk blouse. Still not a word about Dan's spaceplane.

Out of sight, out of mind, Jane thought. Dan launched without telling anyone so the news media are snubbing him. Certainly NASA's not holding news conferences about a private space operation. Not this one, at least.

But that's going to end, Jane knew. The top item on her agenda this morning was to start the machinery rolling for a Senate investigation of Astro Manufacturing Corporation's unauthorized launch. She wasn't on the science committee but Bob Quill was, and he had agreed to call for the investigation.

The nerve of the man! Jane felt all the old anger rising within her. The unmitigated insolence. To launch that rocket without telling anyone, without informing the proper authorities. The gall. That iron-clad ego of his.

Yet, as she checked her lipstick in the mirror by the apartment's front door, she saw she was smiling. That's Dan, she told herself, her anger melting away. If only he'd let me help him. If only he'd play by the rules.

She frowned at her image in the mirror and shook her head. If he played by the rules he wouldn't be Dan Randolph. And you wouldn't still be in love with him.

"Idiot!" Jane snapped at the face in the mirror. Then she left her apartment, heading for a day's work in the Senate. As she went down in the elevator a new thought struck her. Dan's got to land the spaceplane sooner or later. The news media will be all over him then.

There were more than a dozen phone messages on Dan's computer screen that morning, most of them from news reporters. And April hadn't shown up for work. That's not like her, Dan thought. The kid's been ultrareliable. Then he remembered that she had left early yesterday afternoon. He considered calling her apartment, but the upcoming landing of the spaceplane drove that idea out of his mind almost before he had thought of it.

Still, it bothered him. With his computer Dan could run his office pretty well without her, and he could even get his own coffee down at the machine on the hangar floor. Instead, he decided to drive down to the blockhouse and follow the landing on the big screen there.

Before he could get up from his desk chair, though, Claude Passeau barged into the office with two other men right behind him, both of them wearing gray business suits, both looking like high school principals trying to seem tough. A pair of government bureaucrats, Dan realized: Tweedledum and Tweedledee.

"You betrayed me!" Passeau said without preamble. "You launched your rocket without permission. You did it behind my back!"

Dan realized the FAA administrator was speaking for the guys behind him. He smiled pleasantly as he got to his feet.

"I didn't need your permission, Mr. Passeau," Dan said. "I have all the permissions that are required for a launch, all signed on the dotted line by the various local, state, and federal agencies involved."

Passeau pointed a finger at him. "But you'll need FAA approval for landing that aircraft."

"And you won't get it," said Tweedledum, on Passeau's left.

"You're in deep trouble, Mr. Randolph," said Tweedledee.

Raising his hands placatingly, Dan said, "Gentlemen, you're assuming that the plane is coming down in U.S. airspace."

All three men stared at him.

"It's not."

"It's not? How can you—"

Stepping around his desk, Dan said, "Come with me, boys. I was just going over to the blockhouse to watch the landing from there."

Lynn Van Buren was thinking, We're coming up to the point in the reentry trajectory where the 01 vehicle failed. If we're going to have a problem, it'll be in the next few minutes.

"Reentry sequence initiated," called one of her team, sitting in the seat across the aisle from her.

Van Buren realized she was sweating in the plane's cramped cabin, even though the air conditioning was turned up full blast. It was a cloudy morning outside; tropical thunderheads were already building up over the mountains that blocked their view of the sea.

Good thing we're bringing her in now, Van Buren said to herself. Another hour or so and we'll have thunderstorms drenching the area.

"Reentry initiated."

She saw the readings for the temperature sensors on the plane's nose, underbelly, and the leading edges of the wings begin to climb steeply. The rising curves were all well under the red curve that marked maximum allowable temperature, though. So far so good, she thought.

"Pitch-up maneuver in ten seconds."

This is it, Van Buren told herself, her pulse quickening. This is where 01 failed.

"Confirm pitch-up maneuver."

On Van Buren's laptop screen the little icon representing the plane was smack on the curve that displayed the nominal reentry trajectory. No problems, she saw. Then she silently added, So far.

"Max heating."

"Max aerodynamic stress."

She held her breath. The plane was on automatic, guided entirely by its onboard computer. Van Buren knew she could override the onboard system if she had to, but she dearly wanted to avoid that. Let the bird come in on its own, she repeated over and over, like a mantra.

Something flashed. Van Buren winced and glanced out the plane's window. A deep roll of thunder grumbled out there. No! she screamed silently. Hold off! Let me bring the bird back to the ground first!

"Initiating bleed-off turns," said the woman in the seat in front of her. The spaceplane was starting a series of three wide turns to slow itself down enough for the landing.

"Mach eight and dropping."

"Turn one completed."

The Mach numbers were spiraling down. The worst is over, Van Buren thought as she stared at her screen. She's through reentry. No problems.

"Turn two completed."

Another flash of lightning. "Dammit, hold off!" Van Buren grumbled in a whisper. More thunder.

"Turn three completed."

A louder, sharper crack.

"That wasn't thunder," somebody sang out. Sonic boom, Van Buren knew.

"Can you see her?"

They had mounted a camera atop the Citation's fuselage and slaved it to the airport's radar. Van Buren clicked on the camera view.

"There she is!" she shouted. The plane was racing across the clouds, a double vapor trail streaking off its wing tips.

"Come on home, baby," someone said in a fervent prayer.

"Landing gear down."

"Speed two-ten...two-oh-two...one-ninety-six..."

Van Buren shoved her laptop under the chair in front of her, jumped to her feet, and rushed to the plane's hatch. It was slightly ajar. She pushed it all the way open and raced down the metal steps, ducked beneath the Citation's wing just in time to see the sleek silvery spaceplane touch its wheels to the runway with a screech and a puff of rubber.

The rest of the team piled out of the Citation as the spaceplane rolled to a stop well short of the end of the runway.

"Yahoo!" This time the cheer was heartfelt.

Rain began to spatter down. Big fat drops splashed all over them. The Venezuelan soldiers around the perimeter of their area stood in amazement as they watched this gang of loco gringos dancing in the downpour.

LEN KINSKY'S APARTMENT

After Kinsky's explosive flare-up with Dan, and her brief telephone conversation with Kelly Eamons, April had gone through the motions of work while her mind raced. Len couldn't have had anything to do with killing Joe Tenny or Pete Larsen. He just couldn't. But Kelly thinks he's involved in one way or another. And if he leaves the company, goes back to New York or someplace else, we won't be able to find out what he knows about all this.

After more than an hour of such worrying she phoned Kinsky's apartment, only to hear his answering machine's taped message.

"Len, it's April. You're not leaving without saying good-bye to me, are you?"

Kinsky picked up the phone. "April? I'm here."

"Len, you're not really leaving, are you?"

"Yeah. I've got to." His voice sounded shaky, nervous.

"Without saying good-bye?"

"I wish I could, babe. But I've got to split."

"Can't we at least have dinner together before you go?"

"I'm in a big rush, honey."

Taking a deep breath, April said, "I could get a pizza or something and bring it over to your place."

A long hesitation. Then Kinsky said, "Can you get here by five o'clock?"

"I'd have to leave the office early." She knew Dan would be upset; there was always so much for her to do, but Dan's attention was riveted on the space-plane's flight test. He probably won't even miss me until after the plane's landed in Venezuela, April told herself.

"Don't tell Dan you're coming over to see me," Kinsky said, halfway between pleading and demanding.

"Okay," said April. "I'll be there by five. What do you like on your pizza?"

"Doesn't matter, as long as you're with it."

April told Dan she was leaving early; he merely nodded and waved a hand at her, preoccupied with the flight test. As she drove to the ferry she phoned her apartment. No answer. Kelly's already left, she thought. She was about to try the FBI agent's cell phone number, when her own phone beeped.

It was Eamons. "Bad news, April. I've got to head back to Houston."

"Back to Houston? When?"

"Right now. I just finished packing my car and telling the motel that I quit."

"But I'm going to see Len Kinsky," April said, alarmed. "I'm going to his apartment."

Without hesitation Eamons said, "Call it off. I don't want you there without backup."

April pulled into the parking line for the ferry. This early in the afternoon, hers was the only car there. The ferry was at the pier, its ramp down, empty and waiting for cars. But nobody was in sight, and the chain was up, blocking access to the ramp.

"Kelly, if I don't get to Len this afternoon, we'll lose him."

"He's going to New York, isn't he?"

"I don't know. From what he said, maybe not."

"Doesn't matter. We can find him if we have to," Eamons said.

One of the ferry crew came out and took down the chain. Then he waved to April, gesturing for her to pull up into the ship.

Edging her Sebring over the bumpy ramp, April said, "You won't have any reason to search for him if he leaves here without talking to me."

"I don't want you to see him without me to back you up," Eamons said.

"Len's not dangerous. Not like that."

"Maybe not. But the people he might be connected to are probably killers. That's who he's running from, most likely."

Another ferry crewman ambled up to April's car, young, reasonably well groomed despite his tatty T-shirt, smiling pleasantly.

"I'll call you back later," April said.

"I'll be on the road, back to Houston," Eamons replied.

"I'll call you."

"Don't do anything foolish, April."

The crewman smiled at her. "Ticket, please."

April clicked off the phone, put it on the seat beside her, and pulled her wallet out of her handbag. She handed the young man her commuter ticket, noting that it was just about used up and she'd have to buy a new one in a few days.

"Sorry to make you wait," she said.

The young man's smile grew wider. "Got nuthin' else to do." He spread his arms and April turned around in her seat and saw that hers was the only car in the ferry.

Timing is everything, Kinsky told himself as he nervously folded his laptop and slipped it into its black carrying case. He had just closed out his bank account with the local Lamar bank and transferred the funds electronically to the account he kept with the Chase, in New York. Now he had a healthy balance on his platinum Visa card.

He still hadn't decided where he was going. Seattle, maybe. Or L.A. Someplace where Roberto couldn't track him down.

He had received four messages on his answering machine informing him that Roberto was on the road from Houston, coming down to see him in person.

"We gotta talk 'bout this launch you di'n't tell me about," Roberto had said in his last message. The tone of his voice chilled Kinsky to the marrow.

Roberto had said he'd get to Lamar around eight P.M. "Be in your apartment when I get there, man. I wanna have a face-to-face with you."

By eight o'clock, Kinsky thought, I'll be in a plane heading for Chicago, or maybe Canada. Toronto's supposed to be a reasonably livable city.

It was ten minutes before five. I ought to leave. I ought to get out of here right now. But April said she'd be here at five. She's coming here, to my apartment! Five o'clock. Maybe she'll come with me. Maybe the two of us could go to San Francisco. That'd be fantastic.

He shook his head. Stop being such a schmuck. Dan's probably told her to come over, try to talk me out of leaving. Then he thought, Or maybe she's working for them! Maybe she's coming here to make sure I stay long enough for Roberto to get here!

No, that couldn't be, he told himself. If she was working for them they wouldn't have needed me.

Still, he fidgeted nervously around the furnished apartment, eying the hideous clock on the living room wall, above the sofa: it was in the shape of some sort of fish, pale blue and ghastly.

At two minutes before five the doorbell chimed. Kinsky jumped nearly out of his skin. He tiptoed to the door and put an eye to the peephole. April!

He unlocked the door and invited her in with a majestic sweep of his arm, careful to look out into the hallway to see if Roberto or anyone else was lurking out there. Nobody.

While Kinsky bolted the door and rattled the security chain into place, April looked around, then put the big flat cardboard pizza carton she was holding down on the coffee table.

"I got mushrooms and pepperoni," she said. "I hope that's okay."

"Fine." He wiped his suddenly sweaty palms on his slacks.

April stood uncertainly in the middle of the living room. She was wearing a pale green blouse and tan slacks. Kinsky thought she looked beautiful.

"Have a seat," he blurted, gesturing to the sofa. "You want a beer to go with the pizza?"

Stepping around the coffee table and sitting primly at one end of the sofa, April replied, "Do you have anything nonalcoholic?"

He rushed to the kitchen and opened the nearly-empty refrigerator. "I got some frozen lemonade. Take me a minute to make it."

April said, "That's all right. I'll have a beer."

He grabbed two Michelobs from the fridge, then took down two tumblers from the cabinet over the sink. He brought them to the coffee table, where April had already opened the pizza carton.

"It isn't very hot," she said apologetically.

"That's okay." Kinsky poured her beer for her, his hand trembling slightly.

April turned to him. "Len, are you really leaving?"

"Yep."

"But why? Dan—"

"I've got to," he said. "I've just got to."

April looked squarely into his eyes. "What are you afraid of, Len?"

Her gold-flecked eyes were the most beautiful he'd ever seen, Kinsky thought. If only...

He heard himself ask, in a near whisper, "April, would you come with me? Wherever you want to go, the two of us."

"What kind of trouble are you in, Len?"

He nearly dropped his beer. "Trouble? What makes you think that I'm in trouble?"

"You're not mad at Dan. You're scared, I can see that. I can get Dan to help you. He's not angry at you."

She sees right through me, Kinsky thought. "I've just got to get away from here," he mumbled.

April reached out and touched his arm. "Len, please, let me help."

Shaking his head, "You don't want to get involved in this. Believe me."

"Len, I *am* involved in this. So is Dan. So is everybody in the company."

She's not doing this for me, Kinsky realized. She doesn't care about me. She's working for Dan, for the fucking company.

He took a swig of beer from the bottle, then put it down beside the untouched pizza. "You'd better go home, babe, or back to the office or wherever. Anyplace but here."

"Len, I want to help you," April repeated.

Jumping to his feet, Kinsky shouted, "Get out! Get out while you can."

"But Len—"

The front door burst open, the security chain splintering from its mounting on the wall. Roberto pushed into the living room, big-shouldered, scowling, menacing. April shot to her feet, shocked, thoroughly frightened.

Kinsky was stunned. "You're not supposed to be here until eight!" His voice sounded squeaky, terrified, even in his own ears.

"I got here early," Roberto said, kicking the door closed behind him. He glanced through the open door of the bedroom and saw Kinsky's travel bags on the bed. "Looks like a good thing I did."

Struggling to keep from shaking, Kinsky turned to April and said as evenly as he could, "You'd better go now, kid. I need to talk to him in private."

Before April could make a move, though, Roberto said, "Naw, you don' hafta go, *guapa*. Siddown."

April looked at Kinsky.

"Siddown or I knock you down. Both of you."

April sat. So did Kinsky, looking miserable, ashamed, and almost petrified with fright.

MATAGORDA ISLAND, TEXAS

Everyone in the blockhouse stood up and cheered when they heard Van Buren's radio voice announce, "She's on the runway. Mission completed."

Everyone except Passeau and his two gray-suited FAA superiors, although Dan thought he saw a trace of a smile on Passeau's face.

Turning from the blank wall screen toward the three FAA men with a big, satisfied grin, Dan said, "See? No problems."

Passeau said, "Score one for globalization, I suppose. But how do you propose to get your spaceplane back from Caracas?"

"By boat," Dan said cheerfully. "I've already got a freighter under contract for the job. The bird should be back here in a week, ten days at most."

The launch crew was shutting down their consoles, heading for the big steel hatch out into the Texas sunshine.

"You think you've pulled one over on us, do you?" growled Tweedledum as the technicians filed past him.

With an innocent hike of his brows, Dan replied, "No, not at all. I think I've managed to test my bird without breaking any of your regulations."

"You certainly swivel-hipped your way around the regulations," accused Tweedledee.

"I proved my theory," said Dan, much more seriously.

"Your theory?"

"The crash of our oh-one bird wasn't an accident. It was sabotaged."

"Sabotaged?"

"By who?"

"I'm hoping the FBI can figure that out," said Dan, heading for the blockhouse door. "In the meantime, I'm going to apply for permission to resume the flight tests of the spaceplane with a pilot aboard."

"You won't get permission, I guarantee it," Tweedledum snapped, following Dan outside into the warm sunlight.

"There's nothing wrong with the bird!" Dan insisted. "There's no flaw in the design and there aren't any flaws in the manufacturing. The oh-one bird was sabotaged, pure and simple."

Both Tweedledum and Tweedledee shook their heads in unison, like two metronomes.

Passeau stepped between them. "It's quite true that we haven't found any flaws in the design or the construction of the vehicle. Except for the valve in the forward attitude control thruster—"

"Which could *only* have been popped open by a spurious command signal," Dan interrupted. "Which is sabotage, nothing else."

For the first time, the two FAA men looked doubtful. Tweedledee asked his compatriot, "Do you think ...?"

"Hard to prove," said Tweedledum. "Impossible to prove, more'n likely."

Dan let it go at that, satisfied that he had at least planted a seed of doubt in their minds. Doubt is the beginning of wisdom, he told himself.

Dan went back to Hangar A while Passeau led his two superiors off to the engineering building. As he entered his outer office, Dan saw with some annoyance that April still wasn't at her desk. Where the hell is she? he grumbled inwardly. She ought to be on the job, or at least let me know she won't be in.

When he stepped into his private office, though, he saw another woman sitting in front of his desk, a welcoming smile on her heart-shaped face.

"Remember me?" asked Vicki Lee. "I'm working for *Aviation Week* now, thanks to you."

April had spent a sleepless, frightening night. She sat on the sofa in Kinsky's apartment, watching Roberto the way a trapped animal watches a stalking predator. Every time Roberto looked her way she shuddered inwardly. The man's eyes were rimmed with red, and April could see the rage that boiled just beneath his surface. He was like a powder keg, a bomb waiting to be triggered;

she could feel the danger radiating from every move of his big, muscular body. Kinsky sat on the sofa beside her, petrified, silent, unmoving, while Roberto tried time and again to put through a call on his cell phone, to no avail.

At one point he made a connection, only to frown with baffled frustration and yell into the phone, "Whachoo mean he ain't available? You make him available, see? You tell him I got a situation here and I wanna know what he wants me to do."

He listened, his scowl going darker, then shouted, "Hey, slow down. An' speak English, huh? I can't unnerstand when you jabber like that."

Another few moments of listening, then he switched the phone to his other ear and said impatiently, "Well, you tell him to call me and damn quick, too. I got two people here an' I gotta know what to do with them."

He flicked the phone off, muttering in Spanish.

Which gave April an idea. "I've got to go to the bathroom," she said, getting to her feet.

Roberto leered at her. "Okay. I go which you. Give you a hand, huh?"

As coldly as she could, April said, "Certainly not." And she headed for the bathroom, leaving Kinsky sitting inertly on the sofa.

Roberto followed a pace behind her. Her heart pounding, April closed the door firmly in his grinning face and turned the knob to lock it.

"Okay," his voice came through the thin door, "I give you some privacy. I'll wait right here."

Damn! April thought, pulling her cell phone from her purse. If I try to call Kelly he'll hear me and break in and stop me. The last thing she wanted was to give this big bruiser an excuse for violence. She knew where that would end.

She flushed the toilet, then ran water in the sink. Letting the faucet run, April pecked out Kelly's cell phone number and held her breath.

One ring. Two. Come on, April begged silently. Answer the phone, Kelly.

"Eamons here," Kelly's voice said.

Almost fainting with relief, April whispered, "Listen, don't talk." Then, leaving the phone on but blanking its little display screen, she slipped it back into her purse. She had no way of knowing how much the FBI agent would be able to hear, or how far from Lamar she had already driven. But she couldn't think of anything else to do.

She turned off the faucet and unlocked the bathroom door. Roberto yanked it open, surprising her so badly that she flinched away and almost tripped over the toilet.

"You wash your hands?" he asked, grinning. "In the res'rants they always tell us to wash our hands."

April had to squeeze past him to get back into the living room. Kinsky was still sitting as he had been; he hadn't seemed to move, hadn't seemed even to breathe.

"Why are you holding us here?" April said, as loudly as she dared. "What do you intend to do with us?"

Roberto shrugged, straining the fabric of his cotton work shirt. "That all depends."

"Depends on what?" April asked as she sat back on the sofa and placed her purse on her lap.

"Depends on this *fregado* big shot I'm tryin' to get on the phone." He cocked an eye at her. "Also depends on how nice you wanna be to me."

April ignored that. "What big shot?" she demanded. "Where is he?"

"Overseas someplace. Got a palace. Lots of women. Me, I got none. Only you." With one hand he pulled an armchair over to within inches of April and sat in it, so close she could smell the musky aftershave lotion he wore.

Don't give him a reason to do anything! April screamed silently to herself. She thought of screaming aloud for help, but decided that it would only trigger Roberto into violence. Save that for a last resort, she told herself. Play it cool. Keep him cool.

"He won't talk to you on the phone?"

Roberto made a sour face. "He got more assistants than a hotel manager. They say he's busy, can't be disturbed."

"He must be a very prominent man."

"He's a big shot, lemme tell you. I drive him aroun' when he's in Houston. Do special jobs for him."

"Special jobs?"

"Like tonight. I came here to talk to this one." He pointed to the lifeless-seeming Kinsky. "Di'n't espect you'd be here. Makes ever'thing diff'rent."

April jumped to a conclusion. "You knew Pete Larsen, didn't you?"

Roberto's eyes narrowed. "You a cop?"

"No. I'm Dan Randolph's executive assistant."

Roberto's scowl deepened. "Lemme see your purse," he said, grabbing it from her lap. He rummaged through, tossed the cell phone onto the floor without noticing it was on, flipped open her wallet and yanked out credit cards, driver's license, photographs.

April sat there, afraid to move, afraid to say anything. Roberto pulled her Astro Corporation identification badge from the purse.

"Looks like a cop's ID," he growled.

She realized he couldn't read. "That says Astro Corporation. See the big A with the rocket trail circling around it?"

He looked unconvinced, but he muttered, "No gun. No pepper spray, even."

"I'm not a police officer," April said.

"Maybe," Roberto replied warily.

A tap on the front door made him whirl around. The door, still slightly ajar because Roberto had broken the lock, swung inward to reveal an overweight middle-aged man in the tan uniform of the county sheriff's office. He had a heavy black pistol strapped to his hip.

"Pardon me," he said, stepping into the living room. "We got a phone report of a disturbance in here."

Roberto rose slowly to his feet, so menacingly that the policeman put his right hand on the butt of his nine-millimeter.

"Disturbance?" Roberto said. "We di'n't hear no disturbance."

Kinsky stirred to life, shrieking, "He broke in here! He's holding us against our will! He's going to kill us!"

Roberto shot him a murderous glance. "Tha's a fuckin' lie!"

But the police officer pulled his gun from its holster. "Maybe we'd better go down to the station and see what's going on here. He dipped his chin slightly to the two-way radio clipped to his epaulette. "Got a disturbance here. Request backup."

April wanted to cry, she felt so relieved.

WASHINGTON, D.C.

Senator Thornton relaxed in her high-backed leather swivel chair and tried to keep from smiling.

"He actually did it, then?" she asked. "The flight test was a success?"

Sitting before her desk was an associate director of the National Aeronautics and Space Administration. Her lantern-jawed angular face looked far from happy; her lean bony body was all uncomfortable angles. Her hair was dark brown, but with a reddish tinge that told Jane she was dyeing it. Two men sat flanking her. The older of them, from the Department of State, was dressed in a conservative dark blue suit and rep tie, his salt-and-pepper hair carefully styled, his rather bland face even more carefully expressionless. The younger man, who had a receding hairline, chubby pink cheeks, and wore a checkered sports jacket, was an analyst from the National Reconnaissance Office.

"He's done it all right," said the NRO analyst. "Our satellite imagery shows the spaceplane landed at the Caracas airport this morning. His people are already bringing up a mobile crane to haul it onto a flatbed trailer."

Turning to the State Department representative, she asked, "And the government of Venezuela hasn't protested?"

The man blinked slowly once, then answered, "Not a word from them. Apparently Randolph set up authorization to land at Caracas well beforehand."

How like Dan! Jane thought. That's why he wanted a contact in Venezuela. The sneaky sonofabitch. He runs rings around all of us.

The NASA woman spoke up. "I've checked with the FAA. They're furious with him, but Randolph seems to have obtained all the permits he needed to launch from Matagorda Island."

"So he's perfectly within his rights?"

The three of them glanced at one another, then nodded. Glumly, Jane thought.

"I'm not on the space subcommittee," Jane said to the NASA administrator, "so pardon me if this is a naïve question, but couldn't this spaceplane replace your old space shuttle? Wouldn't it be useful for carrying astronauts to and from the International Space Station?"

"It certainly would," the woman replied. "We were working on a similar vehicle several years ago but the program got axed."

"And yet Astro Corporation has one up and flying," said Jane.

The NASA administrator's square jaw went up a notch. "They killed a pilot testing it."

"Yes," Jane conceded. "That's true. Still, today's test was completely successful, wasn't it?"

The administrator understood Jane's implication. "Senator, he doesn't have to work within the government's regulatory environment," she said with some irritation. "I mean, NASA was forced to cooperate with the air force on our spaceplane project. Plus we've got a standing army of scientists, safety specialists, environmental protection people, even trade unions hanging onto us every step of the way. Not to mention congressional committees."

"I didn't mean to criticize," Jane said mildly. "I merely meant that NASA could buy working vehicles from Astro Corporation."

The administrator started to respond, took a breath, then said, "I suppose the agency could do so, if directed that way by Congress."

Jane thought she sounded more than a little resentful. They don't like having Congress tell them what to do. And they don't like giving up their monopoly on the technology, even worse.

The NRO man said, "Senator, we've heard some rumors that Astro's first flight might have failed because the plane was sabotaged."

Jane's brows went up. "I would think you'd know more about that than I would."

With a deprecating little smile, NRO replied, "Now, Senator, you know that the National Reconnaissance Office isn't allowed to run investigations into anything. That's the FBI's turf. Or CIA."

"Of course."

"But if the spaceplane was sabotaged, and if a foreign power or some terrorist group was involved..." He let the implication dangle.

Jane allowed herself a cool smile. "I think I should consult with the FBI about that, don't you? Or the Department of Homeland Security?"

The NRO analyst nodded. "Yes, I suppose that's what you should do."

Sitting up straighter in her big chair, Jane said, "Thank you all very much. This has been very informative for me."

They knew they were being dismissed. Murmuring their deep appreciation and perpetual willingness to be of assistance to her, the three of them left the senator's office.

As soon as the door closed behind them, Jane pecked at her phone console and began to arrange a flight back home to Oklahoma. I've got to see Dan, she told herself. I've got to make certain that this flight doesn't go to his head and he doesn't go tearing off on the wrong track.

Kelly Eamons had arrived at the Calhoun County sheriff's office near midnight, while the sheriff and four of his deputies were still questioning April, Kinsky, and Roberto.

At the station house they had put Roberto in one room, under guard, while they kept Kinsky and April in a separate little room. Kinsky, who had been absolutely silent every moment that Roberto had held them in the apartment, turned into a nonstop fountain of words once the police moved Roberto out of his sight.

April listened as Len repeated over and over his tawdry little tale: He needed extra money to pay his divorce lawyer. Roberto approached him at the motel bar one evening and offered to pay for information about what Astro Corporation was doing.

"Nothing terrible," Kinsky insisted. "Just information on how the company was doing financially, what programs we were pushing, when we'd launch rockets, that sort of stuff."

"Industrial espionage," April had prompted.

"Yeah, that's right," said Kinsky gratefully. "Industrial espionage."

"And when did you first meet him?" the sheriff asked.

Kinsky tried to determine the exact date, but the closest he could pin it down was "a couple months ago."

"Before Pete Larsen was killed?" April asked him.

Kinsky froze, stared at her with horror in his eyes. "You don't think..."

Nodding, April said, "And Joe Tenny, too."

"Oh my god," Kinsky groaned.

The sheriff looked very interested. "Well, was it before those deaths or afterward?"

"After," Kinsky said immediately. "I'm sure it was after. I would've never had anything to do with him if I thought…I mean, I wouldn't. I just wouldn't." He sank his head in his hands. April thought he was going to cry.

Eamons looked tired when she arrived, having driven halfway to Houston and back again. She asked to see April alone.

"Are you okay?" the FBI agent asked, once the sheriff had led Kinsky and his deputies out of the room.

"I'm all right," April said. "I was sure scared, though, until the police showed up."

"That was damned smart of you, turning on your cell phone. I couldn't hear much, but it was enough for me to call the sheriff's office and turn around and head back here."

"You might have saved our lives."

Agent Chavez arrived around two A.M. Kinsky was in the next room, still babbling his story to a pair of deputies and a stenographer. From what April could determine from the sheriff, Roberto had remained silent as a clam.

"Roberto Rodriguez. He's got a rap sheet in California," the sheriff told Chavez. "But he's served his time and he's clean now. There's really nothing we can hold him on, except Kinsky's claim that he broke into his apartment and held him and Miss Simmonds, here, against their will. Any two-cent lawyer'll get him out on bail soon's the county court opens in the morning."

Chavez turned to April. "Did he break into the apartment?"

Glancing at Eamons, April nodded. "You can check the front door. The lock's broken."

The sheriff nodded.

"Let me talk to the man," Chavez said to the sheriff. "Maybe he'll say more in Spanish."

"Hasn't said diddly-squat in English. Hasn't even asked for a lawyer."

Before Chavez could leave the room, April said, "He was calling somebody overseas. He tried several times, and whoever he talked to said the person would call him back."

The sheriff looked at Chavez. "We got his cell phone in my office, along with everything else in his pockets."

They headed for the sheriff's office, with April and Eamons trailing behind. The contents of Roberto's pockets were strewn on the sheriff's desk: a thin wad of folding money, some change, keys, a pack of tissues, a Swiss army knife. And the cell phone.

Sweeping the phone up from his desk, the sheriff asked the deputy sitting just outside his office, "Has this thing gone off?"

"Yes, sir, it surely did. 'Bout an hour ago."

"You answered it?"

"Yes, sir, I surely did."

"And?"

"Some foreign fella, sounded like. I asked him who he was and he hung up."

The sheriff's face flared into an angry red, but Chavez laid a hand on his shoulder. "We can trace it, I think."

"An overseas call?"

Chavez said quietly, "I think so. With a little luck."

LAMAR, TEXAS

As dawn was breaking, April dozed in Eamons's car while the FBI agent drove her back to her place. Once they were parked behind the apartment building, April roused herself.

"I've got to get to the office," she said drowsily. It took her two tries to get out of the car.

Eamons slipped an arm around her waist and led her into the building. "You go get yourself some sleep. You've been through a lot. Forget the office for today."

"But Dan—"

"I'll phone Dan," Eamons insisted as they stepped into the empty elevator. "You get some sleep. That's an order."

April smiled weakly at the FBI agent. Eamons saw her to her front door, hesitated a moment, then went back downstairs to the parking lot. Chavez had parked his gleaming black Chrysler next to her rental and was sitting on its hood, waiting for her. Once he saw her, he got down and ducked back into his car. Eamons opened the passenger-side door and slipped in beside him.

"Still smells new," she said.

Chavez smiled at her. "This is the first time I've driven her out of the Houston metro area. Didn't have time to requisition an agency car."

"You can put in for mileage."

"Yeah." Chavez glanced up at the apartment building. "She okay?"

"I think so. She was pretty scared by that Rodriguez character, and she's been up all night—"

"Who hasn't?"

Eamons nodded, a little groggily. "Yeah, some sleep would be a good idea."

"So what have we got here?" Chavez asked.

"You get anything out of Rodriguez?"

"*Nada.* He wound up asking for a lawyer."

"What about that phone call from overseas?"

"The office is working on it."

Yawning, Eamons asked, "So where do we stand?"

"Rodriguez will be arraigned for breaking and entering, maybe assault, too, as soon as the county court opens. He'll be out on bail thirty seconds later."

"We should put a tail on him. Monitor his phone calls, too. He's our only link to anything."

"Anything?" Chavez snorted. "What anything? All we've got on him is smoke and mirrors. Not a shred of proof."

"But if we keep a watch on him he'll lead us to whoever killed those two men and sabotaged Astro's plane."

"Try telling that to the boss."

"We can't let him get away! He's our only lead."

Chavez looked away from her. "The office isn't going to pay for a watch on him, not unless we can connect him to the rest of it."

"But we can't connect him to anything until we learn more about him: who he's talking to, who he's working for."

"Catch-22," Chavez said, with some distaste.

"I'll tail him," Eamons said. "He hasn't seen me."

Chavez started to shake his head. Eamons said stubbornly, "If the office won't pay for it, then I'll take my vacation time."

"And do it without backup, without electronic surveillance? Who d'you think you are, James Bond?"

Eamons slumped down in the car seat. Chavez thought she looked like a disappointed kid.

"Listen," he said to her, "we know Rodriguez works for a limo service. In Houston. We can check their trip logs and see who he's been driving. That might give us something."

"Check his phone calls, too," Eamons said grudgingly. "We can do that from the office."

Nodding, Chavez turned on the ignition. The Chrysler purred to life. "Let's turn your rental in. Then I'll drive you back to Houston."

"Aren't you sleepy?"

"You sleep and I'll drive. After a couple hours we'll switch off."

Eamons nodded. He's a good partner, she thought. Nacho is smart and dependable. Too damned cautious, but he's got a family to worry about. I can thumb my nose at the suits upstairs if I have to. He won't. But that's okay. He can play organization man and I'm the loose cannon. We make a good team.

Senator Thornton scrupulously avoided using taxpayers' money for her private purposes. Hiring a private jet and pilot to fly to Oklahoma cost a small fortune, but she paid for it with her own credit card. As soon as she got to the ranch she phoned the airstrip and asked for the pilot who usually flew her to Austin.

He showed up at the house half an hour later, while Jane was up in her room, using her desktop computer to check on the afternoon's rollcall votes in the Senate. She had paired her vote with Bob Quill's, so as far as the official record was concerned, she was present and voting.

A tap on her half-open door caught her attention. Turning, she saw Yolanda's swarthy face.

"That crop duster is downstairs waitin' on you," Yolanda said. She had been a family servant all her life, as had her mother before her. Jane smiled at her choice of words. Anyone who flew an airplane was a crop duster, as far as Yolanda was concerned.

As Jane came down the stairs the pilot was standing in the entryway, looking more like a field hand than anything else in his jeans and work shirt. He had flown ground-attack Warthogs in the Middle East, although it took several drinks to get him loose enough to start talking about his "tank plinkin'" days.

"Goin' down to Austin agin?" he asked.

"No, Zeb. Not this time. I want you to fly me to the Astro Corporation complex on Matagorda Island, first thing tomorrow morning."

"You're goin' there on a Sunday?"

"Yes," Jane said, thinking, Dan's office will be closed on Sunday. I'll be able to talk to him without interruptions, without lots of other people in the way.

Zeb's brows crinkled. "That's a private airfield, ain't it? I'll need their okay to land there. Might even be closed of a Sunday."

"I'll take care of that part of it, Zeb," said Jane. "You just pick me up here at seven tomorrow morning."

"Seven, right." He started to leave, then turned back with a shy smile. "Um, maybe I oughtta pack a breakfast?"

Jane nodded. "That's a good idea. Grapefruit juice for me, please."

The pilot left and Jane headed back upstairs thinking, I'd better not let Morgan know about this. He wouldn't understand why I've got to see Dan. She wondered if she truly understood herself.

LA MARSA, TUNISIA

From the rooftop garden of the hotel, Asim al-Bashir could see the ruins of Carthage shimmering in the heat haze. The broad Mediterranean sparkled in the afternoon sunlight; tourists and vacationers frolicked on the narrow beach; expensive yachts and cruise liners dotted the glittering water.

Sitting under the shade of the leafy trellis with a cool breeze wafting in from the sea, al-Bashir looked out at the ancient ruins from behind his polarized sunglasses. Once Carthage was a mighty power, he thought. Once warships from that harbor dominated the Mediterranean. Then came the Romans, the stolid, unimaginative, implacable Romans. No matter how many times Hannibal defeated them, no matter how many Roman armies were slaughtered, they came back with more, always more men, more armies, more battles until they wore Carthage into the dust. They demolished the city, house by house, temple by temple, stone by stone, until nothing was left standing. Then they sowed salt over the foundations so that nothing would ever grow there again. Destruction more savage and complete than a nuclear bomb would have caused.

The final humiliation was that the Romans themselves built a new city alongside the devastated site. It was the Roman ruins that al-Bashir stared at now.

That is the enemy we face, al-Bashir thought. Ruthless, implacable, capable of raising armies against us no matter how many time we batter them.

We cannot conquer them in battle, he knew. We must conquer them from within. Get them to destroy themselves. Make them use their greed and their power against each other. That is what we will do with their power satellite. That will be the first step in our eventual victory over them.

He heard footsteps clicking along the tiled walkway that led to this shady trellis. Nervous, quick steps. Turning, he saw the Egyptian walking toward him, short, spare, his white linen suit looking half a size too big for him, a broad-brimmed hat covering his bald pate.

Al-Bashir rose and nodded perfunctorily. "Salaam, my brother," he said, taking off his sunglasses.

The Egyptian removed his dark glasses, too, and sat on the white-painted cast-iron chair beside al-Bashir's without waiting to be invited.

"Salaam," he murmured.

"To what do I owe the pleasure of your visit?" al-Bashir asked, allowing the irony to show in his tone.

The Nine met as a whole only rarely, and even meetings between individuals were kept to a minimum. But with Western intelligence agencies' abilities to eavesdrop on telephone conversations and computer links, some face-to-face meetings were unavoidable.

"The others grow anxious about your operation with the satellite," the Egyptian said.

"I have spoken to most of them. Everything is proceeding well."

The Egyptian took off his hat and placed it on the table next to them. "This business of your operative being arrested doesn't alarm you?"

Al-Bashir allowed a small smile to curve his lips. "My operative is a chauffeur who was bribing an Astro Corporation employee for information. Nothing more."

"We understand he was the one who caused the explosion of their hydrogen facility."

"The Americans have no inkling of that."

"But if they have him in custody they might get him to talk."

With great patience, al-Bashir explained, "He was in custody for merely a few hours. He said nothing. He is now free. American police are very restricted in their methods of interrogation. We have nothing to fear on that score."

The Egyptian nodded his round, bald head. Watching him, al-Bashir thought that in another time, another era, this man might have been a royal scribe for one of the pharaohs instead of a planner of terrorist strikes.

The Egyptian licked his thick lips, then said, "In the meantime, Randolph has flown his rocketplane. The test was a success."

"All to the good," said al-Bashir.

"You believe so?"

With a small chuckle, al-Bashir said, "If Randolph had been wise enough to ask my help, I could have been of great assistance to him."

The Egyptian looked doubtful.

"My brother," said al-Bashir, "we *want* Randolph to succeed. We need him to finish his power satellite and put it into operation. Only then can we use it for our own purposes."

"To kill many Americans," said the Egyptian.

"Many. Including, perhaps, their president and many of their Congress."

"Really?"

"Really. And the best part is that they will never realize we have attacked them. They will believe the power satellite malfunctioned. They will want to blow that satellite out of the sky. Certainly they will tear Dan Randolph to pieces with their bare hands."

The Egyptian gaped at him in admiration.

Calmly, al-Bashir added, "It will also destroy the political career of the only presidential candidate who might pose some problems for us in the future."

"Indeed?"

"Morgan Scanwell," al-Bashir said. "Him we will not kill, however. He will be humiliated, ruined."

"And Randolph?"

"The mobs will tear down his buildings in Texas." Turning to look back at the ruins of Carthage, he added, "Perhaps they will even sow salt on the site of Astro Manufacturing Corporation."

MATAGORDA ISLAND,
TEXAS

Never let a woman leave a toothbrush in your bathroom, Dan reminded himself as he leaned over the gunwale of the ferry and breathed in the fresh salt-tanged air. It's like allowing the Marines to establish a beachhead on your territory.

The sun was going down as the last ferry of the day chugged across the bay toward Matagorda Island. Dan had spent the previous night and all this Saturday with Vicki Lee, who had come to do an in-depth interview with him, because of the successful flight test of the spaceplane. "In depth," Dan muttered to himself, with a grin. Vicki was fun to be with and energetic in bed. But when she suggested she stay overnight at Dan's apartment instead of returning to the hotel suite she'd rented in Lamar, every alarm bell in Dan's nervous system started clanging.

So he drove her all the way back to Lamar in his newly retopped Jaguar. The hotel there wasn't all that much better than the Astro Motel on the island, but Dan was glad she had decided to stay in Lamar. They spent the night together and most of the warm, humid Saturday languidly poking around the town's meager shops. They had an early dinner in her room—in bed, actually—and then Dan had kissed Vicki good-bye and headed home. Hope I didn't screw up the interview, he said to himself as he watched the sun sink into the scrub pines of the island. *Aviation Week* is the most important source in the industry. Well, he thought, remembering Vicki's passionate panting, at least I screwed the interviewer pretty well.

The hangar was dark and empty by the time he pulled into his parking slot. His apartment was clean and shipshape. Tomasina took advantage of my absence, Dan thought. God, she even stocked the fridge he saw as he took out a cold can of ginger beer. As he sat at his desk and booted up the computer he debated adding a slug of brandy to the spicy, fizzing soda. What do the Aussies call that? The answer came to him as his screen lit up: brandy and dry.

But as soon as he saw the list of messages waiting for him he forgot about a drink. Jane Thornton's name was third on the list. He called up her message before any of the others.

She was at the ranch in Oklahoma, from the looks of it: relaxed denim shirt, reddish-brown hair pinned up off her neck.

"Dan, I need to talk to you in private. I'll be flying down from the ranch tomorrow, leaving here at seven. Could you have your airstrip ready for me to land there, please? Don't call back unless there's some problem with that. Otherwise, I'll see you when I land at your complex."

That was all. About as warm as a form letter from an insurance company, Dan thought. But so what? Jane's coming here, on a Sunday. Tomorrow!

He jumped to his feet and headed for the tiny bathroom. I'd better take a good long shower, Dan told himself.

Feeling like a teenager waiting for his date to appear, Dan paced along the base of the Astro airstrip's pocket-sized control tower as he watched Jane's single-engine plane turn into its final approach, sunlight glinting off its canopy. The guys in the tower had told him the plane was a turboprop TBM 700: fast, pressurized for high-altitude flight, yet with a landing speed low enough to slip into small landing fields.

Engine yowling, the low-winged plane touched down gently on the concrete strip and then taxied slowly to a stop by the tower. Dan fidgeted impatiently, waiting for the hatch to open and Jane to appear. Don't be stupid, he warned himself. She's here on business, nothing else. It's over between us, as far as she's concerned.

But when Jane ducked through the hatch and stepped onto the plane's wing he forgot all that. She was wearing a flowered Western shirt and snug-fitting jeans. Dan raced over to help her down to the concrete apron.

"Hi! Good to see you."

Jane smiled at him. "You can let go of me now, Dan."

"Oh. Yeah." He took his hands from her waist.

The pilot squeezed through the hatch and dropped lightly to the ground. Dan tossed him a set of car keys, then pointed to the company van parked by the control tower next to his own Jag.

"There's a motel about three miles down the road," Dan told the pilot, pointing. "They're expecting you. Whatever you want is on the house."

The pilot thanked him and, after getting a nod from Jane, went to the van. Dan escorted Jane to his Jaguar and drove her, with the car's newly installed top down, to Hangar A.

"I've never been here before," she said, over the rush of the wind.

"I know."

"It looks very quiet."

"Sunday. Day of rest for most of the company."

"I see."

Glancing at her as they neared the hangar, Dan said, "You ought to come for a launch. Plenty of activity then."

"That's what I want to talk to you about," Jane said, looking very serious.

Dan led her into the cool shadows of the empty hangar and up the stairs to his office.

"No one's here?" Jane asked as they went along the catwalk to his office.

"Not a soul." Niles Muhamed was in Hangar B, Dan knew, getting his team ready to pick up the 02 plane when it arrived on the freighter at Galveston. But from inside his office, the complex looked almost totally deserted.

"Just you and me, Jane, practically alone on a tropical island."

She took the chair in front of his desk. "Semitropical, at best," she said.

Dan perched on the edge of the desk in front of her. "That's what I need, a geography lesson."

"Dan, be serious. Please."

He didn't feel serious. He felt like pulling her up from the chair and waltzing across the office with her in his arms. But he said, "Okay. What do you want to talk about?"

"There's a rumor floating around Washington that you believe your first spaceplane was sabotaged."

So that's it, Dan thought. Strictly business.

"I'm positive it was," he said. "My chief engineer was murdered a few days afterward, and they made it look like an accident."

"What proof do you have?"

"None. Not a damned thing. But one of the reasons I flew the backup bird was to prove that there's nothing wrong with the spaceplane's design. She flies fine when nobody messes with her."

"That's pretty thin ice, Dan."

"I know. Nobody believes me. I can't even get the double-damned FBI to take it seriously."

"I see," Jane said. Then she fell silent.

Dan waited a few moments, wondering what to do next. At last he asked, "Is that all you came down here to talk about?"

"No. Not really."

"What else?"

"You."

"Me?"

"And Morgan."

"Him again," Dan grumbled.

"Dan, he's the only man in America who can make this country energy independent."

"And rain makes applesauce."

"It's true!"

Trying to keep his feelings under control, Dan said, "Jane, Scanwell may be the only candidate who wants to make America energy independent, but—"

"He needs your help."

"I am helping him! I'd appreciate a little help coming my way, too."

"We're working on that. I've introduced the bill in the Senate to help raise financing for you."

"Jane, I'm tightrope-walking on a shoelace here."

Despite herself, she giggled. "You always did have a way with words, Dan."

And he grinned back at her. "One of my many talents."

More seriously, Jane said, "This test flight of yours has created a lot of enemies. NASA thinks—"

"I know. They think I'm a loose cannon."

"Worse, Dan. They think you're a threat to their program."

"That's fine by me."

"But they'll oppose you every inch of the way."

"So what? I don't need their help."

"You don't understand," she said. "Government regulatory agencies like the FAA are going to need expert advice about your plans to fly your spaceplane again. Who do you think they'll turn to?"

Dan knew the answer.

"And when you approach private investors for funding, who will they ask for an opinion?"

"The double-damned space agency," he growled.

"Exactly."

"Well I don't have to worry about any of that if I let Tricontinental buy into my company. Or Yamagata."

"We can't have that!" she said sharply.

" 'We'? You mean Scanwell."

"Yes. Morgan can't point to you as part of his energy-independence program if you're owned by a multinational oil company or a Japanese corporation."

"Scanwell won't be able to point to me at all if I don't get some funding damned soon. I'll be underwater."

"We're trying, Dan. But you've got to cooperate."

"I *am* cooperating! I'm pushing as hard as I can to get the powersat up and running."

"But you can't thumb your nose at the FAA the way you just did. You can't turn NASA into an enemy."

"Double-damn it to hell and back!" Dan exploded. "That test flight generated more publicity for the idea of energy independence than anything Scanwell's done! Hell and damnation, I'm even getting nibbles of interest from potential investors, thanks to that flight."

"It's not the kind of publicity we need," Jane said. "It makes you look like a hero, I know, but it's creating more enemies than friends for you."

"You mean it's stealing the spotlight from Scanwell."

"No, that's not what I mean."

"He's making speeches and I'm *doing* something. Maybe *I* ought to run for president!"

Looking up to the ceiling as if seeking divine assistance, Jane said, "Dan you simply don't understand the way politics works. You have to make friends, not enemies."

"I'm not a politician, Jane. I'm just a businessman trying to keep my company from going under."

"You can be a great help to Morgan if you'll just—"

"I don't want to help Scanwell or anybody else!" he snapped. "All I want is to get that powersat operating."

"And the future of the country?"

"The country's future'll be a lot brighter once we have a power satellite showing that we can bring in gobs of energy from space."

"Dan, if you'd only work *with* Morgan instead of running off on your own tangent."

"What good would that do me?" he asked.

Her head sank and for a moment Dan thought she was crying. But then she looked up at him again, dry-eyed. "We could get him elected president, Dan. He's a great man. He could be a great president."

Anger flared deep inside him, but Dan fought to keep it under control. "Look, I like Morgan Scanwell. I really do. He might make a pretty decent president if he can get himself elected. But that's his problem, not mine. I've got problems of my own, plenty of them."

"I know that, Dan, but can't you see that—"

"Jane, can't you see that you're the only person in the world I care about?"

Her breath caught in her throat, then she shook her head slowly. "For what it's worth, Dan, I feel the same way about you."

He felt as if he'd been dropped out of an airplane.

"I wish I didn't," Jane went on, softly, almost as if talking to herself. "You're nothing but trouble for me. But I've never stopped loving you. Even when I was furious with you, I knew I loved you."

"I love you too, Jane," he heard himself say, his voice hollow with wonder.

She rose to her feet, facing him eye to eye. "What are we going to do about it?"

Dan wrapped her in his arms and kissed her. She melted into him and it was if all the years, the separation, the arguments, had disappeared. After a long, long breathless time he slipped his arm around her waist and guided her toward the office door.

He saw the questioning look in her eyes. With a lame grin, he said, "Would you believe that my apartment is just down the catwalk?"

She smiled back at him, her head nestled on his shoulder. "Yes. Knowing you, I'd believe it."

Dan felt very grateful for Tomasina.

They made love languidly, as if they'd never been apart, as if there was nowhere else on Earth that they had to be, no one else that concerned them. But at last, as late afternoon sunlight lanced through the apartment's window, Jane sat up in bed.

"I'm afraid I'll have to get back," she said.

"No," Dan whispered. "Stay with me."

"I wish I could, Dan."

He nodded reluctantly, knowing the moment was gone. "Okay. I'll phone the motel and tell them to start your pilot back to the airport."

She gave him an impish look. "Not yet."

"No?"

"Do you still like long showers?"

He took his hand away from the telephone and got to his feet. "I'll turn on the water," he said, padding toward the tiny bathroom. The shower's barely big enough for one, Dan thought. This is going to be fun.

And it was. Slippery naked bodies slathered with soap suds. Dan banged his elbows on the tiled shower walls more than once, cracked his knee hard enough to make him yowl with pain, but it didn't matter, nothing mattered except that Jane was with him and they were together and none of the rest of the world mattered at all.

Until the water at last began to run cold.

"It's just a small hot-water tank," Dan apologized.

"It's time to go," Jane said, stepping out of the shower stall, reaching for a towel.

Dan patted her dry as slowly as he could, but at last she went back to the bedroom and began picking up the clothes they had strewn across the floor.

Once he was dressed Dan phoned the motel and told Jane's pilot they would meet him at the airstrip in half an hour.

As they walked out into the humid warmth of the late afternoon, Dan asked, "What happens now, Jane?"

With a moment's hesitation she said, "I've got to get back to Washington and you've got to make your power satellite work."

"And Scanwell?"

As if she hadn't heard him, Jane said, "I'll get to the head of the FAA for you. I don't think I can get NASA on your side, but I can at least keep them from publicly criticizing you."

"And Scanwell?" he repeated.

She opened the passenger-side door of the Jaguar and got into the car. Dan walked around to the driver's side without taking his eyes off her.

Once he had started the engine, Jane said, "If you don't go off thumbing your nose at the FAA again, you can be a great help in getting Morgan elected."

"That's not what I mean and you know it," he said.

She did not reply. Dan put the Jag in gear, backed out of the parking slot, headed toward the airstrip.

"Jane, how involved with Scanwell are you? I mean, if we're going to—"

"I'm married to him," she said, looking straight ahead. "He's my husband."

Dan felt as if a ton of ice water had just been poured over him. "Married?" he heard himself yelp.

"Almost two years now," she said, her voice so flat and even that he knew she was struggling inside herself. "He's so straight-laced . . . well, it seemed like a good idea at the time."

"Son of a motherless bitch," Dan muttered fervently.

"We've kept it a secret. Not even our closest aides know. Half my power base in Washington would disappear if they thought of me as Morgan Scanwell's wife."

Dan kept his eyes on the road, his grip tight on the steering wheel.

"You left me, Dan. You went off to Japan."

"I came back."

"But not to me. You came back and started this company of yours. You were more interested in outer space than in me."

"I thought you were more interested in being a senator than in me."

She turned toward him at last. "We're a couple of prime fools, aren't we?"

"I guess we are." He thought a moment. "Do you love him? I mean, you must have, to marry him. But now . . . ?"

"I thought I loved him. I thought the world of him. I still do. He's a great man, Dan. A wonderful man in so many ways. He—"

"Uh, you don't have to tell me how wonderful he is," Dan grumbled. "The question is, where do we stand, you and me, right here and now?"

For the first time since he had first met her, so many years ago, Jane looked uncertain, distraught, close to tears.

"I don't know, Dan. I can't divorce him, not while he's campaigning for the White House."

"And if he wins, you'll be his First Lady. Christ." Dan felt like driving off the road, crashing through the thicket of scrub along the shoulder and plunging into the turbid water of the bay that lay beyond.

"Give me time, Dan," she pleaded. "Let me try to work this out. It isn't easy."

"You're telling me?"

Jane shook her head. "I wish I didn't love you."

"Don't say that."

"I don't mean it. Not that way."

He turned down the little side road, saw the control tower's glass bubble glinting in the setting sun.

"What are we going to do?" Dan asked. "What in the seven circles of hell are we going to do?"

"I don't know, Dan. Not yet. I have to think it out, sort it out in my head."

Anger simmered inside Dan as he skidded the convertible to a stop in a cloud of dust and crunching pebbles.

Jane put a hand on his arm. "Whatever happens, Dan, I love you. Remember that."

"But you're going back to *him*."

"I'm going to my work in Washington. Morgan's in Austin, when he's not off campaigning."

"You'll be with him."

"I'll have to be."

"And us?"

"Just don't do anything crazy, Dan. Get your satellite working, but don't antagonize the FAA or anyone else. And don't sell out to Tricontinental or Yamagata."

"Yeah. Right." He wanted to lean his head on the steering wheel. Or maybe blow his brains out.

HOUSTON, TEXAS

Special Agent Chavez did not like to be summoned upstairs to the field director's office. As far as Nacho was concerned, the people upstairs could go their way and play their games any way they wanted, he didn't care. As long as they left him alone.

But on this Monday morning he and Kelly Eamons rode the elevator up from their own offices to the executive level.

"Look at their carpeting," Eamons whispered as they walked down the corridor to the director's suite.

"We've got carpeting downstairs," Chavez whispered back.

"Not this thick."

The director was new to the job, having been promoted from the Seattle office. She was an African American from Philadelphia, and she had a reputation for being a tough, demanding bureaucrat who worried more about looking good to Washington than anything else. Neither Chavez nor Eamons had met her, except at the formal ceremony when she took over the regional office.

She sure looks tough, Chavez thought as the receptionist ushered them into the director's office. A little bantamweight sitting behind a big government-issue desk with a pugnacious expression on her dried-up face. Her skin was as dark as the office's mahogany furniture. The desk was uncluttered, actually bare except for a phone console, a slim display screen, and a wireless mouse sitting on a pad that bore the FBI's emblem. On the wall behind her, though, he saw photographs of the woman with Philadelphia Eagles football players. Tough, all right, Chavez thought; Eagles fans are killers.

She didn't get up from her desk chair when Chavez and Eamons came in, merely gestured to the leather-covered armchairs in front of her desk. No offer of coffee or chitchat, either.

"Washington just got a request for information from Langley—"

"The CIA?" Eamons blurted.

The director fixed her with a hard stare. "Worse. Homeland Security. The hotshots want to know what we're doing with Astro Manufacturing Corporation."

Eamons glanced at Chavez, who slipped automatically into stiff officialese as he replied, "We've been investigating the possibility that a fatal accident and an apparent suicide were actually murders."

"What jurisdiction do we have?" the director asked.

Chavez unconsciously tugged at his shirt collar. "Um, these incidents might be linked to the crash of an Astro experimental spacecraft," he replied.

"The spaceplane might have been sabotaged," Eamons added.

"Sabotaged?" the director snapped. "By who?"

Before Chavez could respond, Eamons said, "Possibly by terrorists."

The director steepled her stubby fingers in front of her face. "That explains the hotshots' interest."

Both agents waited for the next question.

"Well, what have you come up with?"

"Not a whole lot," Chavez said. "We have one lead, a man who allegedly bribed an Astro employee for information about the company's operations."

"And?"

"There isn't enough to hold him. He's been charged with breaking and entering, and simple assault. He's out on bail."

"Should we be surveilling him?"

"He's all we've got to go on, so far," Chavez admitted. "We were going to check his contacts here in Houston; he's employed as a chauffeur by a limo service."

"I checked him out yesterday," Eamons said.

"Sunday?" The director looked almost startled.

With a cheerful shrug, Eamons said, "The regular dispatcher doesn't work Sundays and his assistant was more helpful than the regular guy would've been. Rodriguez—that's the suspect's name, Roberto Rodriguez—he's been mainly driving executives of Tricontinental Oil."

"Does Tricontinental have any connection to Astro Corporation?" the director asked.

Chavez said, "We could ask Astro's CEO, Dan Randolph. He's the one who came to us in the first place with the story about his plane crash being caused by sabotage."

Turning again to Eamons, the director said, "Get a list of the Tricontinental people this Rodriguez has been chauffeuring."

"I've already got it," Eamons said. "I can flash it to your computer from my desk."

"Do that," said the director. "Now. I need that list before I can figure out how much to tell Washington."

Dan had slept only fitfully, dreaming tangled dreams of Jane and Scanwell and some dark faceless lurking monster looming over him. He got up as the sun was rising, miserable and bewildered and totally unsure of what to do about Jane.

Married. She's married to him. In secret. They don't want anybody to know. But she told me about it. It can't be much of a marriage; they're hardly ever together. But she's married to him. She has sex with him.

And you have sex with other women, that sardonic voice in his head reminded him. Hell, you were boffing Vicki Lee the night before Jane came down to see you.

That doesn't mean anything, he insisted. There's no attachment there, no relationship. But she *married* Scanwell; they're husband and wife.

Arguing with himself, Dan dressed and walked down to his office hours before the official opening time. He had barely settled at his desk when April popped her head through his doorway.

"Breakfast?" she asked, as if everything were normal. "Coffee?"

"Where were you Friday?" Dan asked.

"Didn't you get my phone message?" she said, stepping fully into the office. "I asked Kelly to call you."

"Kelly?"

"Eamons. The FBI agent."

Dan shook his head. "What happened?"

She sat before his desk and went through the story about Kinsky and Roberto and the police.

"Len was selling information to this guy?" Dan asked, unable to accept the idea.

April nodded solemnly. "He's a scary guy, too. Very scary."

"The cops have him now?"

"He's out on bail."

"Great." Dan studied April's face for a moment, thinking, If she's scared, she sure doesn't look it. "So where is Len now?"

"I don't know. Probably on a plane going someplace far from here."

"He's that scared, huh?"

"He was petrified."

"What about you? Should we get you some protection?"

April hesitated. "I don't think Roberto...well, maybe." She shuddered.

"Okay," Dan said, with a grimace. "Get O'Connell from security on the phone for me. And I need to talk to Gerry Adair this morning."

She nodded. "Anything else?"

Dan hesitated a moment, then said, "If Len's really gone, I'll need somebody to handle public relations around here."

"I can call up a few headhunters—"

"Nope. Can't afford 'em." Dan pointed a finger at her like a pistol and said, "You can handle P.R."

"Me?" She looked shocked.

"You. If Len could do it, you can. You're a lot brighter than he is."

"But I don't know anything about it!" April protested.

Spreading his hands, Dan said, "It's simple. When reporters ask you for information, you give 'em our canned answers. Len has a file full of prerecorded statements. If you get a question that's not already covered, I'll help you write a response."

"But—"

"When we want to issue a news release, you've got Len's files, all his contacts, names, affiliations, phone numbers, e-mail addresses. Nothing to it."

April looked dubious.

"You can do it, kid. P.R. is based on contacts, and Len built up a pretty good list."

"There must be more to it than that," April said.

"Nope," said Dan. "I'll even give you a raise. A small one."

She laughed. "Well, I'll try. But I don't know about this."

"You'll be fine. Start a whole new career path for you."

She shook her head warily, but stopped protesting. "All right," she said slowly. "Is there anything else?"

Dan shook his head. "Not unless you can find me a billion dollars someplace. And figure out how I can keep the wolves from the door."

"You mean creditors?"

"I was thinking of Tricontinental and Yamagata, but, yeah, we owe a lot of people a lot of money, don't we?" Despite himself, Dan laughed.

"Speaking of those particular wolves," April said, rising from her chair, "you have calls waiting since Friday from Mr. Yamagata and Mr. al-Bashir."

"Terrific," said Dan.

None the worse for the hours he'd spent at the Calhoun County sheriff's station, Roberto reported for work at the limo service's garage Monday morning. His only assignment was to pick up Asim al-Bashir, arriving just before noon at Houston International Airport.

The head dispatcher, a crusty old African American, eyed Roberto suspiciously. Shaking his head, he said, "You must be some kinda special, this A-rab guy pays to have you sittin' 'round all mornin' just so's he can have you drive him in from the airport. He won't take nobody else."

Roberto's only reply was a grunt.

"What you doin' with that A-rab, make him want you so bad?"

Roberto thought about lifting the shriveled old man off his feet and shaking him like a dried-out gourd, but the dispatcher had the sour courage that comes with age. He knew he was going to die soon, anyway, so he wasn't afraid of much. Besides, the other drivers hanging around would jump in, and Roberto couldn't afford to get himself in trouble with the cops again while this B&E rap was hanging over his head in Calhoun County.

With a glimmer of a teasing grin, the dispatcher said, "I hear them A-rabs a bunch of fags. This A-rab romancin' you, Roberto, my man?"

Roberto snatched the clipboard out of the old man's hand and snapped it in two, then wordlessly handed the broken pieces back to the stunned dispatcher and walked away.

WASHINGTON, D.C.

An unmarked sedan carried Jane from Ronald Reagan National Airport to her apartment building off Dupont Circle, near Connecticut Avenue and Embassy Row.

Being a United States Senator has certain prerogatives. A member of that exclusive, one-hundred-member club can phone the director of Central Intelligence from her private plane on a Sunday evening and get the man to leave his dinner table to answer your call. A U.S. Senator can phone the director of the FBI and ask her to cooperate as fully as possible with the CIA in an investigation of the Astro Corporation's spaceplane crash.

But as she dressed for her working day on Capitol Hill in her tastefully luxurious apartment, Jane realized how quiet the place was, how empty and lonely. Her swirling thoughts kept coming back to Dan, his vigor, his passion, his drive. It was never quiet around Dan, never predictable or routine. Even the thing that had driven them apart, his insane zeal for creating this power satellite, was magnificent, bigger than life. And now it's brought us back together, at least for a moment.

It can't be, Jane thought as she rode the empty elevator down to the garage where her car and driver waited for her, barely hearing the muted music whispering from the speaker in the ceiling. Dan and I simply can't be together. I can't hurt Morgan like that. It would destroy him if I asked for a divorce. It would ruin his chances for the White House.

It had all been planned so cleverly, so completely. Once Morgan had won the party's nomination they would announce their marriage, even go through a formal ceremony. Tremendous publicity. And she would be at his side through the whole grueling campaign. Every minute. Every step of the way to the White House.

I couldn't leave him once he's president, Jane thought. No one's divorced a president. Not even after he's left office. As her sedan took her to the Senate Office Building, Jane smiled bleakly to herself. But if ever a First Lady does divorce a president, it would be over Dan Randolph.

Tell me what happened," al-Bashir snapped, once Roberto pulled the limo away from the airport terminal.

Grudgingly, Roberto explained the fiasco with Kinsky and April.

"Randolph's secretary?" al-Bashir asked. "She was there? She saw you?"

"Yeah," Roberto said, glancing at the Arab's round, brown face in his rearview mirror. "She's a piece, man."

Al-Bashir glared at him. "And you say the FBI was involved?"

"Some Chicano, big guy, he came in while they were questionin' me. Talked to me in Spanish, big deal."

The FBI, al-Bashir mused. This could be serious.

"And what of your contact, this man Kinsky?"

Roberto shrugged his heavy shoulders. "Dunno. From the looks of him, though, he's runnin' fast. Might be halfway to China by now."

How typical of a cowardly Jew, al-Bashir thought. For several moments he remained silent, thinking swiftly while Roberto maneuvered the gleaming white limousine through the crowded freeway traffic.

I'll have to get rid of this oaf, he told himself. I'll get the Tricontinental personnel people to find a job for him back in California. Tricontinental has a rehabilitation program; they'll be happy to add him to their list of good deeds. I can't afford to have him near me; he's too blunt an instrument for what needs to be done now. Besides, he thought, I can infiltrate Astro Corporation myself now, and Dan Randolph will welcome me with open arms. Perhaps his secretary will, too. The thought made al-Bashir smile happily.

Are you ready to fly the oh-two bird?" Dan asked.

Gerry Adair turned toward him. Then he grinned. "Is the Pope Catholic?"

They were standing side by side in Hangar B, where Niles Muhamed was sternly directing his crew as they carefully—tenderly, Dan realized—hoisted the spaceplane off the flatbed that it had been tied to and deposited it safely on the hangar's concrete floor. The air rang with Muhamed's deep-throated shouts and warnings. He even drowned out the electrical whine of the overhead crane.

"You're not rusty since the crash?"

"I've been in the simulator every day, Dan. I'm as ready as I can be."

"Good," Dan said, nodding. "Stay sharp."

"When d'you think we can launch?"

Dan scratched his chin. "Couple weeks. Maybe sooner. The legal eagles are working on clearances from six hundred different double-damned government agencies."

"Will we land in Venezuela again?"

Dan hesitated. "I don't know yet. Maybe, maybe not."

Adair started to reply, but Muhamed strode up to them and jabbed a thumb over his shoulder at the spaceplane sitting now on its three landing wheels. The flatbed truck ground its gears and started out of the hangar with a roar and a stench of diesel fumes.

"Okay, flyboy, you said you wanted to check out the cockpit," Muhamed said.

Adair nodded once and sprinted toward the spaceplane like a kid heading for his Christmas presents. Dan saw that the crew had rolled up a set of metal stairs.

"Don't know why he's gotta go sit in the cockpit," Muhamed groused. "The bird ain't goin' nowhere."

Dan grinned at him. "He's a pilot, Niles. He'd sleep in there if you let him. He'd take his meals in there."

Muhamed shook his head. "Nobody's gonna mess up my cockpit with crumbs and stuff."

Dan laughed, thinking, Maybe I ought to put Niles in charge of security.

April was startled when she returned to her apartment. As she opened the front door she heard country and western music twanging from her radio. She knew she hadn't left the radio on when she'd left in the morning, and even if she had she'd never leave it tuned to *that* wailing of losers.

Cautiously she edged the door halfway open, ready to run back to her car if Roberto or some stranger were in her apartment.

Kelly Eamons was sitting in the armchair, her head bent over the computer in her lap, her fingers pecking away.

Gusting out a sigh of relief, April stepped into the living room and shut the door.

Eamons looked up and smiled. "Hi! I'm back on your case. But don't let anybody know about it."

BOULDER, COLORADO

Len Kinsky sat tensely in the rickety little grillwork chair on the sidewalk outside the Walnut Brewery restaurant. A cool breeze was blowing down off the mountains; the trees lining the street had already started to turn golden. Looking in through the restaurant's big front window, Kinsky could see the big gleaming stainless steel vats of the microbrewery. People were ordering samplers, a row of shot glasses filled with different types of beer. He longed for the old Luchow's in New York, and an honest mug of strong German beer.

Across the table from him sat Rick Chatham, a bland smile on his round, bearded face. Kinsky didn't trust men who wore ponytails, but he was desperate enough to agree to this meeting with the environmental activist.

"Try the wheat beer," Chatham suggested. "You'll like it."

Kinsky did not appreciate being told what he would or wouldn't like. But what the hell, he thought, the guy's just trying to be friendly. Besides, I need him more than he needs me.

Although the pedestrian mall was a block away, Walnut Street was crowded with scruffy-looking students in tattered jeans and T-shirts that were supposed to look impoverished but actually cost a fortune. There were tourists meandering by as well, toting backpacks, bottled water, and babies that either slept or squalled as they meandered along the sidewalk. Up the street Kinsky could see some mountains and clear blue sky, but he preferred to look at the brick and clapboard buildings lining the street. They're trying to make this one-horse burg look like a real city, he thought. But it's just a university town, nothing more.

"So you've quit Astro." Chatham made it a statement, not a question.

"Yeah," Kinsky said with some bitterness. "I'm going to leave the country and see the world."

A waitress asked what they wanted. Kinsky asked for the wheat beer; Chatham went through a long menu of bottled water and finally selected the local offering.

"What made you decide to quit?" Chatham asked. He tried to pose it as a friendly question, but Kinsky knew he was really sizing him up.

Always tell the sucker what he wants to hear, Kinsky knew. That was the secret of successful fortune-tellers, and business consultants, and public relations experts.

"I couldn't take it anymore," he said slowly, as if pulling it from some inner reservoir of conscience. "I mean, they're going to be beaming gigawatts worth of microwaves through the atmosphere and they expected me to tell the world it's all right. Better than all right—they want to pretend it's an environmentally clean source of energy."

Chatham's light brown eyes sparkled.

"Let me play devil's advocate for a minute," he said, hunching forward in his chair and clasping his hands together on the little round grillwork table.

"Okay," said Kinsky. "Go ahead."

"The microwaves will be beamed to a remote location in New Mexico—"

"White Sands. The middle of nowhere."

"Astro Corporation is building an antenna farm there to receive the energy being beamed down from space."

"The rectenna farm, yeah. It's already finished. Just waiting for the satellite to start working."

"That's federal land, isn't it?"

"White Sands Proving Grounds, right. Dan's leased the land for the rectenna farm. Looks like a big set of steel clothes poles stuck in the sand. Thousands of 'em."

" 'Dan'?"

"Dan Randolph. The head of the corporation. Founder and CEO. And chairman of the board, too."

Chatham pursed his lips. "He's got all the power in his own hands, doesn't he."

"He sure does."

"So," Chatham went on, "if these microwaves are being beamed to such a remote location, where nobody's living, not even cattle or grass, who's going to get hurt?"

Kinsky smiled crookedly at him. "Devil's advocate, huh? Okay, yeah, maybe nothing'll get fried except some lizards and snakes."

"So what's the harm?"

Kinsky hesitated a moment. *He wants me to do his thinking for him,* he realized. *He wants me to come up with the ideas he can use.*

Raising an index finger, Kinsky said, "First, if they do kill some wildlife out there in the desert, who's going to know about it? They sure as hell won't tell anybody."

"Ahh. Good point."

"Second," Kinsky raised another finger, "if they make everybody believe that the satellite works and they're getting gigawatts of energy from it, they're going to start building more powersats—with more rectenna farms on the ground."

Chatham nodded hard enough to make his ponytail bob up and down. "And where will they put those rectenna farms? As close to big cities as they can, because those cities will be the market for the energy!"

"Right," Kinsky said.

Growing more excited, Chatham asked, "And what about the long-term effects on the climate of beaming so much energy through the atmosphere? Has anybody looked into that?"

"Dan got a couple of meteorologists from some university to come up with a paper that said the effect would be negligible."

"Negligible! That's the term they use when they want you to look the other way."

"There's more, too."

"What?"

"Those rockets they use," Kinsky said. "Solid fuel boosters. Their exhaust gases are toxic, for chrissake. Aluminum perchloride or something. We can't park our cars within a mile of the launchpad because the exhaust peels the paint off."

"Wow! This is dynamite. We've got to get this information out on the Net, got to organize protests, rallies, the whole nine yards."

Kinsky felt a pang of guilt at having betrayed Dan. *What the hell,* he told himself. *This geek would come after Dan anyway, with me or without me. I've got to look out for numero uno.*

Which reminded him. "You mentioned a consultant's fee when we talked on the phone."

Chatham immediately sobered. "That's right. I have a cashier's check for a thousand dollars right here in my pocket. All I have to do is fill in your name as the recipient."

"We talked about a lot more than one thousand."

"This is just the first installment, my friend. There'll be more, plenty more. I think you're going to be very valuable to us, helping to orchestrate the protests that'll bring this satellite project to a screeching halt."

"I'm heading out of the country," Kinsky said.

"May I ask why?"

Thinking of his ex-wife and her lawyer, and even more of Roberto and the shadowy figures he must be working for, Kinsky replied merely, "Personal reasons."

"But you can stay in touch through e-mail, can't you?"

"Can you set up an account for me? With a new user name. I don't want to be traced."

"Sure," Chatham said easily. "No problem."

"And you can wire-transfer my money."

"Sure," he repeated. "Anywhere you want."

Al-Bashir was tempted to reveal his scheme to Garrison. The crusty old scoundrel would appreciate the beauty of it, and he might even agree to killing the president of the United States. Garrison had complained about "that jerkoff in the White House" often enough.

But he resisted the temptation. Garrison was an American, and even though he had always run the multinational Tricontinental Oil Corporation with the totally unsentimental attitude of a man who puts profits above all else, some shred of national loyalty still might make him balk at the scheme al-Bashir was unfolding.

So I must be clever enough to do what needs to be done without stirring up his opposition. He's still smarting from the realization that I'm the real power in the corporation, and he's working hard to win key members of the board away from me. My best path is to make him a party to the scheme without revealing the entire scheme to him. I want him either on my side or neutralized, not actively opposing me.

The old man hardly ever left the tower in downtown Houston that housed Tricontinental's corporate offices. Garrison kept an apartment on the floor below his own penthouse offices, a spacious suite comfortably furnished with all the latest gadgetry and a handful of servants. Al-Bashir felt quite pleased that Garrison had invited him to his living quarters for a quiet little dinner, rather than to his office for a more impersonal meeting.

This is a sign that he's beginning to accept the situation, al-Bashir told himself, at least a little. He wants to show off his lifestyle to me. All to the good.

The apartment was even more sumptuous than al-Bashir had expected. A young, broad-shouldered butler in a traditional dark suit was waiting for him when the doors to the private elevator smoothly slid open. Al-Bashir found himself in a Texas-sized living room, thickly carpeted, the two farthest walls completely glassed so that he could see the garish majesty of Houston's skyscraper towers, just beginning to light up in the twilight glow that still lingered on the distant horizon. These furnishings and decorations are tasteful—even elegant, al-Bashir thought as the butler led him to the bar of black marble.

Despite the room's size, it seemed comfortable, livable, not like some of the homes al-Bashir had seen, which looked to him more like furniture store showrooms than homes where people actually spent their lives.

Without being asked, the butler poured al-Bashir a tall glass of tea. He sipped at it, appreciating the trace of mint he tasted. Above the bar, he saw, was a larger-than-life painting of a fleshy nude woman.

"Rubens," came Garrison's voice from behind him. Al-Bashir turned and saw the old man wheeling up noiselessly across the plush carpet.

"It's an original, of course." Garrison waved an arm. "They're all originals. Cost a mint, each of 'em. Rafael. Pair of Monet haystacks. That etching over there is by Rembrandt."

"They're magnificent," al-Bashir said.

"Yep. Nice to look at now and then, make you realize what it's all about. Got a mural by Da Vinci on the ceiling over my bed." He cackled evilly. "That one's just a reproduction, though. But it impresses the women."

Al-Bashir smiled down at him. His own home, outside Tunis, had no images on its walls. That was not permitted. But there were many women.

As Garrison led him through the opulent apartment, pointing out artworks as he rolled his powered chair across the plush carpeting, al-Bashir began to understand why the old man had invited him to his home. *He's showing me what he's accumulated over all these years. He's begging me not to take all this away from him.* Al-Bashir smiled tolerantly down at the wizened cripple and thought, *You can keep it all, Garrison. All except the power.*

Dinner was served by the butler, who was the only servant in sight. Garrison sat at the head of the long dining room table, al-Bashir on his right. The old man's wheelchair was a shade lower than the other high-backed chairs; it made Garrison look almost like a child seated at a table too high for him. He ignored that, though, as they ate delicately seasoned veal and talked about business. At last Garrison asked, "Randolph still givin' you the runaround?"

Al-Bashir made a smile. "It's a delicate situation, almost to the point of amusement."

"Nothing amusin' about a billion and a half bucks," Garrison muttered.

"I'm beginning to think that perhaps my approach to Randolph has been wrong."

"Whattaya mean?"

With a rueful little pout, al-Bashir said, "The man seems pathologically unable to make a decision on selling part of his company to us."

"His funeral, then. He needs the money, he sells. Otherwise he can piss in his pants for all I care."

"I would agree, except for one thing."

"Yamagata?"

Al-Bashir dipped his chin in acknowledgment. This old man is no fool, he reminded himself. You must treat him with respect. He's quite capable of ambushing you if you're not careful.

"I don't want to see the Japs get their paws on that power satellite any more'n you do," Garrison said, holding a forkful of veal poised between the platter and his mouth. "I want 'em buyin' our oil, not pullin' in energy from outer space."

"This man Scanwell is a factor, too," al-Bashir said.

Garrison snorted.

"Do you know him? Personally, I mean?"

"I *knew* him," the old man replied. "Before he fixed his eyes on the White House and started all this energy independence bullshit."

"He apparently has allied himself with Randolph."

"Yep. And he won't come within ten miles of me. I'm the big, bad oil industry."

"Scanwell could be trouble if he's elected."

Strangely, Garrison smiled. A sly, knowing smile. "Let him get himself elected. Once he's in the White House we'll show him who the real players are in this business."

Al-Bashir felt genuinely surprised. "You believe you can contain him?"

"Son, we'll *control* him. Same way we've controlled all the other presidents."

"But how can you control the President? After all, he's the most powerful—"

"The hell he is!" Garrison snapped. "You think he's powerful? Hah! We'll lay down the law to him, just like always."

"I don't understand."

"You'll see. Know what they say in Washington? 'The president proposes, but the Congress disposes.' And we've got Congress. Enough of 'em, anyway. Got 'em right here." Garrison patted his pants pocket.

"And you believe you can handle Scanwell the same way?" Al-Bashir felt impressed.

"Presidents come and go," Garrison said. "Some of our congressmen and senators have been there through five and six administrations."

"I see," said al-Bashir with newfound understanding.

"Scanwell and his energy independence." Garrison chuckled. "We'll tie him up in knots."

"That leaves Randolph, then."

"We've gotta keep him from goin' to Yamagata."

"He really doesn't want to sell any of his stock to us," al-Bashir said. "He's deathly afraid that once we're into his company, we'll take it over completely."

"That's the main idea, isn't it?"

"Yes, but we can't do it if he won't sell to us."

Garrison chewed thoughtfully for a moment, then asked, "What do you recommend?"

For a long moment, al-Bashir remained silent. *We both know that what I recommend,* he said to himself, *is what we will do.*

At last he said, "We'll do as he asks. Extend a loan to him."

"Give in to him?"

"Appear to give in to him," al-Bashir said, placatingly. "Let him think that he's won. Loan him what he needs. But only on a monthly basis. Keep him tied to us."

"On a shoestring," Garrison muttered.

"While the price of his stock keeps slipping."

"And we quietly buy it up through third parties, so he doesn't know we're taking him over until it's too late."

"Exactly," said al-Bashir.

Garrison laughed his cackling, rasping snicker. "We won't have to pony up the one-point-five bill. Nowhere near it."

"Probably not," al-Bashir agreed.

"By Christ, you're even sneakier than I am!" Garrison said approvingly.

A win-win situation, al-Bashir congratulated himself as he rode the private elevator to the lobby and the limousine waiting for him at the curb. *Garrison believes we will eventually get control of Astro Corporation. Randolph will believe that he's getting the money he needs to finish the power satellite without selling out his company.*

And I will be able to use the satellite to destroy Randolph and the very idea of generating energy from space. And kill many thousands of Americans into the bargain.

MATAGORDA ISLAND,
TEXAS

Claude Passeau had a quizzical look on his face as he walked with Dan along the stacks. Eight solid-propellant rockets lay on their sides in the big warehouse, each of them bigger than a blue whale, all of them painted gleaming white with Astro Corporation's stylish logo emblazoned along their flanks.

"You seem to have worked some sort of minor miracle," Passeau said.

Dan shook his head, his eyes focused on the crew of technicians who were carefully slipping a cradle around the farthest of the rockets in preparation for lifting it into a sling and carrying it to the next building. There, it would be stood upright and mated with the smaller upper stage that carried the electronic flight systems.

"Getting Lockheed Martin to build these boosters at such a low price?" Dan replied. "No miracle. Just competitive bidding. And mass production. Instead of asking them for one or two, I ordered a dozen. With an option for six dozen more."

"That's not what I'm talking about and you know it," Passeau said.

Dan looked at the smaller man. The FAA administrator looked crisp and cool in a beige summerweight suit.

"Is this silk?" Dan asked, fingering the jacket collar.

"You're avoiding the issue, Dan."

"What issue?"

"The change in the weather."

"Oh?"

With a bemused smile, Passeau said, "The prevailing wind from Washington has changed direction, my friend."

"Has it?" Dan asked innocently.

"Decidedly. Instead of being furious at you for your unauthorized test flight, my superiors have instructed me to wrap up the crash investigation and give you a clean bill of health."

That's Jane's doing, Dan thought. A U.S. senator can make a bureaucracy jump, especially when the bureaucracy's budget is coming up on the Senate floor soon. But then he wondered, Has Garrison anything to do with this? He wants to buy me out, but a defunct Astro Corporation wouldn't be any good to him. Or would it?

Genuinely puzzled, Dan asked, "What does a clean bill of health mean?"

Still smiling, Passeau said, "My final report will not mention the word 'sabotage.' That would be too epistemological. I am merely to conclude that the cause of the crash was specific to your oh-one aircraft and not due to any inherent flaw in its design or your operational procedures."

"That's what your final report's going to say?"

"Yes. I thought you'd be pleased to hear it."

"I am, Claude. Very pleased." Yet Dan felt no elation, no surge of relief.

"Well, it's the truth, isn't it?" Passeau responded, his brows knitting slightly. "Your flight with the oh-two model proved it for everyone to see."

"How soon will you finish your report? How soon can you take the wraps off and let me get back to normal business instead of going to Venezuela?"

Passeau held up a hand. "These things take a bit of time, you know. I can't simply tell my people to wrap up their work and go home."

"Why not?"

"Because government agencies don't work that way, Dan. It would look terribly suspicious if we suddenly put out a report holding you blameless for the crash. We'd be accused of a whitewash."

Planting his fists on his hips, Dan said, "But that's what you're going to do, isn't it? You just told me that your final report will give us a clean bill of health."

"In good time, Dan. In good time. We mustn't rush it; that would look too..." Passeau fumbled for a word. "Too unseemly," he finally said.

"Weeks? Months? Years? How long?"

"Oh, less than a year. Much less. A few months, most likely."

"That's the best you can do?"

"Under the circumstances, I should think you'd be overjoyed."

Dan puffed out a sigh. "I am, Claude. I am. Thanks a whole bunch."

Passeau shook his head and walked away, heading back to his office in the engineering building. Dan looked up at the overhead crane trundling by, then decided to stay in the warehouse and watch the crew wrestling the big booster into its transport sling. It was a lot easier to manhandle a giant firecracker than to fathom the ways of a government bureaucracy.

You have a dinner invitation," April told Dan when he returned to his office. "It's on your screen."

Sliding into his desk chair, Dan tapped his mouse and saw Asim al-Bashir's neatly bearded face.

"Dan, I hope you can join me for dinner tomorrow evening, either here in Houston or down at your Matagorda Island. I have news that you will be very glad to hear."

Everybody's giving me good news today, Dan said to himself as he clicked on the REPLY icon.

"Mr. al-Bashir, I'll be happy to have dinner with you tomorrow. Let's make it in Houston; the restaurants are a lot better there. Let me know where and what time. Thanks."

The restaurant turned out to be an establishment called Istanbul West. To Dan it looked like some Hollywood mogul's idea of a Middle Eastern eatery: pointed archways with elaborate filigrees of traceries, waiters in pantaloons and velvet vests, colorful pillows strewn everywhere. At least the tables are normal height, Dan saw as the maitre d' led him through the big, ornate dining room. Al-Bashir wasn't there yet. Dan remembered that Arabs had a reputation for being loose about punctuality. He also realized that making your guest wait for you to arrive is part of a power trip. Al-Bashir had been precisely punctual the first time they'd met.

So Dan sat at the table. It was on the edge of what appeared to be a dance floor. And there was a small stage where a trio of musicians were unpacking their instruments: some sort of a guitar, a clarinet, and a set of drums. No amplifiers in sight. Dan felt grateful for that.

The menu had regular steaks and chops on one side, more exotic dishes with names that Dan didn't recognize on the other. A waiter came up and, sure enough, he was wearing shoes with curled-up toes. Dan asked for an amantillado. The waiter expressed puzzlement in a down-home accent. Dan ordered a Jack Daniels with water. That, the waiter understood.

I wonder how long al-Bashir's going to keep me waiting, Dan thought as he sipped at his drink and the three-piece combo warmed up.

Then the clarinetist announced that the first oriental dancer of the night was "Yasmin, a lovely Lebanese girl."

She looked more like Texas than Lebanon to Dan: red-haired and billowy in a sequined push-up bra. Once she started dancing, Dan stopped worrying about when al-Bashir would show up.

He finally arrived after "Yasmin" finished her dance, to a raucous round of applause and some howls and hoots from the guys clustered at the bar.

"I'm terribly sorry to be so late," al-Bashir said as he sat at the table. He didn't look sorry to Dan; the man was smiling like a well-fed cat.

"No problem," Dan said glibly. "I've been enjoying the show."

"Ah yes, the dancers. They save the better ones for later in the evening."

Al-Bashir seemed in no hurry to report his good news, so Dan asked him about the Middle Eastern side of the menu. He eventually followed the Tunisian's suggestions and ordered shish kebab with couscous.

When their dinners arrived, Dan laughed. "The locals would call this barbecue."

Al-Bashir smiled tightly. "The locals would never be able to appreciate the spices and sauces. They like their steaks half raw and their beer thin."

Dan accepted that; he even halfway agreed with it.

Through the dinner and into the honey-drenched dessert al-Bashir refrained from talking business. They watched the dancers, chatted about the food and the restaurant, and sipped spiced tea. Dan recognized the game al-Bashir was playing. Okay, he said to himself, you're waiting for me to make the first move, to ask you what you have to tell me. But I can wait as long as you can, pal.

At last the band took a break. Al-Bashir dabbed his lips with his napkin, then leaned close enough for Dan to smell his cinnamon-scented cologne.

"I have good news for you."

"So you said in your phone message," Dan replied.

"I have managed to convince Garrison to accede to your wishes. Tricontinental will loan you the money you need, rather than buy your stock."

Dan couldn't hide his elation. "You will?"

"If that's what you want."

All his reservations gone, Dan grabbed al-Bashir's hand and pumped it hard. "That's what I want, all right. That's exactly what I want."

"Fine. That is what we will do."

Suddenly at a loss, Dan stammered, "I . . . I don't know how to thank you. I mean . . . we'll be able to get the powersat running. We'll be able to beam energy down to the ground."

Smiling benignly, al-Bashir said, "I understand. You see, I want the power satellite to go into operation just as much as you do."

NASHUA, NEW HAMPSHIRE

Jane could feel the tension in Morgan's hand as she sat beside him on the sofa, watching the early election returns on the muted television set across the crowded hotel sitting room. He's trying to appear relaxed and confident, she knew, but she could sense the stress in every rigid line of his body. The suite was jammed with volunteers, aides, a few local politicians, all standing in clumps of twos and threes, their eyes on the TV and the numbers that were slowly accumulating. They spoke in near whispers, tense with expectation, conversations subdued.

More volunteers were gathering downstairs in the hotel's ballroom, ready to party if the returns were good, ready to go home through the iron cold of the New Hampshire night if the results were as bad as most of them feared they would be.

Turning her head to look through the window, Jane saw that snow had started to fall outside, big wet flakes sifting silently down, quiet and serene, illuminated by the tall lights of the Nashua Marriott hotel's half-empty parking lot. A late winter's night in New Hampshire, Jane thought. It's quiet in here, too, despite the press of all these people, she realized. Quiet, but taut with anxiety. You can almost smell the fear.

A good thing it didn't start snowing until after the polling places were closed, Jane told herself. At least the snow didn't keep the voters at home. And we can blame the snow for a poor showing at the party downstairs.

The TV screen showed the local news, with precincts reporting the results of the nation's earliest presidential primary election. The volunteers crowding the modest sitting room were young men and women for the most part, dressed in comfortable, practical tweeds and woolens. No straw hats or garish campaign badges. The older politicians carried on terse discussions with one another, each of them wondering if they had backed the wrong horse, their eyes never leaving the numbers shown on the TV screen.

Denny O'Brien was standing by the well-stocked bar, deep in earnest conversation with the city's leading banker. Jane had to smile at the contrast between them: Denny looked like a sagging, half-deflated blimp next to the lean, flinty-eyed New Hampshireman. No news reporters were among the crowd, Jane noted. Not one.

Well, she thought, we never expected Morgan to carry New Hampshire. He did well enough in the Iowa caucus, but the New Hampshire voters had barely heard of the governor of Texas when the campaign started. Still, we need to make a solid showing here, Jane told herself. The national spotlight is on New Hampshire tonight, and Morgan's got to show that he can win votes.

"...and the surprise of the evening, so far," one of the carefully coiffed TV analysts was saying, "is that Morgan Scanwell appears to be doing much better than the polls indicated."

"Yes," said his partner, smiling with perfect teeth. "Scanwell's message of energy independence seems to have struck a chord among New Hampshire voters."

All the conversations in the suite stopped for a moment, as the TV screen showed fresh numbers. Morgan's in third place, Jane saw! In a field of seven candidates, third place isn't bad. She felt her pulse rate quicken. He's outpolling the Kennedy woman from Massachusetts!

As the evening wore on and the results from across the state came in, the hotel suite became louder and merrier. A couple of news reporters arrived and pushed through the crowd to ask for an interview. Scanwell grinned at them and looked at Jane.

"Let's wait for the final results, shall we?" Jane said.

Nodding, Scanwell said, "Good idea. Shouldn't be long now."

A news camera crew barged in and commandeered one of the big upholstered wing chairs, one guy manhandling it into a corner of the room while his partners set up their minicam and lights.

"All right," said the analyst on the TV screen, "here are the final results."

The room fell silent.

"As expected and predicted, the winner of the New Hampshire primary is Senator Charles Waldron, of New York, with forty-seven percent of the vote."

"Texas Governor Morgan Scanwell," said his smiling colleague, "is the big surprise of the night, coming in second with twenty-two percent, slightly ahead of Michael Underwood..."

The rest was drowned out by cheering. Jane gave Scanwell a celebratory kiss on the cheek, then the governor jumped to his feet and started shaking hands with everybody. Suddenly everyone in the room wanted to grasp his hand. The TV reporter waded through the pack and led him to the wing chair for a congratulatory interview while the volunteers started for the door, heading downstairs to the ballroom for a well-earned celebration.

And Jane found herself wondering what Dan was doing. She knew she had been foolish, stupid even, to go to see him in Texas, to be alone with him, to love him. That was a mistake, she told herself sternly. It won't happen again. It can't happen again. Not now. Not ever.

Still, she wondered what Dan was doing at this very moment.

I never realized it could be so cold in Texas," said Asim al-Bashir as he and Dan hustled from his Jaguar to the bar of the Astro Motel.

Dan grinned at him. "The locals say there's nothing between Texas and the North Pole except a barbed-wire fence."

It was warm inside the bar, although this close to midnight the place was nearly empty. The TV set at the far end of the bar was showing a hockey game. A couple of rednecks were at the other end of the bar, hunched over longnecked beers. Dan saw that the hockey game was in its final minute: the Dallas Stars were ahead of the Redwings, 3–2. As he led al-Bashir to a booth, the Redwings goalie came out to help in a desperate attempt to tie the score.

Don't go into overtime, Dan prayed silently. The barmaid sauntered over to the booth and Dan ordered a Glenlivet on the rocks. To his surprise, al-Bashir asked for the same.

"We're outta Glenlivet," said the barmaid. "How 'bout Johnnie Black?"

"That will be fine," al-Bashir answered. Dan agreed with a resigned nod.

The Stars stole the puck from the attacking Redwings and skated to an easy score at the undefended goal. The Detroit crowd groaned and booed. The final buzzer sounded as the barmaid banged the two scotches onto their table.

"Six fifty," she announced.

"Run a tab for me, okay?" Dan said.

"We're closin' in half an hour. Y'all want me to bring you another round now? Then I can run yer card and get outta here on time."

Dan grinned at her. "Sure, why not? And turn on Fox News or CNN, will you?"

As the barmaid left their booth, al-Bashir lifted his glass. "To continued success," he toasted.

"I'll drink to that," said Dan, touching his glass to the Arab's.

As he sipped the whisky, Dan thought that al-Bashir wasn't one of those fanatical Muslims who wouldn't touch liquor. All to the good, he told himself. That means he isn't a terrorist. Dan smiled inwardly. He doesn't dress like a terrorist. That suit must have cost a small fortune. Silk, it looks like. Probably Saville Row.

"Things are going well," al-Bashir said as the barmaid brought their second round.

Dan fished out his credit card and handed it to the barmaid. Al-Bashir didn't move a muscle.

"Yep, we're perking right along," Dan said. "Thanks to you."

Al-Bashir shrugged modestly. "I'm glad that I was able to convince Garrison to loan you the money you need."

"It's put us over the hump. With a steady inflow of cash we've been able to move right ahead." Dan smiled happily.

"I believe Senator Thornton has been of some help to you, as well."

Dan's smile evaporated. But he admitted, "She's gotten the FAA to back off, that's the most important thing. We'll be flying the spaceplane with Gerry Adair at the controls in another week."

"Despite the cold?" al-Bashir asked. His round, neatly bearded face looked relaxed, at ease, yet his dark eyes were piercing.

"No problem."

"The satellite is finished?"

Dan sipped his scotch. Then, "We're just about ready to turn her on. One more flight to send a crew to check out all her systems and we'll be set to start generating power."

Smiling, al-Bashir said, "The receiving facility at White Sands is ready. I went down there last week."

"Did you?" Dan looked into those steady brown eyes. Al-Bashir's been all over the place, he knew. The man had made himself a familiar figure everywhere in the Astro headquarters. And he went to the rectenna farm, too. Dan felt impressed. He's really made himself a part of the team. Next thing you know he'll want a ride in the spaceplane.

Should I worry about him? Dan asked himself. How much should I let him see? The sardonic voice in his head answered, He's your pipeline to the money, pal. Close him down and you close your whole operation.

Yeah, Dan answered. But still . . .

Al-Bashir broke into his silent debate. "I would like to hire your secretary."

"April?" Dan felt a sudden jolt of alarm.

"April Simmonds, yes. I could offer her twice the salary you're paying."

"To work for you?"

"As my personal assistant, yes."

Stalling for time to think this through, Dan asked, "In Houston?"

"Or Tunis, or wherever I need her. I travel a great deal and she would be of invaluable assistance to me."

"Assistance," Dan heard himself growl. "And what else?"

Al-Bashir smiled smoothly. "Whatever else happens to arise."

Fighting a sudden impulse to punch al-Bashir in his smirking face, Dan said, "I can't let her go. She runs my office for me. She's even doing my public relations work now."

"Is she under contract to Astro?"

Dan shook his head warily.

"Perhaps she would like to work for me. Would you mind if I asked her about it?"

"I'd mind a helluva lot," Dan snapped. Then he recovered his self-control and added, "Go ahead and ask her, if you want to."

"I want to. Very much."

Steaming, Dan saw out of the corner of his eye that the TV screen above the bar was flashing the words NEW HAMPSHIRE PRIMARY against a background of red, white, and blue. Dan turned to look squarely at the screen, glad of the excuse to cut his conversation with al-Bashir. The sound was muted, but the numbers were clear: Scanwell had come in a strong second, surprising most of the forecasters.

The image changed abruptly to a picture of New York Senator Waldron standing at a hotel ballroom podium, waving, mouthing a victory speech to a crowd of cheering, waving straw-hatted supporters. Then it cut to Scanwell, standing at a podium in a different hotel, a wide smile splitting his craggy face, speaking words that Dan could not hear.

And Jane was standing at his side, also smiling, looking radiant and completely happy.

Dan forgot about al-Bashir sitting in the booth with him. He simply stared at Jane. She waltzes down here and pops into my bed and says she still loves me. And then she tells me she's married to Scanwell. Married to him. Her husband. She'll be at his side all the way to the White House. She loves me and she's married to him. Einstein was right: nuclear physics is a lot simpler than politics. And love.

MATAGORDA ISLAND, TEXAS

Hangar B was crackling with activity, al-Bashir saw. The sandy-haired pilot, Adair, was clambering through the open hatch of the spaceplane's cockpit while a team of technicians manned consoles lined along the hangar's far wall. Other technicians were fussing around the plane's landing gear, checking the tires and pneumatic struts that held the wheels.

All under the watchful, baleful eyes of the black man, Niles Muhamed, who stood watching the plane and the people around it, arms folded across his chest. Muhamed wore olive green coveralls, so spotless and unwrinkled they looked almost like a military uniform. Al-Bashir walked up to him.

"The test goes well?" he asked.

Muhamed barely nodded. "So far."

"I've been meaning to ask you," al-Bashir said. "Your name indicates that you might be a Muslim. Is that so?"

"Me? A Muslim?"

"Forgive my curiosity."

"My father was a Muslim," Muhamed said, without taking his eyes from the plane. "Took a Muslim name and all."

"And you?"

"Baptist, like my momma."

"Ah. I see." Al-Bashir started to turn away.

"I got a question for you," Muhamed said.

"Ah?"

"How come Dan's given you the run of the place? You come and go 'round here as if you own the joint."

Al-Bashir smiled. "I may not own the joint, as you put it, but I am the conduit through which the money flows. I suppose Dan trusts me because I have provided the financing that keeps this operation alive."

"You been all over the place," Muhamed said. "Pokin' into everything."

"I'm fascinated by all this high technology. I'm eager to learn everything I can."

Muhamed looked at him with disbelieving eyes. Then one of the technicians called from the line of consoles, "We're ready for the instrument checkout."

"I'll leave you to your work," al-Bashir said graciously, feeling almost relieved that Muhamed turned away from him and started striding across the hangar floor.

Al-Bashir began walking away, too, toward the open doors and the chilly, cloudy weather outside. As he hurried toward Hangar Λ, where Dan's office was, through the damp cutting wind blowing in from the Gulf, he felt glad that Muhamed was not in charge of security for Astro Corporation. The man was suspicious, protective. Thank god Dan Randolph is so trusting, al-Bashir said to himself. If Muhamed were in Dan's place I'd never be able to get the information I need.

By the time he reached Hangar A, al-Bashir was actually shivering. Berating himself for wearing nothing warmer than a silk business suit, he blew into his hands as he climbed the stairs toward Dan's office.

When he stepped into the outer office April said, from behind her desk, "Mr. Randolph isn't in this morning. He's gone to Houston."

Al-Bashir's nerves twitched. "Houston?"

"To meet with Mr. Passeau at the regional FAA office."

"Ah. I see." Houston was also where the regional FBI office was located, al-Bashir knew. The FAA was not troublesome.

"They're working out clearances for the next test flight," said April.

"Of course."

April smiled uncertainly as al-Bashir stood in front of her desk. She is truly lovely, he thought, picturing how she would look in an evening gown, in a bikini, in bed.

"Is there anything I can do for you?" she asked.

Al-Bashir pulled up the little wheeled chair from the corner of the cubicle. "Many things," he said as he sat down.

"I'm really kind of busy, Mr.—"

Al-Bashir interrupted, "I want you to come to work for me, April."

"For Tricontinental? In Houston?"

"No. For me. As my personal assistant. You would travel the world with me. Private jets. The best hotels."

She was clearly surprised, al-Bashir saw.

"A woman of your education and abilities could go far in this world, very far, if you would allow me to help you."

Her look of surprise faded. "I'm happy with the job I have, Mr. al-Bashir."

"Please, call me Asim."

"I'm happy with the job I have," she repeated.

"I'll double your salary. And you would have all the perks you want. You could see the world in luxury."

April smiled again. "I couldn't leave Mr. Randolph, especially with the powersat almost ready to be turned on. He depends on me."

I'd like to depend on you, al-Bashir thought. Aloud, he replied, "Well, will you at least consider my offer?"

She began to shake her head.

"Let's discuss it over dinner," he suggested.

A knowing look came over April's face. "I'd be happy to have dinner with you, Mr. . . . Asim. But purely on a social basis. I have no intention of leaving Astro Corporation."

Al-Bashir shrugged as if defeated. "Very well then. Purely a social dinner. Tonight?"

He saw her calculating in her mind. "I'm busy tonight. How about Friday?"

"Good," he said. "Friday it will be."

And he thought, You won't have to get up early on Saturday to go to the office.

WASHINGTON, D.C.

The cherry blossoms were out early this year. Through the long windows of the Senate hearing room Dan could see the delicate pink blooms on the trees outside. It was springtime out there. Dan sat at the green baize-covered witness table while a battery of photographers blazed away at him, camera flashes flickering so rapidly it felt almost like being in a firefight.

Dan felt tense, almost angry, as he looked at Jane, who was sitting at the end of the banquette before him. Things had been going well for the past seven months, and this Senate hearing was the perfect place to make the announcement he was going to spring on them. Scanwell had rolled through the Super Tuesday primaries so well that he was suddenly the front-runner among the pack chasing after the nomination for president. And Jane was right there with him, every step of the way on the road to the White House. Dan wondered when they'd make a public announcement about their marriage. And there she is, sitting twenty feet away from me and avoiding looking my way.

At least April's stuck by me, he said to himself. If al-Bashir actually did offer her a job with him she must've turned it down. Neither one of them has mentioned it, though. The kid's done pretty damned well as my public relations director, too, he thought as the photographers finally cleared away and the red after-images of their flashes began to fade. Even with those eco-nuts picketing around our main gate, we've had nothing but favorable publicity.

Senator Quill rapped a metal stylus against the wooden block on the banquette desktop and the buzzing chatter slowly quieted. He called the hearing to order and introduced the eleven subcommittee members. Dan noticed that the bank of TV cameras off to one side of the room panned along the banquette, then pointed back at Quill.

"We are also honored to have Senator Thornton, of the great state of Oklahoma, with us this morning in an *ex officio* capacity."

Jane nodded and smiled graciously as the cameras focused on her.

Turning to the subcommittee's chief counsel, a dark-faced younger man with a thick black moustache and an even thicker mop of black hair falling down to his collar, Senator Quill said, "We're ready for the first witness."

Dan rose to his feet as a clerk swore him in. Then he sat down again and faced the chief counsel, who was seated at the same level as Dan, at a small table facing him. Deadpanned, in a voice as inanimate as an automated elevator calling out floor numbers, he asked Dan to state his name and occupation.

"Daniel Hamilton Randolph, CEO and board chairman of Astro Manufacturing Corporation."

"If you have a prepared statement, the subcommittee will listen to it now."

Dan leaned forward slightly, toward the microphones arrayed before him. "I have a statement, but I would prefer to wait until after I respond to the subcommittee's questions."

The young lawyer looked startled for a moment and turned back to glance at Senator Quill, seated above him. Dan kept a straight face, but he enjoyed that momentary look of consternation. Quill nodded, and Dan flicked a glance at Jane, down at the end of the table. She looked slightly nettled.

The chief counsel began questioning Dan about the solar power satellite. Dan had already set up a video presentation and for the next ten minutes the computer graphics played their animated scenes on the big high-definition screen that hung on the wall of the hearing chamber opposite the TV crews.

Once the video ended, the lawyer said, "This subcommittee has heard testimony to the effect that the microwave beam coming from the satellite to the ground is environmentally dangerous."

Dan nodded. "Testimony from Rick Chatham and his people, I know."

"What is your response to their assertions?"

"Are any of his assertions backed by scientific evidence?" Dan asked, with a patient smile on his face. "Does Chatham have any expertise in climatology, or radiology, or any other -ology?"

Dan heard a few titters behind him.

"Can anyone in his group program a kitchen appliance without asking some teenager for help?"

Laughter, even among some of the senators.

But the lawyer frowned and repeated, "What is your response, sir, to these assertions?"

Putting on a serious expression, Dan said, "Sir, we have done several scientific studies of the effects of beaming those microwaves through the atmosphere. I have provided the subcommittee with the relevant reports."

Before the chief counsel could respond, Dan added, "The long and short of it is that we keep the beam so diffuse that birds can fly through it without harm. Cattle can graze on the ground where the antennas receive the microwave energy. We know the numbers and we have added a safety factor of one hundred percent specifically to make certain that there won't be any harmful effects."

Senator Quill broke in: "Your animated video didn't show how you keep the beam so spread out."

Wondering if Jane had prompted him to ask that question, Dan said, "Senator, the satellite's downlink antenna defocuses the beam. The system spreads the beam as it leaves the satellite. If that system should fail, the whole power satellite shuts down automatically."

"I see," said Quill, although he looked slightly puzzled.

The other senators began popping questions at Dan, each one of them eager to get their face on camera. Most of the questions were soft. The subcommittee's on my side, Dan thought. Gradually the questions drifted away from the environmental effects and began to center on the actual operation of the satellite and the spaceplane.

"You've had two flights of your spaceplane since the fatal crash last year," Senator Quill said.

"Three flights, Senator," Dan replied. "The first one was unmanned. I mean automated."

"And the more recent two flights?"

"Both were piloted and both were completely successful."

"What about that first flight, the one that crashed?" asked the senator at the far end of the banquette.

Dan gave his carefully prepared answer. "The FAA and the National Transportation Safety Board have concluded that the accident wasn't caused by a generic flaw in the spaceplane's design or manufacture. Our successful flights with the second spaceplane show that the crash was caused by the malfunction of a thrust actuator, which has been corrected."

"Isn't the FBI investigating the crash? Isn't there a possibility that it was caused by sabotage?"

The crowd stirred and reporters began whispering into their phones. Dan suppressed a frown. He had agreed with the FBI people in Houston to keep their investigation hush-hush. Not that they've found anything, he reminded himself. But there aren't any secrets when a U.S. senator wants to get his face on national TV.

Aloud, he answered, "Senator, we just do not know what caused that actuator to fail. Even NASA is stumped by the accident."

"Was it an act of terrorism?" the senator insisted, looking straight into the TV cameras.

Dan shook his head glumly. "You'll have to ask the FBI about that, sir."

More questions, none of them hostile. Finally Quill looked down the table toward Jane. "I invited Senator Thornton to these proceedings because she has introduced legislation that has a bearing on financing high-technology ventures such as yours. Senator Thornton, do you have any questions for this witness?"

Jane sat up a little straighter as Dan thought, I have a question for you, Senator: When am I going to see you again?

"Mr. Randolph," Jane said, coolly impersonal, "what effect would it have on financing ventures such as yours if the government offered guarantees for long-term, low-interest loans?"

Dan had rehearsed the answer with Jane for a week before this hearing. But only over a videophone link. In the seven months since her surprise visit to Matagorda, Dan had been in the same room with her exactly twice, and both times there had been a crowd separating them. And Scanwell.

Almost automatically, Dan went through their prepared tutorial on financing high-technology ventures.

"There are three factors involved," he told the subcommittee. "First, high-tech ventures are almost always high risk. In my business, for example, every rocket launch has a considerable amount of risk involved, although we're reducing those risks quite a bit."

Quill nodded and Dan got the impression that Jane had already briefed him about this.

"Second," he went on, "high-tech ventures usually involve a large investment. You can't build satellites and spacecraft on a shoestring budget."

"You're talking billions of dollars?" asked one of the senators.

"Hundreds of millions, at least."

"What's the third factor?" Quill prompted.

"Time," said Dan. "The investor's money is going to be tied up for a long time, years, maybe a decade or more."

"Not a ninety-day turnaround," Jane said with a smile.

"No, not at all," Dan replied. "If you put all those three factors together—high risk, high investment cost, and a long time before payout—you can see why it's so difficult to raise investment capital."

"Would a government guarantee of long-term, low-interest loans be of help?" Jane asked.

"It already has," Dan said. "Astro Corporation has been working from loans raised in the private sector for the past several months. I'm certain that this legislation you've introduced in the Senate has opened that door for us."

One of the senators quipped, "Well, if it's worked that well for you, maybe we won't have to pass the bill."

A few of the other senators chuckled tolerantly. Jane did not, Dan noticed. He suppressed an urge to snap a snotty answer at the flippant senator.

"Any other questions for this witness?" Quill asked, looking up and down the table. "If not, then the witness is excused."

"Before I go," Dan said, "I have a short statement to make, Senators."

Quill looked down at Dan. "As long as it's short."

Dan didn't quibble with the senator's choice of words. "I just want to tell you, Senators, that we intend to start beaming power from the satellite in two weeks."

The hearing room erupted. The cameras all focused on Dan. Reporters flicked open their cell phones and began yammering into them. The senators looked at each other up and down the long banquette while the audience burst into dozens of chattering conversations.

In the midst of it all Rick Chatham leaped to his feet, ponytail flying, and shouted, "You can't do that! I'll get a court injunction!"

Quill began tapping on the wooden block in front of him, harder and harder, the impatience on his face morphing into red-faced anger. But it did no good. The reporters swarmed around Dan yelling questions at him. Vicki Lee was among them, but Dan looked past them all to search for Jane. Her chair was empty. She had already left.

DUBAI INTERNATIONAL
AIRPORT

Asim al-Bashir strode along the sand-toned carpet, which was patterned in curling arcs such as the wind would stir on the desert floor. Golden replicas of graceful palm trees lined the corridor of the Sheik Rashid terminal. Tourists and pilgrims thronged the duty-free shops where goods from all over the world were on display for the avid travelers. Al-Bashir disdained the merchants and buyers alike. Beyond the terminal's windows he could see the garish skyline of high-rise office towers and hotels, including the thirty-story-high sail shape of the Burj al Arab Hotel. Western ostentation, he sneered inwardly. Instead of resisting the West's garish culture, they imitate it and even exceed it.

When he entered the private lounge that had been reserved for him, the Egyptian was already there, looking distinctly morose in his poorly fitted white linen suit. Al-Bashir himself wore a hand-tailored silk suit of royal blue.

No, al-Bashir decided, the Egyptian is not depressed; he's apprehensive, fearful. This business of the power satellite is beyond his capacity.

Al-Bashir had bowed to The Nine's wish for a face-to-face meeting between the two men; the Egyptian had insisted it be in a location in the Moslem Middle East, where they would be relatively safe. Relatively, al-Bashir thought, with a thin smile. The United States Army occupied Dubai and the other Emirates; despite occasional suicide bombings the Americans were tightening their stranglehold on the Gulf. Well, that will change soon enough, al-Bashir thought.

The Egyptian sat with his back to the window and its view of the skyline while a uniformed airline employee poured coffee for the two men and then made his quiet departure.

"You seem apprehensive, my brother," al-Bashir said to the Egyptian.

"Randolph plans to turn on the power satellite in ten days."

"Yes. He made his grand announcement at the Senate hearing last week." Al-Bashir picked up the delicate cup and sipped at the coffee.

"Randolph made a bold gesture."

Al-Bashir smiled. "I have come to know the man. He is an egomaniac at heart."

"Still … will we be ready in ten days?"

Tapping the data disc encased in the breast pocket of his suit jacket, al-Bashir replied, "I have the complete blueprints of the satellite. Once it begins beaming power to the ground, we will seize it and shift the beam to Washington."

"You can do that?"

"Quite easily. While Randolph's technicians in Texas are trying to determine what's gone wrong with their satellite, we will concentrate the microwave beam and kill thousands."

"Including their President?"

"It is all arranged. Despite his own high opinion of himself, Randolph is a trusting soul. A typical American. I helped him to get the financing he needed, so he believes I am his friend. He has opened his entire operation to me. They are all pathetically naïve."

"You are certain this will work?" the Egyptian asked, reaching for his own coffee cup. "The others of The Nine are rather … concerned."

"Tell them it is written. Once the power satellite begins to work we will turn it into a death weapon against the enemies of Allah."

The Egyptian smiled minimally and appeared to relax somewhat. Al-Bashir smiled back at him. As they sipped the strong, hot, sweetened coffee al-Bashir told himself sternly, Let him believe that we strike in the name of Allah. Let the others believe that I am a fighter in the war between Islam and the West. But don't let yourself fall into such a belief. Religion has its purposes. Use their faith, but remember your goal: Tricontinental Oil, and the power to bend nations to my will.

The skyline of Houston was almost as garish, and much larger, than Dubai's. Sitting behind his desk in the FBI building, Nacho Chavez took a bite of the breakfast burrito he was holding in his right hand, wrapped in a napkin that was already soaked with grease.

"It's got to be al-Bashir," said Kelly Eamons.

"What evidence do you have?" he demanded.

"This Roberto goon was working for al-Bashir," Eamons said, sitting tensely on the front three inches of her chair. "Al-Bashir didn't use any other driver when he was in Houston."

"So?"

"Roberto was the muscle. He probably killed Larsen."

"The Astro employee who committed suicide?" Nacho asked through a mouthful of burrito.

"It wasn't suicide. Roberto murdered him."

"Prove it."

Eamons's blue-green eyes snapped at him. Redheads and their Irish temper, Chavez thought.

"Okay," she said slowly. "We have his voiceprint from that phony message he left on Larsen's answering machine. We need to find him and get a voice match from him."

Still playing the devil's advocate, Chavez replied, "We don't know where he is, and even if we did we don't have anything to hold him on."

"He jumped bail on the assault charge."

"Local rap. Not our jurisdiction."

"He's probably fled the state, gone back to L.A."

Chavez chewed thoughtfully, then said, "Probably."

"That makes him a fugitive, doesn't it? Interstate. That's our jurisdiction, isn't it?"

Chavez had to grin at her earnestness. "Kelly, do you think for half a microsecond that the suits upstairs are going to okay a manhunt for a guy who's jumped bail on a measly assault charge?"

Eamons said immediately, "Nacho, you could phone the L.A. office and ask them to look for him."

"Yeah, L.A.'s so small that one particular Hispanic guy will be dead easy to find."

"Come on! It can't hurt to ask. He's got those gang tattoos, according to his sheet. That'll help, won't it?"

Putting the remains of his burrito on his desk, Chavez asked, "Wait. Back up a minute. Why are you so interested in Roberto?"

"Because he murdered Larsen. Maybe Tenny, as well."

"And you think if we nail him he'll roll on whoever hired him."

"Right. Al-Bashir. The man's probably a terrorist. He's the one who sabotaged Astro's spaceship and he hired Roberto to cover his tracks."

"How do you know that?"

"He was part owner of the tanker that blew up beneath the Golden Gate Bridge, Nacho."

"And the other tanker? In Florida?"

She shook her head. "Different company. But I bet if we keep digging we'll find he had a hand in that one, too."

"Maybe," Chavez admitted. "But what of it? He owns a chunk of Tricontinental Oil, too. Does that make him a terrorist? Hell, they're funding Astro Corporation and the power satellite project."

Eamons said nothing.

"It's too thin, Kelly," said Chavez. "You don't have anything except your suspicions. There's no real evidence at all."

"The voiceprint."

"Well, that *might* be useful," Chavez agreed. "If we had Roberto and could match him to it."

"So try to find him!"

With a patient sigh, Chavez said, "I suppose I could call a guy I know in the L.A. office. But I don't think anything will come of it. Hell, Roberto could be in Hong Kong, for all we know."

Eamons nodded glumly. It was very thin, she agreed silently. We're just spinning our wheels, trying to find Roberto. Al-Bashir's the one we're after and I've got to figure out a way to get to him.

BAIKONUR COSMODROME, KAZAKHSTAN

Welcome to purgatory!" said Yuri Vasilyevich Nikolayev, jovially. He wore a heavy overcoat and a fur hat squashed down on his thick eyebrows. His breath made clouds in the chill air.

The two men who had just alit from the wearily chuffing old train looked around uneasily. As far as the eye could see the land stretched away, flat, brown, and dusty. The sky was enormous, bright blue, cloudless. They were both bundled in thickly padded coats; one wore a woolen watch cap, the other was hatless. The wind whipping in from the arid wasteland blew what was left of his thinning hair.

"You come on good day," Nikolayev said as the two others hefted their travel bags and followed him toward the train's baggage car, where their equipment was being unloaded. "Fine weather. Maybe spring will arrive, after all."

Nikolayev spoke in thickly accented English, the only language that all three men understood. The other two said hardly a word as they toted the bulky loads of equipment to the minibus Nikolayev had waiting for them. They allowed no one to touch their packages, not even the Russian cosmonaut.

Gilly Williamson coughed as he climbed into the ice-cold minibus. "Dust in me throat," he said, half apologetically.

"Much dust," said Nikolayev, nodding sympathetically. Clambering into the driver's seat, he pointed skyward. "Soon we will be above it all."

Williamson's face was a map of Ireland: pale skin, green eyes, light brown hair that fell boyishly across his forehead. But his face was old, aged beyond his years. His eyes were guarded, suspicious. Born in bloody Belfast, at age three he had been orphaned and nearly killed himself by a car bomb that had been set off in a crowded shopping street. By the time he was old enough to go to university he was an expert wiring man for an offshoot group of the IRA. The organization helped to pay for his schooling, but once he graduated with an engineer's degree he left Ireland for good and built electronic systems for a major American aerospace firm. Then the company had been bought out in a hostile takeover and Williamson was laid off. Worse, a routine physical for another firm that was about to hire him revealed he had lung cancer. He was unemployable.

That was when a former IRA man contacted him and told him about a job that was available. Very hush-hush. At first Williamson was puzzled: What would an ex-IRA man be doing working for the bloody government? Soon enough, Gilly discovered this was not a government job. Far from it. For nearly a year he had trained for this job in space. He couldn't help feeling nervous about flying into orbit, but he was determined not to let anyone see his fear. After all, why should a man diagnosed with terminal lung cancer be afraid of flying into orbit?

The third man of the team was Malfoud Bouchachi, a slim, balding, dour Algerian engineer who had helped to devise the plan for destroying the Golden Gate Bridge. Slightly older than Williamson, Bouchachi was a veteran of several terrorist strikes. Possessed of iron self-control, cold and calculating, he trusted no one, not even this Russian who was supposed to fly them up to the Yankee power satellite.

Nikolayev chattered happily as he drove them and their equipment in the minibus from the train station toward the wooden barracks where they would be quartered until their flight.

"Not a luxury hotel," he warned them, "but toilets work most of time and food is passable. You get the joke? Passable!" He laughed by himself.

Once they cleared the train depot they could see the cosmodrome's rows of gantry cranes standing against the empty sky, steel latticework towers, silent, rusting.

"My grandfather helped to build those," Nikolayev shouted over the grumble of the minibus's engine, pointing as he drove along the rutted road with one hand. "Back in Khrushcheff's time this was busy place, spaceport to the universe, let me tell you."

The Irishman and the Algerian said nothing, simply gaped at the long rows of rusting towers.

"Now, not so busy," Nikolayev went on. "Government doesn't have money for space anymore. Private companies—maybe sometimes. Not much, though."

Williamson said, "Our people are paying quite a lot for this flight."

And Bouchachi thought, Quite a lot, considering that this will be a one-way mission.

Dinners with al-Bashir ought to be pleasant, April thought. Yet she always felt tense near him, wary. The best restaurant in Lamar wasn't all that much for a man of the world like him, she supposed, but he gave every appearance of enjoying his steak and never let the conversation go dull. At least once a week they dined together. Sometimes they went dancing afterward, although it wasn't easy to find a place where they played anything other than country and western stomps.

April enjoyed the attention and al-Bashir never got grabby or demanding afterward. She would kiss him good night at the door of her apartment building and that was it. He didn't even try to get her to invite him upstairs to her apartment.

Yet there was something in those dark brown eyes of his, some secret amusement or anticipation that he wasn't sharing with her. Does he really like me, April wondered, or is he just dating me to find out more about what Dan's doing? It can't be that, she told herself. Dan's given him free rein to go everywhere and talk to anybody he wants to.

For weeks April puzzled over the situation. An American guy would have made his move long before this, she knew. And from all she had heard about Arabs, they treated women like possessions. Yet al-Bashir was outwardly gentle and pleasant. A good conversationalist, good dancer. She thought that she should enjoy being with him. Except—his eyes bothered her. The way he looked at her, she felt like a deer being watched by a wolf. He strips me with his eyes, April realized. It made her uneasy.

She found herself wondering what it would be like to go out with Dan. Would he be gentle and patient and pleasant? She knew he wouldn't. And she realized that she wouldn't want Dan to be.

Al-Bashir enjoyed his dates with April, as well. She was lovely, intelligent, and eager to learn from him. He especially liked the way she listened, wide-eyed, to his tales of world travels and international business affairs. She was reluctant to get romantically involved, but he knew that there was plenty of time for that. And there were plenty of women in Houston to satisfy his sexual needs.

April is like a beautiful, sensitive doe, he told himself. She's not to be hunted so much as won over, like the ancient story of beauty and the beast.

After the power satellite has done its work, he told himself. After I've destroyed Astro Corporation and Dan Randolph has been crucified by the politicians and the news media. After she has no job and no hope. Then she will turn to me and offer herself. I will get her and get rid of Garrison at the same time. I will be the most powerful of them all.

Al-Bashir smiled to himself. The future will be sweet, indeed.

HOUSTON, TEXAS

From her little cubicle down the hall from Chavez's office, Kelly Eamons phoned April at her Astro Corporation office.

April's image on Eamons's desktop screen looked surprised once she recognized the FBI agent.

"Hi, Kelly! How are you? Have you found out anything new?"

Wishing she had something positive to say, Eamons replied guardedly, "Not really. What's happening with you?"

"This place is jumping. We're going to turn on the powersat next week. Every news outfit in the country is buzzing around. They all want to interview Dan and Gerry Adair, our astronaut. They're even asking for interviews with the engineers."

Eamons tried to hide her disappointment. She'd been hoping that April wasn't too busy to help her stalled investigation.

"I thought Dan made a mistake to schedule the turn-on for the Sunday of the holiday weekend," April was rattling on, "but he's a lot smarter about these things than I am. It's a slow news day, and the media's practically frothing at the mouth to have a big story for Sunday."

Big story if the satellite works, Eamons thought. But, she realized, an even bigger story if it doesn't work.

To April she said, "I understand that one of Tricontinental Oil's directors is spending a lot of time down there in Matagorda." Before April could ask, she added, "Asim al-Bashir."

"Oh, yes. Asim's here all the time."

"Asim?" Eamons's ears perked up.

Lowering her voice slightly, April said, "I've been dating him."

"You have?"

"Nothing serious. Just dinner."

"Really?"

"He's very nice. Sort of."

Her mind racing, Eamons tried to make small talk while she decided how much to tell April. The kid's not a trained agent, she told herself. You got her into enough trouble with that Kinsky guy and Roberto. If al-Bashir really is the brains behind Roberto and everything else...

"He's invited me to come up to Houston for a visit," April was saying. "Maybe we could get together then."

"That sounds a little like walking into the spider's parlor," Eamons said, still wondering what to do.

"Don't worry. I can't get away from the office until after the powersat's turned on," April said.

"Still..."

"I'll get my own hotel room," April said, her smile brighter. With a laugh she added, "If you're worried about me you can have an agent follow me wherever I go."

Or plant a bug on you, Eamons said to herself.

For months Jane had ignored Dan's phone messages. In truth, she had been too busy to see him, with Morgan Scanwell's constant campaigning across the nation. New Hampshire, Iowa, South Carolina, the smashing Super Tuesday victories and now the California, New York, and Texas primaries coming up. The major leagues.

Dan had called insistently, almost every day since their brief foolish fling at his place in Matagorda. Stupid thing to do, Jane told herself every time she saw his name on her list of unanswered messages. You allowed your hormones to overwhelm your good sense. If Morgan ever finds out...! But coldly, logically, she told herself that if Morgan found out he would do nothing. He might be hurt, crushed even, but he would neither do nor say anything that would sidetrack his campaign to the White House.

Nor will I, Jane decided. I owe Morgan that much. I can't let Dan interfere, can't let him muddy the waters no matter how much I love him. Not now. It's too late for that now. Maybe not ever.

Still, her heart had nearly stopped when she'd seen Dan at the Senate subcommittee hearing. She'd known he would be there, she'd thought she'd steeled herself for the moment, yet still her knees went weak at the sight of him. It had taken all her strength, all her resolve, to sit through his testimony and remain cool, unmoved.

Now, as she sat alone in her office at the end of a long, draining day, his name appeared again on her desktop screen, right at the top of calls she should answer.

Almost without her consciously willing it, Jane clicked on his name.

Dan's face appeared on the screen. He was grinning happily. "I know you're busy but I just wanted to say thanks for helping us. Sunday morning we're supposed to turn the powersat on. Maybe you can come down here Saturday. I'll have a surprise for you."

His image froze, a set of telephone numbers superimposed over it: office, personal direct line, cell phone.

A surprise, she thought. I'll bet. Probably a bottle of champagne and a freshly made bed. Despite herself, Jane smiled. Then she thought, Morgan ought to be at the Astro facility when Dan turns the power satellite on. After all, he is the governor of Texas and Astro is in his state. It would be good publicity, a fine chance to show his energy independence ideas can really work.

She brought up Morgan's schedule for the coming week. He'll be spending the next three days in California and New York, she saw. Friday night back to Austin, ostensibly attending to his duties as governor but actually mending fences and shaking hands for the upcoming Texas primary. Monday the Memorial Day barbecue. Jane called Austin and spoke to Scanwell's travel aide.

"He can jet down to Matagorda for a few hours on Sunday," she said. "He'll get more news coverage there than in Austin."

The travel aide, a lank-haired, sleepy-eyed brunette, nodded unenthusiastically. "Yes, Senator, I suppose so. But he's got a full schedule of meetings set for Sunday and then the barbecue on the holiday."

"Bring the important ones along on the jet with him," Jane told her. "They'll appreciate being on the plane with the governor and then seeing the kickoff of the power satellite."

"I don't know if I can do that this late," the aide complained. "It's already Tuesday and—"

"You can do it," Jane said firmly. "I have every confidence in you."

The aide nodded again, even more glumly. They both understood quite well that when the governor's campaign manager makes a suggestion, it's really a command.

That done, Jane clicked to her own schedule for the Memorial Day weekend. The Senate would be adjourned until Tuesday noon. Friday she had meetings scheduled with Denny and the rest of the strategists to plan the final weeks of the campaign leading up to the party's convention in Denver.

I could fly home to the ranch Friday night, she told herself. I could pop down to Matagorda early Saturday and be there when Morgan arrives on Sunday.

I could, Jane thought. But I won't.

MATAGORDA ISLAND,
TEXAS

You jes keep that A-rab away from my hangar," Niles Muhamed said, almost in a growl.

Dan leaned back in his desk chair and stared at the scowling technician. He couldn't remember the last time Muhamed had made the hundred-yard trip from Hangar B to his office.

"What's the problem, Niles?"

"No problem," Muhamed said, standing tensely before Dan's ornate desk. "I jes don't like him snoopin' around the oh-two."

"Has he been in the cockpit?" Dan asked.

"That'll be the day!" Muhamed snorted. "I don't let nobody touch that baby 'cept Gerry and his ground crew. Nobody else gets closer'n ten feet."

"So what's al-Bashir done that bothers you?"

Muhamed's frown turned from suspicious to puzzled. "Nothin' I can put a finger on. He's jes slippery, you know, like he's always askin' questions and tryin' to figure out what's goin' down."

Spreading his hands, Dan tried to explain, "Niles, he's our pipeline to the money that's keeping us going. It's natural that he wants to know what we're doing."

"Natural, huh?"

"I've given him a pretty free hand to look at anything he likes," Dan admitted. "He's been all over the place."

"Yeah, well you jes tell him to stay outta Hangar B. I don't want nobody messin' with the oh-two."

Dan thought, I can tell al-Bashir that we're closing off the hangar as a security measure, this close to starting up the powersat. He'll see the necessity of that.

"Okay," he said to the scowling technician. "I'll tell him. In fact, you can keep the hangar closed to anybody but the plane's crew."

With a single curt nod Muhamed turned around and marched out of the office, leaving Dan musing about security. Wouldn't hurt to keep Hangar B sealed off, he thought. Al-Bashir can poke into the control center or anyplace else he likes, but we'll keep tight security on the spaceplane. That's our most vulnerable spot. We'll keep him away from it. Probably not necessary, but Niles is right: don't let anybody screw around with the plane. One crash was more than enough.

Later that day Dan was in the satellite control center, trying to look calm and confident, but he could hardly restrain an urge to jump up and down like a little kid or turn cartwheels all along the rows of consoles. He settled for loosening the tie that was already pulled away from his unbuttoned collar. Lynn Van Buren stood beside him, wearing her usual dark pantsuit and string of pearls.

Standing at the double-doored entrance to the big room, Dan and his chief engineer watched with a mixture of admiration and excitement as the engineers went through their checkout routines at the rows of consoles lined across the windowless cinderblock control center. An oversized display screen covered one wall. It showed an electronic map of the southwestern part of the United States, northern Mexico and Baja California, and a large swath of the Pacific Ocean. West of the Galápagos Islands, precisely on the equator at 106 degrees west longitude, glowed a single bright red dot: the location of the powersat 22,300 miles above the ocean.

"It's all going smoothly," Dan said, rubbing his hands together nervously.

"Smooth as a baby's bottom," agreed Van Buren. She looked serious, even dour, her round face unsmiling.

"White Sands checks out okay?" he asked.

Van Buren nodded. "They're ready to receive right now."

"We could turn the bird on now, couldn't we?"

Van Buren hesitated a fraction of a second. "Give us the next two days to triple-check everything, chief. You don't want a fizzle on Sunday in front of everybody."

"Yeah, right," said Dan. "But I want a preliminary start-up Saturday afternoon."

"I know. We've got it in the schedule. Ten-minute test run."

"Make it half an hour."

She cocked a brow at him. "Chief, the magnetrons and everything else come up to full power output in less than a minute. A ten-minute prelim run is plenty of time to make sure it's all working."

"Half an hour," he repeated.

"It's not necessary."

Dan grinned at her. "Do it for me, okay?"

With the resigned expression of an engineer who is doomed to satisfy silly demands from management, Van Buren shrugged her chunky shoulders and acquiesced. "Okay, half an hour."

"Good."

He practically danced out of the control center and across the parking lot that separated the building from Hangar A. A crew of safety-masked painters up on scaffolds were spraying robin's-egg blue over the gray cinderblocks. Dan wanted the place to look new and clean and bright for the camera crews that would descend on them Sunday morning.

He was still in a happy mood as he breezed past April's desk and entered his private office. She came in right behind him, a PDA clutched in her hand.

"We just got a call from Governor Scanwell's office," April announced as Dan slid into his desk chair. "He'll be here for the turn-on ceremony Sunday morning."

Dan's heart skipped a beat. That means Jane will be here, too, he immediately thought. Maybe she'll come Saturday. No, he warned himself. Don't expect that. It's too much to hope for.

"He'll be flying in from Austin with six or seven guests," April added.

"Great," said Dan. "The more the merrier."

"You can expect a lot more pickets out by the gate on Sunday, too," April said.

"More than today?" Dan's security chief, Mitch O'Connell, had told him that the ecofreaks were waving placards at the cars coming in for work in the morning and screaming obscenities at their drivers.

"Mr. O'Connell says there'll be a lot more. He's worried they might try to get through the gate Sunday and disrupt everything."

Dan thought for a moment. "I'll have to talk to Mitch about it. Maybe bring in a crew of rent-a-cops for the day."

"Governor Scanwell will be flying in, so he won't have to come through the gate," she said.

"Yeah. But when those nuts see the TV trucks rolling up to the gate they'll get frantic. Their big chance for publicity."

April looked worried. "You don't think they'll actually disrupt things, do you? Or cause damage?"

"Maybe we ought to hire a SWAT team," Dan grumbled.

Late that afternoon Asim al-Bashir walked into Dan's office unannounced; he simply smiled at April as he went past her desk, rapped once on the jamb of Dan's open door, and stepped in.

Dan looked up from his computer screen, more curious than annoyed.

"I just want to let you know," al-Bashir said without preamble, "that I'll be out of town for the next day or two."

"Houston?" Dan asked. "Don't tell me you're going to get Garrison himself to come down for the turn-on."

Al-Bashir chuckled. "No, Garrison isn't interested. Actually, I've got to fly to Europe for a meeting."

"Will you be back Sunday?"

His smile remained in place, but the expression in his eyes changed subtly. "Oh yes," said al-Bashir. "I'll be here Sunday. I wouldn't miss it for the world."

Aren't you the least bit nervous?" Gilly Williamson asked.

Malfoud Bouchachi closed the drawer into which he had placed the few clothes he'd brought with him. "No," said the Algerian. "I find that I am strangely calm."

Williamson shook his head in admiration. The two men were in the bedroom they would share until they were launched into space. Outside the room's only window the flat parched vastness of Kazakhstan stretched to the bare brown hills on the dusty, barren horizon.

"A strange place to die," Williamson muttered.

"We will not die *here*," said Bouchachi.

"I know. But still..." Williamson took in a breath of dry, dust-laden air, and coughed. "Better than a fucking hospital ward, I suppose."

"We will accomplish much more than we ever could otherwise. Our deaths will be meaningful."

Sitting on the thin mattress of his bed, Williamson smiled bitterly. "Nobody's death is meaningful, friend."

"You are a Christian?" Bouchachi asked.

"I was a Catholic."

"And now?"

"Nothing. Nothing at all."

Bouchachi nodded knowingly. "Ah, I understand. I have been promised a martyr's reward in Paradise."

"D'you believe it?"

"Sometimes. It doesn't really matter. At least, that is what I tell myself when my faith weakens."

"Fuck all," Williamson said fervently. "We're all going to die, no matter what we do. Sooner is better than later."

"If your death accomplishes something."

"Oh, we'll accomplish something, all right. We'll take half a million with us."

"That many?"

"At least."

The two men had trained separately for six months, Bouchachi at Star City, on the outskirts of Moscow, Williamson at the Chinese space center near Beijing. Neither of them knew how to pilot a spacecraft; that would be Niko- layev's task. Their assignment was to reach the power satellite and turn it into an instrument of mass murder. Money from The Nine fueled their mission: al- Bashir and his cohorts funneled tens of millions of carefully laundered dollars into Russia, China, and Kazakhstan. Williamson's family would be told that he died in an automobile accident in Hubei Province, near the site of the Three Gorges Dam project; they would receive a hefty pension from a construction firm owned by al-Bashir. Bouchachi, whose family had been killed three years earlier in an Algerian government raid against a fundamentalist sect's home village, had no need of such arrangements.

Williamson got up from the creaking bed and walked to the screened window. Bouchachi went back to meticulously rearranging his few clothes and moving his prayer rug from the bottom to the top drawer of the room's only bureau. By standing to one side of the window and craning his neck, Williamson could see a tall, white-painted rocket booster standing on one of the launchpads.

"Come look," he said to his comrade. "They've got our bird up."

Bouchachi turned and glanced out the window. "Our ride to Paradise," he muttered.

THORNTON RANCH, OKLAHOMA

The Senate had adjourned just after noon on Friday so its members could rush home for a three-day Memorial Day weekend of mending fences and twisting arms. Jane had flown to the ranch in a private jet, looking forward to at least one day of rest out of the three-day "holiday." Morgan's campaign was rolling smoothly, but there was still so much more to be done.

She was in the sitting room of her master suite and had just poured herself a nightcap of straight golden tequila when Tómas, her majordomo—a bald, spare, elderly Mexican of great dignity—quietly announced that Dan Randolph had arrived and was waiting in the entryway.

Her first reaction was anger. How dare he come here, uninvited, unannounced? she demanded silently as she wrapped a floor-length robe around her nightgown. Yet by the time she had reached the ranch house's entry her anger had largely melted away. And when she saw Dan standing there, in jeans and an open-necked sports shirt, smiling sheepishly like a boy who'd done something he knew wasn't right but had done it anyway, she couldn't keep herself from smiling back at him.

But she quickly stifled her smile and demanded sharply, "What are you doing here?"

Dan made a vague gesture with both his hands. "You wouldn't come to see me, so I came to see you."

Before she could ask the next obvious question, he explained, "Your office said you were spending Saturday at home and your next public appointment is at Astro Corporation headquarters on Sunday. I thought I could fly you down to Matagorda tomorrow."

Making certain that her robe was tightly belted, Jane led Dan into the spacious living room.

"I flew in by myself," Dan said. "Landed in the dark. Rented a car at the Marietta airport under a phony name. Nobody knows I'm here."

"Except every servant in the house," she snapped.

Dan replied ingenuously, "I thought they were all old family retainers, loyal unto death."

Despite herself, Jane laughed. "You're incorrigible."

"I try to be."

"Well, as long as you're here you might as well sit down."

Dan went to the sofa, under the Vickrey painting of a little girl standing beneath an umbrella on a rain-slicked parking lot. He sat squarely in the middle of the plump cushions. Jane took the armchair at one end of the sofa, so Dan shifted over toward her.

"Would you like a drink?" she asked.

"Do you have any Armagnac?"

Jane called for Tómas and asked him to find the tequila she had left in her bedroom. "Do we have any . . ." She turned to Dan. "What was it?"

"Armagnac."

Tómas's gray brows rose a millimeter. "I will look in the bar, sir."

Once he left the room, Jane asked, "What in the world made you fly up here in the dead of night like this?"

"I wanted to see you."

She tried to frown at him. "Dan, what happened the last time—"

"Was wonderful."

"I'm a married woman."

"You don't love him. You love me."

"But I'm still married to him."

His brow furrowed. "Yes. We'll have to do something about that."

Tómas returned carrying a colorful ceramic tray that bore Jane's shot glass of tequila and a trio of bottles.

"There is no Armagnac, I'm sorry to say," he reported. "Perhaps one of these will do?"

Dan scanned the labels and found a bottle of Presidente. "This will be fine," he said.

Tómas poured him a snifter of the brandy and departed.

Dan sipped, then said, "I had hoped you'd pop down to Matagorda to-morrow instead of waiting until Sunday."

"I have a full day tomorrow," Jane lied. "Then your ceremony Sunday morning, and then I've got to fly to Los Angeles for Morgan's big rally there Sunday night. Monday I've got to get back to Washington for the Memorial Day ceremony at Arlington National Cemetery."

"That's a full weekend, all right," Dan admitted. "The Memorial Day ceremony'll be at the Tomb of the Unknowns?"

"Monday afternoon. The president's going to be there, of course."

"Of course. But do you have to be?"

Ignoring his question, she asked, "You said you had a surprise for me."

"Yep."

"What is it?"

"If I tell you, it won't be a surprise."

Jane studied his face for a moment. Then, "I'm not going down with you tomorrow, Dan. I'll be there first thing Sunday morning, when Morgan and the other VIPs arrive."

"Chaperons," he muttered.

"You don't need a chaperon," she said fervently, "you need a keeper."

Dan laughed. "Yeah, maybe."

Very seriously, Jane said, "Dan, there's nothing we can do. I can't risk upsetting Morgan's campaign. We're planning to announce that we're married just before the convention starts, for god's sake."

"Okay. After he's elected and all safely ensconced in the White House you can announce that you're divorcing him."

"Be serious!"

"I am serious," he said. "About you."

She said nothing for a long moment. Dan got up from the couch and bent over and kissed her.

She pushed away. "You're sleeping in one of the guest bedrooms tonight."

"Sure," he said. They both knew it wouldn't work that way.

High over the Atlantic Ocean, al-Bashir stretched out in his bed. One of the advantages of leasing a private jet plane, he thought, is that you don't have to sit up all night in one of those uncomfortable reclining chairs.

He had spent the day in the hilltop villa just outside Marseille, inspecting the makeshift control station that his aides had installed there. Much of the equipment was old, almost antique, but al-Bashir satisfied himself that it would work well enough. Not up to NASA standards, of course, but it would get the job done. Some of it was stolen. Most of it had been leased from the Russians. It had worked well enough for them over the years. The technicians would be able to disassemble it quickly and leave no trace of their work for the police or Western intelligence agencies to find.

Al-Bashir had barely caught a glimpse of the beautiful Mediterranean during his hurried last-minute inspection of the control station. He flew in, let the technicians demonstrate the equipment for him, and immediately took off for Texas again. He kept his clock on American Central Daylight Saving Time throughout the trip.

As he drifted to sleep, lulled by the steady thrum of the jet engines, he fantasized about having April in bed with him. She'll be thrilled to fly a private jet to France, he thought. She'll be happy to please me for that.

LANGLEY, VIRGINIA

The director of the Central Intelligence Agency was not happy about coming in to the office on the Saturday morning of the long weekend. "It's a good thing the Orioles aren't in town," he muttered darkly to his aides as he took his chair at the head of the long, polished table.

Only three other people were in the conference room with him, two of them women. The long windows that swept across one entire wall were covered with thick drapes. The air conditioning was so frigid that the director felt slightly uncomfortable even with his vest and jacket on. The entire front wall was a smart screen that showed, at the moment, a map of the world.

One of the women, a top analyst from the Asia desk, took the chair at the director's right and pecked at the laptop computer she had brought with her. A grainy telephoto image of a freighter tied to a dock appeared on the smart screen.

"Our people in Singapore," she said, "reported a shipment of arms and explosives arrived in port last night."

"From?" asked the director.

"Calcutta, if the ship's manifest can be believed."

"What do you think?"

"Satellite tracking shows the freighter originated in Shanghai."

The director rocked back in his chair. "Chinese weaponry. Damn."

The man sitting across the table from the analyst was from the satellite surveillance office. He chimed in, "It could be heading for the rebels in Myanmar."

"Or Sri Lanka," said the other woman.

With a shake of his head, the director asked, "Then why put in at Singapore?"

"They're not off-loading," said the analyst. "Not yet, anyway."

For this they called me in on a holiday morning, the director groused to himself. Aloud, he said, "What's your assessment?"

"Terrorism," said the analyst.

"In Singapore?"

She shook her head. "Indonesia. The fundamentalist guerrillas must have closed a deal with the Chinese. Oil for guns."

The surveillance man on the other side of the table countered, "The guerrillas don't have control of the oil fields."

"Not yet."

They argued the point back and forth until the director silenced them. "Okay," he said. "Notify the authorities in Singapore. They can search the ship, impound the arms."

The analyst grinned. "And they'll be a lot tougher on the smugglers than we could be."

"If they're not bought off," muttered the surveillance man.

The director pointed a finger at him. "They won't be, if they know that we know what's going on." Turning to the analyst, "I don't want our source of information compromised."

She nodded agreement.

"Anything else?" the director asked, anxious to get back to his home and an afternoon of gardening.

"Some unusual shipments of electronics gear near Marseille," said the other woman.

"Drug equipment?"

"No," she said. "Electronics. Several truckloads."

"Maybe some frogs are starting a rock band," snickered the surveillance guy. The others chuckled.

"That's it, then?" asked the director.

"Unannounced rocket launch from Baikonur," the man said. He tapped at his laptop, and a crisp satellite view of the launch center in Kazakhstan filled the screen.

"Anything unusual?"

"We don't know what the payload is, but it's big. They used their heaviest booster." With a pencil-slim laser pointer he highlighted one of the launch stands. "And it looks like they're setting up for a manned mission, as well."

"Resupply for the space station?"

The man shook his head. "Wrong orbit for that."

"It's not a missile, is it?"

"No, no worries about that. But it's a big payload, unidentified and unannounced. Might be a scientific mission. Or a communications relay."

"Why wouldn't they announce it?"

The surveillance man shrugged exaggeratedly. "You know the Russians: a riddle wrapped in a mystery inside an enigma."

The director frowned at him. "Our job is to solve riddles, whatever they're wrapped in."

Nodding glumly, the surveillance man said, "We're watching, sir. Wish we had some humint on the ground, though."

"I'll see what I can do," said the director, already halfway out of his chair. "Tomorrow."

Dawn was just beginning to brighten the Oklahoma sky when Dan awoke gradually, like a scuba diver rising slowly from the dark depths toward the sunlit surface of the sea. As he opened his eyes, for an instant he didn't recognize where he was. Then he turned his head and there was Jane sleeping peacefully beside him. He grinned and turned on his side to cup his body against hers.

She awoke with a start, then relaxed and grinned over her bare shoulder at him. "You're poking me."

"Your snoring woke me up," he said.

"I don't snore. And you're *poking* me."

"Natural reaction," said Dan. "There's only one way to cure it."

"Only one?" she teased.

"There are certain variations," he admitted, stroking her flank.

"Such as?"

It was full morning when they finally got out of bed and showered. Dan made an elaborate show of peeking out into the corridor to make certain none of the servants saw him coming out of Jane's bedroom.

"I'll go mess up the bed in the guest room," he whispered to her.

She tossed a towel at him. "Go to the kitchen and tell the cook what you want for breakfast. I'll be there in a few minutes."

Dan waltzed down the corridor and found the kitchen.

"Buenas dias," he said brightly to the cook.

She gave him a fishy look. "What you like for breakfast, sir?"

Dan almost blurted that he needed a batch of vitamin E. He caught himself, though, and ordered huevos rancheros with grapefruit juice and black coffee.

Jane came in just as the cook put Dan's eggs on the table before him. She slipped into the padded chair in the breakfast nook beside him, her expression very serious.

"Dan" she said, leaning close to him, "this isn't going to work."

His lighthearted mood evaporated.

"What we're doing is wrong, Dan," Jane said earnestly. "Just plain wrong."

"Felt good to me," he mumbled.

"Be serious!"

He looked into her beautiful, troubled eyes. "For what it's worth, this is driving me crazy."

"We've got to stop."

"Or tell Scanwell what the score is."

"No! We can't do that."

"I could."

"Dan, no!"

"I could walk right up to him tomorrow and say, 'Hey, pal, your wife and I are in love with each other.' "

"Please, Dan."

"It's the truth, isn't it?"

"That's only part of the truth."

He felt a dull, sullen resentment building up inside him. "And the rest of it is that you think his becoming president is more important than you and me."

"It is, Dan. It truly is."

"Is it?"

"It's important to your work, too," she said earnestly. "It will mean so much. To all of us. To everyone."

Glancing down at his untouched breakfast, Dan pushed his chair back from the table. "Okay, you go get your husband elected president. I've got to get back to the office and get that satellite running."

Jane made no attempt to stop him.

MATAGORDA ISLAND, TEXAS

Dan's foul mood only worsened as he flew the Staggerwing back to Matagorda. He tried to forget about Jane and the mess his personal life was in. Yeah, he told himself as he banked the biplane around a massive thunderhead that was building up above the Texas plain. Forget about her. That's easy. Like forgetting about breathing. Think about business, he commanded himself. Get your mind off Jane and Scanwell. Stop thinking about them together.

All right, concentrate on business. What if something goes wrong with the satellite? You'll have every VIP you could coax down to Matagorda standing there watching. What if something goes wrong? You'll be laughed out of business, that's what. Like that old Vanguard rocket, back in the beginning of the space age. Everybody in the world watching and it blows up four feet above the launch stand.

So what can I do about it? Dan asked himself. We push the button and the powersat doesn't turn on. Some glitch. Something goes wrong. The Staggerwing bounced through a layer of turbulence as he began his descent toward the airstrip at Matagorda. I ought to have the spaceplane ready to go, Dan realized.

Have the bird on the pad with Adair and a maintenance crew ready to take off at a moment's notice. That's what the spaceplane's for, after all. Quick reaction. Immediate access to orbit.

As he cranked down the biplane's landing gear and lined up on the airstrip Dan made up his mind. Put the spaceplane on the pad, have her ready to go if an emergency comes up. That means the launch crew has to come in to work today and the rest of the weekend, too. Garrison's comptroller won't like that.

The plane's wheels touched the concrete with a screech and twin puffs of rubber. Dan let it roll to the end of the strip, thinking, If we have the spaceplane ready to go, even if there's a glitch the news media will have a launch to photograph. So we'll spend a little more of Garrison's money, so what.

It was nearly noon by the time he pushed through the double doors of the newly painted control center building. Standing in the midst of the quietly tense technicians, Lynn Van Buren yanked off her headset when she saw Dan coming up the aisle between the consoles toward her.

"Glad you could make it," she said, a grin dimpling her cheeks. "We were about to start her up without you."

"I was unavoidably detained," Dan muttered.

Eying him up and down, she said, "My god, chief, your clothes look as if you've slept in them."

Dan broke into a wolfish grin. "That, I did *not* do."

"Lucky girl."

"Are we investigating my sex life or getting the powersat on the air?" he demanded, trying to sound severe.

"Everything's up and running, chief. Everybody's in place. Even Mr. al-Bashir dropped in." She pointed to the Tunisian, who was sitting at one of the spare consoles, a headset clamped over his dark hair. Dan felt his face tighten into a frown. Al-Bashir's sticking his nose into every damned thing, he grumbled silently. Then he thought, He's your conduit to the money; you'll just have to put up with him.

Everything seemed to be humming along efficiently, Dan saw. The technicians were bent over their tasks at their consoles, display screens flickering with images and data.

He went to the console where al-Bashir was sitting and tapped him on the shoulder. Al-Bashir looked up, startled for a moment, then relaxed into a smile.

"This is exciting," he said.

Nodding, Dan said, "It sure is."

Something in al-Bashir's eyes troubled Dan. There was more than excitement there, more than anticipation. The man's eyes glowed as if this moment was going to be a personal triumph for him.

Dan heard himself warn, "Don't touch any buttons."

Al-Bashir chuckled politely. "Not to worry. Your Mrs. Van Buren has disconnected all the controls on this keyboard. I am a passive spectator, nothing more."

But his eyes told Dan there was a lot more going on than that.

Excusing himself, Dan went back to where Van Buren was standing in the central aisle.

"I want the spaceplane on the pad, ready for launch. Now."

"Now?" she gasped.

"Now. This afternoon. Get Gerry Adair and the maintenance geeks and tell them to hold themselves in readiness for an immediate launch."

"But why? What's—"

"Today is Saturday," Dan said, jabbing a finger at her for emphasis. "Tomorrow's the big turn-on in front of all the VIPs, right?"

Van Buren nodded, still confused by his insistence.

"If anything goes wrong with the test today, if anything screws up at the big ceremony tomorrow, I want a crew ready to belt the hell out of here and get up there and fix the bird. Understand?"

Recognition finally dawned in Van Buren's eyes. "Oh. I see. But everything's been going so well—"

"Murphy's Law, Lynn. If anything goes wrong I want us to be able to fix it. Pronto."

"For what it's worth, chief, I don't think it's going to be necessary."

"Do it anyway."

"It'll be so damned expensive."

"Do it!" Dan snapped. "To hell with the money. I want to be ready for any emergency." Then he let a hint of a smile bend his lips slightly. "Besides, it'll give the camera crews some sexy footage, with the spaceplane sitting up there ready to go at an instant's notice."

"Okay," she said reluctantly. "We'll have to get some LOX and hydrogen here, PDQ. They'll charge premium rates, you know."

"Let 'em," Dan said. "It's Garrison's money."

Van Buren went to the central console and picked up its phone. After a few minutes she returned to where Dan was standing, arms folded across his chest.

"Okay. Adair and the crew are entitled to overtime pay, and flight pay, too, if they have to go up."

Dan grunted.

"Strictly business, chief," Van Buren said, fixing the headset over her mouse-brown hair. "Strictly business."

They went through the final checkout swiftly. One by one, the technicians reported that the subsystems they were monitoring were set to go. It's a simple machine, Dan told himself as the technicians went through their checklists. No moving parts, practically. But it's got a lot of pieces to it. A lot that can go wrong.

The last item on the checklist was the receiving antenna station. One hand pressing the earphone to the side of her head, Van Buren called White Sands. "Rectenna farm ready and waiting," she announced.

Dan wet his lips, then said, "Okay, let's do it."

The head engineer gestured to the master console. No one was sitting at it.

"I thought you'd like to press the button yourself, chief," she said.

Dan hesitated, then shook his head. "No, Lynn. That's your job. I won't deprive you of it."

Her brows hiked up. "You certain?"

"The pleasure is all yours," Dan said, surprised at the superstitious dread that kept his hands jammed in his trousers pockets.

Van Buren wasn't superstititous. "Okay then." She raised her voice so that everyone in the crowded, tense room could hear her. "On my mark, five seconds and counting. Mark!"

Dan knew that the team at White Sands heard her, too.

"Three . . . two . . . one." Van Buren leaned ostentatiously on the red button that activated the satellite.

"Section one is go," sang out one of the techs.

"Section two, full output."

"Section three okay."

One by one the fifty component solar panels began converting sunlight into electricity.

"Inverters powering up."

"Magnetron one, on."

"Magnetron two . . ."

The magnetrons converted the electricity into microwave energy.

"Antenna powering up."

The antenna was a compartmented metal box nearly a mile long that focused the microwave power and beamed it toward Earth.

Suddenly Dan realized he didn't remember if the checklist included making certain that the antenna was pointed correctly at the rectenna farm. It has to be, he told himself. They use a laser beam as a guide. If it strays out of the rectenna field the magnetrons turn off automatically. Yet he couldn't recall if he'd heard anyone check out the beam's aim.

Van Buren gave a sudden whoop. "White Sands is receiving power!"

Dan raced her to the console that displayed the data White Sands was transmitting. Leaning over the seated technician's back they saw the power curve ramp up almost exactly along the predicted curve. Five hundred megawatts. A thousand. Dan's insides were churning. He could feel his heart thumping so hard it was threatening to break through his ribs. Two gigawatts. Four. Six.

"Ten gigawatts!" Van Buren hollered at the top of her lungs. Everyone roared. Dan grabbed his chief engineer and danced in the aisle between consoles with her. Technicians threw their headsets in the air.

"Break out the champagne!" somebody yelled.

Dan waved his arms and shouted as loudly as he could, "No celebrating until she's run for thirty minutes! Then we'll shut her down and head for Hangar A. That's where the champagne's stashed."

More quietly, he said to Van Buren, "And I want the bird on the pad, ready to go."

"You won't need it," she said confidently.

"I hope you're right," said Dan. "But get her set on the launchpad, anyway."

Then he noticed that al-Bashir had his cell phone pressed against his ear, jabbering away over the noise of the impromptu celebration.

BAIKONUR, KAZAKHSTAN

It was just after three A.M. when the van carrying Nikolayev, Williamson, and Bouchachi stopped at the base of the gantry tower. The three men clambered down stiffly from the van onto the steel flooring, each of them encased in a cumbersome, dull orange spacesuit, the visors of their fishbowl helmets open. A dozen technicians in quilted coats and leather hats with earflaps bustled around them. The big Proton rocket loomed above them all, illuminated glaringly by huge spotlights, icy white vapor wafting from its upper stage.

"The world's most reliable rocket," Nikolayev said cheerfully. "Safer than driving automobile."

Williamson scowled at the Russian and his faked joviality. "Let's get on with it, then," he said, heading for the open cage of the elevator.

Bouchachi, shivering from the cold even inside the thick spacesuit, clumped glumly after him.

As the elevator creaked and groaned slowly upward, Nikolayev asked, "You know of red hands disease?"

Bouchachi's eyes widened. "What are you talking about?"

Nikolayev explained that in the old days of the Soviet Union, guest cosmonauts from communist nations were allowed to ride up to the Salyut space stations for short visits. When a Hungarian cosmonaut returned to the ground after a week in orbit, the medics were disturbed to find that his hands had turned red. They feared some strange space malady and wondered what to do about it.

"Finally, one of doctors asks Hungarian about his red hands," Nikolayev went on. "Hungarian says, 'Of course I have red hands. I am guest on Russian space station. Every time I went to touch anything in space station one of Russians slapped my hands.' "

Nikolayez laughed heartily, while Bouchachi managed a polite smile and Williamson frowned.

"I understand," Bouchachi said as the elevator stopped at the uppermost level. "We are guests aboard your spacecraft. We are not to touch anything."

"Or you get red hands," Nikolayev warned, still laughing.

There were six more technicians waiting for them at the top level. The wind was howling up there, cutting icily. The sky was dark and full of stars. Williamson turned a full circle on the steel platform, searching for one particular star that should be bright and steady low on the horizon. The powersat. He couldn't see it. Of course not, he realized. It's on the other side of the world.

Two of the technicians touched his shoulders and nudged him toward the hatch of the Soyuz TMA spacecraft. Williamson had practiced this a hundred times in the simulators, but somehow this time was different. He stubbed his booted foot on the lip of the hatch and would have toppled to his knees if the technicians hadn't been there to hold him up. They literally lifted him off his feet and shoved him through the hatch, boots first.

Inside, the spacecraft was as cramped as a sardine tin. Grumbling inwardly about how stiff his spacesuit felt, Williamson clambered over two of the couches that had been shoehorned in among all the equipment and controls, then slid awkwardly into the farthermost couch, banging his helmeted head on a protruding electronics box as he leaned back.

Nikolayev slipped in next to him, so close that their shoulders pressed against each other. "Is easier once we reach orbit," the Russian said confidently. "In zero gravity this coffin gets bigger. You'll see."

Bouchachi clambered in hesitantly. He was still settling into his couch when the technicians closed the hatch and sealed it.

We're in for it now, Williamson thought. No way out.

Nikolayev adjusted the pin microphone inside his helmet and began chattering with the controllers in Russian. After several minutes he said, "Down visors." He slid the visor of his helmet down and sealed with a click. Williamson and Bouchachi did the same.

"Now we wait," Nikolayev said, his voice muffled by the closed helmets. His cheerful demeanor was gone. He looked totally serious to Williamson.

Got to piss, Williamson realized. There was a relief tube in the suit, but he wasn't certain he was connected to it properly. The dour technicians, mostly Asians, who had helped them get into the spacesuits had paid little attention to the plumbing. Would it short out some electrical circuits if it leaks? Williamson wondered. He decided not to try it. I'll wait. I can hold it.

He heard thumps and grinding noises. Pumps starting up? he wondered. Or something gone wrong. The tight, hot little metal sarcophagus started vibrating like a tuning fork.

"Ten more minutes," Nikolayev said.

More bangs and groans. Metal expanding, Williamson told himself. Or contracting. He thought he heard the wind keening outside. A storm coming up?

"Five minutes," said the Russian. "Everything automatic from here on."

The big rocket was coming to life. Pumps gurgled, pipes shuddered, the lights on the instrument board six inches in front of their faces blinked several times, then steadied. Most of them were green, Williamson saw. A display screen lit up with a complex of grid lines and colored curves.

Nikolayev adjusted a dial below the display screen, but it didn't seem to have any affect on the image.

Williamson and Bouchachi had radios in their suits, earphones built into their helmets. But Nikolayev had not bothered to patch them in to the circuit he was listening to.

The cosmonaut said something in rapid, fluent Russian. Then he broke into a big grin and nodded inside his transparent bubble of a helmet. "Da, da! Dah sveedahnyah!"

Once they lifted off, Williamson knew, there would be no more communications with Baikonur.

Something exploded. For a flash of an instant Williamson was certain that the rocket had blown up and they were about to be killed. Then an enormous invisible hand squeezed down on his chest so hard he could barely breathe. His arms were too heavy to lift off the seat rests. Pain and terror flaring through him, he managed to turn his head toward Nikolayev. The Russian's face looked as if someone were flattening it out with an invisible pressing iron.

The noise and vibration were terrifying. Williamson couldn't see Bouchachi, on the other side of the Russian. The pressure got worse and all of a sudden Williamson's bladder let go. He heard a moan and wondered if it was his own tortured voice or Bouchachi's.

And then it stopped.

It all just suddenly stopped. No noise, no vibration, no pressure. Williamson saw his arms floating up off the seat rests as if they had a will of their own. He turned his head to look at Nikolayev and a surge of dizziness made his eyes water. He felt as if he were going to upchuck.

"Zero gravity," said Nikolayev happily. "In forty-five minutes we make rendezvous with transfer rocket."

Williamson wondered if he could survive forty-five minutes without heaving up his guts into the fishbowl helmet.

MATAGORDA ISLAND,
TEXAS

Now remember," Dan shouted, standing in the middle of the hangar floor, "this was just a rehearsal. Tomorrow's the real thing."

Hardly anyone paid any attention to him, they were all swilling champagne, laughing, pounding each other on the back. Even Niles Muhamed, normally as grim as the angel of death, was shaking up bottles of champagne and spraying them on whoever happened to be in range of the cold, white geyser.

"Give it up, chief," said Lynn Van Buren, her inevitable dark pantsuit stained with Muhamed's champagne spray. "They've earned an afternoon of fun."

Frowning with helplessness, Dan said, "I don't want them hung over tomorrow."

"They'll be okay. Let them let off steam. They'll get a good night's sleep."

Van Buren drifted off into the crowd and Dan slowly realized that he was alone. Joe Tenny wasn't there to share this moment with him. Claude Passeau had gone back to New Orleans. Even April was nowhere in sight.

I wish Jane could've been here, he said to himself. She'll come down tomorrow but Scanwell will be with her. And six hundred other VIPs and news people. Vickie Lee, most probably. Wonder if she'll stay the night.

Feeling suddenly unbearably sad, drained, disappointed like a man who had spent his last ounce of energy to reach a mountain peak only to find that it wasn't worth the struggle, Dan walked slowly toward the stairs leading up to his office and his apartment. Then he stopped. No sense going up there with all this noise going on down here.

There's no place for me to go, he realized. No place at all. He began to drift through the crowd, looking for April. She's going to have a lot to do tomorrow, with all the news media coming in. Better make sure she doesn't get too much champagne into her.

Off in the farthermost corner of the hangar, away from the whooping, sloshing crowd, al-Bashir was speaking quietly, intently, to April. One hand holding a plastic cup of California champagne, he leaned against the metal wall of the hangar with his other hand, neatly pinning April against the wall.

"France?" April asked. "You mean Paris?"

"Marseille, actually," he said smoothly. "On the Mediterranean. We can go to Paris afterward, if you like."

April looked surprised, almost alarmed. But she murmured, "I've never been to France."

"Marseille is not far from the Riviera," al-Bashir said. "They make the world's best bouillabaisse there."

"I've heard of that. It's like a sort of fish stew, isn't it?"

"With certain exotic ingredients added."

"Like saffron?"

Al-Bashir smiled. "You'll love it."

"But there's so much to do here," April said, her eyes evading his.

"We can leave tomorrow afternoon, after the turn-on ceremony. Surely Dan owes you a few days' vacation."

"I really don't think I could..." Her voice faded away.

Al-Bashir put his arm down and stood up straight, almost at attention. "You will have your own hotel suite, I promise you. You'll be perfectly safe."

A slight smile touched her lips. "Can I trust you?"

"Of course," he lied.

As soon as she got to her apartment that evening, her head buzzing from the champagne, April phoned Kelly Eamons in Houston. No answer. She left messages on both Kelly's office line and her cell phone.

Saturday evening, April thought. She's probably out on a date.

April fell asleep as she sat in her living room recliner watching a detective show on television. It always worked out so neatly on TV: they caught the murderer in one hour flat, even taking time-outs for commercials.

The phone rang and she instantly snapped awake.

"Hi, April. It's me, Kelly."

Holding the cordless phone as she got up from the recliner, April said, "Let me put you on the computer, okay?"

"Sure."

It took a few moments for April to boot up her desktop machine and get Kelly's freckle-faced image on her screen. Once she did, she told the FBI agent about al-Bashir's invitation.

"To Marseille?" Eamons echoed. "That's a major narcotics port."

"Narcotics? Do you think . . . ?"

Eamons's brows knit. "There's nothing linking him to drugs. Nothing linking him to much of anything, outside of his connection with that bozo Roberto."

"He seems nice enough," April said half-heartedly.

"I don't like the idea of you being alone with him. In France, yet."

April tried to make light of it. "What's he going to do, kidnap me and carry me off to his harem?"

"He has a harem, you know. In the city of Tunis."

"Really?"

Frowning, Eamons said, "We've checked with the CIA about him. He seems to be nothing more than a big-time international businessman. A billionaire."

"But you think he might be linked to the murders here at Astro."

"It's only a straw," Eamons admitted. "But it's the only straw we've got."

"Maybe if I go with him we can learn more," April suggested.

"Maybe if you go with him you could get hurt. Badly."

April replied, "He doesn't want to hurt me. He just wants to go to bed with me."

"And what do you want?"

Without an eyeblink's hesitation, April said, "I want to find out who killed Joe Tenny. And Pete Larsen."

"And that test pilot."

Nodding, April said, "And what they're planning next."

"That's damned dangerous, April."

"But he doesn't know I'm working with you. He just thinks I'm an available woman."

Eamons's scowl deepened. "He wants to fly off to Marseille tomorrow afternoon?"

"After we turn on the powersat, yes."

"We'll have to act fast, then."

"And do what?"

"I've got to round up a medical team and get them down there tonight," said Eamons.

"A medical team?"

"You're going to get an implant."

"I'm on the pill," April blurted.

Eamons shook her head. "Not for contraception, silly. This implant is a microtracker. We've got to know exactly where you are every second you're with him."

GATHERING FORCES

Sunday dawned cloudy and gray. Not a good omen, Dan thought, looking out his window as he got dressed. Shirt and tie this morning, he told himself. You've got to look like the successful, prosperous captain of industry.

April was at her desk, on the phone, when he entered his office. But she looked drawn, tired, as if she hadn't slept all night. Nervous? Dan wondered. Well, she's had an awful lot to do these past couple of weeks, and today's going to be the busiest day of her life.

Once he had booted up his computer he saw that Mitch O'Connell's name was at the top of his to-call list. Dan clicked on the name and the phone made the connection.

"There's about a hundred and fifty of 'em picketing out by the main gate," the security chief said, his heavy-jawed face grim.

"Are they making any trouble?" Dan asked.

"Not yet. But wait till the VIPs start showing up."

Dan thought swiftly. Jane and Scanwell were flying in, as were many of the other invited guests. They'd come right in to the airstrip, bypassing the perimeter gate. But the news people would be coming in their vans and they're the ones the pickets want to impress. Soon as they see the TV vans they'll start harassing the limos trying to get through the main gate.

"Send a set of cars to the ferry dock," he said to O'Connell, "and have the drivers guide the arriving guests down to the secondary road. Let 'em in through the back gate."

O'Connell said worriedly, "That way they'll be driving right past the launchpad."

"That's okay. Fine, in fact. Give 'em something to gawk at before they park at the control center. The TV crews'll love it."

"I don't know if I have enough people to do it."

Dan sighed. The ultimate bureaucratic ploy: I need more people. "Call in as many people as you need. Holiday pay scale. Call in the state police, for double-damn's sake."

"Okay, boss," O'Connell said, brightening. "I'll get right·on it."

Just outside the wire fence that marked the perimeter of the Astro facility, Rick Chatham was giving instructions to his volunteers. Most of them carried placards professionally printed in red, white, and blue:

STOP THE POWERSAT
DON'T MICROWAVE THE WORLD
SPACE IS FOR SCIENCE, NOT PROFIT

"When the TV trucks come down this road," he said, pointing with an outstretched arm, "we've got to swarm around them, wave our placards in front of their drivers so they have to slow down and stop."

"We can lay down on the road," a balding, overweight man in khaki shorts called out. "Then they'll have to stop."

"If that's what it takes, that's what we'll have to do," Chatham agreed. "Make them stop and turn their cameras on us."

"Make the world see what's going on here!"

"That's right," said Chatham. "We're going to make the world realize that what these industrialists are trying to do is evil. They're stealing energy from the sun and beaming intense microwaves down to the ground. They're threatening to upset the balance of nature and destroy our environment."

"We've got to stop them!" a woman cried out earnestly.

"Remember, we're on state-owned land here," Chatham said as loudly as he could. "We have a perfect right to be here, and if they try to force us out *they're* breaking the law, not us."

On the other side of the gate a quartet of uniformed security officers stood by uneasily. They wore no guns, but each of them carried a fully charged cattle prod strapped to his hip. A fifth officer, wearing a sergeant's stripes on her sleeves, stood scowling at the group of volunteers gathered in the road.

Once Chatham finished his little oration she called out to him. "Sir? May I speak to you for a moment?"

Chatham ambled over toward her, leaned one arm on the wire mesh of the gate.

"You've got a legal right to demonstrate," the sergeant said, "on that side of the gate."

"I know that," said Chatham. "That's the law."

"Right. But if your people try to cross over the property line once we've opened this gate, that's trespassing, and we are under orders to deal with trespassers."

Chatham smiled lazily at her. "All five of you? How could you stop us? I've got more than a hundred people here."

"A detachment of state police will be arriving on the first ferry, sir," said the sergeant. "And if you put one toe on this side of the gate I'll make it my personal business to split your skull open."

She smiled sweetly at him.

Asim al-Bashir drove his rented Mercedes off the ferry and past the line of cars that seemed to be waiting at the edge of the parking lot. Behind him a long black limo with a State of Texas emblem jounced across the ferry's ramp and onto dry land, followed by a heavy TV van bristling with antennas. Al-Bashir saw one of the waiting autos cut in front of the limo. He watched in his rearview mirror as a young man got out of the car and started talking with the chauffeur. The TV van stopped behind the limo. Cars waiting behind the van bleated their horns angrily.

Wondering what that was all about, al-Bashir leaned on the gas pedal and sped down the main road toward the Astro facility. The limo, he noticed, turned off on the side road, led by the unmarked automobile, and the TV van followed it.

As he neared the Astro complex al-Bashir saw that a crowd of people was blocking the road. He slowed down and saw that most of them were carrying colorful placards. Demonstrators, he realized. Ecology fanatics trying to block the gate.

Al-Bashir knew how to deal with demonstrators. He slowed the Mercedes to ten miles per hour and kept boring straight ahead. They waved their placards in front of his windshield and yelled at him; he couldn't hear their shouted curses through the car's luxurious insulation. Smiling tightly, he edged the car through the angry crowd. The Astro guards had opened the gate and he inched through. None of the demonstrators tried to get through the gate, and a women in a sergeant's uniform threw him a salute as he accelerated past her.

Al-Bashir laughed to himself as headed for Hangar A. What if we turned the powersat beam onto this spot? he thought idly. What if we cooked those demonstrators where they stood? How poetic! What a sensation that would cause!

But he commanded himself to be serious. You have more important victims to deal with than a ragtag band of do-gooders, he said silently. And besides, you don't want to hurt Dan Randolph. He is the real enemy. The devil incarnate. He must die, and his satellite with him, if we are to win. But not until we strike. Randolph has to be alive to be the focus of the people's wrath after their president is killed.

Then he thought of April. You don't want to hurt her, either, he reminded himself. By this time tomorrow, she'll be flying to Marseille with you. She'll actually be safer with me than here, when the mobs start to tear this place down to the ground.

NEAR-EARTH ORBIT

Williamson's stomach still churned queasily and his head felt as if it were stuffed with snot-soaked tissues. He tried to keep perfectly still, strapped into the couch of the Soyuz spacecraft. Like three corpses wedged into a metal bucket, he thought. The Russian said it would seem bigger once we got to zero gravity, but it still feels like a bloody coffin in here.

"You okay?" Nikolayev asked.

Before Williamson could think of a reply, Bouchachi groaned, "I believe I'm going to die."

Nikolayev laughed. "No, you won't die. You might want to, right now, but in few hours you'll feel better. By time we make rendezvous you'll be okay to get up and move around."

Williamson realized he was hearing them through the headphones in his sealed helmet. The Russian had turned on the intercom system.

"Everything is fine," Nikolayev assured them, pointing with a gloved hand to the curves on the display screen before them. "We are on track for rendezvous with transfer ship. In two hours, eighteen minutes we go to transfer ship waiting for us, then we ride out to powersat. Then I sit and wait for you while you go outside and fix satellite."

No, Williamson countered silently. Once we reach the powersat I kill you, you stupid Russian bastard. If he hadn't felt so sick, Williamson would have smiled.

We should have hired a band," Dan said to April as they stood at the base of the airstrip's control tower, watching Scanwell's private jet making its final approach. Wind's picking up, he noted, watching the distant trees tossing. We're going to have to turn on the powersat in the middle of a rainstorm.

April squinted up at the darkening clouds piling up in the sky and said nothing. Dan wondered if she were nervous, worried, or just tired. Probably all three, he decided. Al-Bashir stood at her other side, chatting quietly with the representative that NASA had sent for the occasion.

"A brass band would've been a nice touch," Dan said to no one in particular. He was talking to cover his own nervousness, and he knew it. "We could've had them play 'Hail to the Chief' when Scanwell gets out of his plane."

April said softly, "He isn't president yet."

Forcing a grin, Dan replied, "Well, he's still governor of Texas. We could've played 'The Eyes of Texas Are Upon You' or something like that."

That brought a smile to her lips. Dan felt better for it.

Eight TV trucks were lined up in the parking area, their cameras tracking Scanwell's approaching jet. Dan turned the other way and saw the booster standing on the launchpad, with the spaceplane sitting atop it. Ready to go, he thought. Just like a Minuteman. I only hope we don't need it.

The business jet touched down with a screech of tires and rolled to the apron where Dan and the others were waiting. News reporters surged toward the plane. Dan congratulated himself that none of the TV vans had been accosted by the eco-nut demonstrators; his little detour had worked.

The plane's hatch swung open and Morgan Scanwell appeared at the top of the stairs, tall and rangy, smiling confidently, waving to the crowd—which was mostly news media people. Vicki Lee was among them, Dan saw, representing *Aviation Week*. He wondered if she planned to stay overnight and, if she did, what he would do about it.

Jane followed Scanwell down the plane's stairs, looking splendid in a soft green-skirted suit. Regal, Dan thought. That's the word for her. She should be running for president, he told himself. She'd be much better at it than he would.

Nacho Chavez looked decidedly unhappy, Eamons thought. Not angry, not frightened, just plain unhappy, miserable, like a little boy who got caught doing something naughty.

The regional director, on the other hand, looked outright furious. She sat behind her desk like an enraged gnome, anger radiating from her frowning, hard-eyed face.

A helluva way to spend a Sunday morning, Eamons had to admit.

"You implanted a tracking beacon on her body?" the director growled.

"I did it," Eamons said. "Agent Chavez didn't know about it until after it was done."

"You did the procedure yourself?"

"No, Ma'am. I requisitioned the electronic device from logistics and got a local surgeon to do the implantation last night. It's really a simple procedure."

"And you expect this office to pay for it?"

Chavez shifted in his chair and said, "For what it's worth, I agree with Kelly's initiative."

"Initiative? Is that what we're calling this?"

Hunching his heavy shoulders, Chavez pointed out, "The woman voluntarily accepted the implantation."

"It's the only way to keep track of her," Eamons said with some urgency. "The suspect wants to take her out of the country and we need to keep track of her. For her own safety."

"Out of the country? You mean they're going to Mexico?"

Eamons shook her head and answered in a lowered voice, "No, Ma'am. France."

"France!" the director exploded. "They're going to France?"

"Marseille, apparently. They're leaving tonight, according to my information."

"On a private plane," Chavez chimed in.

"We don't have jurisdiction!" the director yelled. "What in the hell was going through your brain when you dreamed up all this bullshit?"

Eamons stiffened. "Ma'am, we have reason to believe that this man al-Bashir was involved in the sabotage of the Astro Corporation spacecraft and the murders of three Astro employees."

"And now he's going to Marseille," Chavez added.

"And you'll have this woman going with him. A civilian!" The director glared at them both. "For Christ's sake, you could both be accused of promoting prostitution, you know that? If you don't get her killed first."

Chavez's face reddened.

"And you still don't have any real evidence about this so-called suspect of yours, do you?"

"He's our man," Eamons replied stubbornly. "I'm sure of it."

The director snorted disdainfully. "Marseille," she growled.

"I could phone her and tell her to cancel the trip," Eamons said.

"We'll have to get the satellite spooks to track her," the director grumbled.

Eamons sat up straighter. "Nacho and I could fly to Marseille," she suggested.

"Like hell you will," the director said. "You've spent enough of my budget as it is."

"Why is he going to Marseille?" Chavez wondered aloud.

The director glared at him for a moment, then said quietly, "Latest poop from Washington, the spooks have found some unusual electronic activity just outside Marseille. It was in Friday's summary from Homeland Defense."

"Electronic activity?"

"They don't know what it is. They're trying to home in on it, but it's intermittent, comes and goes."

Eamons said slowly, "Dan Randolph believed that his spaceplane crashed because somebody sent spurious electronic commands to it."

With a disgusted sigh, the director said, "I'll have to kick this upstairs to Washington."

As they left the director's office, Chavez whispered to Eamons, "Are you sure you want to let this woman fly out to Marseille with al-Bashir?"

"She wants to do it," Eamons said.

"You could be putting her neck in a noose."

"That's why I had her implanted with the tracker."

"Big help that's going to be."

MATAGORDA ISLAND, TEXAS

Despite the frigid gusts blasting from the air-conditioning shafts that ran along the ceiling, the control center felt hot and stuffy to Dan, with all the VIPs and news people squeezed inside its cinderblock walls. He stood by the closed double doors, pressed next to April, cold sweat trickling down his ribs.

Scanwell was standing on Dan's other side, his eyes sweeping the quietly intense room. Jane was beside the governor; aside from a completely impersonal handshake and greeting, she had said nothing to Dan.

Lynn Van Buren was on her feet in the midst of the consoles, headset clamped over her short brown hair. The technicians were bent over their keyboards, their backs to the spectators. The big wall screen displayed an animated drawing of the Earth, with Astro headquarters and the receiving station at White Sands identified in big white block letters, and a square representing the power satellite high above. A dotted red line flickered from Matagorda to the satellite.

"Can we get a picture of the satellite out there in space?" Scanwell asked, leaning slightly toward Dan.

Shaking his head, Dan replied, "We don't have cameras up there. It's an extra expense we don't need."

"But what about NASA, or the Air Force?"

Dan grimaced. "We're not a government operation, so they've steered clear of us. Maybe the news services will turn one of their satellites around for a picture, but their birds are all focused on the ground. We couldn't even get imagery from them when our first spaceplane crashed."

Scanwell shook his head. "Seems to me there ought to be some video coverage of your satellite."

Pointing to the news people, Dan said, "Tell them." Silently, he added, Maybe once you're in the White House you can change things that much.

In addition to her normal headset, Van Buren had the tiny microphone of a portable amplifier clipped to her blouse, just beneath her inevitable necklace of pearls. She reached for the power pack tucked in the waistband of her skirt and turned it on. A blood-curdling howl of electronic feedback shrieked through the control center.

"Sorry about that," Van Buren apologized, fiddling with the power pack. "Can everybody hear me?"

A ragged chorus of assent rippled through the crowd. Some of the onlookers raised their hands like schoolchildren.

"Okay. Fine," said Van Buren. Pointing to the big clock on the wall, she told them, "We're in the final countdown now. In two minutes the satellite will start beaming power to the rectenna farm...I mean, the receiving antennas, out at White Sands."

It was like New Year's Eve, Dan thought. Every eye turned to the big clock and its steadily clicking second hand. Van Buren turned off the amplifier. Dan knew she was going through the final checkout with the technicians: solar cells, inverters, magnetrons, output antenna, receiving antennas.

People started counting the seconds aloud, "Thirty...twenty-nine..."

Unbidden, the old joke about the world's first totally automated airliner came to Dan's mind: The plane's computerized pilot speaks to the passengers through its voice synthesizer circuitry and assures them that the flight would be under perfect control at all times. The automated little speech concludes, "Nothing can go wrong...go wrong...go wrong..."

"Fifteen...fourteen...thirteen..."

My whole life's tied up in this, Dan told himself. If it doesn't work I'm finished, down in flames.

"Eight...seven..."

He leaned forward slightly to look past Scanwell at Jane. Her eyes were on the clock, too. And her hands were clenched into tight little fists. This means a lot to her, too, Dan realized. But is it because of me or Scanwell?

"Transmitting power!" Van Buren called out.

The animation on the wall screen showed a solid green line running from the satellite to the rectennas at White Sands. Somebody gave a cowboy whoop. Other cheered. April jumped up and down and threw her arms around Dan's neck. Shocked, he wrapped his arms around her waist.

"Ten gigawatts on the line!" Van Buren shouted. "All systems up and running!"

Even the technicians joined the celebration, whipping off their headsets and grabbing each other in bear hugs. Dan disentangled himself from April, who looked suddenly embarrassed.

"We did it, kid!" he shouted at her over the blare of the crowd's cheering. "We did it!"

Scanwell grabbed him by the shoulder and stuck out a big hand. Dan shook it while two dozen cameras flashed away. Then Jane shook his hand too, smiling her politician's smile while her eyes focused on April.

Every reporter in the room started shouting questions at Dan and Scanwell. Out of the corner of his eye Dan saw that the wall screen now displayed a graph of the power being received by the rectennas. The curve climbed steeply to ten gigawatts and stayed there.

Grinning, Dan thought that he could start making some money now by selling that power to the Western electric utilities. California won't have any blackouts this summer, he told himself happily.

MARSEILLE

The Egyptian was too nervous to stay in the makeshift control center, so he went outside into the garden and sat in the shade of an ancient, gnarled olive tree. It was too hot and intense down in the basement with that quartet of bearded young electronics specialists, with their multiple earrings and other piercings defacing their lips and brows. He could barely understand what they were saying, their English was so studded with arcane jargon. Besides, they had turned the basement into a pigsty, littering it with emptied fast-food cartons and crumpled papers and plastic bottles; the floor crunched with crumbs when you walked across it.

It is going well, the Egyptian assured himself as he gazed out on the calm Mediterranean. Below this hilltop villa sprawled the city, dirty, noisy and dangerous. But from up here he could watch the placid sea glittering as the sun set at the end of a lovely springtime afternoon.

It is going well, he repeated to himself. The astronauts have reached their transfer ship. The new antenna was precisely where it was supposed to be, and now they are taking it up to the power satellite. If the American TV news can be believed, the power satellite is already beaming power to Earth.

Soon that power will kill thousands. And the Americans will never know that we caused it to be so. They will think their satellite malfunctioned. They will believe that it is dangerous. They will demand that it be destroyed.

Not a bad result for the cost of three martyrs. And one of them doesn't even know he will become a martyr.

One should never give news reporters free liquor, thought al-Bashir. He stood in the corner of Hangar A and watched the reporters and camera crews swilling the champagne and harder spirits that Dan Randolph had provided, making asses of themselves as they got gloriously drunk. Dan had wisely made arrangements to have his own security personnel drive the louts to the Astro Motel for the night. No fool, this man Randolph.

Governor Scanwell and Senator Thornton had taken a perfunctory sip of champagne and then flown off to their next campaign stop. The noise level in the metal-walled hangar was becoming intolerable. Al-Bashir finished the plastic cup of cola that he had been holding for nearly an hour, then walked out into the parking lot and got into his Mercedes.

He started up the engine and turned the air-conditioning on high, then pulled out his cell phone and called his office in Houston. They would patch his call to Tunis, where in turn the call would be forwarded to Marseille. The roundabout routing was time-consuming, but al-Bashir wanted to make certain his call would not be traced.

Perhaps I should speak to Garrison, he thought, and inform him of Randolph's success. With a slight smile, he wondered if the news would give the old man a fatal stroke or heart attack. Not likely. Garrison is made of stronger stuff than that.

His conversation with the Egyptian in Marseille was brief.

"It is a success," al-Bashir said, without even identifying himself.

"It goes well here," the Egyptian replied.

"Good. I will arrive there near dawn tomorrow, I should think."

"We will expect you then."

Al-Bashir clicked the phone off. Now to find April, he thought. It's time to take her away with me.

Once Jane left the celebration, Dan decided he'd had enough of it, too. He saw April in the crowd, talking to al-Bashir. Then the Arab went out and didn't come back, leaving April to chat with a couple of the news people. Some chat, Dan thought. You have to scream at the top of your lungs just to hear yourself think. The noise level was starting to hurt his ears. Vicki Lee was somewhere in the crowd; he'd lost sight of her.

So he made his way through the drinkers to Niles Muhamed and asked his help in loading a carton of champagne bottles and a cooler of ice into one of the company minivans.

"You goin' to have your own party?" Muhamed asked, his face glowering with suspicion.

"Sort of," said Dan with a lopsided grin.

With Muhamed in the passenger seat beside him, Dan drove out to the main gate. The state police contingent had gone, but the Astro guards were still there, and a handful of demonstrators were sitting disconsolately on the hoods of their cars, their placards down on the ground.

Dan told the guards to open the gate, then drove the minivan a few yards up the road and pulled over to the side.

Hopping out of the car, he went to its rear hatch and popped it open.

"I thought you guys might like some champagne," he said brightly.

A short, compactly built man with a sandy ponytail walked up to Dan, suspicion etched on his face.

"Champagne? For us?"

"Why not?" Dan said, grinning. "Just because we don't agree doesn't mean we have to be sore at each other."

Rick Chatham stared at Dan. "You're Dan Randolph, aren't you?"

"Right," said Dan, handing Chatham a bottle of champagne.

"I don't get it."

With a quick shrug, Dan said, "Look, you made your demonstration. You did your thing. And we did ours. The satellite's beaming power and the world hasn't come to an end. Let's have a drink."

Several more of the demonstrators came up behind Chatham, eying the champagne.

"This isn't over, you know," Chatham said. "We haven't given up."

"Fine," Dan replied. "In the meantime, have some bubbly. It's kind of warm, but there's a cooler of ice here."

The demonstrators crowded around the rear end of the minivan, grabbing bottles.

MATAGORDA ISLAND, TEXAS

Al-Bashir turned off the engine on his Mercedes and walked back into the hangar. The noise was still painful, although the crowd was noticeably smaller.

April was still there, and when she caught sight of al-Bashir she looked slightly startled, almost afraid. He smiled at her from across the crowded hangar floor, then went to the makeshift bar and asked for two colas.

As he threaded his way through the crowd toward April, he saw a dusty minivan pull up directly in front of the hangar door. Dan Randolph got out with the scowling black technician. I wonder where he was, al-Bashir asked himself. No matter. His fate is about to be sealed. And I have a rendezvous of my own to make.

He stopped at one of the shaky little round tables that had been set up across the hangar floor. Putting down the two plastic cups of cola, al-Bashir reached into his jacket pocket for the little vial of pills he had brought with him from Marseille. He shook one out and made a show of putting it in his mouth, then taking a swallow of his cola. Actually, he palmed the pale pink lozenge and dropped it inconspicuously into the other drink. Somatomax, it was called. A gamma-hydroxybutrate, used for bodybuilding in Europe; illegal in the United States. Its side effects included euphoria and drowsiness. An admirable date-rape drug, much more subtle and effective than the roofies and clonazepam that American college boys used.

While Jane was present, Dan had stayed as far from Vicki Lee as he could, but now that the senator had left with Scanwell, Dan simply drifted through the crowd, nursing a plastic cup of flat and warm champagne, thinking, What the hell, if she comes over there's no harm being sociable to her. He still worried about allowing her into his apartment upstairs, but he realized it would be damnably awkward to steer her out to whichever motel she was staying in.

We'll see what develops, he told himself.

Even across the crowded, noisy hangar, April was alarmed by what she saw in al-Bashir's eyes. A cold shudder ran through her. You must be crazy, she told herself. Go to France with him? In his private jet? That's like saying yes to him before he even asks.

And yet she had told Eamons that she would go. They wanted to get evidence against al-Bashir. The man might be the one behind the crash and the murders, the one who was trying to ruin Dan.

But she fished her cell phone out of her purse and tapped out Eamons's personal number. One ring. Two. Come on, April said, seeing that al-Bashir was pushing his way through the crowd toward her, a drink in each hand.

"Eamons here."

"Kelly! It's April."

"Where are you?"

"I'm still at Matagorda." She hesitated a moment. Al-Bashir was almost within earshot.

"Can you talk any louder?" Eamons asked. "There's a lot of noise in the background."

"I'm not going," April said, as loudly as she dared.

"What?"

"I'm not going through with it. I'm sorry, but I just can't do it."

Eamons said nothing for a long moment. Then, "Can't say I blame you, kid."

"I'm sorry."

"Don't be. It was a crazy idea in the first place."

Al-Bashir stepped up to her, smiling, holding the two drinks.

"I'll call you later."

"Okay. Call me when you get home. No matter what time it is."

"All right. Thanks." April clicked off the phone and put it back in her purse.

"Have a drink, April," said al-Bashir, proffering one of the plastic cups. She hesitated.

Smiling more broadly, al-Bashir said, "It's nonalcoholic. Coke. Coca-Cola, that is, not cocaine." He laughed mildly.

April took the cup. It felt cold and slippery in her hand. Then she looked up and saw, halfway across the hangar floor, that a buxom young news reporter was sidling up to Dan and he was grinning at her. April felt her innards tense.

Al-Bashir said something to her, but she didn't hear it. She watched as Dan slipped an arm around the woman's waist. The woman looked familiar to her. Vicki Lee, she recalled. From *Aviation Week*. She's been here before, April knew. The way Dan was looking at her, there was far more than publicity on his mind, she could see.

Al-Bashir lifted his cup in a mock toast. April made herself smile at him and sipped at the drink he had given her.

Williamson found that if he didn't move his head he was all right. His stomach had settled down, just as Nikolayev had foretold. That's the one thing they can't train you for in the simulators, he told himself. Zero gravity screws up all your body fluids. His head still felt stuffed, as if he had a monster of a sinus infection. But he didn't feel as if he had to puke anymore, for which he was bloody grateful.

I wonder if Bouchachi's going through the same ordeal, Williamson asked himself. He's damned quiet. Bloody martyr. Maybe he's afraid that if he complains Allah won't let him into Paradise after all. Williamson laughed inwardly. Maybe I can get his seventy-two virgins then.

The transfer ship was slightly bigger than the Soyuz they had ridden to low orbit. Now Nikolayev was steering them to the powersat itself, high up in the synchronous twenty-four-hour orbit. Their equipment package was flying formation with them, guided from the ground control center, wherever that was.

It's like a fucking computer game, Williamson thought. None of it seemed real to him. He sat inside a bulky spacesuit topped by a fishbowl helmet, inside a cabin that was crammed with gauges and dials and lighted boards that winked and clicked at him. No way to see outside, which was probably just as well. Nothing out there to see, he figured.

Ann's face came to his thoughts, despite his best efforts to drive her image out of his mind. She had been beautiful once, young and lovely, with a laugh that could charm the angels down from heaven. But the face he saw now was pale and strained, lined with worry, old before her time. She knew Williamson was going to die, slowly and painfully as the cancer ate away his insides. She knew she'd have to support their two children by herself. He hadn't told her about the money he'd get for this mission. He'd left a letter for her, to be delivered in three days. It'll all be over by then, Williamson knew. I'll be dead. Bouchachi and Nikolayev will be dead. And so will a whole shitload of Yanks.

ABOVE THE ATLANTIC

April awoke slowly, reluctantly, dragging herself out of a deep and deliciously relaxing sleep. A soft, droning sound was lulling her, urging her to rest, easing her body with a soft, gentle vibration. Then her eyes popped open. She was in a plane, sitting in a wide, comfortably cushioned seat. The sound and vibration were from the engines, muted by ample insulation. Through the little round window at her left elbow she saw nothing but steel-gray water far below.

"Where am I?" she muttered, then immediately felt foolish.

A slim young Asian woman in a tan flight attendant's uniform bent over her, smiling. "Would you like some breakfast, Miss? Coffee? Tea?"

Turning in her seat, she saw al-Bashir making his way up the aisle from the rear end of the cabin.

"Good morning!" he said cheerfully. "I trust you slept well."

April blinked at him. She was still wearing the dress she'd worn at work and, later, at the party. Was that yesterday?

"How did I get here?" she asked, feeling confused and more than a little afraid.

Taking the chair across the aisle and swiveling it toward her, al-Bashir said smoothly, "We drove to my plane after the party ended. We're going to Marseille, don't you remember?"

"But I don't have any clothes," April blurted. "I left my luggage in my apartment."

Smiling, al-Bashir said, "Not to worry. We'll buy everything you need once we land at Marseille."

April tried hard to remember going to the plane with him, but her mind was a foggy blank.

Al-Bashir reached across the aisle and patted her knee. "You're going to have a wonderful time in Marseille. You'll see."

The phone in Dan's apartment didn't just ring. Lynn Van Buren's voice called sharply, "We've got trouble, chief."

Dan sat up in bed, instantly wide awake. If Lynn's using the voice override circuit—

"Phone answer," he called out. The digital clock said 5:58 A.M.

Vicki Lee stirred beside him. Dan had been reluctant to allow her up to his one-room apartment, but as the party down on the hangar floor broke up, there didn't seem much else to do. Champagne clouds the mind, Dan told himself.

"Dan," said Van Buren, the image of her face dark and grave on the desktop screen. She seemed to be wearing a striped pajama top. "White Sands reports power's out."

Dan's guts clenched. "What happened?" In the back of his mind he realized Van Buren could see him and the woman in bed with him but that didn't matter.

"Don't know. Diagnostics show the solar cells are generating electricity, but they're not getting anything down at the rectennas."

"Jesus Christ!"

Dan jumped out of bed, naked, ran to his desk and sat his bare rump on the fuzzy-covered little typist's chair.

"Show me the diagnostics."

"What's going on?" He heard Vicki's sleepy voice from over his shoulder.

"Go take a shower," Dan snapped as he peered at the numbers and curves flowing across his screen.

"The magnetrons shut down," Van Buren was saying. "They're not functioning."

Dan saw a series of red lights blinking balefully at him against a schematic of the satellite's power antenna.

"That can't be!" he snapped. "You can't have a couple dozen magnetrons just suddenly shut down."

"Everything else is working," Van Buren countered.

Dan pressed his lips together, thinking furiously. "Round up the maintenance team. Get them ready for an emergency launch."

"Dan, today's a holiday. Memorial Day. They're scattered all over the place. And probably hung over from last night—"

"Get them!" Dan shouted.

"Right, chief."

Vicki Lee peeked out from the bathroom door. "Trouble?" she asked.

Dan nodded as he pushed past her into the lavatory. "You stay here. Don't leave this room until I come back for you."

"What's going on?"

"You'll get an exclusive, but not until I come back. Understand? Don't leave this room."

He pushed her firmly out of the lavatory and quickly showered. She bombarded him with questions as he dressed. He ignored her, except to take her cell phone from her purse while she watched, flabbergasted.

Dan rushed down the catwalk to his office. April wasn't there this early in the morning, so he hurriedly called O'Connell's office. A sleepy-eyed young man in a security uniform appeared on the screen.

Dan gave him three orders. Get O'Connell to the base right away. Shut down all outgoing phone calls unless authorized by Lynn Van Buren. And don't let Vicki Lee out of Hangar A until Dan himself gave permission.

Then he sprinted toward the control center.

In addition to being an excellent engineer, Malfoud Bouchachi was a religious man. He prayed silently as he worked on the powersat's huge antenna, a mile-long assembly of copper alloy attached to the immense structure that floated in the emptiness of space. One by one, with the patience of a truly dedicated man, he was unbolting the connectors that held the huge antenna to the massive power satellite, using a cordless contrarotating power tool. He had gone through two batteries already and was not even halfway through his task.

Williamson should be here assisting me, he thought angrily. But he knew that Williamson had other tasks to perform, tasks that Bouchachi himself shrank from.

Below him was the Earth, looming huge and blue with gleaming white clouds scattered across its curved face. He thought of it as below him, although in the zero gravity of space *up* and *down* were meaningless concepts. Yet Bouchachi felt that if that enormous ponderous planet were above him, hanging over him like the giant fist of Allah, it would crush him, squash him like an insect, eliminate him utterly from existence.

So, as he bent over his work and waited for Williamson to join him, he forced his mind to accept the idea that the Earth was below him, down, and he was floating high above it all. He had lost track of time and did not know when he should stop for prayer. Allah would forgive him for that, he felt. This work must be completed. There will be plenty of time for prayer afterward, once the work is completed and we have nothing to do but wait until our oxygen runs out.

That must be South America, he thought, gazing past the straight metal edge of the giant antenna. The Pacific Ocean glittered bright and deeply blue, although there were lighter hues around the islands that were almost directly beneath them. South America darkened the edge of the curving globe, smeared with clouds, creased with mountains that looked like puny wrinkles from this height. Mecca is on the other side of the world, Bouchachi knew. The Holy City can never be seen from this satellite.

He looked up from his work and blinked sweat from his eyes. He felt hot inside his spacesuit, soaked with perspiration, despite the fact that just outside the fabric of the suit the temperature must be close to absolute zero. No air. No life.

I cannot see Mecca from here, he repeated to himself. This giant machine is the work of devils, put into space as far away from the Holy City as the godless Americans could place it. It took an effort to straighten up from his bent posture. Turning his entire weightless body, he looked out at the vast expanse of the power satellite. It stretched for miles, huge, glittering darkly, a mammoth construction of evil. Its very size frightened him; that, and the knowledge that evil men could construct such an infernal machine.

Straining his eyes, he thought he could see the brown bulk of Mexico and the barren gray desert of the southwestern United States. Yes, and farther north, beneath a swirl of clouds, lay Florida. And beyond that, Washington. The capital of the Great Satan. Where their president will make his last speech later this day.

WASHINGTON, D.C.

Senator Thornton rode with Senator Quill to Arlington National Cemetery. The Memorial Day service at the Tomb of the Unknowns was an annual observance, a chance for the president to use the emotions of patriotism and sacrifice to further his own political agenda. The president was fighting for his political life, Jane knew; the latest polls showed that Morgan Scanwell was within twelve percentage points of the president, and the national conventions hadn't even convened yet.

Quill wore a lightweight gray suit with a carefully knotted lavender tie and a jeweled American flag pin in his lapel. Sitting beside him in the rear seat of the limousine, Jane was in a conservative coral pink knee-length sheath. Both senators would accept red poppies from an amputee veteran in a wheelchair when they got out of the limousine. The photo opportunity had been set up by Quill's publicity aides.

"Where's Morgan this fine morning?" Quill asked cheerfully.

"In Austin. He's meeting with the delegation chairmen this morning, and then there's a big barbecue later this afternoon."

"He wasn't invited to Arlington?" Quill teased.

"The president's going to invite the candidate who'll oppose him in November? Be real, Bob."

"Morgan doesn't have the candidacy sewn up yet. Jackson's close enough to make a real fight at the convention. Especially if he picks Roswell as his running mate."

Jane scoffed at the thought. "Liz Roswell would lose more votes than she gains."

Quill pursed his lips thoughtfully. "You might be right."

"I know Morgan's got a lot of work ahead of him," Jane said, more seriously. "But he's going into the convention as the leading candidate and we're going to go for a first-ballot win."

"Jackson won't accept the number-two slot."

"Our people are talking to his people."

"He won't go for it."

Jane let a knowing little smile curve her lips. "Then maybe I will."

"You?" Quill's mouth hung open.

Laughing, Jane said, "That's the first time I've ever seen you really surprised, Bob."

"You're not serious."

"We've talked about it," Jane said lightly.

"Pillow talk."

Her smile disappeared. "It's more than that. We might have a big announcement to make just before the convention opens."

His composure recovered, Quill leaned back in the limousine's plush seat and chuckled quietly. "Let me guess."

"Go right ahead."

"You're going to get married."

Jane smiled again but said nothing. In her mind, though, she wondered how Dan would react to the announcement. Stop that! she commanded herself. Put Dan out of your mind. You're heading for the White House, that's the important thing. The nation needs Morgan and nothing's going to stop us from making him president, not Dan or anything else.

By the time the limousine pulled to a stop in front of the waiting Marine Corps veteran in his wheelchair, Jane had almost succeeded in forgetting about Dan.

Standing at the base of the launchpad, Dan looked over his maintenance crew with a jaundiced eye.

"By damn, you guys look like something the cat dragged in."

Gerry Adair grinned wryly. "It was your party, boss."

"Start sucking oxygen," Dan snapped. "You've got to be ready to launch as soon as the spaceplane's fueled up."

One of the technicians stared at him. "We're going up? Now? Today?"

"Damned right," said Dan.

"But it's the holiday!"

"You'll get double pay."

Shaking his head, the technician said, "It's not that. We got a picnic planned. My wife's family came down from Nebraska, for chrissake."

"We've got an emergency on our hands," Dan said.

"My wife's gonna kill me."

Looking at the dark clouds piling up over the Gulf, Dan thought, If Mother Nature doesn't kill you first.

The director of the FBI's Houston branch did not appreciate having to come into the office on Memorial Day, especially when she'd been there the day before.

"What's all this hysteria about?" she snapped as she stormed into her office. She was wearing a loose sweater over a tee shirt and cut-off jeans that exposed her skinny, knobby-kneed legs.

Kelly Eamons was already there, pacing nervously. "April Simmonds isn't at her apartment."

"So? It's a holiday, for god's sake. Most people spend holidays with their families."

The director's acid-dripping irony made no impression on Eamons. "You don't understand. She said she wasn't going to France with al-Bashir. But now I can't find her."

"Use the tracking beacon."

"I tried! The guys downstairs claim they can't find her signal."

The director slammed down onto her desk chair muttering, "This was a screwball operation from the beginning."

"She's out of range of our local equipment," Kelly said, pacing again.

"I thought you said she'd decided not to go to France with the suspect."

"She did. Yesterday afternoon. But now..."

Agent Chavez barged into the office, looking distressed. He was wearing shorts, too: picnic clothes.

"I got your message," he said to Eamons. "The guys downstairs still can't pick up her signal."

"She's gone with him after all," Eamons muttered.

"But you said she'd decided not to," said the director.

"Something changed her mind."

"Or somebody," Chavez chimed in.

"She could be in trouble."

The director shook her head, glaring at them both. Then she reached for her telephone. "Do you two loose cannons have any idea of the levels of hierarchy I'm gonna have to go through to get the satellite spooks to see if they can pick up her signal?"

Eamons brightened. "She must be in a plane, heading for France."

"Or already there," said Chavez. "In Marseille."

"Sit down," the director said, pecking at her quick-dial keyboard. "This could take hours."

GEOSYNCHRONOUS ORBIT

Gilly Williamson had killed men before. The first time was when a daft policeman barged in on him in the cellar of the safe house where he was wiring a car bomb. Before he could even think about it, Williamson put four nine-millimeter bullets through the fool's chest.

He expected to feel guilty about it. He expected it would give him nightmares. But it didn't. It was him or me, he knew. The damned idiot hesitated and I didn't. That's the difference between life and death.

Of course, the bombs he devised killed dozens, perhaps hundreds. He had never kept score. But *personal* killing, face to face, that was a different matter. There was the informer that was going to rat out the whole cell to the Tommies. He was stupid enough to warn Gilly over pints at a pub in London. Gilly had thanked him from the bottom of his heart and then, after they walked together to the bastard's car parked back in the alley, Gilly had brained him with the fool's own electric torch. He'd looked so surprised when the first blow cracked his skull open. In a few seconds you couldn't recognize his face at all.

That was when Gilly had to leave the United Kingdom, leave his wife and kids and travel to blasted North Africa. Casablanca. Nothing like the movie, he found. Then Oran, another cesspit full of gabbling Arabs. In Tunis he was recruited by The Nine, although he never met any of the mucky-mucks, just their flunkies.

He knew he had cancer, he'd known it since he'd been diagnosed by the Public Health doctors back in London. Cigarettes, they claimed. Bad genes. Bad luck. What difference? He knew he was going to die and the only question was: How could he provide for his wife and kids?

This one-way mission to the satellite was his answer. Williamson had mailed the bank receipt to his wife before he'd gone off to the remote training base in the stark granite-gray mountains of northern China.

Now he hung suspended on a tether halfway between the enormous satellite and the transfer craft where Nikolayev waited for them to finish their tasks. Below him glowed the blue and white-flecked Earth. Beyond it he could see a crescent Moon, small and slim like the symbol on Arab flags. There were stars out there, too, but Williamson could only see a few of the brightest through the dark tinting of his helmet visor and he paid no attention to them.

He had finished his wiring task nearly half an hour ago. The satellite was no longer beaming power through its antenna. Once they removed the antenna and attached the new, special one they'd carried up with them, their job would be finished. Then it would be up to the crew on the ground to point that antenna where they wanted it.

But before that could happen, Williamson had one additional task to do. Nikolayev. The Russian was a mercenary, a professional cosmonaut who'd been paid to carry these two men to the power satellite. He didn't know what they were doing to the powersat and he didn't care. He expected to wait for them to finish their work, whatever it was, and then fly them back to a landing in Kazakhstan.

But that wouldn't do. The plan called for no witnesses. The whole point of this operation was to make it look as if the powersat had malfunctioned. Accidentally. Williamson and Bouchachi were even going to reattach the regular antenna once they got word from the ground that they had accomplished their mission. Then they'd fly off into deeper space, where nobody would think to search for them. And die there.

Nikolayev had no inkling of that part of the plan. He expected to return home.

Time to disabuse him of that, Williamson told himself as he made his weightless way hand over hand along the tether that connected to the waiting transfer craft.

"I'm coming in," he called to Nikolayev through his suit radio.

"Come ahead," came the cosmonaut's bored voice. "Hatch is open."

Everything took an extra effort in zero gravity. Williamson had thought it would all be easy when everything was weightless, but he found that it was hard work even to stretch out his arms. Maybe it's the bloody suit, he thought. It's as stiff as a corpse.

Slowly, sweating with the effort, he hooked his boots on the rim of the open hatch, then wormed his way inside the spacecraft. Nikolayev was strapped into the middle seat, sealed up in his suit and fishbowl helmet.

"Close the hatch," the cosmonaut said, "and we can fill cabin with air again. Take off helmets, relax a while."

"Not just yet," Williamson said. He pulled out the knife he'd carried in the pouch on his trouser leg and slipped it out of its sheath. The blade was clean and slim and sharp.

Nikolayev looked puzzled. "What's that for?"

"For you."

With a swift slash, Williamson sliced open the chest of the cosmonaut's suit. Nikolayev's eyes went so wide Williamson could see white all around the pupils. The suit material was tough, layer upon layer of fabric and plastic. Williamson hacksawed through it, laboring hard. The Russian tried to parry the knife slash, but in the spacesuit he was hopelessly clumsy. And far too late.

"What have you done?" Nikolayev screamed.

Williamson said nothing. The Russian gasped for air, clawed at his helmet with both gloved hands, then suddenly lunged at Williamson. Gilly pushed him off easily and watched him shudder inside his cumbersome suit as the air ran out of it and the fabric decompressed like a punctured balloon. Niko-layev's screams and flailings faded away and he slumped in the seat, quite dead. Williamson said to himself, I've done nothing that I won't be doing to myself soon enough.

"Sorry, mate," Williamson whispered. "No witnesses, you know."

MARSEILLE

The young Asian flight attendant still wore her tan uniform as she led April up the main stairway of the villa and showed her to a wide, airy bedroom. Feeling confused and scared, April asked her, "Where did Mr. Al-Bashir go?"

They had driven together from the airport up to this hilltop villa, but al-Bashir had been on the phone almost every moment of the drive, speaking in French and sometimes in what April assumed was Arabic. The uniformed woman sat up front with the liveried chauffeur. Once the limousine had pulled up on the gravel-topped driveway, al-Bashir had smilingly helped April out of the car, then turned her over to the Asian woman.

Ignoring her question, the woman went to the French windows at the far end of the spacious bedroom and threw them open. April saw a sizeable balcony lined with large clay pots filled with thickly blooming red and pink geraniums and, beyond, the tranquil deep blue of the Mediterranean Sea.

"You will be very comfortable here," said the Asian woman, smiling.

April looked around the room. Tile flooring. Heavy dark furniture. A four-poster king-sized bed.

"But I don't have any clothes with me," she said, almost pleading.

"Mr. al-Bashir has already seen to that," the woman said. She strode to the closet and slid its doors open. April saw a long row of what looked like evening gowns. Or maybe they were nightgowns.

"Why don't you take a nice shower and get into some fresh clothes? You'll find makeup and toiletries in the lavatory."

With a final smile, the Asian woman walked to the door and left the room, leaving April alone.

April slumped down on the bed and fought back an impulse to cry. Am I a guest here, she wondered, or a prisoner?

It had started to rain in Matagorda. Dan could hear the drops drumming heavily against the roof of the blockhouse. Inside, the launch crew were at their consoles, the quiet tension of the countdown starting to notch upward.

"It's just a squall," Dan said, peering at the weather radar display in the control center. "It'll pass in half an hour or so."

Lynn Van Buren tapped a red-lacquered fingernail against the screen. "There's more coming in behind it."

"So we'll launch in between 'em," said Dan.

The door from outside opened, allowing a gust of wet wind to blow through the blockhouse. Dan saw Gerry Adair come in, stooped against the wind, his yellow slicker glistening wet.

"Crew ready?" Dan asked.

Adair's freckled face looked somber. "Max isn't going."

"What?"

"He said you can fire him, but he's not going up today."

Dan resisted the urged to slam a fist against the nearest console. "Double-damn it, he's not going to have any family picnic in this weather!"

"I've been on the phone with him for the past twenty minutes, boss. He just won't go. Says his wife'll divorce him."

"And rain makes applesauce," Dan muttered.

"The rest of the crew is ready, pretty much," said Adair.

"What do you mean, pretty much?"

With a hike of his pale eyebrows, Adair answered, "We don't know what we're going up there for, boss."

"The double-damned power's off!" Dan shouted. "You're going up to find out what the hell's wrong and fix it!"

"Without Max? He's our structures man."

"I'll take his place."

"You?" Adair and Van Buren said in unison.

"Don't look so damned stunned," Dan told them. Jabbing a finger at Adair, "I've put more hours in orbit than you have, kid."

"Yeah, but boss—"

Dan wheeled on Van Buren. "You run the countdown like normal. I'm going to get suited up."

Van Buren fingered her pearl strand nervously. "Chief, do you think that's wise?"

"I won't ask these guys to do anything I won't do myself," Dan said. Then he headed for the door. Adair scrambled to catch up with him.

Down in the basement of the hilltop villa, al-Bashir paced nervously along the row of technicians bent over their miscellany of computers. He accidentally kicked a crumpled can of soda; it clattered out of his way. The room looked like a pigpen. Al-Bashir wrinkled his nose in distaste; it smelled like a sty, too.

"How soon can we begin to move the satellite?" he asked the Egyptian.

"Bouchachi reports that they are nearly finished attaching the new antenna."

"So?"

"Once it is attached they can begin beaming power at high intensity."

Al-Bashir looked at his wristwatch. He had set it to Eastern Daylight Time, the time zone for Washington, D.C.

"The president will begin his speech in another hour."

Perspiration sheened the Egyptian's bald head. "They should be finished by then."

"Can we begin to move the satellite now?"

"It would be better to wait until they are finished with the antenna."

Al-Bashir frowned, stroked his beard impatiently, then said, "I want it moved now. I want that antenna aimed at Washington. *Now*."

"But—"

"You have the proper coordinates."

"Yes, but—"

"But what?" al-Bashir snapped.

"We can activate the attitude control thrusters through the relay satellite," the Egyptian said, his eyes shifting nervously, "so that the antenna points at Washington."

"Then do it."

"But we can't uplink communicate with our workers on the satellite. We only have a downlink from them."

"The plan calls for our maintaining radio silence, except for sending the command codes to the attitude thrusters. What of it?"

"They might be hurt when the satellite begins to shift its position."

"Hurt? How can they be hurt? Everything is weightless up there."

"But not massless. Objects still have mass."

Al-Bashir shook his head angrily. "Bah! An academic quibble."

"It's more than that," the Egyptian insisted. "If we don't warn them that the satellite will begin to shift its position before they are finished attaching the new antenna—"

"Are you afraid they'll float off the satellite?"

"No, they're attached by tethers."

"Then start the maneuver now."

"It's wrong—"

Al-Bashir slapped him. Hard. Without his consciously deciding to, his hand flashed out and caught the Egyptian flush on his round, stubbled cheek. The crack made the technicians look up.

"I am in command here," al-Bashir said, his voice cold with fury. "You will do as I say." Looking at the staring technicians, he added, "All of you!"

The Egyptian stood speechless, the finger marks of al-Bashir's hand white against his nut-brown cheek.

"Move the satellite to its proper position," al-Bashir said.

The Egyptian turned and nodded to one of the technicians, who began tapping quickly on his computer keyboard.

GEOSYNCHRONOUS ORBIT

D'you think that thing will be in the way?" Williamson asked, pointing a gloved thumb toward the powersat's original antenna, floating free now and drifting alongside the satellite like a huge metal ice floe.

Bouchachi shook his head inside his helmet. "No, it is already far enough to be no problem."

"Good."

The two men were bolting the new, smaller antenna onto the output port from the magnetrons, working slowly in their cumbersome suits. Even though no sound could be heard in the vacuum of space, Williamson could feel the vibration of his power drill through the thick fabric of his gloves. Bloody gloves are a pain in the arse, he said to himself. The gloves were as stiff as thick cardboard; it was hard to flex the fingers enough to grip the power tools firmly. He had almost fumbled the drill out of his reach twice now.

Bouchachi worked steadily and kept himself from asking about Nikolayev. He knew that Williamson had killed the Russian. Can an infidel become a holy martyr? Bouchachi asked himself. What matter? That is for Allah to decide. Allah, the all merciful, the all compassionate. He hoped that Nikolayev might find a place in Paradise. Even though he had not been fully aware of the purpose of this mission, they could not have accomplished anything without him.

In his helmet earphones Bouchachi could hear Williamson breathing hard. The work was much more difficult than they had anticipated, and it was going slowly. Panting with exertion himself, he raised his left arm to look at the watch on the set of instruments fastened to his wrist.

"Nearly finished," Williamson said.

Bouchachi blinked sweat from his eyes. I wish I could wipe my face, he said to himself. I'm drenched with perspiration. Suddenly he lurched with fear. Are the microwaves cooking me? Am I being boiled alive by the microwaves?

No, he told himself. We turned off the power output. There will be no microwaves coming out of this infernal machine until we finish attaching this antenna and turn on the power once more.

Still, it took an effort for him to make his hands stop shaking.

"Hey, what's that?" Williamson said.

"What?"

"Thought I saw a puff of smoke or something."

"Smoke? Impossible."

"It was something."

"It couldn't be smoke. Not here."

"There it is again!"

This time Bouchachi caught it, out of the corner of his eye. A wisp of glittering gas, gone almost before the eye could register it.

"The attitude control jets," he said. "They're moving the satellite."

"But we're not finished yet!"

"They grow impatient, down below."

"I don't feel us moving."

Bouchachi almost smiled. He started to explain, then thought better of it. Why try to teach the laws of inertia at this point?

"Good thing we've got the new antenna almost nailed down," Williamson said. "We'd have a helluva time if it'd still been hanging loose."

Ah, thought Bouchachi. He does understand Newton's laws, at least a little.

Aloud, he said, "We still have much work to do."

"We'll finish on time," Williamson answered. "Or close to it."

Dan felt excited as a schoolkid as he tugged on the leggings of the spacesuit. He realized he hadn't been in space for more than five years.

What was it Da Vinci said? he asked himself. Something Leonardo wrote after he tried out one of the man-carrying gliders he'd built. The words came to him:

Once you have tasted flight, you will forever walk the Earth with your eyes turned skyward. For there you have been and there you long to return.

Something like that, Dan said to himself as he wormed his arms through the sleeves of the spacesuit. Smart cookie, old Leonardo. Pretty good painter, too.

Tucking his bubble helmet under one arm, Dan clumped out to the briefing room, where the rest of the crew waited. *For there you have been and there you long to return,* he repeated silently. I'm going back into space!

The briefing room was small, most of the floor space taken up by eight comfortably padded astronaut-type reclining chairs. Five spacesuited people were already seated, two of them women. Gerry Adair stood in his suit at the front of the room and led the abbreviated briefing. Dan waited in the back and listened respectfully. Ride the spaceplane to low orbit, rendezvous with the OTV parked there and ride it to the powersat. Then find out what's wrong with the bird and fix it.

"That's why we make the big bucks," Adair kidded. "So let's get this bird back on the air."

Before they could push themselves out of their chairs, Dan said, "One other thing, people. This is a test of our whole concept. If we can fix that beast and get it running properly, we'll have proved that the powersat idea will work. Everything we've done so far is hanging on what we do in the next few hours."

Adair grinned at him. "Gee, boss, I thought you were going to give us that old 'band of brothers' bullshit from Shakespeare."

"That too," Dan quipped back at him. "Now let's get going."

Al-Bashir peered at the small TV perched on a tabletop in the villa's basement. Satellite news was showing the assemblage of notables gathering at the Tomb of the Unknowns in Arlington National Cemetery.

"The president of the United States is due to arrive in less than half an hour," the news commentator was saying. "In the meantime, a crowd of more than twenty thousand has gathered for this day of remembrance..."

Al-Bashir smiled grimly. They'll remember this day, he said to himself. Oh, yes, they will remember it.

April found that the door to her bedroom was not locked. She pushed it slowly open and looked down the hallway. No one in sight.

Walking slowly, she approached the staircase leading downstairs. She went down the carpeted stairs and looked around. No one in the spacious, well-appointed living room, either. The house seemed to be deserted, although through the living room windows she could see several cars and vans parked out front.

If I had the keys I could drive out of here, she told herself. But to where? I'm in a foreign country. I don't know the roads. I can't even speak the language.

"Can I help you?"

Whirling about, April saw the same Asian woman standing at the opposite end of the living room. She had changed from her flight attendant's uniform into a flowered bikini, topped with a gauzy see-through cover-up over it. April suddenly felt shabby, wrinkled and grubby in the same dress she'd worn for—how long now? It must be twenty-four hours, at least.

"Can I help you?" the woman repeated.

"I . . . I got hungry," April said. "I was looking for the kitchen."

"I'll fix you a luncheon tray," the woman said, smiling. "I'll bring it up to your room."

"But I—"

"Please return to your room. Mr. al-Bashir left very specific instructions. He wants you in your bedroom when he finishes the work he's doing."

MATAGORDA ISLAND, TEXAS

As he sat in the last row of the spaceplane's cabin listening to the count-down in his helmet earphones, Dan realized that all seven of the crew were lying on their backs with their legs up in the air, like women in the throes of passionate sex. He grinned to himself. They were all completely enveloped in their spacesuits, encased in thick layers of plastic and fabric. We couldn't even masturbate in these outfits, he thought.

This is the first time I've ridden the spaceplane, he realized. All his other trips to orbit had been aboard Soyuz-type capsules either made in Russia or manufactured under license by a commercial builder. He wouldn't pay the $10,000-per-pound price NASA wanted for the space shuttle, nor was NASA comfortable with the thought of carrying a money-grubbing industrialist into space instead of a scientist or engineer.

"T minus two minutes," Dan heard in his earphones. "Internal power on. All systems go."

Gerry Adair sat up front at the controls. Not that there was anything for him to do; the countdown and launch were all automated. Adair's work would come later, once they had achieved orbit and had to make a rendezvous with the orbital transfer vehicle that was waiting up there.

"T minus ninety seconds. LOX pressure in the green. Hydrogen pressure in the green."

Still no word about what caused the outage, Dan thought. Guess we won't know for certain until we get there and see for ourselves.

"T minus sixty seconds. Life support on internal. Fuel cells on."

Van Buren would call if she'd found out what's wrong with the bird. Good thing this didn't happen yesterday with all the VIPs here. Vicki must be throwing a fit by now, threatening to sue if we don't let her leave the base. Tough. We can't have her blabbing this story before we fix the satellite.

"Ten . . . nine . . . eight . . ."

Dan closed his eyes and gripped his seat's armrests as hard as he could through his thick gloves. This beast kicks like a mule, he knew.

Worse. The rocket engines ignited and Dan felt as if he were being fired out of a cannon. A forty-ton anvil slammed into his chest; his eyeballs started sinking into his head. There were no windows along the cabin to look out of, and he couldn't have turned his head anyway. He just sank into the cushioned acceleration couch and tried to breathe. He couldn't lift his arms off the seat rests, couldn't even wiggle his toes inside the heavy boots.

His vision blurred and everything turned a lurid reddish tint, like being in a photo lab with the safety lights on.

I'm too old for this sort of thing, Dan told himself. What in the Seven Cities of Cibola made me think I should take this double-damned roller coaster?

After several lifetimes, the pressure eased somewhat. Dan heard a bang and felt the cabin shudder. Booster separation, his mind told him. The booster's dropped away and we're riding on the spaceplane's engines now.

And then it all went away. The pressure vanished. Dan's arms floated off the armrests. His stomach gurgled, but he remembered to refrain from making sudden head movements.

"Woo-ie!" one of the women whooped. "That was a *ride!*"

"Let's do it again, Daddy!"

Dan grinned weakly and concentrated on not throwing up.

There was plenty of handshaking to do at Arlington National Cemetery. While the honor guard of soldiers, sailors, airmen, and marines got out of their trucks and began to arrange their ranks and flags, Senator Thornton worked her way through the VIP stand, saying hello and exchanging greetings with politicians and bureaucrats.

She noticed that Secret Service bodyguards were arriving now, trying to look unobtrusive as they scoped out the crowd with special electro-optical scanners disguised to look like fashionable sunglasses.

The president would be arriving soon, Jane knew. His motorcade of limousines and motorcycles has probably already left the White House and is making its way around the Lincoln Memorial.

It was somewhat ironic that the nerve center for the nation's elaborate network of spy satellites was buried deep underground. Beneath enough reinforced concrete to survive even a nuclear strike, dozens of technicians monitored screens that showed virtually every square inch of the Earth's surface, land and sea. Ships were being tracked, even submerged submarines. Not a truck or a train moved without some satellite high up in orbit watching it.

The room hummed with electrical power; it was large and generously air-conditioned, yet it still felt sweaty-hot and crowded, with all the technicians seated at row after row of consoles. Even on this holiday afternoon there was an intent man or woman hunched over each console monitoring each screen. The strip lamps along the ceiling were dim; most of the light came from the display screens, flickering eerily against the concrete walls.

Nothing much out of the ordinary was happening, though, so the duty officer should have been relaxed. She was not. A Navy lieutenant commander, she was a woman who ached for command of a capital ship at sea but instead was stuck with babysitting a bunch of spy eyes in the sky. She had been surprised when the deputy director of homeland security entered the monitoring center escorted by a pair of marines. In quick order, her surprise gave way to interest, and then to irritation.

"Track an electronic beacon?" she asked the deputy director for the third time. She looked again at the flimsy sheet of specifications he had handed her. "With this low a signal?" She shook her head.

The deputy director was in his midfifties, a lifelong bureaucrat who had been in the Treasury Department before Homeland Security had opened new paths for career advancement. He was good-looking in a chisel-featured, cosmetic-surgery way. He was accustomed to persuading people who were reluctant to comply with his wishes. He was not accustomed to being rebuffed, especially by a woman in uniform.

"Commander," he said softly, over the muted hum of the consoles, "this request comes from the very highest level of the Homeland Security Department. The request originated with the FBI. It also has the CIA's approval, I might add."

"I don't care if it comes from the Oval Office," the lieutenant commander said. "That signal is just too weak for our birds to pick up. What kind of a freaking dumbjohn set up this pitiful little squeaker?"

"Ferret satellites have picked up signals a lot weaker than this one."

Waving the spec sheet in his face, the captain said, "Yeah, but it's not just the power of the signal all by itself. It's the signal-to-noise ratio. Your beacon's too goddam close to the port of Marseille. There's all kinds of chatter coming out of the city, on every frequency you can imagine. It'd be like trying to listen to a mouse fart in the middle of some Italian opera."

The deputy director performed a dramatic sigh. "So am I supposed to go back to the director of homeland security and tell him that you won't even *try* to track their beacon?"

The lieutenant commander heard his unspoken words: *That would not be a positive career move for you.* She also realized that this must be just as important as he claimed, to get a deputy director down here on a holiday afternoon.

She stared at the spec sheet again, grumbled something too low for the deputy director to make out, and walked off to one of the monitoring consoles.

WASHINGTON, D.C.

From the giant structure of the power satellite, 22,300 miles above the equator, an invisible sword of energy lanced down toward Washington, D.C., powerful enough to kill anything in its path. It touched the ground in Bethesda and marched south-southeast, piercing the fat little clumps of cumulus cloud that floated across the land as it swept inexorably toward its target: Arlington National Cemetery.

Birds fell out of the sky, their feathers scorched, their innards exploded by the sudden blast of heat. Grass curled and browned as the beam swept by. Newly leafed trees puffed tendrils of smoke. Like a finger of death the energy beam swept slowly across the District of Columbia. The water of the Potomac sizzled briefly as ten thousand million watts of energy crossed the river and reached Arlington.

Automobile ignition systems conked out. Cars on the Key Bridge suddenly lost power and banged into a snarl of dented fenders and crumpled trunks. People inside the cars fainted from sudden heat shock; several died, slumped over their steering wheels. Electronics systems shut down in home after home; children wailed that their computer games had crashed while their parents clicked fruitlessly at the remote control units of their suddenly blank TV sets.

A power transformer on a telephone pole just outside Meriden Hill Park blew out in a spectacular shower of sparks and smoke. The children playing on the grass were startled.

Mrs. Rhonda Bernstein, minding her grandchildren at the park while her daughter and her fumble-fingered son-in-law prepared their backyard picnic dinner, was alarmed enough by the transformer's blowout to fish out her cell phone and call 911. The phone didn't work. Frowning, she shook it and pecked at the minuscule keyboard again. Not a peep.

These damned cheap things never work when you need them, she thought angrily. Some bargain. She was perspiring, she realized. I haven't had a hot flash in five years, she thought. But this was worse. She couldn't catch her breath. The blood was thundering in her ears. And the children had stopped playing. None of them was running around anymore. Two of them had fallen to the ground; the others just stood there looking scared.

Then she saw that the grass was turning brown. Before her eyes it was curling up and browning, just as if somebody had thrown it into an oven.

She had strength enough to get to her feet before she collapsed to the ground with a fatal heart attack.

Hey, the magnetrons have come back up!" called one of the technicians at the control center in Matagorda.

Lynn Van Buren hurried over to the woman's console and saw that indeed the satellite's magnetrons were up to full power again. It can't be Dan and the crew; they're not even halfway there yet.

She had to stand on tiptoes to see over the console and yell to the guy two rows away, "What're you getting from White Sands?"

"Nothing," he answered. "Not a milliwatt."

Van Buren frowned, thinking, The powersat's beaming power again but the rectennas aren't receiving a thing. Her pulse began to race; she could feel her heart thumping beneath her ribs. This could be bad. Really bad.

"Something screwy here," called one of the other technicians. Van Buren hurried over to his console.

"Look at the accelerometer record," he said, tracing a finger along a curve that glowed red on his screen against a rapidly changing set of alphanumerics. "The bird's moving."

"It can't be!"

"Look at the friggin' numbers!"

Van Buren stared. "It's being maneuvered!" she blurted.

"Not by us," said the technician. "We haven't budged her since we settled her in that geosynch slot months ago."

Van Buren raced to the communications console. "Pipe me through to the boss."

"They're in the OTV now," said the communications technician.

"I know that!" Van Buren snapped. "Get him!"

The comm tech stared up at her. Van Buren never lost her temper.

How can it be so hot all of a sudden?" asked Irv Lamont. "One minute it's nice, all of a sudden it's like August."

Eighty-six-year-old Lamont was playing chess at the sidewalk café with Cass Bernardillo, his friend of sixty-some years.

Bernardillo looked up from the chessboard. "Clouding up. We might get a shower."

"The weather forecast was for sunny and mild," Lamont grumbled.

"The weather forecast. What do they know? Remember last February? I had to shovel four inches of 'sunny and mild' off my driveway."

"You should have moved to a condo," Lamont said. "Let them do the outside work."

"I've lived in that house for fifty-three years. The only way I'm gonna leave is feet first."

Lamont made a sour face at his old friend. Then he ran a hand inside his shirt collar. "Christ, it's *hot*."

"Let's go inside the restaurant. It's air-conditioned inside."

"They always keep it too cold."

"So you want to broil yourself out here?"

Lamont started to answer, but collapsed over the chessboard, scattering the pieces to the sidewalk. Bernardillo slumped in his chair and slid to the pavement, too. Half a dozen people walking along the street keeled over. A car slammed into a light pole and then a city bus careened into a line of parked cars with a screeching, rending tearing of metal. People screamed. And more fell, dead and dying.

Al-Bashir's eyes were riveted to the television screen. The president of the United States was getting out of his long black limousine, smiling at the crowd of people lining his path to the dais where he would deliver his speech and then present a ceremonial ring of flowers at the Tomb of the Unknowns.

"The beam isn't there!" he shouted without taking his eyes from the screen. "It's not there yet!"

The Egyptian, standing behind one of the seated technicians, said, "It isn't easy to move that huge satellite. This has to be done carefully, delicately."

"Get the beam on its target!" al-Bashir insisted.

"It's moving across the city. Give us a few more minutes."

Al-Bashir tried to control his impatience. A few more minutes won't hurt. Let him begin his speech. Strike him down in the middle of his oration. Let the whole world see him broiled alive, him and his lackeys around him.

Then he smiled to himself. In a few minutes, half an hour at most, it will be done. Then I go upstairs for my reward. I deserve a reward for this. She'll be mine, whether she wants to be or not.

Jane Thornton took her place beside Senator Quill as the president glad-handed his way along the line of VIPs waiting beneath the long plastic awning. Everyone put on their best smiles for the cameras.

Every time Jane saw the president she was struck by how small he was. Strange, she thought. American presidents tend to be either six-footers or little bantam cocks. Washington, Lincoln, even Reagan were all tall men. Teddy Roosevelt wasn't all that tall, but he was dynamic, energetic.

This president was at least two inches shorter than Jane, even in the elevator shoes that everyone in Washington knew he wore. She smiled down at him as he took her hand. He smiled back warmly while the cameras clicked away.

"I ought to thank you, Jane."

"Me, Mr. President?"

"Sure, You're pushing Scanwell into a first-ballot nomination."

"I'm certainly trying."

"Great. You think he can beat an incumbent president? I'll whup his ass in November. I'm looking forward to it."

Without letting her smile slip one millimeter, Jane said, "Good luck, then. You'll need it."

"I hear you might be his vice presidential choice," the president added.

Jane murmured, "You have long ears."

"Take the slot if he offers it to you. Then I'll whup your sweet little ass, too. That'll be even more fun."

The orbital transfer vehicle looked like a barbell-shaped ocean buoy encrusted with barnacles. Designed to operate in space and never come back to Earth, it did not need to have a sleek aerodynamic shape like the spaceplane. Its exterior was studded with antennas, tool kits, grappling arms, and life-support packs.

Inside, it resembled a sardine can. Built to hold ten spacesuited people, it seemed jammed to bursting with only the seven of them standing in it. No seats; they weren't necessary in zero gravity. Dan's team stood with their boots slipped into fabric foot loops fastened to the metal decking.

Adair stood up at the front of the circular cabin, his attention on the beeping, flickering readout screens surrounding him, rather than the curving window of thick quartz glass in front of him. Dan stood just behind him, peering out that window. It was black out there, as deep and dark as infinity. Only a few very bright stars could be seen through the quartz's heavy tinting.

"Rendezvous with the beast in eight minutes," Adair called out.

Like the spaceplane, the cabin of the OTV was pressurized. The crew could lift the visors of their helmets and breathe the air the vehicle stowed in its internal tanks. It was a small luxury, but Dan felt glad of it. Eight minutes, he thought. Then the work begins. For now, the seven men and women simply stood there, with nothing to do but wait. There was no sensation of motion; they didn't even sway in their foot anchors.

"Getting a flash from Matagorda," Adair said. "On two."

Dan touched the stud on his wrist band that activated radio frequency two.

"This is Dan," he said.

A crackle of electronic hash in his helmet earphones, then, "Van Buren here. Our monitors show the magnetrons have come back on, but White Sands still isn't getting any power."

Dan felt his brows knit. "That doesn't make any sense."

A fraction of a second's delay, just enough to make him realize he was nearly twenty-two thousand miles away.

"And the satellite's being moved," she added, her voice edging up a notch.

"Moved?"

"Somebody's repositioning it. And it isn't us."

"Away from White Sands?"

"Right."

"To where?"

"We're trying to figure that out."

"Get on it! Right away!"

"We're on it, chief."

"Call me the instant you figure out where it's being pointed."

"Right." Van Buren clicked off.

"Hey!" Adair hollered. "I can see the beast!"

Dan followed the astronaut's pointing arm and there it was, a thin flat square hanging against the black of space, its edges glowing in sunlight. They were coming up from below the powersat; Dan saw the rows of boxlike structures and domes that housed the inverters and magnetrons and other equipment. Down at the end, as far from the output antenna as possible, was the dome for the satellite's control systems. There was a docking port next to it. That was where Adair was aiming the OTV.

A glint of light caught his attention. Leaning forward, one hand on Adair's back to steady himself, Dan peered out the window and saw a long, slim metallic object floating off a few hundred yards from the powersat, rotating slowly, catching the sunlight as it spun.

"That's the output antenna!" he shouted.

"Jeez, boss, I think you're right," said Adair.

"How'd it get loose?"

"Beats me."

"Swing us up toward that end of the satellite," Dan commanded. "I want to see what's happened up there."

MATAGORDA ISLAND,
TEXAS

Looks like the East Coast, maybe Washington," said the technician.

Van Buren was tugging nervously on her strand of pearls, leaning over the seated man to study his console screen.

"Washington," she muttered. And her mind raced. *The magnetrons are putting out power. Some sonofabitch has moved the satellite out of its normal position. They're pointing it at Washington. The beam's too diffuse to hurt anybody, but . . .*

She straightened up and yelled across the rows of consoles to the communications tech, "Get Dan on the horn. Right away!"

By the time she had rushed to the comm console, she could hear Dan's voice, "What've you got?"

"Dan, this is just preliminary, we don't have it nailed down all that firmly yet, but I think they're moved the beam to Washington."

There was a tiny lag, just long enough to be noticeable. Then Dan exploded, "Jesus Christ on a motorcycle!"

"It's all right, Dan," Van Buren said, unconsciously fingering her pearls. "The beam's too diffuse to do any damage."

Again the lag. Then Dan's voice answered tightly, "Maybe not."

"What do you mean?"

"Somebody's removed our antenna from the powersat and put up a different one."

"What?" Van Buren's necklace broke, pearls clattering all over the control center's tiled floor.

It's an Astro Corporation craft," said Williamson. "I can see the logo they've slapped on her side."

"Have they seen us?" Bouchachi asked, alarmed.

"Dunno. Maybe."

The two men were huddled in their own transfer vessel, still in their spacesuits. Williamson had shoved Nikolayev's body out the hatch so Bouchachi wouldn't have to share his final hour or so with the corpse. Neither of them had expected Astro to react so quickly to their tampering with the satellite. They'll try to set it right, Williamson thought. We'll have to stop them. Or at least delay them.

He wondered how they could accomplish that. From all he knew about this mission, they wouldn't have to delay the Astro people for long. The job would be completed in a few minutes. Just hold them off for a few minutes, he told himself. We're going to die anyway, so what difference does a few minutes make?

"Come on, then," he said, grasping the edges of the open hatch to pull himself outside.

"Where are you going?" Bouchachi asked.

"To the control station."

"But that's all the way at the other end of the satellite!"

"Right. We'll have to hurry."

In the underground satellite monitoring center, the lieutenant commander walked briskly to where the Homeland Security guy sat impatiently sipping at a Styrofoam cup of coffee.

He looked up at her expectantly, got to his feet. "You've got something?"

"Not your dinky li'l beacon," said the commander.

"Then what?"

"A wicked powerful beam coming from a location just a few klicks outside Marseille. Looks like a communications signal uplinking to a satellite."

"A satellite? We're looking for a tracking beacon from an individual—"

"I know that," said the commander. "But this signal wasn't there yesterday. Wasn't even there when I came on shift this morning. We—"

An Air Force tech sergeant came up, saluted smartly, and handed her a photograph. "Just in, ma'am. The location of the signal near Marseille."

The homeland security deputy director looked over the commander's shoulder at the picture.

"It's a villa."

"Nice place," said the commander.

"There's a lot of cars parked out front."

"No antennas in sight. But that doesn't mean anything."

"Do you think that's where our person is?"

The commander shrugged. "Maybe. But we'll never pick up her beacon while they're beaming out that whopping signal."

Dan heard the anxiety in Van Buren's voice. "If they've concentrated the beam they could do some bad damage."

"I know," he said. "Get Senator Thornton on the phone. Her private number's in my computer. Tell her everything we know. Tell her it's from me."

"Okay. I'm on my way."

Dan clicked his suit radio back to the suit-to-suit frequency. "Gerry, how soon can we dock?"

"Which docking port do you want to use?"

"The one back down by the control shack."

Adair nodded inside his fishbowl helmet. "Okay. Gimme five minutes."

"Make it three."

Adair laughed.

"What's funny?" Dan snapped.

"I was going to say three, but I figured if I did, you'd say two."

Jane glanced past the edge of the awning up at the sky as the president droned on. Clouds were building up, looking grayer and more threatening every moment. She suppressed a giggle. Maybe the big bore will get rained out. What a pity.

The president and the VIPs stood beneath the plastic awning, but the crowd gathered out beyond them was in the open. We'll stay dry enough, Jane thought. But they'll all have to run for shelter. Such a shame—they won't hear the end of the president's platitudes.

Denny O'Brien was out there, sweating in the midst of the crowd. Damned hot for May, he thought. Looking up, he saw that the rain clouds which had been building thicker and grayer for the past hour or more were breaking up. No, he realized. They're not blowing away. A hole's opening up in the middle of 'em. Like somebody's carving a hole right through the thick bank of clouds. And the hole's getting bigger. He could see blue sky through it.

His cell phone buzzed with the signal it gave when the call was intended for the senator. Her cell phone was turned off, of course. Nobody took incoming calls when they were standing near the president, especially when the man was giving a speech.

While the people around him glared disapprovingly, O'Brien flicked his phone open and squinted at the screen. Matagorda? That's where Dan Randolph's outfit is.

He put the phone to his ear. There was so much static on the phone that he could barely understand the caller.

"Slow down!" he hissed. "Talk slower and clearer."

"Get the president under shelter!" Van Buren's voice said urgently. "Not in a car or anything metal. They're beaming a lethal level of microwaves at him!"

"What kind of a stunt do you—"

"It's no stunt!" Van Buren screeched. "They're trying to assassinate the president! With microwaves from the powersat!"

P O W E R S A T

Dan was the first one through the hatch and into the docking port. Without waiting to see who was following him, he cracked open the port's outer hatch and pulled himself out onto the flat surface of the powersat.

And his breath caught in his throat. Stretching out in every direction was the vast sunlit surface of the satellite, like a huge man-made plain set in the midst of the star-studded infinity of space. The flat surface glinted darkly, like polished obsidian, as tens of thousands of solar cells greedily drank in the Sun's unfailing energy. Beyond the edge of the powersat he saw the gleaming blue sphere of the Earth, flecked with swirling white clouds. Farther still, the small pale battered crescent of the Moon grinned lopsidedly at him.

No time for sightseeing, Dan told himself sternly. The broad surface of the powersat was studded with cleats, handholds where safety tethers could be attached. Dan had no time for that. He grabbed the nearest cleat and began pulling himself down the hundred-yard-thick edge of the satellite, heading for its underside and the bulbous enclosure of the control station, zipping along from one handhold to the next like a speeding torpedo.

"Hey, boss, you're supposed to use the tether!" a distressed voice sounded in his earphones.

"You use 'em," Dan said. "I'm in a hurry."

Back when he had worked for Yamagata, Dan had won bets from other workers in sprints across smaller structures. He grinned to himself. I haven't lost the knack.

But then he saw two other figures in dull orange spacesuits heading for the control station, coming up from the other direction. This is going to be a race, after all, he said to himself.

Although Denny O'Brien was in terrible physical shape, his mind was sharp. While the president droned on, O'Brien pushed through the crowd toward the nearest Secret Service agent. There may have been a dozen others that he didn't notice, but this guy had the stone face, the special eyeglasses, and the sports jacket that covered his Uzi, despite the wilting heat.

"I'm Senator Thornton's senior aide," O'Brien said breathlessly, holding his plastic ID under the agent's nose. "I've just got word there's an assassination attempt going down."

The agent's stone face went slack-jawed.

"Who's in charge? We've gotta get the president to safety right away!"

Dr. Supartha could not believe her eyes. Usually the emergency room was fairly quiet on a holiday afternoon; it wasn't until the night shift that the drunks got themselves into accidents or fights. But here in the middle of the afternoon, almost a dozen people had come into the hospital, seven of them already dead, all of them showing the strangest symptoms.

Dr. Supartha had thought it merely a coincidence when the first two came to her attention. Heat prostration? She shook her head. The outward symptoms might have suggested that, but this was something far different, far worse.

By the gods, she thought, these poor devils look as if they'd been *cooked*.

There was always the danger of missing the next cleat and going sailing off the powersat out into space, Dan thought as he sped along toward the control station. Without a tether to anchor you, you'd go sailing into the wild black yonder forever. Unless one of your buddies came out and picked you up.

No time to worry about that. Those two strangers were heading for the control station, and they weren't up here to do any good. They've already replaced our antenna and moved the satellite to aim at Washington.

Jane's there! he suddenly realized. These bastards could kill her!

He redoubled his efforts to get to the control station before they did. In his helmet earphones he heard Adair and the others shouting to him, warning him that he was taking foolish chances. Yeah, he answered silently. Let me slow down and play it safe while they wipe out Washington with Jane in it.

A Secret Service agent slipped up beside the president and placed a handwritten note on the rostrum.

The president glared at the woman, angry at the interruption, then glanced at the note. And paled.

He bit his lip for a moment, then looked up at the audience. "Ladies and gentlemen, please excuse me. An emergency has come up and I must return to the White House immediately. Thank you."

The crowd stood stunned as the president abruptly turned away from the rostrum and a squad of Secret Service agents surrounded him.

Jane Thornton was just as puzzled as everyone else. For a few moments she stood beneath the protective awning, not knowing what to do. She turned to Quinn, who looked just as confused as she felt. Then she saw Denny O'Brien struggling through the crowd toward her, waving his cell phone in one extended arm like a signal. As she watched, O'Brien staggered and sank to his knees, his suit obviously sopping with perspiration.

And others were dropping to the browning grass, all around him.

MARSEILLE

It's working!" Al-Bashir clapped his hands with a loud smack. "Look! Look!" He pointed to the TV screen.

Pandemonium had broken out at Arlington National Cemetery. People were falling to the ground by the dozens, by the hundreds. The TV cameras' picture became grainy, splotched with interference.

"But the president is getting away," said the Egyptian, standing beside al-Bashir.

With a grim smile, al-Bashir replied, "Let them bundle him into his limousine. The metal shell of the limo will serve as an oven very nicely."

The Egyptian nodded, then turned back to the technicians at their laptops. One by one, he checked them and satisfied himself that the satellite was still beaming out power and still aimed at Arlington.

Al-Bashir was practically dancing across the basement floor. "In an hour, at most, the vice president will order their military to blow the powersat out of the sky."

"And the evidence of our work will be destroyed," said the Egyptian.

"Exactly," said al-Bashir. "They will never know that this was a deliberate attack on them. They will think the satellite malfunctioned. This will kill the idea of solar power satellites forever!"

"A great victory," the Egyptian admitted.

"Indeed."

Al-Bashir headed for the door that led to the stairway.

"You're not waiting to see what happens now?" the Egyptian asked.

"No need. It is written. Now I go to reap the fruits of victory."

The Egyptian nodded, barely. He knew that al-Bashir had brought a woman with him.

"I will remain here," he said to al-Bashir's back. "I will monitor the situation until it ends."

Al-Bashir waved a hand in acknowledgment, thinking, The man is an engineer through and through. He wants to make certain of every last detail.

The Egyptian, meanwhile, was thinking of a dictum he had heard from some American funnyman: It's not over until it's over.

Dan was racing across the broad surface of the powersat, flicking hand over hand along the cleats, heading for the control station. One thought burned in his mind, They're trying to kill Jane. These sons of bitches are trying to kill Jane.

In his helmet earphones he heard Adair and the others of his crew calling to him, urging him to slow down, to be careful.

"You're gonna get yourself killed, boss!" Adair warned.

The hell I am, Dan replied silently, puffing too hard to speak aloud.

He could see the two cosmonauts in their dirty orange suits making their way to the control station. The bastards had a head start, but Dan was catching up swiftly.

Then he heard one of his crew saying sternly, "You two are trespassing on private property! Identify yourselves immediately!"

Dan almost laughed. I didn't realize we had a double-damned lawyer in the crew. The intruders did not respond. Probably their suit radios are on completely different frequencies from ours, he reasoned.

He knew what had happened, and with the clarity born of a massive adrenalin surge he understood exactly what the intruders were going to do. They had already concentrated the microwave beam being broadcast by the powersat and maneuvered its attitude thrusters so that the beam was pouring onto Washington. Now they were heading for the control station to wreck the controls and prevent Dan and his crew from turning off the power.

At Arlington National Cemetery hundreds were collapsing onto the grass while a squad of Secret Service agents huddled around the president beneath the heavy plastic canopy that stretched over the speakers' platform.

Jane stared at Denny O'Brien's prostrate form, his cell phone still grasped in his dead fingers.

"What's happening?" Quill asked, his usual unflappable calm completely shattered. He looked frightened, dazed, as he hunched on his knees in the mass of terrified, whimpering VIPs.

"Get down!" said one of the Secret Service agents. "Somebody's shooting out there!"

Jane remained on her feet and pulled her cell phone from her shoulder purse. Turning it on, she saw that she had received a call from Matagorda. She pecked at the recall button.

Harsh static hissed in her ear. Then a voice she didn't recognize, high and tight with tension, answered, "Who is this?"

"Senator Thornton," Jane replied.

"Thank god and all his saints," said Lynn Van Buren. "I've been trying to reach you. The powersat's gone wonky. It's beaming microwaves at you. High intensity."

"I'm with the president—"

"Is he safe?"

"So far. They're going to take him—"

"Don't move him!" Van Buren snapped. "If he's protected from the microwaves where he is, don't move him! For god's sake, don't put him in a limo or any other car. That'd be like sticking him in a microwave oven!"

Jane felt an ice-cool calm envelope her. Now that she knew what was happening, she knew what to do.

"Stay on the line. I'm going to give this phone to the head of the president's security detail."

The chief of the Secret Service bodyguards was also on his feet, an Uzi cocked in his right hand, scanning the crowd. He was saying into the pin mike at his lips, "I don't see any shooters."

Jane stood before him. "You know who I am?"

"Senator Thornton, yes."

She shoved the phone at him. "There aren't any shooters. We're being baked by a microwave beam from the power satellite."

"What?"

"Listen to what this woman has to say," Jane said, thrusting the phone into his empty hand. "She's from Astro Corporation, in Texas—the people who built the satellite."

April felt her insides jump as al-Bashir came through the bedroom doorway. She stood tensed by the open French windows that led onto the flower-rimmed balcony.

"Still in the same dress?" he asked, looking slightly disappointed. "I thought you would have showered and changed by now."

April had examined the clothes hanging in the closet. Nothing but slinky, sheer stuff. "I'm not a *Playboy* model," she said.

Al-Bashir ignored her sarcasm. "I'm sorry to have kept you waiting. I had business to attend to. Important business."

"I'd like to go home, Mr. al-Bashir," she said as firmly as she could manage.

His smile turned smug. "I don't think that would be advisable under the circumstances."

"I don't know how you brought me here," April said, feeling like a trapped animal. "I mean, I never agreed to come here with you."

"Yet here you are."

There was a light rap on the door. Al-Bashir opened it, and the Asian woman came in, dressed in a miniskirted skintight outfit, pushing a rolling cart covered with a damask tablecloth. It bore a dinner for two in covered dishes, an ice bucket containing a bottle of champagne, and two long-stemmed glasses.

In silence, the woman wheeled the cart to the middle of the room, then looked questioningly at al-Bashir.

"You may go," he told her, "for now. I'll call you when we're ready for you."

April felt icicles prickling along her spine.

"Look, Mr. al-Bashir—" she began.

"Call me Asim."

"I didn't ask to be brought here, and I'd like to go back home. Right now."

Al-Bashir shook his head pityingly. "I don't think you'd like to be back in that pig's nest in Texas, April. It's going to be very ugly there. In a few hours mobs will be tearing down Astro Corporation and looking for Dan Randolph's blood."

Her knees went weak. "What? What do you mean?"

"Several thousand Americans have been killed, including the president of the United States, very possibly. They were all killed by Dan Randolph's power satellite."

April sagged down onto the bed, speechless. Smiling contentedly, al-Bashir went to the champagne bottle and began undoing its cork.

POWERSAT

Williamson saw the American in his snow-white spacesuit racing like a lunatic toward the control station. But the bugger's too late, Williamson told himself. He and Bouchachi reached the hatch of the domed enclosure well ahead of the Yank.

"You stay at the hatch and hold him off," Williamson told Bouchachi. "I'll go in and knock out the controls so they can't turn the power off."

"Hold him off?" Bouchachi asked, his voice little more than a squeak in Williamson's earphones. "How? With what?"

Williamson considered giving the Algerian the knife he'd used on the cosmonaut, but thought better of it. Better save it in case *I* need it, he said to himself. Tapping the array of wrenches and other tools attached to Bouchachi's belt, he said, "Whack him on the helmet hard enough to crack it open."

"But the others!" Bouchachi pointed to the half-dozen other Americans making their way slowly, hand over hand, toward them.

"By the time they get here it'll be too late."

"But they'll kill us!"

"We're goin' to die anyway, right? In another little while you'll be in Paradise, chum, with your seventy-two virgins."

Williamson ducked through the hatch, into the control station. Bouchachi turned and saw that the American was only a bare few meters away. He fumbled at his waist for the biggest wrench he had.

Too late. The American launched himself like a missile at Bouchachi. The two spacesuited men collided soundlessly. Bouchachi felt the wind knocked out of his lungs. He grappled with the American, trying to keep him away from the hatch, and they both went sailing, tumbling head over heels, across the broad expanse of the powersat.

Dan wrenched one arm free of his opponent and grabbed a cleat. He felt his shoulder pop from the sudden strain; a streak of agony ran along his whole right side. The other guy was hanging on to him with both arms, their helmets bumping. Dan could see that the guy was some sort of Arab.

With his free left hand Dan reached behind the guy's helmet and pawed at the strap holding the man's life-support backpack. The guy's eyes went frantic and he pushed away from Dan. Still hanging onto the cleat despite the pain in his shoulder, Dan pulled up both his booted feet and kicked the bastard in the gut as hard as he could. The man went spinning away, arms and legs flailing as he tumbled off into space, dwindling rapidly in the distance.

With his usable left hand, Dan made his way from cleat to cleat until he was at the hatch of the control station.

The other intruder was inside the dome, his boots hooked into foot loops on the floor, his body half bent in the simian crouch that people unconsciously assume in zero gravity. The only light inside the dome was from the control board's colored display screens and lighted gauges. Dan saw it reflecting off the intruder's helmet. He was poring over the board, Dan realized, trying to figure out how to disable the controls. Then he pulled a sizable wrench from the tool set at his belt.

He's going to smash everything! Dan saw.

With a roar that the intruder couldn't hear Dan launched himself at the man headfirst, banging into him and sending the two of them bouncing off the curving wall of the tight little control dome. Fresh agonies of pain shot through Dan's right shoulder. Where the hell's the rest of my gang? he wondered as he recoiled away from the intruder.

The bastard still had the wrench in his fist, and he pushed off the wall to fly straight at Dan.

With a grim smile, Dan realized that this bozo didn't know shit about fighting in zero *g*. Flicking his boots against the loops studding the floor, Dan edged sideways and his attacker sailed right past him and into the other side of the dome. He bounced away, turned an inadvertent somersault, then righted himself and faced Dan again.

By now Dan had moved to the control panel, standing in front of it. "You want to wreck the controls," he said, knowing the other couldn't hear him, "you'll have to get past me first."

The intruder hesitated, hanging weightlessly a few inches above the floor. He threw the wrench at Dan, sending himself into a hopeless spin. Dan caught the wrench in his good hand and hefted it menacingly. "Thanks, pal. Now come on over here so I can give it back to you."

But there was a knife in the man's gloved hand now. Dan saw its slim blade glint in the faint light from the control screens.

Anchoring one boot in a foot loop, Dan hurled the wrench back at the intruder. The man ducked in reflex action, and the motion started him tumbling again. Dan glided out from the foot loop and slipped behind the flailing intruder, locking his legs around the guy's waist and grabbing his knife hand. The two of them bucked and banged off the control board and the dome's curving wall for what seemed like an hour to Dan.

At last he heard Adair's voice, "What's going on here, a rodeo?"

"Ride him, boss!"

"Christ, the sumbitch's got a knife!"

All six of Dan's crew jammed into the dome and overpowered Williamson. One of the women ended up with the knife.

"Why don't we just stick this up his ass?" she snarled.

Dan was already at the controls, shutting down the magnetrons. "Uh-uh. We want him alive and able to answer questions."

One by one, in swift succession, Dan turned off the magnetrons, poking at the control board with his left hand. A string of red lights sprang across the control board. His right shoulder was flaming with pain now, as the adrenaline ebbed out of his blood.

"Radio Van Buren and verify that we've turned off the power," Dan said, suddenly so tired and hurting that he wanted to curl up and go to sleep.

THE OVAL OFFICE

The president was livid.

"They tried to kill me!" he kept repeating, shouting almost, as he paced furiously back and forth behind his huge ornate desk. "Some mother-fucking bastards tried to kill me!"

The director of homeland security had never seen the president so enraged. "It wasn't just you, Mr. President. More than six hundred people have died—"

"I don't give a shit! They were after *me!*"

The secretary of defense—an old friend and a veteran of many private tirades—just sat on the plush little sofa by the empty fireplace and bided his time. Sitting across from him in the Oval Office were the secretary of state and the president's national security advisor.

"We're getting information on what happened," the national security advisor said, trying to calm down his president. "Apparently a terrorist group took control of that power satellite up in space—"

"Blow it out of the sky!" the president snarled, turning to the defense secretary. "We've got missiles! Blast that sonofabitch to hell!"

The defense secretary hiked his eyebrows. "It's owned by an American corporation, Mr. President."

"I don't care! That damned thing is *dangerous!* Blow it up!"

The secretary of state, very aware that she was the only woman in the room, decided she had to say something. "Mr. President, wouldn't it be better—"

But the president ignored her. Pointing at his chief of staff, he said, "Get the Air Force on the line. I'll give the order myself."

The chief of staff glanced nervously at the others, then walked slowly across the carpet that bore the Great Seal of the United States, heading for the president's desk and his telephone console.

"There's a team of Americans aboard the satellite," said the director of homeland defense.

"Americans?" the president snapped.

"They went up there and grabbed the terrorists. They've shut down the satellite. It's not beaming power anywhere now."

The defense secretary asked, "How'd they get up there so quick?"

The homeland defense director smiled knowingly. "Better than that, we know where the terrorist base is. The ground control base where they directed the satellite."

The Oval Office went silent for several moments. Then the secretary of state asked, "So soon? It's been less than an hour."

Almost smugly, the homeland defense director pulled a photograph from his inside jacket pocket, walked over to the desk and placed it in front of the president.

"It looks like a house," the president said, settling slowly into his desk chair.

"It's a villa outside Marseille."

"That's where the terrorists are?"

"There were two on the satellite itself. The American team from Astro Corporation got them." Tapping a finger on the photo, the homeland defense director went on, "But this is where the radio signals that controlled the satellite came from."

"You're certain of this?" the president's chief of staff asked.

"Dead certain."

The president looked up from the photo. "Are they still in there?"

"We've got three different satellites watching. None of the cars parked in that photo have left yet."

"It hasn't even been an hour."

"They're probably dismantling their equipment and getting set to skeedaddle," said the homeland defense director.

The president shifted his red-rimmed eyes to the defense secretary. "Can you put a smart bomb on that villa?"

The defense secretary smiled tightly. "Which window would you like it to go through?"

The national security advisor said, "But that's in France! Sovereign French territory!"

"How quickly can you get it done?" the president asked the defense secretary.

"We have a carrier group in the Med. No more than an hour. Maybe a little less."

"Do it."

The secretary of state shot to her feet. "Mr. President! You can't bomb a building inside a sovereign nation! France, for god's sake!"

"We have an antiterrorism agreement with them, don't we?"

"Yes, but—"

"You get the French ambassador on the phone and explain it to him."

"Lord knows where he is this afternoon," she said. "It'll take more than an hour to track him down."

"Good. Take your time. And when you get him, explain this to him slowly."

Dan had expected to be angry, to be in a killing rage as he heard from Van Buren what had happened at Arlington National Cemetery. But once he learned that Jane hadn't been harmed, all the fury leaked out of him. I'm coming down from an adrenaline high, he told himself. But a voice in his head kept repeating, Jane's all right. You saved her. She's all right.

He sat in the last row of the spaceplane, his shoulder throbbing painfully, as Adair went through the checklist preparing to break orbit and fly back to Matagorda. In the cushioned seat next to him sat Gilly Williamson, looking exhausted, grimy, totally spent.

Like the six others in the cabin, Dan and Williamson were still in their spacesuits, although they had removed their helmets. Makes a big difference, Dan thought, when you can rub your eyes or scratch your nose.

Williamson scratched his stubbly chin and stared straight ahead, his eyes focused on some inner demons.

"Sorry we couldn't pick up your buddy," Dan said, keeping his voice low. "He was too far out for us to risk chasing him with the OTV."

Williamson turned his head toward Dan slightly. "It's okay. He wanted to be a holy martyr, anyway."

"And you?" Dan asked. "You wanted to be a martyr, too?"

"I already am one, mate."

Dan pondered that for all of a second or two. "You're not Moslem."

"Not bloody likely."

"Then what's the suicide bit all about?"

"I'm already dead, pal. Cancer. It's just a matter of time."

"So you wanted to go out in a blaze of glory? Is that it?"

Williamson smirked at him. "I've got a wife and kids to support. This was my pension plan."

Comprehension dawned on Dan. "Pension? Really? Tell me more."

"Why the fuck should I?"

Dan beamed his brightest grin. "Because I'm a greedy Yank capitalist, and whatever they promised you, I'll double."

USS HARRY S. TRUMAN

As the massive aircraft carrier plowed across the Mediterranean Sea, her skipper and his flight operations officer huddled over a display table with the commander of the carrier's attack squadron, their faces underlit by the light coming from the table's electronic screen. It showed a satellite picture of the hilltop villa outside Marseille. The squadron commander was in his olive green flight suit; the other two officers in tropical tan uniforms.

"This comes from the SecDef himself," the skipper was saying. "Ultra Top Secret. Only the three of us are in on it."

"What about my GIB?" the squadron commander asked.

"Your weapons man sits in that back seat and does his job," the flight operations officer said sternly. "He doesn't have to know where the missile's going."

"As far as your guy in back is concerned, this is just a weapons test. Nothing more," said the skipper. "You are not to fly within twenty miles of French airspace."

"Yes, sir. I'll keep her on the wavetops, under their radar."

"You've got half an hour to get to the release point," said the flight operations officer. "Maintain radio silence, but keep your receiver open in case there's a recall order."

"Satellite navigation all the way?" asked the squadron commander.

"That's right. No contact with the ship once you've been launched," the flight operations officer said.

"And the missile will follow satellite guidance once it's launched?"

"It better."

The three men straightened up. The squadron commander grinned tightly. "Holy Mother of God, the frogs are going to go apeshit over this."

The skipper was not amused. "If we carry this off properly, the French will believe a group of terrorists were attacked by a rival group. At least, that's the cover story our people will put out."

"I hope it works," the squadron commander said.

"You just do your job," said the flight operations officer. "Let the politicians in Washington worry about the rest."

"Yes, sir." The squadron commander saluted smartly, then turned and started for his plane, already warmed up and in place on the carrier's forward catapult.

As al-Bashir poured champagne into the two fluted glasses, April heard a timid knock on the bedroom door.

Looking annoyed, al-Bashir slammed the champagne bottle back into its bucket and strode to the door. He opened it only a crack. April glimpsed a round-faced, bald man out in the corridor. He looked upset. The two men spoke rapidly—in Arabic, April guessed.

Al-Bashir's face was dark as he closed the door and turned back to April.

"It appears that your president escaped with his life," he said, scowling. "But more than a thousand Americans have been killed. And the power satellite has been shut down completely."

"You did this?" April asked, still sitting on the bed. She felt breathless, weak.

"Yes," said al-Bashir. Then he smiled again. "With a little help from my friends, as your Beatles sang."

"And Dan?"

"Randolph? He'll be blamed for the disaster, of course. His power satellite will be cursed by everyone. No one will know that we engineered it."

"You engineered all this?"

His smile widened. "Yes, I did. And you're not returning to the United States. You're going to Tunis, with me."

"But I don't want—"

"What you want is of no consequence. I promised myself a little reward when this operation with the satellite was finished, and you are my reward."

He held out one of the glasses of champagne to her.

April stared at him for a long, wordless moment. He's smiling, she thought. He's just killed a thousand or so people and he's smiling about it. He's ruined Dan, destroyed the very idea of the powersat, and it makes him smile.

She got her feet, surprised that she had the strength to stand without trembling. Without a word, she stepped toward al-Bashir and accepted the champagne.

"You'll enjoy my home in Tunis. You'll have every luxury, so long as you behave yourself properly."

"Every luxury except freedom," April murmured.

He made a disappointed cluck of his tongue. "You Americans always talk about freedom."

"Yes, we do."

"Enjoy life, lovely one. With me you will live far better than you ever could in miserable Texas."

April sipped at the champagne, her mind whirling. I'm his prize for destroying Dan. I'm his reward. He's captured me and I'll have to do whatever he wants.

Al-Bashir put his glass down on the damask-covered cart and began uncovering the dishes. "Ah, you see? A steak dinner, just as you would have in Texas. All the comforts of home."

The spaceplane was starting to rattle as Adair jinked it through the first of several high-altitude turns aimed at killing speed before it could come in for a landing. At least the worst part of reentry is over, Dan thought. Everybody sat tight in their seats as the craft blazed back into the atmosphere, leaving a brilliant flaming meteor trail behind it.

Dan had to put his bubble helmet on again to use the radio link to Matagorda. Williamson still sat beside him, looking less surly than he had before Dan began promising him the best medical care in America and a whopping insurance policy for his family—in exchange for his telling the FBI what he knew.

Van Buren's voice sounded close to tears. "Hundreds have been killed, Dan. Roasted alive. The TV's full of it."

"What about Senator Thornton?" he asked.

"I don't know. They haven't mentioned her name. The president's okay, though."

"Can you contact her by phone?"

"I talked with her when this all started, but then all the phone links went down," Van Buren answered.

Double damn it to hell and back, Dan grumbled to himself. Jane must be okay. If they didn't get the president they didn't get the VIPs around him. She's all right. They didn't kill her. She's okay.

He wished he were certain of that.

MARSEILLE

The French call it entrecôte," al-Bashir was saying as he pulled up a chair for April. "Much better than the grilled steak you get in Texas."

April sat at the wheeled cart and stared at the dinner laid out before her. Steak with some sort of sauce on it. Vegetables. A salad in a separate little plate. The silverware looked like solid silver. She picked up a fork. Yes, it was heavy.

"You must be famished," al-Bashir said as he sat on the opposite side of the table. "Dig in, as you Americans say."

April nibbled at the salad, sliced a piece of steak and tried to eat it. She had no appetite whatever.

Al-Bashir put down his knife and fork and looked across the table at her. "I understand," he said softly. "This is all very strange to you, even a little frightening."

April said nothing. She couldn't look at him. She stared down at the table setting in front of her.

Getting to his feet, al-Bashir came around the cart and grasped her by the arm. "You've got to face the facts, April. There's no life for you in America anymore. Your life is here, with me."

"I want to go home."

"Forget about America. Forget about Dan Randolph. His corporation will be destroyed and him along with it."

She turned her face away from him.

His grip on her arm tightened and he pulled her to her feet. "Come to bed with me, April. You'll enjoy it, I promise you."

With one swift move she grabbed the steak knife from beside her plate and rammed it into al-Bashir's soft belly. He grunted, his eyes went wide.

"How did you enjoy that, wiseass?" April snarled at him.

Al-Bashir tried to speak, but his knees gave way and he sank to the carpet, the silver knife sunk into his gut all the way up to the hilt. Blood was seeping. He tried to say something but all that came out of his mouth was a strangled little squeak.

They'll kill me, April told herself. They'll beat the hell out of me and gang-rape me and kill me. But at least I got him. She looked down at al-Bashir. His hands were twitching, trying to grasp the hilt of the knife.

"You've destroyed Dan? Well, I've destroyed you. How's it feel?"

Bending over the prostrate, staring al-Bashir, April yanked the knife out of him. He screamed and blood spurted from the wound.

Holding the bloody knife, April waited for the Asian woman to return. I'll slit the bitch's throat, she told herself. I'll kill as many of them as I can.

But nothing happened. No one rapped at the door. No one tried to enter. Al-Bashir was groaning, still breathing shallowly, but his eyes were closed. A growing pool of blood stained the carpet around his body.

She heard a car door slam. Going to the open French windows, she saw several men loading electronic equipment into a van. One of them looked up and pointed. For an instant April thought he was pointing at her but then she heard a roar like a rocket engine and the world exploded in a flash of fire.

Back on the *Truman*, the skipper stared at the satellite imagery. The hilltop villa was obliterated: nothing left standing except a few blackened stones. Even the cars and vans were only twisted wreckage now.

The steel hatch opened and the flight operations officer stepped in and saluted. The skipper dumped the satellite image and returned his salute.

"Scotty's back. Picture-perfect trap."

The skipper nodded. "Tell him 'well done' for me. And then neither of you is to say a word about this again. Ever. To anyone."

"Aye-aye, sir."

MATAGORDA ISLAND, TEXAS

It was a week later: a balmy, sunny Sunday afternoon. The Astro complex was quiet. Most of the staff were home enjoying the weekend. A skeleton crew stood by the launchpad, where the spaceplane had been mated with a fresh booster, ready for another flight to the powersat if necessary.

Nacho Chavez sat glumly in front of Dan's desk. Beside him, Kelly Eamons looked on the verge of tears.

"It was my fault," she said to Dan. "I encouraged her to play up to al-Bashir."

"You warned her it was dangerous," Chavez said. "You planted the tracker on her."

"A lot of good it did."

Dan could barely believe what they'd told him. "April's dead? She was killed in the bombing of that villa?"

"With al-Bashir and almost a dozen others," Chavez said.

"And al-Bashir was behind it all?"

"All of it. The crash of your spaceplane, the murders of Dr. Tenny and that technician, Larsen."

"And they used my powersat to try to assassinate the president."

Chavez nodded. Then he said, "None of this leaves this room, Mr. Randolph. We're depending on your discretion."

"We thought you'd want to know about April," said Eamons.

Dan felt stunned. April got herself mixed up in this cloak-and-dagger stuff? he kept repeating in his mind. And she's dead? Killed. He couldn't get himself to believe it. He expected her to pop through his office doorway any minute. But she's dead. They killed her.

"Why in the ever-loving, blue-eyed world would she get herself involved so deep—?"

"For you," Eamons replied. "She did it for you. I think she was in love with you."

Dan grunted as if he'd been punched in the gut. He opened his mouth to say something, but no words came out. His breath caught in his throat.

"She was a very wonderful woman," Eamons went on. "More wonderful than you know."

Dan's head sank halfway down to his chest. "Jesus," he mumbled. "Sweet Jesus Christ Almighty."

"We're getting a good deal of information out of this Williamson guy," Chavez said, trying to sound brighter. "He's being very cooperative."

So what? Dan wanted to say. Instead, he heard himself ask, "And the French? How do they feel about us bombing one of their villas?"

Chavez put on an innocent expression. "Who bombed one of their villas? The terrorists blew each other up."

"The French are going along with that?"

"We've allowed them to participate in Williamson's interrogation. I'm sure we'll make other concessions to them, as well."

Dan shook his head wearily. "I suppose I could offer them electricity at a cut rate."

"The powersat is back in operation?"

"Since yesterday. Delivering ten gigawatts to White Sands, day and night. I'm getting bids for the electricity from six different power utilities in the States, and another one in Canada."

They chatted for a few minutes more, never mentioning April again. Then Chavez got to his feet and Eamons followed suit.

"We've got to get back to Houston," Chavez said.

"I can fly you."

The FBI agent shook his head. "We'll drive. Officially, we haven't been here. This is all on our own time."

"I'm really sorry about April," Eamons said, her voice trembling.

"Yeah," said Dan, his own voice faltering. "Me, too."

And then there was nothing left to say. Dan shook hands with the two agents and went out to the catwalk with them. He watched them walk slowly down the metal stairs, their footsteps echoing in the empty hangar, and walk out to where Chavez's car sat parked in the nearly empty lot.

Chavez drove away, and the hangar grew very quiet. Won't be for long, Dan said to himself. We'll start building two new spaceplanes in a few weeks. And laying out plans for the next power satellite.

He walked back into his office and booted up his computer to look at his appointments for the coming week.

"Testimony to Senate science subcommittee," he read from the screen. I wonder if Jane will be there? he asked himself.

WASHINGTON, D.C.

So you're telling this subcommittee that your power satellite is not dangerous?" Senator Quill asked sharply.

Seated at the green baize-covered witness table, Dan said crisply, "That's right, Senator. A power satellite is no more dangerous than any other electrical power station, if it's operated properly."

"But terrorists turned it into a death ray!" snapped an angry-faced white-haired senator several seats down from Quill. "Nearly a thousand people were killed!"

Dan had expected that. "Senator," he replied patiently, "how do you prevent terrorists from blowing up a nuclear power station?"

The senator's white brows knit. "Why, you have guards and such."

"Right," said Dan. "You protect the facility. And that's what we're going to have to do with power satellites. Protect them. Guard them. They are very valuable assets, and just because they're in space instead of on the ground doesn't mean that they shouldn't be protected—or can't be."

"Protected how?" Quill asked, anxious to retake control of the hearing.

Dan started his prepared little lecture on building fail-safes into the satellite controls and having crews standing by with spaceplanes ready to fly out to a powersat in case of any emergency. As he spoke, though, he wondered where Jane was and why she hadn't attended this hearing.

By day's end Dan felt bone tired and ready to fly back to Texas. The Senate subcommittee hearing had gone favorably, he thought. Quill had even broached the idea of proposing to the Department of Defense that the air force take on the task of protecting American assets in orbit.

Dan ate dinner with his new Washington-based public relations staff, who congratulated him on his testimony before the subcommittee. Then he rode out to Reagan National Airport in a hired limousine. The Astro corporate jet was parked outside the general aviation terminal. As he ducked out of the limo Dan saw that a dank, chilly fog was rolling in from the Potomac. He heard the thundering roar of a commercial jetliner taking off. The fog won't keep us grounded, he thought, with relief. I'll be home by midnight.

And then his heart flipped as he saw Jane walking toward him from the terminal building. She was wearing a fitted suit—modest, yet it showed her figure to good advantage. Light color; it was hard to make out the shade in the dim, foggy evening light.

"You're leaving without saying good-bye?" she asked, trying to smile.

"I was hoping we could get together while I was in Washington," he said, "but then I figured it wasn't going to work."

"You're going back to Texas."

"And you're going to the White House."

She hesitated a heartbeat, then stepped closer to him, so close he could feel the warmth of her, smell the delicate scent of her perfume.

"Dan," she breathed, "maybe I should go to Texas with you."

His jaw dropped open.

"I could give it up, the whole thing, all of it," Jane said.

"Leave Scanwell? Leave Washington?"

She didn't reply. He saw tears welling in her eyes.

"You can't do that, Jane," he heard himself say. "You'd hate yourself in the morning."

"Be serious—"

"I am. You'd hate *me,* sooner or later. If Scanwell doesn't win the election, you'd be miserable."

"But what about us?"

Now he fell silent for a long, agonizing moment. At last, "It just won't work, Jane. There's too much between us."

"Your satellite."

"Your career. Scanwell. The White House."

"My God, Dan . . . I wish it wasn't like this."

"But it is."

She leaned her head on his shoulder and he slipped his arms around her waist. Dan's mind was racing, trying to find a way, thinking of what would happen if...

He lifted her chin and looked into her misty green eyes. "I love you, Jane. I always will."

"And I love you, Dan."

She kissed him lightly on the lips. He let his arms slide away from their embrace. They stood face to face, almost touching, silent and miserable.

"Well," he said, "good luck. After you get elected, invite me to the White House."

"The Lincoln Bedroom," she said, trying to smile.

Dan realized there were no more words in him. He walked past her to the plane that was waiting for him. It was the most difficult thing he had ever done.

MATAGORDA ISLAND, TEXAS

Several weeks later, Dan sat alone at his desk in the evening shadows and watched Morgan Scanwell make his acceptance speech at the convention.

"...and more than mere energy independence, the United States will become the supplier of energy to the world, energy to raise the living standards of the poor: clean, renewable energy to build new industries, new cities..."

His phone called out, "Mr. Yamagata on line one, boss."

Dan frowned at the synthesized voice's interruption, but he realized that it must be lunchtime in Tokyo. Despite himself, he grinned at the thought of Saito delaying a meal just to talk to him. So he muted the TV and shrank the scene from the convention to a small box at the bottom corner of the screen.

Saito Yamagata's round face beamed a big smile at him. "Congratulations, Daniel, my friend. You have a president that will be very helpful to you."

"He's not elected yet," Dan said.

"He will be. My experts assure me that Scanwell will beat the incumbent by a comfortable margin."

"Let's hope so."

"We should discuss a strategic partnership between my corporation and yours," Yamagata said.

Dan felt his brows hike. "Scanwell's preaching energy independence, Sai. He wants us to stand by ourselves."

Yamagata's smile didn't falter one millimeter. "What he says now to get elected and what he finds as realities once he's in the White House are two very different things."

"Meaning?"

"The Japanese ambassador and his technical aides are already discussing cooperation between Japan and the United States in building power satellites. Surely the global energy market is big enough for us both."

Dan nodded, thinking, Sai's no fool. "I get it," he said to Yamagata. "If Scanwell partners the U.S. with Japan it'll cut the legs out from under OPEC and the guys who fund terrorists."

Yamagata made a polite shrug. "It might help Scanwell to overcome the pressures from Garrison and the oil industry, as well."

"You know that double-damned Garrison cut off Tricontinental's loans to me as soon as we got the powersat working again."

"I'm not surprised. Garrison has no interest in helping any form of energy that competes with oil."

"Maybe."

"Don't you worry about him, Daniel. I predict a very bright future for us."

"Us?"

"Astro and Yamagata. An alliance beneficial to both corporations and to both nations."

Dan saw in the corner of the screen that Scanwell had finished his acceptance speech. Jane came up beside him and he put an arm around her. Husband and wife.

That's it, he thought. The whole world knows about them now. It's over. You'll never have her. You had your chance and you threw it away. Beau Geste, that's who the hell I am. A double-damned idiot.

Yamagata was saying, "You're going to become a very wealthy man, Daniel. An extremely wealthy man."

"Yeah," said Dan sourly. "I guess so."

And he thought about Hannah, Joe Tenny, Pete Larsen, April. Is it worth the cost? Nearly a thousand killed by the terrorists. Is anything worth all those lives?

His eyes strayed from the images on the screen to the models on his desk: the powersat and the spaceplane. We're going to change the world, Dan told himself. We've paid the price, and now we're going to start bringing the world energy from space.

I'll get filthy rich, just like Garrison. And Jane's going to be president of the United States one day. Big fucking deal.

He said good-bye to the still-smiling Yamagata and shut down his screen. Sliding out from behind his heavy dark desk, Dan went out to the catwalk, still half-expecting to see April as he passed her desk. He climbed the metal stairs and stepped out onto the hangar's roof. The sun had set more than an hour ago, but the sky was still aflame with deep reds and violets. A fresh breeze was blowing in from the gulf, carrying the rich scent of pines and the salty tang of the sea.

Turning toward the southwestern horizon, Dan saw a single bright star gleaming against the growing darkness. The power satellite. The future. With a sardonic smile twisting his lips he stared at it and promised himself he'd build a whole constellation of them.

He heard Yamagata's voice in his head: *You're going to become a very wealthy man, Daniel. An extremely wealthy man.*

Maybe so, he thought. But the real job is to make the world wealthier. That's what's important.

His bitterness ebbed a little. Not a bad goal for a man to have, he told himself. Saving the world.